This Proud
and Savage Land

Alexander Cordell

This Proud
and Savage Land

WEIDENFELD & NICOLSON
LONDON

For
William Faulknal Jenkins,
and children everywhere.

Acknowledgements

I am indebted to many for help in research, especially to authors Chris Barber and his father, W. T. Barber, who suggested the title. To many librarians I am grateful, my friend Mr John Bowring, ALA, in particular. The old gentlemen of industry have helped me again; men like Mr John Jones, an old collier who knows Clydach Vale like his hand, and to Mr Trevor Rowson, the Nantyglo historian, my thanks for reading the manuscript.

I have also had assistance from the following: Mr Emrys F. Evans, ARICS, and Dr B. C. Burnham of the National Trust Land Agency and the University of Wales respectively; the Dyfed County Archivist; Dr Anne Digby (University of York); Mr Roy Williams; Mr John Davies of Llanwrtyd Bookshop; Mr D. G. Edwards; Mr Martin Farr of the Cavers' Association; Mrs Mercedes Waters of the Moss Rose Press; and Mr E. E. Edwards, the Rhymney historian. Lastly, my thanks to Messrs Gollancz Ltd, the publishers of *Rape of the Fair Country*, for granting me the use of extracts from that novel.

'History,' said Mr Ford, 'is bunk.'

English history is a record of events that never happened compiled by charlatans to misinform the young.

This story, however, is true, for only a true story is worth telling. Its facts are supported by Parliamentary Commissions.

Author's note

Reference to Gwent within the novel complies with the Welsh refusal of the period to recognize the ceding to England of the county then known as Monmouthshire.

Children, stumbling through the stews
Reviled and spat upon and shocking.
Cheer up! Some day you may have shoes,
And, who knows, a stocking.
Meanwhile, listen to grown-ups, and heed 'em.
Then you'll have a future – Freedom.

After Heinrich Heine (1797–1856)

Book I

1800–1805

One

I sat in a corner of the swaying coach and watched my
father's sleeping face. With his long legs thrust out, he slept
in a fumbling dream of money-lenders, pawnbrokers and
bailiffs, to all of whom he owed money.

Closing my ears to the galloping hooves in a vain attempt
at sleep, I braced myself to the onward dash for the first stop
at Llandovery. It was supposed to be summer, but since we'd
left the Grouse Inn in the foothills of the Cambrian mountains a storm had beaten about us, mumbling and clattering
among the distant peaks and lashing us with stair-rod rain – a
fine way to celebrate a sixteenth birthday.

Now the coach skidded precariously on the flooded road
and the two mares beat their hooves in a quieter, rhythmic
pattern: rubbing at the misted window, I stared out over the
dull forbidding country fifty feet below; one false hoof could
send us somersaulting down into the flooded river. And then
I heard the voice of Old Amos, our coachman, a wail on the
wind.

'What you think, master? Road might be topped over
south o' Bryn. And if the weir be awash we'll not get through
where Sarn Helen crosses the Main. I says to turn back and
run for Builth, eh?' And my father awoke with a start, flung
open the door beside him and yelled back:

'What ails ye these days, Amos? Whip us on or I'll be up
there and drive the thing myself!' Wiping rain from his face,
he slammed shut the door and glanced at me as the coach
lumbered on. 'You all right, son?'

'Aye, sir.'

'Cold?'

'No, sir,' and my father tossed me the Cyfarthfa blanket, saying:

'Put that over your knees.' He jerked his thumb up at Old Amos. 'The damned idiot. I've known the day he'd have tackled the Devil's Staircase in worse weather than this. A man gets old . . .' Tipping a flask to his mouth, he swallowed greedily and the fumes of brandy swept over me. 'Dear Christ! If ever ye see me aimin' in that direction, lad, put me down six feet.' Grinning wide, he made a fist of his hand, reached out and put it on my chin. 'You like travelling with ye father?'

'Yes, sir.'

'Now your mother's gone we'll do more of it, eh?'

It was dusk. Crippled hedgerows raised threatening arms at us as we clattered along, every one a witch of my nightmare dreams these days, for my father was on the road to the Devil: swigging again from a flask, he cried, 'Try to sleep, lad. It was a windy old ride coming horseback over from Tregaron – lucky we didn't strike footpads, eh? But, unlucky for them with you six feet up beside me! Now first stop Abergavenny – a bath, a steak and a bed, if the money runs to it, Hywel. Then on to Chepstow and over the ferry for London in the morning – that suit you?'

'Yes, sir.'

He roared, 'In the name of God will ye cease the in-ordinate bloody politeness, lad! I'm ye father, not your headmaster.'

'Yes, Dada.'

The previous night we had spent at the Grouse Inn, at Abergwysen: Old Amos, our family retainer – the only servant left to us – had waited there with a coach and pair to begin this final leg to London.

At the Grouse Inn lace-hatted girls had waited upon us at table; bosomy pieces with red lips and curtsys serving in the gentry room while ragged, lusty drovers hung their boots on to the tables in another: beards went up and ale went down like lift and force pumps, while Shadrach and Mesdach, the sister landladies, plus Poll Plenty, the barmaid, rushed around with trays of foaming jugs.

The Grouse proved worse than Sodom and Gomorrah, said my father, and this I could well believe from what I saw going on downstairs; what went on upstairs was nobody's business. But despite his criticism, he was worse than any of them; cuddling bare-bosom ladies in the snugs and dancing fandangoes with old Shadrach, a glass in each hand, and this went on until the crows of dawn. All of which was a little different from the good taste of my school in Canterbury, which I had now officially left because Father hadn't paid the fees.

Therefore it was with a bit of a shock that I found Poll Plenty with a leg in the bed beside me come dawn, and without so much as an invitation; which is going some for a bare fourteen.

'For God's sake!' I cried, easing her out. 'What you doing here?' and she went all pouty and made big eyes and said, pathetic:

'Ach, be a sport, Hywel Mortymer? Isn't ye pa upstairs in the feathers with Shadrach and Mesdach, and me shiverin' cold in me little bare attic? While you're here with the big Cyfarthfa blanket. Och, fella, be a sport!'

'Cold me eye, missus, it's the middle of June!'

'Mind, you're a marvellous six footer for all you're a lad. How old are ye, for God's sake?'

'Sixteen today,' said I, holding her off.

'And me two years younger! Let me in, me son, and you'll be two years wiser in the mornin',' and she shoved me over and came in head first.

'There now, what about that,' whispered Poll Plenty, shivering still, and she'd got me shivering, too, for I'd never been up against a lady before, and there happened upon me a strange development that had only occurred before in

5

dreams. Which is all right, I suppose, if this sort of thing is done by mutual agreement, but I knew what would have happened if the Canterbury headmaster had caught me at it, so as Poll came in one side, I came out of the other, and I went up the rickety stairs to her attic in my nightshirt with her hanging on to my leg.

She was right: it was as cold as an Eskimo's heart up there on her mattress, and I shivered and dew-dropped until the bell clanged for breakfast.

But you get no thanks from some people for kindly acts like giving up your bed, and Poll was huffy cool with me when serving at table with my father; like slapping down my egg and bacon with her nose up, and not so much as a good morning.

'What's wrong with her, I wonder?' asked my father, buttering toast.

'Can't think,' I replied. 'She came into my room last night saying she was cold, so I put her under the Cyfarthfa blanket in my bed and went upstairs to the attic.'

'That,' said my father, 'was generous. Doubtless she appreciated it.' He munched his toast. 'But some women, you'll find, are never satisfied. Do they instruct you in the behaviour of the gentle sex in your school?'

'Oh aye, about mothers and sisters mainly – being above rubies.'

'Excellent. However, there are others who may not be relatives, Hywel. Remind me to talk with you on the subject at the first available opportunity. This afternoon, of course, will be taken up with meeting some of our creditors.'

'Creditors?'

'Your esteemed Uncle John, and Tom and Kent Mortimer. Relatives on your mother's side, I fear, have always brought me trouble.'

There was no affection between my family, the Mortymers, and Sir John Mortimer, my dead mother's brother; he and

6

his two sons, Kent and Tom, were our sworn enemies, according to my father.

The similarity of our family names requires explanation.

My uncle, Sir John, was of an aristocratic line; indeed, my mother could trace her family back 400 years to the Battle of Mortimer's Cross; and before that, even, to Edmund Mortimer who married Jane, one of Owain Glyndwr's daughters, following a Mortimer defeat at the Battle of Pilleth.

But, somewhere down the ancestral line things had gone awry.

Rumour had it that Edmund had abandoned a lady who was in child by him in order to placate Glyndwr, who was pushing him into marriage to Jane. The court would have been scandalized, so the illegitimacy of the lady's child was hushed. And, to differentiate the offspring from the noble Mortimer line, Glyndwr named him as a *Mortymer*, which to him was an indication of the bastardy.

Thus began the Mortymer ancestry, of which I was the last, and, when my father married my mother, the sister of Sir John and a daughter of the true Mortimer dynasty, a vendetta between the two families began.

It was a quarrel that had come to a violent head with the suicide of my mother two years ago; from that moment, my father and Sir John Mortimer became enemies.

This had now expressed itself in the financial ruin of my family, brought about by my uncle and my father's own dissolute existence.

I did not know on that afternoon in the Grouse Inn that this family hatred would follow me down to my sons.

Awaiting our meeting with Sir John and his sons, I wandered alone on the cobbles outside the inn and watched the blacksmiths shoeing our two horses, with Old Amos fussing and fuming about them.

Earlier, I had seen these smiths fitting tiny iron shoes to the feet of rams and ewes; also soling and heeling a hundred

7

geese for the squawking, jabbering thirteen-mile walk through the Cambrians to Tregaron. After fashioning for them little leather boots, he chased them through a patch of warm pitch and sand, and the old things came out on the other side wearing boots I'd have bought for myself. The sight of them, sheep, pigs, geese and cattle, took my mind back to my childhood when I'd lie hand in hand with my mother in the belly of the bed and listen to the pattering of their feet as the drovers brought them into Tregaron market.

This, for as long as I could remember, was the music of my childhood; the obscene bawling of the drovers, the bellow-ing of worn-out cattle and the lamenting shrieks of the porkers coming to town. At first this used to terrify me; as did the gilded portraits of my ancestors lining the walls of a house that was dead, but would not fall down. And, hearing my cries, my mother would draw me down into her warmth.

Sometimes, on these occasions, my father would come.

I can see him now, his great bulk filling the doorway of the bedroom.

'Jesus Christ, woman, do we have to have a bloody audience? Is that wee crot always going to be here when I come to you on a hungry midnight?'

At this my mother would hold me closer, and my father would go, leaving behind him a stink of brandy.

I was still with Old Amos, watching the smiths at work on the horses, when I saw Sir John Mortimer and his two sons arrive.

I'd never had a really good look at Sir John, my mother's brother, but now I saw him in bright, pitiless sunlight.

He was small; almost completely bald, and of shifty eyes; his dainty air and foppish manner contrasted with the bulky masculinity of my father; one could be forgiven for mistaking the illegitimate line.

Tom and Kent, his sons, followed their mother for size and deportment, being tall and muscular; Tom, near my own age, was friendly; Kent, mature, was an elemental snob – one

8

determined, it appeared, to put the bastards in their place. By a strange presentiment I knew, at that first meeting, that he would prove my lifelong enemy.

Seeing them arrive, I joined my father in an ante-room of the inn; he said as I approached: 'They have come.'

I nodded, taking a seat beside him. He added, 'Listen, Hywel; you are the equal of this lot, so remember it. But, whatever they say, however quick your temper – keep it – or you will answer to me, you understand?'

'Yes, sir.'

'We may be the poor relations, but we will leave this room with our pride, though we leave our assets behind.'

I glanced at him in the moment before the others entered.

'They have broken you?'

He nodded. 'Every penny, every acre, every slate. As I told you, you won't be going back to school in Canterbury.'

He did not say more for then they were in, Sir John leading his sons; all of them evincing that aristocratic indifference that told they were not to be tampered with: sitting down, they faced us across the highly polished table. Poll Plenty entered, asking, with a curtsy: 'You require tea, gentlemen?' She fluttered an eye at me.

'Get out, woman,' snapped Sir John, 'I want no witnesses to this.'

He scowled at my father. 'By the living God, Mortymer, you'll leave here penniless. This time I'll relieve you of your property; next time, with half a chance, I'll have your lives.'

'I'll give it a go with pistols, if you like?' My father winked.

'Death with honour, eh?' The man's voice was low and husky and never, before or since, have I seen such hatred in a face. He said: 'An ignominious death for the pair of you – it's all you're entitled to as a legacy of your bastardy . . .' Suddenly he got to his feet, his features contorted. 'Make the most of what you have left, Mortymer. You sent my sister to a felon's death: only through bribes does she lie in consecrated ground. You made her life a living hell, and in her name I will hound you, your son and his sons to shameful deaths. Only through this expiation will my sister know peace.'

With his hands forming a cage over his mouth, he wept.

Kent Mortimer, the elder son, glared at us. 'By God, you've got something to answer for, you lot,' he said, and Tom sat silently.

My father said, 'And so have you, if you make me late for my afternoon punch. Come now, it's a tipple we need to make us all sociable. *Girl!*' And he snapped his fingers at Poll Plenty.

For the first time I realized the indelicacy, the studied vulgarity of my father in the face of another's grief: for the first time, too, I understood the suffering of Sir John Mortimer, and the reason for his hatred.

Two

Because the victory of our relatives was a shock to his system, my father spent the rest of the day in a drunken haze, wenching and roistering, and we didn't leave the Grouse Inn for London until night was coming on.

At the gaming tables of high society, he declared, he would now proceed to make a fortune.

The storm, roaring among the peaks of the Cambrians, swirled about us furiously as Old Amos whipped up the horses, and we were off.

With four guineas in his pocket, my father departed with all the *bonhomie* of a self-made millionaire. Subject to immediate eviction from our Tregaron mansion, we left with hurrahs and catcalls from the Grouse servants, one of whom blew a hunting horn. We left with the sale of our lands properly concluded by deed, with what small assets we had in the Llandovery bank sequestered by my uncle's lawyers to pay my father's debts. We travelled now in a coach and pair owned by Sir John, with his express intention of removing us from the area: we went carrying on our backs our only possessions – clothes.

'I give your uncle credit,' said my father with a yawn as he settled himself comfortably in the coach. 'I always admire good organization; his intention being to break us down to the sixth generation, I couldn't have done a better job myself.'

'So what now?' I asked him as Amos whipped the horses to greater speed.

'I shall tell you, my son,' cried my father. 'We plunge. For, when the chips are down and your luck is out, this is the moment of greatest fortune. My credit is still good in Jackson's Rooms, is it not? Gentleman John Jackson will give me a loan and at his expense I shall recoup the family wealth.' Tossing up his flask, he snatched it, uncorked it and drank deep, wiping his mouth. With a big fist up, he quoted, '"He either fears his fate too much, or his deserts are small, who dares not put it to the touch to gain or lose it all,"' and he threw back his head and bellowed a laugh. 'You hear that, what? Long live the Mortymers spelled with a y!'

He was sickening me; I did not reply. This, I thought, was what my mother had suffered for years: life with a bellowing, brandy-soaked bull of a man who spent his life with drink and whores, branding his insensitivity upon her soul. Now he opened the window beside him and shouted up into the storm:

'Come on, Amos, what ails ye? We're away to London, not a trot to Michaelmas Fair. Get the whip to them!'

The whip slashed down, and we broke into a gallop along the precipitous Treachery Pass. Propping up his riding boots, my father shouted above the thunder:

'Some June, eh, me son? True Welsh mountain weather, so to hell with gentry farming – it don't need carding and wagerin' to lift the roof, ye know – a couple o' dirty harvests'll do it quicker.' And he grinned and thumped my knee. 'You understand, I take it, that we're down to grub tacks?'

'Of course.'

'It bloody looks like it, for your face is as dull as tomorrer. Come on, man, shiver up your herring-roes! You're done with that rotten English school, haven't ye? – your mother sent you there, you know, not me – but if you're short on education you'll be into a fortune if you stick with me.' He swigged at a flask. 'Father and son, eh? – the bastard Mortymers! Dear God, I do 'em credit – your uncle handled it fine! But, if we're groggy, we ain't laid out, eh?' His voice lowered confidentially. 'Ye see, lad, the tables down in Jackson's were supposed to raise us, but the luck went cold.

But luck, son, is the essence of living: old Lady Luck, she downs ye one minute, then lifts ye up.'

The rain lashed down: thunder clouds barged themselves across the caverns of the sky as if in haste to deluge the earth; vivid lightning flashes blazed on my father's haggard face, and he cried:

'Anyway, to hell with property – it isn't worth a fig these days – lazy tenants, repairs, poaching, land taxes, unpaid rent – we'll be better off without the old pile, now your mother's gone.'

The memory of her suicide momentarily stilled him, then he added, 'Ever since she died her bloody relatives have been after the house and land, and now they've got it. God alive and reigning, fellow, have ye nothin' at all to say?'

I shook my head.

For in the woodshed down on the bank of a little brook outside Tregaron, I had cut my mother down. Seeing her, I had expected to find her face contorted by the rope, but it was not. Indeed, it was an astonishing hanging, said the surgeon who attended her, for there was an expression of inestimable peace upon her face: no swelling of the features, no bulging eyes; she who had fought for family piety with all the district wenches, and begged him to farm instead of wager. But the attractions of Jackson's Rooms and its gaming tables had beaten her. She had married a gentry farmer against her family's wishes, and paid the price; proving no match for the riotous larkery of Jackson's in Old Bond Street, where fortunes could be lost on the turn of a card.

Here gamed the fops and dandies of the day: the Dukes of York and Clarence; the amorous Duke of Marlborough, who bought and sold his pugilists like horseflesh to satisfy his love of The Fancy.

Here in Jackson's met the millionaire Baldwins and Vernons; the aristocratic lay-me-downs of the turf – Lord Barrymore for one – now in the heyday of their riotous living; dining in sumptuous houses while the starving languished in London's fetid slums. Here in Jackson's establishment old

13

scores were paid off and duels arranged that never took place in cowardice: over its gaming tables our family fortune had vanished into the laps of a clique whose pursuit in life was pleasure. In this palace attended by Royalty, my father had even exploited me. Now he said:

'Once we bed down in Jackson's we'll find you a more able opponent than young Tom Mortimer, I vow. Have you been keeping up the art of self-defence under old Dai Bando at school?' He leaned back and surveyed me with untainted pride.

'Boxing's a prime subject in the curriculum, yes.'

It pleased him and his grey eyes momentarily shone. 'But, ye've never had a black eye to prove it!'

'The Noble Art, as taught by Dai Bando keeps your eye out of the way.'

'One thing's certain, though I've never approved of his methods, he taught ye enough to give young Tom, your cousin, a dusting!' He kicked up his boots and shouted laughter. The coach rocked on the rutted road, nearly unseating us, and he took out his monocle and screwed it into his eye and adopted the effeminate manners of supporters of the Fancy, saying, '"By gad, Mortymer, where did ye get such bloodstock? From your loins, did ye say? Who, then, was the filly? For I vow, given two more years, I'd put the lad in with Game Chicken."'

He could be entertaining, too, and I rocked with laughter. He continued, removing the monocle, 'But I tell ye this, me son, it did your father's heart a world o' good to see ye dust up Tom to such effect – giving him two years and a stone to boot.'

It was the first and only time I had met my Cousin Tom in private; facing each other, on a family wager, within the roped square in Jackson's Rooms. I replied: 'But it was unfair. Tom had never donned a muffler in his life.'

'But now ye'll meet others who have, me lad – young up-and-comers like you, the sons of the finest blood in London. Dear God, if we play the cards right – you with the mufflers and me on the tables – we could raise a fortune that would set us high and mighty. And where would our relatives be then, poor things? Are ye on?'

'I'm not taking the prize ring for a living, Dada.'

'God alive, would I be suggestin' it? Just a bout here and there to keep us fed till I get upon me feet – look, look, son – where else are you likely to meet the Marquis of Granby, the King of Prussia and the Duke of Mecklenburgh in a single afternoon? – to say nothin' of bare-knucklers like Tom Cribb and Belcher . . . and Gentleman John Jackson, the king of 'em all?' He swung himself over and sat beside me, his enthusiasm growing. 'You're a natural, don't ye realize? You've fast hands and a dig in them both. Do ye realize I won a pony off the Prince of Wales when he wagered on Tom for size instead of ye for quality? And do ye know what he said to me when they brought Tom round? "Mortymer," he said, "henceforth, Sir, we can keep our rough-meat pugilists safely grazed and watered in our stables, and wager, instead, on the prowess of our sons." Now then, will you give it thought?'

I did. I thought of Cousin Tom's bloodstained face and I pitied him, yet marvelled at his dignity in the face of that thrashing – doled out by someone akin to his little brother. But, and I knew this, Tom Mortimer would never forget the degradation of this defeat, and neither would his father.

The coach lurched along the rutted, flooded road; the hooves were a drumming rhythm above the wind. As we skidded past Rounder Bend I saw the signpost of the white mare's skull: bright its bones in the light of a scudding moon, and the voice of Old Amos was a wail: 'Road blocked fifty yards up, sir! Strangers about, too – and it dunna look healthy!'

Reaching under his seat, my father drew out the big horse pistol he used for highwaymen; furiously he powdered it; rammed in the ball. And, as the wheels locked and we ground to a halt, he cocked the weapon, sighted it, and kicked open the coach door. Instantly, it was slammed shut. A bludgeon shattered the glass, striking him in the chest and forcing him backwards. All in seconds: one moment security, next moment panic. And, as my father fell, the face of a man appeared framed in the broken window, to disappear instantly as the pistol exploded: dropping to my knees I heard the ball whine off into space, and a faint, distant cry. Hauling my father up, I saw, in horror, two men gripping Old Amos: saw them run him, his boots skidding on the road, to the edge of the drop to the river below; and propel him, his arms and legs flailing, into space.

Silence now.

No sound but the blustering wind and our own heavy breathing: blood from my father's face dripped monotonously on to my hand. And then a man's voice bawled:

'Is he alone?'

'No, the lad's with 'im. They got young Tom, mind!'

'What?'

'They got young Tom.'

'Don't be bloody daft – he were here a second back.'

'Not no he anna – look, somebody fired from the coach. He's dead.'

'Jesus Christ!'

'Aye, there'll be hell to pay rent to when we get back home.'

'Stop bloody talking and get this thing over . . .'

I risked a look through the broken glass: two men were stooping over the prostrate body of another. One said, getting up. 'It's only a graze, I tell ye. Give 'im a minute and he'll be up. Come on, come on, you know what the old man said.'

'All of it over?' a man cried. 'Look, Musker, them's fine mares!'

'Never mind that, get the whole lot over,' and before I could gather myself the coach tipped beneath me. The horses shrieked as the coach went higher and the shaft took them.

Gathering my wits, I stooped, hauling my father up against me, and he moved feebly in my arms, semi-conscious from the blow of the bludgeon. As I reached out a hand for the door the coach tipped higher still, sending me sprawling back with my father in my arms. The horses were shrieking; men were shouting incoherently. If there was one out there, here was ten: a man roared:

'And again so, *lift!*' and the coach reared up beneath me, sliding us both into a corner.

'Get another hold, I say. Lift, lift! Come on, Musker, get your back into it.'

Another voice shouted, 'He's only a lad, ye know – ain't we after the old man?'

'Shut your mouth and *lift!*'

And, in the moment before the coach overturned and teetered on the lip of the road berm, I saw through the shattered window the face of a man: he was wearing a French cockade hat and one side of his face was scarred as if blown away, muscle and bone, by shot: the face disappeared as the coach rolled over, and I saw below me the foaming Cledan River in full spate twenty feet down: flying hooves I saw, and a single spinning wheel, and felt my father's arms go about me as a lanthorn flared and we dropped into space.

Now, locked in his embrace, I somersaulted in a mad world of scarlet and gold; into a topsy-turvy crescendo of thumps and smashes and pain: in a jack-in-the-box coffin we struck impeding rocks in our downward plunge, upright one second, upside down the next, but my father, not I, was taking the impact of the collisions. And then, in one last explosion of pain and light, the coach crashed into the mud of the river bank: glass tinkled, I remember, as I drifted into silence.

Utter silence, broken only by the rippling of the river.

All was stillness in my world of returning consciousness: then I heard the river again and the cadent voice of a solitary bird on the soft-breathing air. My eyes, but not my brain, saw weak sun-shafts filtering down through rents in the roof of the wrecked coach; I shivered to the sudden touch of lapping water.

Now I realized that I was lying face down upon the body of my father, and that his arms, still about me, clutched me in a vice of death. And the river, flooding into the half-submerged coach, was slowly embracing him so that his face was already covered.

I saw this face in all its mutilation, wavering in water below my eyes. Sickened, I prised myself free of his arms, and saw his body beneath me in all its ragged decimation; the once live bones jutting up, blood-smeared; the broken hands that clasped mine. Now a new phenomenon as the dawn sun blazed, lighting up the coach interior to a new brightness: the vision beneath me snatched away my breath as I stared down.

For the face that, but a few hours before, had been lined by dissolution had vanished, and a new face had replaced it. As if a magician's wand had been waved above it, this new face was that of youth. Unlined and handsome, the youth of my father wavered before me as if in a holy transfiguration: his hair, but a few hours before sparse and gray, was now a shining black, as I had seen it in the portraits of his youth. But, young or old, he was still a corpse, and I dragged away the blanket that covered us like a shroud, and crawled painfully to an upturned seat.

Looking up through the smashed roof I saw above me the berm of the road that led to Llandovery, and high on a pole, glinting bone-white in the dawn sun, shone the white mare's skull on Rounder Bend.

Nothing moved.

It was as if there was nobody else in the world but me and my dead father.

Then I noticed the little silver locket round his neck that held a portrait of my mother; the crash had upturned it and it was lying upon his breast. Bending, I removed it, then pulled out the Cyfarthfa blanket and folded it inside my coat.

Three

Easing my cramped limbs, I climbed on to the roof of the coach, to find myself staring into the beaked face of a giant red kite; I don't know which was the more surprised, it or me: it shrieked, its taloned feet scrabbling for a hold on the wood; then, fighting for balance, it spread great wings and sailed upward into the vaporous blue of the sun to join its mate. Together they indulged in cat-like mewing at my interruption: high above them a procession of white-gowned monks, having just finished St Peter's weekly wash, waddled across the dawning sky. Filled with disgust and loathing at the birds, I raised a fist at them, shouting abuse. But they circled still, impatient for the prey: soon, I knew, they would descend again to rip and tear at my father.

Now I climbed from crag to crag and reached the berm of the Llandovery road; to sink down, sobbing, at the foot of the gibbet that bore the white mare's skull.

From this high vantage I heard the snarling of dogs. A wolf pack, splitting into groups, was fighting over the carcasses of the horses, one of which was half submerged in the river: near by the body of poor Old Amos, as yet unnoticed, lay face down in the mud of the bank. Sickened, I watched the two kites descend and disappear like burrowing moles into the coach in search of my father. Then pain and weariness swept over me in waves of increasing intensity: wrapped in the Cyfarthfa blanket, I wept, until sleep claimed me.

It was near midday when I awoke, cramped and sore: over my body was a pattern of bruises. It was only when I rose and began to walk that I realized the miracle of my escape. Limping away from the gibbet, I saw below me a swath of mist filling the valley; and heard the wolves, unseen, still at feed.

This was true wolf country: Wolf's Leap, the gorge near the Devil's Staircase, was the haunt of at least one savage pack; home, too, of the red kite, the carrion-eaters of the Irfon Valley, and more than one drover, in my time, had provided a meal among its jagged crags.

Although I had known this land since childhood, I had never considered its dangers. Now, alone and unarmed, I gritted my teeth to the pain and broke into a loping, swaying run. I'd considered returning to Abergwysen, but since it was probably the Mortimers who had mounted the attack upon us, this could prove dangerous: my longing was to go home to Tregaron House; then I remembered that this now belonged to them.

Finally, with the sun rising over the mountains, I went west, making for Pumsaint and the old Cothi Inn where Cushy Cuddlecome, one of my father's paramours, held court – a woman to be trusted, if there wasn't a man about.

Crossing the Twyi near Cilcwm, I left the forest to the east: I made across open fields to Caio, and the ancient road called Sarn Helen.

This was Roman country. The road I had just left entered a great forest to the west and stretched to Neath, which the Romans called Nidum, then wound north to Chester.

Through this forest had moved the procession of Roman wagons bearing the mineral wealth of Wales.

Bound for the Severn estuary, it was then shipped to Rome and Syracuse, Etruscan outstations, and the Roman Western Empire. Indeed, it was for Welsh gold that the Romans had first invaded Britain. Ravaging the country, they had put down resistance from the Celtic tribes and built a fort beside the River Cothi: 20,000 soldiers guarded the nearby Dolaucothi goldmines in the year AD 78.

All this I had learned from my scholarly father, when we came for fishing trips to Pumsaint and stayed at the Cothi Inn – whose little tap-room actually lay within the confines of the Roman commandant's office.

Although nothing can be seen of this today, I would lie abed at nights in the attic room at the stop of the stairs and dream of flying chariots and legions of marching men; hear the clash of alien swords . . . amid the laughter of a tipsy Cushy Cuddlecome and the booms of my father in his cups.

Down in the tap-room where walked the ghosts of legionnaires, I would listen to the old goldminers' tales: of the discovery of golden spears and breastplates; of hoards of bangles and trinkets hidden away for soldiers' sweethearts, but which never reached Italy: they would tell, too, of the silly gentry toffs of Llandovery market, who, greedy for anything of gold, would buy paint-gilded ornaments of iron and brass.

After old Grancher Saul, Cushy's relative, had eased out the drunks, I'd sit by the fire and watch Cushy's eyes as she weighed up my father for a night of frolic. Aged six, I was an innocent in their world of lust. Big and busty was Cushy, with lace across the front of her bosom; paint and powder on her face and lavender water under the arms, so she always smelled as sweet as a nut. She moved like a great, animated corpse, with her curly hair hanging past her ears like twenty-five pounds of black Christmas candles. I usually had a pretty good scratch, I recall, when parting company with these. For Cushy was a great one for heaving lads up: lifting them high in *aoohs* and *aahs* and anna he a pretty lad and what big eyes he's got, and all this usually ended with a slobbering kiss in the chops, and I nearly twisted my farmers off once, trying to escape from Cushy in her happy-kiss-children mood.

Later still, I'd climb the stairs to my bed in the attic which I shared with Grancher, who slept in the big armchair by the door, and listen to him getting another cartload of porkers off to Lampeter market.

Yes, I'd lie there wondering why I had to sleep with

Grancher, while my father slept with Cushy in the suite, as she called it; which was a big four-poster with balls on each corner, and a portico over the top plus gilded angels with harps. It used to beat me how either of them got any sleep, what with the thumping, giggling, humping and heaving that went on in there all night; for my Dada was no pygmy and Cushy was an outsize piece even with her corsets on, being large in the front where ladies are inclined to be. No, I never really discovered why he slept with her and not with me; he'd have had a much better night in my attic, despite Grancher's snores. For next morning at breakfast they were very different people, him and Cushy, with him dopey and her throwing things at the dog.

Later in life I realized, of course, why my mother used to cry herself to sleep in Tregaron – worried, I suppose, about my father not sleeping so well whenever he was away from home. For when we arrived back with her he had bags under his eyes like the fleshpots of Jerusalem.

The dinners of the whitewashed farms were delicate on the wind as I staggered along the flinted tracks called roads. This was a stagecoach route for mail and probably I could have sought help; instead, I found myself lying in the roadside ditches like something hunted as they and farmers' traps clattered past. Tears scalded my eyes at the loss of my father; thoughts of the Cothi Inn reminded me of happier days in Tregaron. Alone, in pain and hungry, I felt I was the only person in the world.

Indeed, hunger was now overcoming weariness: thirst could be quenched at wayside streams, but now I went under the heat of the sun in visions of strings of hot, brown sausages flying in the breeze. I swam in bowls of oxtail soup, climbed slopes of steak and kidney pudding and hummocks of fried onions laced with gravy. Suddenly, rounding a bend in the road, I saw the ancient inn stark white against the midday sun, for the gold of the day had cut the throat of the sky and the River Cothi was sparkling like chain-silver: such was this beauty that it momentarily smothered my lust for food.

Light and smoke struck me as I pushed open the inn door.

Now, whenever I'd had dealings with Cushy while my father was alive, I always had a weather eye open, since it seemed to me that she'd just had the meat course and was weighing me up for afters.

Though one could scarcely call her gentry, she was a member of the property-owning classes, said my father; the Cothi Inn having been left to her by a doting mother who had entertained three husbands and then passed on with a biological deficiency. So Cushy, approaching middle age, was alone in the world save for Grancher Saul who lived in a wheelchair. Her devotion to Grancher was clear to me from the start, for she kept him in her private room during the day, then lifted him plus wheelchair into the servants' hoist and hauled him up, wheelchair and all, into the attic for the night; 'For he do prefer to sleep near Heaven, mind, the dear little soul,' said she.

Until I came to the Cothi that night I had never really got to the bottom of Grancher Saul, having never seen him with an eye open since I was twelve. But, despite Grancher's afflictions, Cushy was a happy big soul, with an outsize heart and a bosom for weeping on: she also had two minders – Swillickin' Jock, who was ginger all over, and Ham Bone, who was six-foot-six – both there in Cothi's for protectional purposes.

Under ordinary conditions I would have entered her tap-room unobserved, since Cushy's batting blue eyes were usually reserved for my father: not so this time.

All round the walls sat the customers, intent on tying biblical quotations on to the legs of their fighting cocks, for the place was like a church vestry come summer, said my father. If it wasn't cock-fighting it was badger-baiting, with Black Jack and Snap and Spot the Codger thrown in, and

23

more money changed hands in there than the London Stock Exchange just started up, said he.

Later, when the ale was down and the moon high, there'd be sand thrown on to the floor and squeaking and squarking and a flying of feathers in blotches of blood. My father was a dab hand at relevant quotations, such as: 'The Pope did a lot for adultery when he called it a mortal sin', and 'God did more for the lower classes when He invented cockerels'.

Beneath my feet were stains of scarlet as I pushed my way to the bar where Cushy, showing enough bosom to kill a drover, was pouring cask ale into mugs. Now she lifted her big blue eyes at me.

'Jesus alive and reigning!' said she, and went on pouring, and the ale swilled over the teak and splashed on to my boots. But, equal to any occasion, she thrust out a fat arm and lifted the flap of the counter beside her.

'In here quick,' she whispered, 'or the Mortimers will 'ave the bloody roof off.' I ducked under it and she assisted me into her private room and slammed the door.

Silence; dead silence in a world of purple drapes and gilt and gold furniture; of ancient relatives with side whiskers and beards, and matriarchs in black bombazine staring at me in disapproval. The carpet was red and the ceiling bright blue, with shining stars: very conservative was Cushy when it came to internal decoration.

The first thing she did was to feed me, for Cushy understood male appetite: a bowl of tripe and onions enough to fill a horse, with the top of a cottage loaf thrown in and lashings of salted farm butter: this and a pint of home-brew for me and a quart and two whisky chasers for herself, for she didn't drink a lot, did Cushy, and I was ready for the interrogation.

'Tom Mortimer's dead, ye know.'

'*What!*' Slowly, I rose, staring down at her painted face.

'Aye, me son, and talk has it that you and your father done it, God rest 'is soul,' and she dabbed at her eyes with a little lace handkerchief.

I told her what had happened in gusty breath.

'Aye, well, be that as it may, the Mortimers are holding you and your pa to account for it. Making their peaceful way along the road from the Grouse Inn, they was, after the meeting what wound you up, and in revenge you comes along and shoots poor Tom in the back.'

'Good God,' I whispered.

'Ay ay, let's hope so,' rejoined Cushy. 'For it was a terrible thing to do to a young man in 'is prime – shoot him down like a dog.'

I raised my voice. 'Do you think we'd do a thing like that?'

'*Heisht*, you, of course not!' She was sober serious now. 'I reckon it was an accident when the Mortimers pushed the pair of you over at Rounder Bend like you say, but that's what the Mortimers are letting forth, and that's what the magistrates will 'ave at the Assizes. You 'ave to sleep wi' a fella to know him, and I knew your father, God rest him. He got up to most things, but he'd never shoot a man in the dark.' She sniffed and wiped, smearing her mascara. 'They've been 'ere, you know.'

'Who, the Specials?'

'No, the Mortimers. They know you got clear, see?'

I said, 'They must have searched the coach. When did they come here?'

'Soon after dawn, breathing fire and brimstone, with a rope for hanging you to take revenge for their Tom, they said. And my two pansy minders under the bed, the sods. But I took a rabbit gun to 'em – "Get off me lawful property, ye scallywags," I said. "Hywel Mortymer only shoots on the duelling field," I said. "You got any complaints against me, Sir John, you takes it to the law – this is a respectable establishment" – well it is, ain't it?'

'Of course. What happened then?'

'Then him and Kent and the men ride off, don't they? – with me firing buck-shot, and there was a fella with a cocked hat on, and I got him in the arse.'

We sat together within an affinity born of tragedy, and she

25

said then, with a dimpled hand on my knee, 'It do go hard on a lad like you, really speakin', and you can depend on Cushy because of your pa, for I go honey-like inside at the thoughts of 'im. He weren't everyone's cup o' tea, mind, but he were good and kind to Cushy for a fancy: most times fancies are rough wi' a lady, you understand?'

'Yes,' I said.

'How old are ye now, Hywel Mortymer?'

'Sixteen.'

'Gawd, that's a pity, because you'll 'ave to sleep wi' Grancher. Not in the same bed, of course, for all the beds are singles, as ye know. And he dunna snore like he used to, and keeps himself to himself, does Grancher.' She added, 'And he prefers 'is wheelchair to a mattress.'

'I know. I've slept with him before.'

'Just for the night, ye understand, and after you're bedded, watered and fed in the mornin', you'll 'ave to be off, lest the Mortimers come again, understand?'

'I'll never forget you, Miss Cuddlecome.'

Taking a clay pipe off the mantel, she stuffed it with tobacco, lit it and blew out smoke, coughing and wheezing, then led me to the stairs, saying, 'Later, when you're a man and not a crot of a lad, you can come back to the Cothi and attach yourself to Cushy, will ye do that, my lovely?'

'You can bank on it, missus.'

With a candle held before me I followed her up the rickety stairs to the attic, and there was Grancher in his wheelchair with his chin sunk on his chest, and I confess right away that I didn't like the look of him, but Cushy kissed the top of his head, saying, 'Sleep tight, the pair of ye, and I'll see you both in the mornin'.'

I flung off my clothes after she'd gone and climbed into an iron ball of a bed with a feather mattress and real sheets; the cold of it caressed my aching body, with the June moon hanging in the leaded window and filling the room with a strange, unearthly glow.

Then I wept again, remembering my father.

26

Sleep shut me off like a tap: I didn't see the going of Grancher.

Deep in duck-down feathers, I slept as never before, but awoke around dawn when an icy hand seemed to touch my face in dreams. Sitting up, I stared across the room at Grancher in that grey light, for the moon was gone and red was painting up the sky. And it seemed to me, in that vacuum between sleep and waking, that Grancher's wheelchair had moved, for I swore that when I came in with Cushy he was in the other corner.

So I called softly to him, 'You all right, Grancher?'

Chin still sunk on chest, he sat, and his little bald head was shining in the faint dawn light. No reply; not even a whimper to say he'd heard me, so I got out of the bed as naked as with the midwife, and tiptoed over the boards to the wheelchair, and knelt before it.

'Are you all right, Grancher?' I asked again, but so still and quiet was he that I wondered, with an icy shiver, if the poor old sod had passed on in the night: there was no real fright in me at this suggestion, because death is only an extension of life, my father had taught me.

So I raised a hand and put it inside Grancher's coat to feel the old chap's heart, and my fingers touched a rib cage which was bony and cold; as cold as the grave was Grancher, poor soul, so I went back to the bed, collected the Cyfarthfa blanket and put it around his shoulders.

It was then that I saw a little silver chain around Grancher's neck, and on the end of the chain was a little silver plate. I lifted this up and held it to the window.

SAUL RHYS CUDDLECOME,
BELOVED OF THE FAMILY.
DIED 10th JUNE 1796.
Embalmed by H. Jones,
taxidermist of Lampeter
with deference and
respect.

'Bloody hell!' I ejaculated, and crossed the floor at speed, dived into the bed and got under the sheets.

I hadn't been back two minutes when all hell came loose in the inn yard, with men shouting and women shrieking and horse hooves clattering on the cobbles: then feet came thumping up the stairs to the attic and the door burst open and there was Cushy in a shimmy and breastplates and flinging up her arms, and she had a gun.

'Out, lad, *out*! It's the Mortimers come after your blood!' and I heard Sir John's high, throaty voice shouting: 'Open up, Miss Cuddlecome – we know he's here. Open up or it'll be the worse for you!'

'Open up, is it?' cried Cushy, rushing to the window while I fought my way into my trousers. 'Sure to God, ye'll not set foot in here, ye murderin' bunch of scallywags!' and she flung back the window and levelled the gun, and by the way it was waving the only safe ones were the Mortimers. 'I'll blow the arse off any man who puts a finger on me private property!'

'Produce the son of Hywel Mortymer, woman, and we'll leave you in peace!' Kent shouted up. And I peeped past Cushy's shoulder and saw him astride his horse, calm and dignified.

'Quick, son, *quick!*' whispered Cushy, tucking in the tail of my shirt, and she pointed. 'Out of the other window, shin over the tiles and it's a six-foot drop to the front entrance. It's the way me fellas come and go, and they're half dead, so it's nought to a sprightly lad like you. *Away!*' and she kissed me and pushed me off.

I hauled up the sash, cocked a leg over the sill, slid down the tiles and hung on the gutter, before dropping down at the front door.

With my boots in my hand and my shirt tail out again and flapping, I made for the open fields, and had the legions of Rome been after me they wouldn't have gained a yard.

'Right, ye bloody rapscallions, you've asked for it.' They were the last words I heard Cushy shout before she blasted them with a gun, and the night was quiet then, save for galloping horses.

'Hey, you!' called Cushy, halfway out of the bedroom window, and I came out of the shadows and caught the Cyfarthfa blanket she tossed down to me.

'God go with you, Hywel Mortymer's son,' said she.

I hoped so, for I needed all the help I could get; certainly the Mortimers hadn't wasted much time before discovering I hadn't died in the coach.

Four

My father always said that the safest place away from your enemy is to hide within his lines: this, said he, Colonel Wintour did when pursued by Cromwell's Roundheads: remembering that the Mortimers were seeking me in the area of Dolaucothi, I decided to go down its mines in search of gold.

Now, the village of Pumsaint gets its name from a famous Standing Stone that commemorates the resting place of the five saints – Gwyn, Gwyno, Gwynore, Celnin and Ceitho – who once journeyed here: indeed, one can see on the stone the ground hollows of their shoulders. Later, the Romans tunnelled the place for gold, constructing adits that burrowed into the hills, using Celtic labour working under the lash. On and off this prospecting had continued down the centuries.

Hearing the crush and stamp of a working mill; seeing the wavering light of compound flares, I made my way towards it.

Here a little mill was running to a waterwheel which tapped the flow of the ancient Cothi. Ragged men, women and children were labouring in the red light, shovelling up the broken ore the miners were digging out of the adits, and spreading it for crushing under the hammers: then the milled stone was sprayed with water to catch the specks of gold and channel it down to the trappers: isolated groups of little children, the end of the night shift, were on their knees over puddling holes, wearily jigging reed baskets into pools of Cothi water. About them, sticks in hand, walked the overmen with measured tread, eyes skinned for the gold thief. A few specks in the lining of a coat could bring in more than a twelve-hour shift of labour.

The foreman I found was big and beefy, and he put his calloused hands on his hips and eyed me for an interloper. 'What you want?'

'I'm after a start,' I said.

His sloe eyes drifted over me; the trapping women chanced a peep from behind their red kerchiefs: the man walked round me like a butcher at a meat auction.

'You ever tram-hauled?'

'Tram-hauled?'

His white teeth split his face; a woman giggled. Said he, 'If you'd tram-hauled, Daio, you'd know what it was. But ye've got bull shoulders on ye – so threepence a day on a twelve-hour shift; take it or leave it.' He turned away.

It began to rain: diadems of water threaded the shoulders of the labourers. Somebody hit a bar triangle; the night shift began to gather their few possessions; from the vicinity of the road the day shift, moody and sulked with sleep, moved in with the lethargy of humans already dead. I caught the foreman's eye and winked, and he curved his hands to his mouth, shouting: *'Bimbo!'* A little lad aged about five appeared barefooted before me in rags. His Welsh eyes, dark, shone in his high-boned face: cupped in his grubby hands was a tame linnet.

The foreman said: 'Lovely posh fella by 'ere, Bimbo, so treat him gentle – take him up to Bill Smalley at the face – for haulin', say – no soft capers.'

'You come to stay, mister?' asked Bimbo, as I followed his little drumstick legs into a tunnel.

I spoke his dialect: lovely posh fella, indeed. 'Only time to earn a butty – you been here long?'

The entrance faded and brought us into near-blackness; but fifty feet ahead a lamp burned in a niche. Hands outstretched against bumps, we went to it, Bimbo leading.

In a piping treble he replied over his shoulder, 'Only two weeks, but soon we'll be off, says Rhian.'

'Rhian?'

'My sister.' We paused and his face danced before me in the flickering light like a disembodied ghost.

'You travel together?' I asked.

'Ay ay, from Water Street Poorhouse, down Carmarthen way. Ten stripes Rhian got for bustin' out, and I got six for being her brother. "Bimbo lad," she says to me, "this anna fair; it was me, not you, who potted 'em."'

'Potted who?'

'The Poorhouse maister. He do come free with Rhian and squiggled up her dress, so she hit him with a poker.'

'And that's what you got the stripes for?'

'That's right. Mind, old Bill Smalley's a right bastard, too, but he don't tickle women up so much, says Rhian – ain't that good?'

'Marvellous.' I gave him a grin. 'Some sister.'

'Aye, but she's a tidy old bitch if you cross her, mind.'

'Most sisters are,' I said, and he reached out a hand behind him and hauled me on.

Now the tunnel deepened in a sweep of slush and from the roof came the dull, musical plopping of water. But the lights brightened as we floundered onwards, now calf-deep in mud and filth, and the floor drifted more as we neared the working face. As we rounded a bend in the adit I saw them at it full flush: a dozen men and more, some stripped to the waist, some naked, hewing at the rock in a thunder of picking, shovelling and gasps; the wounding thumps of the mandrels, the crashing of falling debris, the soprano music of the spades.

Bimbo gripped my arm and we stood waiting, for these were the sinews of the gold adits; the experts of brain and muscle who could trace the invading arsenopyrite that geology had folded into the pyritic shales: aye, I learned it all later, for there was a lot more to this than dig and shovel and tram. Shale and siltstone, lode and quartz that stand within the sheer zones that only the geologist knows – the magical ingredients that give birth to the ultimate magic – *gold*. Gold, not Fool's Gold (this they spot with half an eye). Real gold that spins the earth. The Romans knew the trade as well, the old chaps said reluctantly: the chemists and geologists of 2,000 years ago intimately knew the metal that ruled the world.

Now a big man turned at the face, and this was Foreman Smalley.

'What's on, Bimbo?'

'Lovely posh fella come by 'ere, Foreman, and Compound chap do say to treat him gentle.'

'What doin'?' The voice was double bass.

'Hauling, sir,' I said.

'Age?'

'Sixteen.'

'With them shoulders ye look like twenty. Women and kids on trams, lad – I can use you here,' and he tossed me his pick and I caught it in mid-air. 'Hewing. But put it up your mate and you'll be out feet first – eh, lads?' The hewers paused for a breather and I saw their sweat-stained faces riven with rock dust and the wide breadth of their shoulders.

'He's only a lad, though, Foreman,' said one, and his eyes shone like rubies in the dancing light.

'We've all been lads, mun. He'll be a man when the shift is over, eh?' and he clapped a ham hand on to my shoulder. 'You'll strip your fingers in the first hour, but you've got six more skins, remember: when I see blood on the haft I'll know you're working.'

'You'm a hard bleeder, Foreman,' said a man, and he was north country.

'If you think I'm hard you should meet the owners. Come on, get movin', or I'll put you to bed wi' a shovel!'

I spat on my hands (which was my first mistake) and got going: and I remember thinking that it was a far cry to the silver-laid table of Tregaron House, and the preening aristocracy of Jackson's Rooms.

Come midday it was snap time, and I had no snap. The others tossed bits and pieces at me as if I were a dog, but I tossed them back, saying I wasn't hungry. After a bit Bimbo arrived and stood to attention before me. Sprawling on the heaps, in attitudes of exhaustion, the hewers regarded him.

'Hey, Bimbo, where's ye sister?'

'If she'd hew for me, lad, I'd call her Foreman!'

'Hoi hoi, Bimbo, where do she sleep nights?'

'With me,' said Bimbo, and added to me, 'Missus says you're to come.'

'Oh dear me, bloody hark at it!' cried a man. 'What about us?'

'It never happens to me, Sam?'

'Cut it out, lads,' said Foreman Smalley, 'leave the little sod be.' And added, 'Tell her I'll put a pillow under her ears and teach her how to be a wife,' and this went right over Bimbo's head; he said:

'You got no bait, says Rhian, so you'd better come, or she'll get her rag out.' He gripped me, hurrying me on.

'Best you go,' called Foreman, grinning.

'Can't get back in time, sir.'

'Take an hour – cool your hands, lad – you've done good.' And Bimbo explained over his shoulder: 'Mind, Smalley's worse than the lot, really, but my Rhian mentioned as how she potted the Carmarthen fella with a poker, so now he only pinches her bum. What's your name?'

'Hywel Mortymer.'

This was the first decision, and I took it. It was my father's name; more, it was the name my mother had taken in love. I wondered what my father would have done, and got the instant answer. When once a man is ashamed of his name he can only sink lower; and once you turn your back on this bloody world, said he once, the world kicks your backside.

'Hywel what?' asked Bimbo, peering.

'Mortymer – Hywel Mortymer.'

'It's a bloody queer name is that one. Come.'

❧

34

There was a journey of empty trams linked for a run to the Smalley face. Beside each tram sprawled its hauliers; sometimes a woman and a child; often just two children, a lad and a girl.

The lad was called a foal and he hauled in front, the girl or woman they called a half-marrow, both of which were north country terms: names brought down by men like Smalley, who hailed from Lancashire.

Down at the face they used corfs; wicker baskets holding four hundredweight; these took the immediate fall of the face rock, and men, not children, tipped them to fill the trams; they were called Headsmen, the strongest of the team. Now the foals and marrows were lying along the road, or sat propped up against the adit walls: they sat in rags, most half naked, the women with sack bands round their waists and their breasts hanging bare; some were old, with feeding paps dragged by children; some were young; thick-chested Amazons with firm strong breasts untouched by the hands of men: a few, like Rhian, who was covered in the breast, were beautiful despite the dirt.

Rhian got up as I approached. She was small and dainty, her features dark and well defined, and her hair was a mass of tumbling blackness. She had tied it back with string and it reached in blue-black waves to her shoulders. Her voice, when she spoke, had the sing-song music of Carmarthen Welsh.

'You Hywel Mortymer?' She raised her face, for she scarce came up to my shoulder.

'Ay, ay.'

'Bimbo do tell that you've got no bait. You share with us?'

'I'd be glad to.'

I squatted beside her on the rail and she gathered the neck of her sack dress about her and turned her face this way and that, as women do when they don't know what to say.

'You like fishes?'

'When you're as hungry as me, you like anything.' It broke the silence of unspoken words that had come between us.

Bimbo squatted between us with his linnet held against his face, and his eyes like stars under the lamp.

I watched as Rhian took a little sprat from her bait tin and carefully broke it in her fingers. A slice of black bread top and bottom, and I had a sandwich with the tail sticking out; had it been boiled lobster and caviar, it wouldn't have tasted better.

'*Diawch!* Dear me! Oh, look at your hands!'

Reaching out, she caught my hands and turned the palms upward: red and raw and with rolled up, broken blisters; claws for fingers and palms like boiled bacon. Then she raised her eyes to mine in that moment, still holding me, and there was born an affinity and affection.

She is gone now, my Rhian: aeons of time divide us, but always will I remember the look of compassion upon her face in that filthy place.

'He's got gent's hands, mind,' cried Bimbo, treble. 'That's what old Smalley said.'

'If I had Smalley I'd give him a basting for putting a gentleman on the face.'

'No gentleman, just ordinary,' I said.

'Oh aye? Hold on.' As I ate the bread and fish she filled a tin with water and washed my hands with a strip of her petticoat; the pain flushed me, yet scarcely did I feel it. Then she knelt and pulled up her dress to her thighs and Bimbo held it there while she knocked off more strips of the white petticoat and bound up my hands and tied the knots with her teeth, and her teeth, I saw, were white and even against her curved red lips, and I judged her age at twenty.

She said, 'If the skin weren't broken I'd fetch a cow-pat from outside, to heal; but these won't heal till you're done with Smalley. You realize he's testing you?' She raised her dark eyes.

'Testing or not, I need the money.' Chewing, I lay back against the tram and regarded her. 'You on bad times too?' I asked.

She answered, 'When times were good our mam took us

down to Flannel Street, Abergavenny, for red and yellow petticoats; even some with lace on, and white, like this. When times got bad she took us on the roads with cans and pegs and landed us in Carmarthen Poorhouse . . .'

'Gypsy travellers?' I asked, for you could see these any time on the roads of Wales with their little mountain ponies in the shafts and their bob-carts rattling along with cans swinging on the back; and more, when she turned up her face to the light, this one had the cut of the gypsy on her, as had Bimbo. I smelled in them the peat smoke; saw the ring of faces at the bonfires come Brecon Fair.

'No,' said she curtly. 'Welsh, not gypsies.'

Now the triangular iron bar was rung again and the women and children rose in sighs; the foals harnessed up, the half-marrows prepared to push behind.

These trams did not run on wheels on a line, but on skids; bumping and carving a groove in the mud which greased their path. I offered to help push, for the journey of trams was going up to my face, but Rhian shook her head.

'Two to a tram; third one could collect a yardstick on the bum. Smalley don't go for three-ers.'

They pushed off in grunts and *hey-ya-hup, hey-ya-hup,* getting the trams swishing on the skids: the foal worked low, with a chain between his legs; the half-marrows pushed behind, their bare feet splayed to the rock crops; head bent, one arm hanging to the ground for purchase. No identifiable words accompanied the haul, only sighs and grunts and groans: gasping in the dust-laden air they went, one tram after another; the draught donkeys called humans who had been hauling in this adit since the start of civilization.

But these were slaves to a modern purpose; the economic boom that plundered their strength for the profits of present-day Romans; a new, baser breed of old speculators who hung their bullion on the backs of the younger generation; and who, had the law allowed them, would have had them under the whip.

As I overtook sledge after sledge on my way up the road, I passed a girl whose breasts were small: pretty was she with her dancing blue eyes and her hair hanging down either side of her face, and she smiled up at me as I passed her. Foreman had bought her from Irish lands, snatched the straw out of her mouth, said Rhian, and paid for her at the Hiring Fair: twopence a day or five pounds a year plus water and wheat. Aged six.

Presently, I stood in a wall niche and watched the journeys go by: one by one came the trams, turning off on the passing road; and I stood there until the last tram came, and this was pulled by Rhian with the chain between her legs and her sack dress rolled up to her waist to show her drawers. At the back of the tram, his small body rigid to the load, pushed Bimbo.

'See you later, Mr Mortymer,' cried he, and the linnet he had tamed was perched upon his shoulder.

A man was standing beyond the parting when I came back to the face; I saw him clearly, despite the gloom, for he was silhouetted against the lamps where the hewers were working: a gentleman, this one, and I couldn't think how he'd missed me coming in: the hewers were grouped around him: Bill Smalley, the foreman, was standing to attention, screwing at his cap, as a peasant faces authority. I slowed my pace as I heard Smalley say: 'No new men taken on this past week, sir – only a lad or two; I took one on this morning.'

'Describe him,' said the gentleman, and I recognized the voice: it was Kent Mortimer; the usual autocratic gestures now, slapping his horsewhip against his riding-boot.

Foreman said: 'Young, sir, like I said. About sixteen, sir – no more; but a well-set-up boy, so I took him on, but he cut 'is hands up som'at dreadful.'

'His name.'

'No name, sir. Didn't ask 'im.'

'Do you usually take on workers without knowing their names?'

'I'd 'ave his name in the mornin', sir, begging ye pardon.'

'And I'll have yours tonight, my man. I'll talk to your owner about this, by God. Is this the way you run an adit?'

'You hang on here a coupla minutes more, sir, for he'll be back any moment, I vow . . .' said Smalley.

'I very much doubt it, knowing the Mortymers,' snapped Kent, and turned, ploughing his way through the mud in my direction.

He was quick, but I was quicker.

Dousing the wall lamps as I went to make pursuit more difficult, I made my way back to the adit entrance, and came out into the golden ball of the sun. The day shimmered in warmth and birdsong; it was like the beginning of the earth.

Once clear of the Dolaucothi mines, I ran, and did not stop until Pumsaint was a long way behind me.

In a lonely place on the road I came across a gang of Poorhouse road-menders; men, women and children, working under an overseer who strolled among them with a stick.

Time was, back in Tregaron, I'd see these paupers, who wore a purple badge of shame, carrying big stones up a hill, dig them in and bury them, then dig them up and carry them down the hill again: the intention, said Old Amos, being to keep them gainfully employed; the County ain't puttin' 'em up for nothing.

And one of these, a little dwarf-like lad of about twelve years, raised his face and stared at me as I passed. I saw in his eyes the boy he might have been, before his death at the hands of people.

Long after I saw the spires of the town coming up, the look upon his face haunted me.

Pursued by my stomach, I hurried on, but turned once.

The little crippled boy was still there among the other paupers, looking back.

There was born between us an unspoken affinity.

Five

I was getting close to Llandovery now and the only friend I had in the world, my mother; her grave and her nearness called me.

Sun-bright urchins, spindle-legged and rickety, were playing on the cobbled streets as I entered the market town: hoopla, toss-a-farthing and pitch-for-marbles: one-two-three O'Leary, the ancient game of girls, was chalked on the pavements outside the church, now performed by hopping shrews in clogs with their skirts tucked up into their drawers; pinafored wives sat on their doorsteps in the sun, the rosebud mouths of their suckling infants slobbering with milk; it revived new memories of my hunger.

Boozies were already tipsy on the rutted roads, parting their beards in the four-ale taps and pouring down pewters without so much as a swallow: fine gentlemen in well-cut jackets and trews were arming beautiful women in silk, and the air was perfumed with the waft of lavender. Now a massive bull being led by the nose, followed by a clutch of leashed and snarling terriers . . . to the baiting bull-ring where the torture would make him tender. Near me, head bowed and haltered on her way to market, a wife, pulled by a drunk, was led for sale.

Now the clanging of an urgent bell forced me into a thicker crowd; I took refuge in a doorway, and the excitement grew, for there arose a cry from the mob: 'Poppie May's comin', lads! Poppie May's a'coming!' and I looked down at an old crone tugging at my trousers; she croaked in Welsh: 'You stand by me, young sprat, lest the gaoler do 'ave you, for he's always after fresh blood. Don't ye hear, lad? Poppie May's comin'!'

Through an avenue formed in the mob came a procession of dancing, cheering people: acrobats were handspringing and cartwheeling on the edge of the crowd. Standing in an ox-cart, crammed like herrings in a barrel, was the bewigged judiciary of the town: bowing right and left, they were accepting the obeisance of the fair-day crowd. Tipstaff and gaoler, town crier and special constable, mayor and Corporation, waved as applause grew about them.

Behind them came a lunatic in a cage: something less than human of drumstick limbs and a wasted body; a living skeleton with excrement in its matted hair and tatters draping its naked body: a man by the look of it, but I couldn't be sure. The creature shrieked and tore at its bars while the refuse of the street was flung at it: weeping, clutching at its hair, it yelled its invectives back at its tormentors: the people surged around the cage, bawling abuse.

The old girl sitting at my feet cried: 'Old Mad Casker do put on a rare good show, mind, but you anna seen nothin', son, till you seen our l'il Poppie.'

Now, the lunatic cage passed, a donkey pulling a trap came into view, and I stood on tiptoe for a better look.

Tied to the trap, stripped to the waist and with her arms tied outstretched, was a young woman; half conscious now, for she had been flogged through the town: her long hair dragged the mud of the road, her bare feet scraped along the cobbles. Behind her came two gaolers, and their whips cracked down. Blood had soaked the waistband of her bodice; her eyes were open as she was dragged past me; blood and froth was upon her mouth.

'Mind you,' cried the old girl, 'she do ask for it no end, do Poppie May. Every Fair Day she do come up before the beaks, this time for a sixpenny bonnet.'

'Bonnet?'

The old woman champed her toothless jaws. 'Bonnets – and if it anna bonnets it be pretty scarves – can't do without

41

'em.' And she cupped her hands to her sagging face, and yelled, 'Go on, Tom lad, give her one for me!'

Behind the gaolers walked three of the woman's children; skeletal waifs, in rags.

Later I saw Poppie May laid out on the roadside while a blacksmith pinned fetters on her wrists and feet.

Seven years transportation to Australia.

The old woman had followed me, intrigued by my tears. 'Jesus, mun, what you cryin' for?' asked she. 'She be liftin' babies' bonnets off the market stalls every bloody Fair Day.'

I never got rid of the scene; the woman fainting by the road; the ringing of the blacksmith's hammers.

On a corner near the market stalls I recognized a face I'd seen before; the thin, sallow features of the lad with the work-house road gang outside Llandovery. Broken-backed and crippled, with one hand on the ground helping his progress, he looked like a zoo monkey, and he leered at me with his twisted mouth. For a moment we stared at one another in recognition, and then I went in search of my mother.

My mother, two years ago, had been buried in Llandovery; the knowledge of her always brought to me a sweet, intimate joy.

I remembered the black shine of the funeral horses stamping on the cobbled yard of Tregaron House; the hearse with its gleaming black mahogany and shining brass; the manes decorated with ostrich feathers, the gleam of the coffin.

I remembered, too, my father's stoic grief as I walked with him in the churchyard; the bruised grass, ragged grave-diggers, the vulgarity of the upturned soil so soon to embrace one I loved. Her beauty, her refinement, made an outcry against such barbarity. My father had told me to kiss my mother's face, and this I had done, seeing on her throat the burn of the rope that had choked out her life, despite the undertaker's efforts to conceal it.

'You realize, I hope, that she was out of her mind, Hywel,' said my father.

'Yes,' I had replied.

'Only a woman whose reason had gone would do to herself so terrible a thing, you understand?'

'Of course.'

'You found her. You know what she did; it was unforgivable, wasn't it?'

'Yes,' I had said, 'it was unforgivable.'

And I saw in his eyes the light I have seen in the eyes of an animal as it awaited the sharpening of the knife.

Now the spire of the church in Llandovery was ringed with a halo of light as I knelt by the grave of my mother. Because of my bandaged hands I opened with difficulty the silver locket at my throat, and gazed at the silver-framed portrait; she was in her wedding dress: dark eyes and olive skin; hair shining black, falling in ringlets to her shoulders. I looked again at the inscription on the gravestone before me:

LADY JANE MORTYMER (*née Mortimer*)
Born August 15th 1760, died June 1st 1798
Beloved wife of Hywel Iestyn Mortymer of Tregaron House;
daughter of Lord and Lady Mortimer of Llandovery

The sun was going down when I arose; the churchyard was empty save for a sea of monumental stones, flying cupids and faceless angels; yet I felt my mother's friendship closer to me then than I had known before.

As if she knew I was in need of a mortal friend, she sent me Bendy Oldroyd.

Two little girls, Mamie Goldie and Billa Jam Tart, were dancing a fandango in Market Square when I got back to the stalls; later, I knew these in Blaenafon before two old drunkards got them. Now the mob, its mood of cruelty changed after Poppie May was dragged away, was clapping the time to dancing; gentlemen were crossing their boots, arms balancing; young girls holding up their petticoats to show their knees. Fiddles were playing, melodeons going, and the sun burned down before shutting up shop for the night.

Starving to drop my teeth out, I pushed through the dancers to the stalls. The crowd was even thicker here; old girls in hooped crinolines of bombazine and alpaca, young girls in white smocks and pinafores, with flower chains in their hair, and loungers in farm trews weighing up their chances; waiting for nightfall and their evil intent. Posh toffs were here with monocles and big bellies, furtively followed by ragged pickpockets, chancing their arm with a length of rope. Tipsy dumpies out of the taverns were there sweating ale, their faces bunches of laughs, their boots clattering to the dance; monkeys on sticks with organ-grinders; tame bears, their teeth drawn, being led on chains. Young dandies with silver-knobbed canes and lace at their wrists and throats were eyeing up the chance of an heiress, for the powder-puff damsels were home on school holiday, usually under the eagle eyes of brooms in stays.

Starving orphans were grouped around the pie-stalls where big-chested matrons, their hair tied in top knots, were duffing up butter pats: beyond them, on a raised dais, stood the children of the hiring fair – standing like cattle with straw on their mouths, proof that they were up for sale – one meal a day and five pounds a year. God help the little orphan girl, I thought, among these beefy farmers.

There was lava bread from Swansea, black puddings, chopped lights and buttered bacon in garlic to keep vampires off; and strings and strings of widows' memories: tables were laden with bread-and-butter pudding and Chinese wedding-cake. Upon the air came the sweet brown smell of baking bread which you eat with the nose.

One old girl was pulling out little brown loaves from a wayside oven, and setting them out to cool; one of these, I noticed, had tipped over the edge and was steaming in the grass. I moved closer, for my stomach, ever since Rhian's sprat sandwich, had been rumbling for pounce thunder.

Nearer now, nearer, I pushed through a clutch of pearl-buttoned waistcoats, and the spit was already on my mouth when I took a last glance about me, and stooped.

'Touch that, me son, and you'll dance on a rope,' said a voice; I looked at the owner: it was the crippled lad I had seen before.

I whispered, 'Christ, I'm starving!'

'Ye might be, gent, but that's not the way to do it. My mate tried it down in Lampeter last spring and they got him in the van, had him in chains at the Assizes, and topped him – he was twelve years old.' He peered up at me, an apparition of crippledom made more dreadful by the sun.

I stared down at him, and he said, 'You want to eat real bad?'

I nodded, taking in his wasted body, his strange pallor; his tattered clothes hung about him, and through their rents his skinny limbs projected.

'You ain't done so well, neither,' I said, speaking his language.

'Nor I ain't done so bad,' and he eased a little gold watch out of his pocket, gave me its gleam, then dropped it back. His perky little face went up. 'Stands to reason, don't it? If you're going to be topped, marrer, it's best to be topped for somethin'!' He jerked his head. 'Follow me,' and he pushed through the crowd to a cider stall where a beefy publican was holding up bottles of brown scrumpy, and bawling from a cavernous mouth:

'Here it is, men, one tot o' Bill Bogg's elixir and your bloody nut comes off. Allsops, do ye call it? Gnat-piss, ye mean,' and he clanged two bottles together. 'A quart o' this and your missus becomes Lady Godiva. Roll up, roll up!'

My new companion elbowed me in the ribs. 'You fancy a plate o' jellied eels – some folks don't like fish, ye know.'

The publican roared, beetroot in the face: 'Come on, you

lucky men – as cheap as dirt, mun – a penny a pint to put ye on the right side of the wife . . . Roll up, roll up!'

'Watch this,' whispered my friend, and shouted, 'I'll take a gill, mister!' and he fished in his rags for money.

'A gill? A *gill*?' The publican's red face turned down to us. 'Oho, my friends, we have a north country booger down by 'ere, 'ave we?' and he waved his bottles. 'No gills served in Wales, me son, get back up there to Lancashire,' and my friend, unperturbed, bawled back:

'A gill's a gill, up north or down here, because Mr Downey, the fishmonger over there do say so – he's been a publican for years. He wants a gill, he says, and a gill he's goin' to have – or a half pint – same thing.'

'Two gills to a half, my lad,' said the publican.

'That anna what Mr Downey says,' cried my companion.

The publican went purple. 'I am being accused, I take it, of not knowing my job? – and me in the trade for forty year?' Reaching down, he got my friend by the lapels and shook him to rattle. 'Listen 'ere, Lancashire – you go and tell that fishy bugger that I'll sell him a half-pint bottle, but he ain't getting gills. There's *two* gills to half a pint – I anna dealing in farthings.'

'Yes, sir,' said my friend, and gripped me, towing me off behind him. 'We're halfway home, gent – come on,' and we stopped over the road at Downey the Fish.

'Two bowls of stewed eels, Mr Downey,' cried my comrade, and white-smocked Downey, as big as a brewer's dray, cocked his face to the sky and ladled them out, crying:

'A bowl a piece for two fine gentlemen. A penny a bowl, remember!'

'Bill Bogg, the publican's paying,' came the reply. 'My mate and I worked all mornin' for him,' and he took the bowls and set them on our laps and we spooned up the eels, and never in my life have I tasted such delicious fruits of the sea.

Because he was getting nowhere by holding out his hand, Mr Downey went on tiptoe, shouting over the heads of the

crowd to Bogg the Publican, and the essence of the fraud, I
discovered, was timing, for my companion leaped to his feet
and bawled shrilly, 'That's right, ain't it, Mr Bogg – *two?*'

'Of course, you fishy idiot,' cried back the publican. 'And
it'll always be two, in Wales or up north.'

Downey the Fish scratched his ear and regarded us with
small, fishy eyes. My friend got up, elbowing me to do
likewise, and as I got the last bit of eel down me he cried up,
'A penny a bowl for this is daylight bloody robbery, ye know.
I can get three buns for a penny over at Mrs Evan Evans.'

'Then go, in the name of God,' said Downey, still perplexed, and he called to the publican. 'What you on about,
Boggs? You do sound like real offended . . .'

'What's your name, gent?' asked my friend, wandering
away.

'Hywel, Hywel Mortymer.'

'Ach, that's too much of a mouthful – "Gent" I'm callin'
you, for you're a hoity-toity.'

'What's yours?' I asked.

'Bendy, they do call me. Bendy Oldroyd.'

Out of the corner of my eyes I saw publican and fishmonger in animated conversation in the middle of the road,
and I mentioned it.

'What happens now?' I asked.

'We bugger off,' said Bendy.

Six

Night threatened like a ghost with an empty sleeve; then came dusk, a mysterious creeping of starlight and hobgoblin gloom. I followed Bendy's strange, loping gait across fields and meadows until darkness dropped like a conjurer's cape and the moon came out.

'Sleep now,' said Bendy, 'until they call the dogs off.'

'They're after us?'

'Maybe. Folks eating proper don't like losing jellied eels,' and he sank down into a mattress of leaves, the refuse of a thousand autumns; sighing, I lay beside him, pulling the Cyfarthfa blanket up around my ears, and his face was shadowed in that moonlight; hollows for eyes had he, like an undertaker's corpse.

'What about them eels, then?'

I sat up. 'What about them?'

'I got the eels, you got a blanket. Don't you share?'

'Sorry,' I said.

'That entitles you to a meat course in the mornin'. Twice today you've 'ad fish – that piece in Dolaucothi gave you a sprat, you told me, I gave you eels – now you're on meat – we go hare-bonkin' in the dawn.'

'Hare-bonkin'?'

'Jesus, Gent, don't you know nothin'?' and before I could reply he was fast asleep.

It was incredible; I leaned above him, listening; he was breathing for a boy embalmed. And then: 'Good night, Gent,' said Bendy.

I awoke to find blood dripping over the earth, for the dawn had razored the throat of the sky. All was beautiful in a

48

bright, roseate hue, with the forest leaves turned up as if in benediction. Earlier, I had awakened in memory of my father, and the night was hoarding up moonlight in its cupboards; the forest full of rip, claws and shrieks.

'You all right, Gent?' said Bendy, for I must have sobbed in sleep.

'Yes,' I replied.

'Too late for snivellin' now, remember, your pa's gone.'

Earlier I had told him of the death of my father.

'Like my pa, really speakin',' said he. 'He popped his clogs down Top Town way; he dunna mean a lot to me, but he were a good old boy to my mither. He never got pissed when she was birthing the nippers, like most old chaps do, she said. "And it anna his fault we're poor – there's heat in gentry boots, but only coal in a collier's – so don't go blaming your pa, said she. It comes the way you're born." But your old man do sound a right old sod, by what you tell me.'

It angered me, but I didn't reply; my own fault, I supposed, for confiding too much. And then, to my astonishment, Bendy clambered up to his knees, put his hands together and said in prayer: 'God bless the eels and God bless me – and Gent, too. You ready for a wash?'

Together we went down to a little brook, and knelt, splashing icy water into our faces.

'Right, you,' cried Bendy, getting up. 'Hare-bonkin'. You hungry?'

'Starved!'

'Reet, you – but first we cut the bonkers,' and he produced like magic from his rags a wicked-looking knife, and I wouldn't have slept had I known of its existence: with this he nicked and broke off two thick cudgels, each about two feet long, and tossed me one. 'Come on,' he said. 'These are the bonkers; sit ready and do what I tell you, Gent, or you'll get bonked by me – understand?'

I nodded, and followed him through the trees. He moved silently, despite his crippled walk, until we came to a meadow fringe; here he went slower, creeping on all fours out of the forest to sit cross-legged. Strange and lovely smells arose from the earth, I remember; dandies and early hare-bells were yawning at the sun. Over his shoulder, Bendy beckoned, and on all fours, too, I joined him, my rear soaking up the spit-gobs of the grass, very uncomfortable.

'Where's the hares?'

'Hush you. Speak when you're spoken to.'

'I can't see any!'

'God's grief, Gent, don't you know anythin'? Listen,' and he cupped his grimy hands to his mouth and made a soft lamenting sound, like an animal in pain.

I peered through the sun-shot mist of the meadow. It was empty.

I looked past the snub profile beside me; at the little twisted body, the deformed legs and hunched shoulders: yet there was about Bendy Oldroyd an unaccountable beauty.

Again the soft, sighing sound came from his tiny hands. The forest echoed it; the world seemed to stop and listen; there was no sound but this pleading cry.

'Here they come, the silly old sods,' said Bendy.

I saw, as the mist rose slowly, five big hares approaching from a distant hedge: in line they came in staccato, hopping runs, ears erect; I swear I saw the anxiety upon their whiskered faces.

'Keep still,' commanded Bendy.

I kept still.

'Now slowly raise the bonker and rest it on your shoulder.'

I obeyed, ready for the downward strike. He whispered: 'Listen. The doe will come first, they always do, for she thinks her son is dyin', understand?'

'No.'

'Bloody hell, you're dull. She made the leveret, don't she? Right. Now she thinks he's got 'is neck in a thicket, or something. But you never kill a doe, ye hear me? Ye can have a dozen old bucks jumpin' her, but only the doe makes leverets.'

'You never kill the source of leverets, you mean?'

'Don't know about that, Gent, but you never kill a doe. Right, lad, here they come.'

They were coming, all five; hopping closer to the sound of a trapped leveret: now they came in line, suspiciously sniffing at the stink of humans, but mesmerized by the primeval call of their injured young: on, on, nearer, nearer: we sat like dawn statues.

'Don't blink,' whispered Bendy, and I stared ball-eyed at the approaching dinners.

'Don't even breathe,' whispered Bendy: rigidly I sat, the bonker trembling in my hand. Of a sudden, one hare disengaged itself from the others in a run of courage and appeared before me with a snitching mouth, and I brought down my bonker and hit it flat: the rest scampered off in a mêlée of cloven feet and buttoned tails.

'Oh, you silly sod,' cried Bendy. 'You've bonked the doe!'

The quivering body of the doe lay before us.

Reaching out, Bendy picked it up and put it against his face, and then, almost as quickly, he dropped it and swung to me, his bonker laid back, but I ducked away and on all fours, and faced him.

He cried: 'You toity old bugger, I ain't teachin' you nothing. Just look what you've done. You'm no better than gentry fox hunters!'

Picking up the doe again he cradled it in his arms.

'I'm sorry,' I said.

'Sorry's no good, Hywel Mortymer.' For the first time he used my name. 'You know something? I reckon's you've just killed 10,000 leverets.'

'There's another 10,000 in the forest,' I said, tiring of him, and he raised his tear-stained face to mine.

'Oh, no there ain't, Gent. I been taught by my ma to treat women special, for they're the mothers o' the earth.'

For a little while we sat apart.

Later, within the restricting bounds of injured friendship, we buried the doe on the edge of the forest where the dawn comes first, and she'd like that she would, said Bendy. Then he went back into the meadow and again I heard the crying of an injured leveret, and when he returned he was carrying a fine big buck. This we gutted, cleaned, beheaded, chopped his legs, and crucified him on sticks over a peat fire with his innards turned to the sun.

The smell of that roasting buck would have brought spit to the lips of Lucifer.

I was dusting out the fire before we began our journey onwards when Bendy saw the silver locket I wore round my neck: reaching out greasy fingers, he turned it this way and that in the sun.

'What you got in there, Gent?'

'A portrait of my mother.'

By some trick of the day, amid the drowsing hum of bees, I knew resentment: his twisted body, his filthy hand and the smoke of the dying fire drifting up between us turned him into a little Beelzebub.

'Can I see her?' he asked.

'No!'

Anger blazed suddenly in his eyes, large and beautiful; the only good feature of his face.

'Why not?'

'Because you can't.'

He said, 'I feed you eels and hare, Gent. I saved your neck back there in the town, and the first thing I want from you, you turn me down. I anna got a mother, so I wants a look at yours.'

I didn't reply. To show him my mother's face would be a betrayal: it was akin to showing her to a beast.

'Then fook you, Gent. I ain't doin' nothin' for you no more – understand? Nothing no more!'

'Suits me,' I said, and I folded up the Cyfarthfa blanket and he marched off without a backward glance until I called him.

'Bendy Oldroyd!'

He came running back to me, one hand helping his progress, and knelt before me. Because my hands were still bandaged, I took the locket off my neck and he took it in cupped hands and gently opened it, his face alive with unfeigned joy.

'Oh, my Gawd,' said he, 'ain't she beautiful!'

Kneeling there, his eyes grew brighter, and he added, 'She's nearly as pretty as that little doe.'

Come close to midday, with the sun almost directly over-head and Bendy leading the way along an isolated path, he suddenly turned, caught me and swung me down into the grass.

'Horses!' he whispered.

'What?'

'Horses!'

I sat up. 'Don't be daft, there's nothing round here for miles!'

'Oh yes, there is,' and he parted the grass about him, peering down a hill. 'Horses these past five minutes, and now they're on the gallop.' And he lifted his nose to the wind and scented it, as does an animal.

'Suppose there is – what's it to do with us?'

'Militia horses; I heard a stallion, and clanks.'

'Clanks?'

'Sabres and saddles; they're coming after those eels.'

'They're a bit late for that,' I said, and rose.

Now, within a bower of branches we rested because the day was hot; drank with cupped hands from a stream, and ate what was left of the hare.

Earlier I had asked him where he was leading us, and he'd said anywhere clear of Llandovery; then wiggled out of his pocket the watch, a fob on a golden chain, which he had lifted off a gentleman. I didn't pursue it at the time, but we couldn't just keep on running, so I asked, with a straw in my mouth: 'Where are we bound? We're miles from Llandovery!'

'I'm away to the fire towns, I don't know about you.'

We were around Trecastle way now, on the Sarn Helen road again, and the mountains danced like silver dragons in the sun, veiling the horizon like a shroud; above a brook a ballet of gnat-flies danced, curtsying to one another in the early sunlight, and it seemed to me, watching that road ribboned away to the west, that I was looking down the vertebrae of the centuries; I mentioned this, but Bendy shrugged.

'What's so good in the fire towns, then?' I asked.

'I got an aunt there.' He propped his back against a tree and screwed up his wizened little face. 'I reckon I can eat on her, till I find work in coal, for I'm not going back to the Poorhouse.'

'You always worked in coal?'

'Since I can remember.' He made a face at the sun. 'Since I was five, perhaps – don't really recall.' He added, 'My pa was a horse-whisperer, you know.'

'A what?'

'A horse-whisperer. He could whisper sweet nothings into a nag's ear and that thing would do anything he asked. Actually, he was a farrier working down the Percy pit outside North Shields – you been there?'

I shook my head.

He continued, 'Nags are queer fish, especially pit ponies, and they'll boss along wi' ye until you do something wrong. One day my pa picked up a shire's shoe-nail instead of a pony's, and drove it into a pony's hoof, and the nags gave him a bad name round the stables and he couldn't do anything right. So he were down-graded to a collier.'

He delighted me. 'Go on!'

'And to get another tram – one tram per human head, see – he took me underground, for he had mouths to feed.'

'At five years old?'

'That's nowt,' asserted Bendy. 'I've known babies in long clothes go down for a tram. I knew a man – and this be true – who made a clay doll in swaddling clothes, and took that down. "That baby's mighty quiet," says Foreman. "Ay, ay," said the collier, "it's well behaved." "Don't it ever breast-feed?" "Aye," said the collier, "barely once a fortnight," and though Foreman knew he were spoofing, he still got another tram.' Bendy smiled at his thoughts. 'My Grancher lost a foot and went to London. But that's when he were ten years old. He pickpocketed wi' other urchins, living on the streets, he said. Way back fifty years or so, that was, and he saw a girl o' ten burned for a witch in Smithfield. Every Sunday mornin' he went to London Bridge to see the pirates drown.'

'Drown?'

'Aye, they'd chain 'em hand and foot to the ring-bolts – captured pirates, see – and he'd pay a ha'penny to see the tide come up the Thames and drown 'em.'

'Good God.'

'No, he ain't,' said Bendy. 'And he ain't in Heaven, neither, says my old man, but you keep praying, Bendy son, in case he is, my ma told me.'

We fell to quiet and lay immersed in gold; in bee-hum and the chatter of rooks.

'What happened to him – your pa, I mean?'

'I told you recent – popped his clogs up in the Top Towns – Blaenafon town ironworks when he were living with my aunt. He was mending a five-ton drop-hammer when some-body pulled a handle, and he come out flat as a bloody pancake. That's why I'm off there now.'

'Blaenafon? Where's that?'

'Search me, but I'm going there – you coming?'

I shrugged. One place was as good as another, it seemed, so I asked, 'What's so special about these Top Towns, then?'

'Work in plenty – in iron, in coal. Fire-paint-red places, my pa called them. When the furnaces are a'going ye don't need lamps.'

The sky was the colour of topaz now; a skylark was weaving its dot in the sky, its song cadent.

He continued, 'I likes coal, though it's better pushing than hauling because of the chafes. Bound to have chafes, ain't ye, pulling with a chain between your legs?' He sighed in deep reminiscence. 'Like I said, I were five when I went down Blackboy; she was a wet old bitch with water round your knees, but she fetched good coal. I were a trapper in her barrow-ways.'

'A trapper?'

'Aye, they gave me a place to sit in the dark, and when the trams came through I had to lift the brattice door with a string —'

'Brattice door?'

And he sighed at my ignorance, saying: 'The door stops the foul air travelling, for you can't see nor smell the Foul, see? Sometimes I had a candle for the dark, sometimes not, for a pound o' them cost twopence and bread was a penny; so you eat in the dark or light up the rats – take pick. I was six when that old Blackboy fired; it killed ten of us, mainly kids.'

'You were hurt?'

'Not a lot,' and he turned his face to me. 'I lost the skin and flesh one side, see? Mind, it were Susie Thomas's fault – she pegged up the brattice, then fell asleep. She was only four, but she was Welsh and should 'ave known better, said Bert Fart, our overman, and he were a real sod with the yardstick. Although she was scorched in the legs and bum he basted her all over, drawers off, for you never peg up the brattice. I mean, it's dangerous, ain't it? I lost my singing hinni in that explosion, too.'

'Singing hinni?'

'North country plum puddin' cake. My ma was a Scot, and she made it proper way, with rice; when she put it on the griddle it sang a little song. Mind, the rats liked singing hinni no end, too, so you ate it early on. My ma died down Blackboy.' He looked away.

'Down Blackboy?'

'Well, down Dial Drift, really. But she drank fever water down Blackboy just when she was comin' up for her ninth, and you ain't birthing underground like a pony, said my pa. "Aw, Catcheen, me lovely," she says to him, "don't be daft, for there's weeks in me yet; hang on till I get me show, lad, for we needs the money." "No," my pa said back, "you've had eight out decent in straw, and you ain't bedding on a coal mattress; I'm havin' you up, woman." But while he were on Blackboy shift with me and our lot, she went down Dial half-days, got caught down there with her stomach, and died half-birthed.'

We sat in silence. I thought he was going to cry, but he did not.

'Can I look at your ma again, Gent?'

I nodded.

Bats and blackbirds were dropping around us before we continued the journey east to Blaenafon, for that's where the work is, said Bendy.

'With folks following us, it's best to travel by night,' he added.

'There's nobody following us, don't be daft.'

'Oh yes, there is, my son.'

Now we were in Fforest Fach, south of Senny and to the east of Crai, and that night we stripped off and bathed in the old Senni and the stars were as big as lanterns, the moon a fractured opal in the big black sky.

Later, near dawn, south of Brecon in the foothills of the Allt Ddu, we rested again because I had blisters, and the trees above us were a black tracery of branches against a sky of fleece, with Orion beaming searchlights and Sirius making her archeries of red and gold.

In that beauty the Mortimers came.

'Horses again,' said Bendy, shaking me into wakefulness. 'Your people on to us, I reckon, and this time they've got a dog.'

'What makes you think it's the Mortimers?'

'From what you told me, Gent. Folks don't travel this far after jellied eels, look!'

I followed his pointed finger; down in the valley three

horsemen were coming straight up the mountain slopes towards us; faintly on the wind came the barking of a dog. We lay flat, parting the vetch grass, the hair of the mountain.

I said, 'Look, they're following our tracks!'

'Aye,' answered Bendy. 'Sod that old dog. Why the hell did I get mixed up wi' you, Gent. Before you come I had no trouble.'

He stared belligerently at me in the moonlight, and added: 'Bollocks to you, Gent. I'm off.'

'Please yourself, and bollocks to you, too.'

He made a wry face. 'We could always swim the river.'

I spoke his language so he fully understood. 'All right, go and swim the bloody thing. If you don't want to stay, I'm better off without you.'

'Aw, Jesus, come on!' said Bendy, and caught my arm and hauled me to my feet. 'I done this country before; if I leaves ye now you'll hit the bogs, or something. Can ye swim?'

'Of course.'

'I can't, so you can float me over.'

'So that's why you're staying with me!'

'Give me three guesses,' he replied, and towed me after him. 'Come on!' and together we pelted east to a rushing stream which was a tributary of the River Usk, having its source on the highest point of the Beacons. Down this we paddled north to put the dog off the scent; we travelled, weary and footsore, until we reached the mothering river.

Having lost us, our pursuers must have galloped across country to the Brecon to Abergavenny road.

Lying in the roadside ditch, fearful of the dog, we watched them come: clip-clopping in the dawn's red light to Llechfaen, going in the wrong direction, three horsemen: Sir John, Kent Mortimer, and the man with the shattered face, his cocked hat hanging down the back of his neck. There was no sign of the dog.

'They the relatives?' whispered Bendy.

I nodded.

'Dear God, you must 'ave done something real terrible, Gent, for them to want you this bad.'

'One day I might explain it to you,' I replied.

It isn't wise, my mother once told me, to tell a stranger secrets, and one was stirring within me now.

His mention of the iron Top Towns had reminded me of my father's financial interests in these places. Yes, I knew a bit about the Top Towns: stocks and shares he'd handed over to my Uncle John in return for his debts.

But one thing was certain – Bendy Oldroyd was the last in the world I'd tell of such things.

Seven

Now, a day later, miles further east and free of the pursuing Mortimers, we found the land bathed in a magical brightness as we washed away the dust and dirt beneath drooping willow trees: the lake called Tal-y-Bont, iron flat to a sheeny loveliness, sparkled silver in the hot June day: wading deeper through the shallows, I dived, seeing a new world of waving fauna and flowers, and rose into sunlight, spraying water.

Instantly, I saw a trout swimming close by: a trout of great size – feet long if she was an inch, with long black hair streaming out as she went in an ungainly dog-paddle; a hen fish I had seen before, one with Welsh-dark eyes.

Years later another like this was seen by my son; but a salmon, swimming in the shallows of the Usk.

Now this particular trout waded out of the lake and threw herself down on to a grassy bank in my full view; she looked like a primeval maiden spewed up from the earth.

Bimbo's sister; her name, I remembered, was Rhian.

But I didn't come out of the water quickly; despite my nobler instincts I trod water and peered with eyes on corn-stalks . . . aware that I was looking at the secrets of my mother.

Later, at moon-come-high, as Bendy called it, we went out to search for drunken pheasants: that afternoon he had soaked a pocketful of wheat in a handful of whisky stolen from a drover, and sprinkled it along the edge of a wood where pheasants nested. Sure enough, not a minute after we arrived, along comes a beautiful cock three sheets to the wind, and staggers up to us like a man about to ask the time, and Bendy knocks him off.

Transportation for seven years if you're caught with pheasant feathers – dished out by clergy magistrates who were saving them up for slaughter on the Glorious Twelfth.

'Wouldn't be the first time I've eaten the feathers, either,' remarked Bendy, and I tell you this: the smell of that cock pheasant blowing over quicksilver Tal-y-Bont must have raised every sporting gun for miles. Eaten hot to the scald was he, with the juice running down our chins, and we oohed and aahed to the pain of our fingers while the moon, round and full with him, sat on the rim of the world like a pumpkin.

'You like boiled salmon, fresh from the river?' asked Bendy. 'I've got that next on the menu.'

There was being born in me a small if undefined affection for Bendy Oldroyd; strangely enough, it had little to do with the stomach.

Perhaps it was the perfume of roasting pheasants that brought Rhian into my life again; I never really knew, for she didn't stay long enough this time for me to ask her.

All that afternoon, giving her time to get her dress back on, I had combed the lakeside for a sight of her, but she had vanished as if aboard a magic carpet.

Night fell; wrapped in the Cyfarthfa blanket, we slept, and there was nothing to sully that sleep until sun-come, when a twig snapped.

'We got company, Gent,' my friend whispered into my ear, and I opened an eye to the astonishing beauty of the morning.

Amid sun-shafts and mist something made shape not ten feet from where we slept, and it was Rhian.

She had appeared as Rhiannon might have done from the mists of the Mabinogi: dreamlike, unearthly. I peered about her for her magic horse.

So quiet and still she stood. She wore the same ragged clothes as she had in the Dolaucothi mines, but round her waist now was a silver girdle, and round her forehead a band of gold; upon her feet were little leather slippers. Now she came to the white ashes of our fire, staring down at the bones of the pheasant.

Her beauty took my breath, but not Bendy's. 'What you after?' he demanded.

I rose, but Bendy was quick, and pulled me back down.

'I know her,' I whispered.

'I don't.'

'She's hungry – this is the girl who gave me the sprat . . .'

'Oh aye? Well, she ain't getting any of this,' and he snatched at the can that held the bits of pheasant and put them behind him, and I yelled, trying to get at them:

'Hey you! Give over!' I spoke his language. 'She fed me good and I'm goin' to feed her!' I wrested the pieces of pheasant away from him, and between us they fell on the hot ashes and the fat of them flared and burnt into a flame that sizzled. As Rhian backed away, her hands to her face, Bendy pulled a faggot out of the fire and brandished it.

Rhian shrieked, and fled, and I raced after her, shouting, 'Come back, come back!'

She disappeared into the trees as if plucked off the earth.

'Rhian! Rhian! *Bimbo!*'

The trees echoed; the lake flung back my voice.

In desperation, I ran round to the place I had seen her when bathing, and found footprints, big and small, leading down to the water. Then I saw something else, and stooped to pick it up.

It was an empty canvas purse of cheap but intricate design. Dropping it into my pocket, I went back to the camping place, where Bendy was on his knees, damping down the fire.

'You're a hard old bugger, ain't you, Bendy Oldroyd?'

To this he did not reply, but went on killing the fire, and the bits of pheasant he had salvaged he held hard against him.

'One would think you've never gone hungry.'

'I been hungry all my life.'

'She could have had my bits.'

'Give her your bits, Dafto, and she'd 'ave been after mine.'

'Her name's Rhian. She fed me, so I owed her one. The least you could have done was tickle her a fish.'

'Give her a fish and she'll want the loaf as well. This ain't the miracle of the multitude, ye know. Up to now I've fed you, but I anna feedin' your mates. If she was my marrer, it'd come different, but she looks a tarty old bitch, and she's nothin' to me.'

'Don't you speak bad of her, Bendy Oldroyd. We're all entitled to food.'

'Maybe, but not off me – I've got me hands full seein' to you. You gentry sods are all the same – feed one and up comes all the bloody relatives.'

I sat in silence, watching the tree fringe for a sign of a movement, but there was nothing to tell Rhian was coming back. After a while I rolled up the Cyfarthfa and stamped out what was left of the fire, and the little bits of pheasant bones were sticking up out of the sand.

'I hate your guts now, Bendy Oldroyd. You're a right bugger.'

He climbed to his feet beside me and looked me up and down. 'That makes two of us,' said he: he was a foot the smaller, but I reckon he'd have taken me on.

The smoke rose about us in the acrid stink of lost friendship.

Within the pocket of my coat I held the little purse, and as we walked on, Bendy leading, the bitterness of our rejection of Rhian grew like a cancer within me.

Two days later, coming over the top of a moonscape land called Trefil, it was like walking on the roof of the world.

Here were great stone quarries that sent their limestone to the furnaces of the Top Towns; the awaking centres of industry where iron was moulded into shape – Sirhowy and Tredegar, Merthyr Tydfil and Beaufort, Ebbw Vale and

Nantyglo. From our high vantage on the edge of this lunar country we could see long lines of horses and carts coming and going along the Rassau stone-road that soon would become a tram-road.

Pack mules and horses, each loaded with three-hundredweight panniers – the rough pig iron straight from the Sirhowy furnaces – were trudging, linked by a tethering rope, in long lines of misery to forging mills of works like that at Glangrwyney; there to join the canal and tram-road system for shipment to the ports of the world.

As we descended to the plain, the mule-train drivers called to us, but keep clear o' that lot, advised Bendy, for we don't know the time o' day with them: tough fellas these, said he; many tipsy drunk, and brutalized by their vagrant trade. Meeting other mule trains head on, they fought like animals for right of way.

Under the rising of a quicklime moon, there arose from the earth strange and lovely smells, and I saw spread about me the red sunlight of a million forests; the trees dozing after the sad heat of the afternoon. Now arrived new smells from the cooking fires of an evicted army of tattered people who were resting for the night along the road to Merthyr. As Bendy and I walked through them, they begged for alms.

They had been evicted by the aristocracy who made parliamentary laws to suit their pockets, but you'll never read this in school books. What the absentee landlords were doing in Ireland – hoarding up vast estates under the new Land Enclosure Acts – they were doing in Britain – six million acres of common land now became their own by legal theft under iniquitous English laws.

Forty thousand acres of arable land here was plundered by these bandits of the Houses of Parliament. And protest by these small farmers would bring in two horses and a chain, and down would come their house. If you banded together and rioted, in would come their hired thugs, the yeomen militia or garrison military. They would break your heads or have you up before their corrupt magistrates for transportation, even hanging.

My father was afflicted by the sins of Adam, but he was never a disciple of the Old Traitorous, our despised Anglicized Church that supported this theft from small Welsh farmers, and drove them from their homes.

Indeed, said he, they are a perverted class of traitors pandering to English rule for the subjugation of all things Welsh: they used the Reformation to suppress our customs and beliefs; stripped the wealth of our ancient monasteries and sold their souls for English favour.

What, I wonder, has Wales done to deserve these *bradwrs*? These apologies for Welshmen who exchange their country for an English fart?

And so, they lined the road to Merthyr, these evicted farmers, their faces riven by the toil of the land that they once owned, but now had lost to another's greed.

Bendy cried: 'What's wrong, Gent, did they upset you?'

I didn't reply. The smell of their poverty and hunger had replaced the perfume of their roadside fires.

'That's nowt,' said Bendy. 'It don't only happen in Wales, you know, it's on the go all over England. You should see the dead babies when they turn 'em out in December.' And he winked at the sunset. 'This is the middle o' June.'

We walked on, and as we went I remembered the old ballad that the evicted peasants sang to the Land Enclosures Acts:

> The law locks up the man or woman
> Who steals the goose from off the common.
> But leaves the greater villain loose
> Who steals the common from the goose.

Already I was sickening of this primeval freedom with its dirt, misery and injustice.

This world into which I'd been pitchforked was one of unfettered savagery, and I was already sure that I would not have survived this far, had it not been for Bendy Oldroyd.

As we walked on, now under a threatening sky, I remembered the warm comfort of genteel living; the warm beds, the carpeted floors. In happier times when my mother was alive, one snapped one's fingers – yes, even as a child – everything happened. Hunger was unknown; cold was a stranger: joints of beef and venison came steaming to the silver table; we in Tregaron House gave little thought to the beggars at the gates.

Now, as it began to rain in blusters of wind, and icy fingers searched my body beneath my stained clothes, I remembered the great log fires of Canterbury; the arched dignity of the school halls. Remembering, too, that I had no kith or kin in the world save those who hated me, I knew an overwhelming sense of loneliness.

The rain swept into us with renewed fury. I wiped it from my face and glanced at Bendy; he slowed his loping stride to give me a watery grin.

'You all right, Gent?'

'Yes,' I lied.

'Tricky for you, Gent. But you're doin' fine,' said he.

Eight

Now we were in the wilderness between Brynmawr and Blaenafon, a place of stunted trees and scraggy bushes bent into crippledom by the winds of the Coity mountain; itself a coal hill honeycombed by generations of miners and delvers since the start of Time.

Once this land had been a bedspread of forests, but Iron Age men had felled the trees for charcoal; proof that they knew the construction of their little bloomeries and forges. After this spoliation, great herds of goats and wandering cattle had eaten what was left of the vegetation, leaving the mountains bald; even the lovely Blorenge looked like a man after a pudding-basin haircut.

It was night now, and we were in dangerous country; later, this was Scotch Cattle land, its caves and outcrops infested by unemployed ironworkers who, led by their 'bulls' (the biggest and fiercest of the group) broke the legs of men and burned the furniture of workers who worked on after the embryonic union said 'Stop'.

The eerie silence of the plateau was broken only by a small, buffeting wind and the music of night birds, their trilling, exuberant songs an accompaniment to distant, reverberating thunder of iron-making.

Most beautiful was the sky above us now, for the rain had washed it clean: the clouds reflecting pulsating rainbow colours as the world began to catch alight all over The Top from Nantyglo to Hirwaun. Never will I forget the sight as we neared Blaenafon; the colours of lonely bloomeries shooting their rockets at the stars.

Music was coming from the Whistle Inn, where off-shift

workers thronged; a man was singing a plaintive song in Welsh, his voice bass and pure on the wind: the pace of industry quickened as we neared the Brynmawr Corner and turned down North Street into Blaenafon. And such was the flashing and baying of furnace glare that I thought it was the end of the earth.

'Fire towns,' announced Bendy. 'What did I tell you?'

Past the Stinchcombe collier cottages we went, and through the Works entrance I saw the furnaces simmering and gangs of pygmy workmen labouring half-naked against the glare. The air was filled with clanging, banging, the cracking of whips and bawled commands; a fizz-gig of activity.

The Drum and Monkey pub sign was creaking in the wind, and beyond this anxious-looking women with babies in shawls were looking at the food in the Company Shop window, which was filled with sausages and pies. Maimed beggars with skeletal children in their laps were squatting on the road opposite Staffordshire Row, this being built, we were told, for incoming Midlands specialists who knew the colour of the flame: ostlers and farriers were to live here, too, said Billy Handy, who, drunk, came clattering out of the Drum and Monkey. Doing a light fantastic with his boots on the metalled road, he swept off his hat and bowed low before us.

'Strangers, is it, me fine fellas?'

'It is,' I replied.

'And can I be of service to you? For I'm Welsh, like you, though I go Killarney when I'm in me cups, like now. Is it someone you're after, me lads?'

'Aye,' I said. 'This chap's aunt; her name is Flo Oldroyd and she comes from North Shields,' and he answered:

'Number Ten Shepherd's Square; least she's due there after it's built, but she died a week last Monday. Anyone else?'

'She had a friend who runs the Royal Oak, a fella called Selwyn ap Pringle – is that near?' asked Bendy, sad.

'Ach, dear me, you're talking about a bad fella indeed,'

announced Billy Handy. 'For I run the Drum and Monkey, and he's the landlord of the Royal Oak, so we're in competition. And since I cut the throats of pigs spare time, it's me ambition to cut the throat of Selwyn ap Pringle.' He pointed uphill. 'Follow the road up the mountain; go straight past the honeycomb Irish, and it's the first on the right: you'll tell it's him when you taste his beer, and don't mention the name of Billy Handy.'

'Thanks,' said I.

'And dunna stop when the poor Irish hail ye, or they'll have you for tomorrow's dinner.'

'*Arrah!*' shouted someone. 'Where are you bound, Welsh lads?'

We were over the mountain slope now and on the Abergavenny stone-road, and the voice came from a hole in the ground, which was one of the ironstone mines that fed the furnaces. She came out of her hole in the mountain like a mole, this one, and her tatters flew about her in the dusk wind.

'Welsh boys, Welsh boys! Have ye a leek, for we're on the starve?'

'Bloody hell,' I whispered, 'let's get going!'

But she ran into the middle of the track and barred our way, and others came crowding out of nearby shanties and soon there was a score of them, their hands out like claws, begging for food. These were the starvers of the Irish famines who had arrived in Fishguard as walking ballast and eaten their way through the cornlands of west Wales, following their noses for food and work.

Escaping from the evictions of brutal landlords, tempted by Anglican priests to spit in the face of the Virgin for a bowl of stir-about, they had climbed out of the bottomless coffins of Clare and Mayo, and raced for Wales. Sleeping along the highway, raiding barns, they possessed nothing but the rags they stood up in and the kindness of the Quakers who sent them daily soup carts.

Now, whenever they were seen along the roads the cries went up, 'Mary's Children! Everyone inside! *Mary's Children!*'

In their droves they beset the Top Towns, undercutting the wages of the Welsh. So the Welsh drove them out of the towns, and this lot was living on the mountain. At the first blow of winter they would die like flies, the children first.

We pulled out the linings of our pockets to show we were penniless; they turned away and began a keening we could hear all the way down to Selwyn ap Pringle, who, let me say, had all his buttons about him.

'Is this the Royal Oak Inn?' I asked, and its landlord was pedalling his boots at the sun; sitting on his bum without a care in the world.

'It is, me lucky men,' cried he.

He was a battered old bugger with a stove hat upon his head, a collar back to front, a gum-bucket in his mouth and a cheeky old face cocked up.

'Welcome to the Royal Oak, lads – Selwyn ap Pringle at your service,' and he spat at our feet. 'Is it ale and women you're after?'

'It is not, it's work,' said I.

'Well now,' he answered, getting up in creaks and groans. 'I once had a pull in that direction till Sod-O Digby, the Pwll-du agent, died, and right now he'll be readin' the Book of Lamentations. Do you want to hear the story about him and me?'

'We do not,' cried Bendy, bravely.

'Mind, it's a tale of good fortune, and whoever I relate it to falls straight on their feet.'

'Tell us,' I said, for I knew we were bound to have it.

'Well, Sod-O Digby and me were in lodgings up Doncaster way. Do ye know those parts?'

'Aye, sir,' said Bendy, intrigued.

'And she was a landlady to dream of – the one who lodged Sod-O and me.' He made a shape in the air with his hands.

'She were the loveliest bit o' crackling for miles, and rich, too – she only did it for a hobby.'

'Go on,' I cried, for some sorry old frumps are out and about in the mountains, and this one delighted me, and he cried, falsetto:

'Now, unknown to me, Sod-O was sleeping with her and giving her my name in case he hit a paternity order, and there was me thinkin' theirs was a pure and holy friendship. More, when we left Doncaster and came down here, I was on me uppers and Sod-O was in the money, for he got a job as Agent while I was beggin' for a crust. And all of a sudden our rich landlady dies and leaves Selwyn ap Pringle £6,000, for this was the name poor Sod-O gave her!' and he threw up his fist and shouted at the sun.

'And then?' we asked, together.

'Then I bought the Royal Oak and set myself up, and last week somebody dropped a seven-pound hammer and Sod-O forgot to duck. Which goes to show the twists of Fate, me darlin's. One moment you're up, next moment you're down, like Annie Oh-No's drawers.'

'Who's Annie Oh-No?'

'Never you mind, son, for I've taken to the pair of you for hearing out me yarn,' and he pointed. 'Cross the road, go round the Tumble, ask for Mr Effyn Tasker – he's the overman round the Pwll-du drifts – and say that Selwyn sent you. All right?'

'Aye, you're not so bad, mister,' said Bendy, happily.

'I give you a start and you drink my ale – what about it?'

'You're on,' I said, and steered Bendy away in the moonlight, for darkness had fallen over the Golden Valley below us like the drop of a witch's skirt, and lights were twinkling along the silver Usk.

Some queer old buggers were abroad after dusk up here, apparently.

Long, long before the Garndyrus Inn was built, which was later called the Old Victoria: even before the Blaenafon furnaces down in the valley were in full blast, Pwll-du (pronounced by the English ironmasters 'poolth-dee') was a thriving community. Coal, not iron, was its main product: and Abraham Harry, old when Pwll-du was young, dug his drift and sent his coal to the fires of Wales.

Before that the Marquis of Abergavenny, whose seat was Neville Hall, converted to his possession 12,000 acres under the Enclosure Act. Evicting tenant farmers, he leased this land to Messrs Hopkins, Hill and Pratt, speculators who sunk £40,000 into its potential, realizing it was a source of ironstone, timber for charcoal, coal and limestone – the ingredients in great demand for war.

So Pwll-du sprang up, and was peopled by immigrant Irish, English, and evicted Welsh farmers and labourers, and this gave the village a soul.

Upper Row, a terrace of fourteen cottages, was built, followed by Lower Row, one of twenty-eight cottages: two public houses followed – the Lamb and the Prince of Wales, later becoming the Company Shop. St Catherine's Church came next, then a little chapel called Horeb, and the community thrived. Drifts and levels were sunk and the coal was good. And while Mr Effyn Tasker bossed the output here, it was in the chapel that Tomos Traherne held court.

Father to the community but parent to none, this pastor governed with a rod of iron; his voice booming in pursuit of harlots and wayward children. It appeared that he was at this now, for we heard him shout, like Bason's Bull: 'This, my people, is the time of boils and blains when God is sickened of your sins! And if you do not repent, his fevers will come among you and mow you down like chaff!'

'Dear me, hark at that,' whispered Bendy, and we went closer and saw before us a crowd of people in chapel black, and standing on a stone in the midst of them was this pastor; immense in size and domination was he, and he bawled: 'Reach up, good people!' and he raised great arms skyward and shook blue-veined hands, 'Reach up and clutch at the Lord as a drowning man clutches at a lifebelt! Reach up, *Reach u-u-u-up!*'

The mass of people, swaying and moaning, reached up a forest of hands.

A drumbeat began then, a mesmeric thumping that filled the wind, and the pastor, his great belly shaking, leaped up, clutching at the air. 'Jump, jump up, my lovelies! Jump out of the pit dug deep for you by the Incarnate Fiend! All you like sheep have gone astray, but there's still a bit o' wool on those poor shoulders, so jump, jump up into the arms of God!'

Men and women, from brawnies to toddlers, leaped up and down, their hands waving, fingers clutching, and Tomos Traherne cried: 'Old Beelzebub has got you by the ankles! Shake him off or he will draw you down into his caverns of fire! Jump, jump, or you will incinerate in his bosom! Oh, that Ishmael should live in Thee! Reach down for us, O God!'

Everybody in the place was at it now; in paroxysms of fear, they leaped about and shrieked in a medley of skirts, petticoats and drawers: hair came down, bonnets fell off, caps went awry and boots went up, and the preacher bawled, 'Come from the taverns! Reject strong drink! Despise the lusts of the flesh! For the wind of a new Revival is blowing like a gale across these mountains. Jump, jump!'

Even Bendy was at it now, leaping about, his arms and legs akimbo, and before I knew what I was doing, I was jumping, too, for the magnetic gaze of the holy man was fast upon us now. Singling us out as strangers, he pierced us with small, black eyes from under bushy brows, and shouted: 'And you, newcomers! Aye, you I mean, *jump!*' and we obeyed, floundering about.

All over the field the jumpers were dropping like flies, the old ones first, the young ones prancing around the corpses, with husbands patting the cheeks of fat wives and slapping the backs of their hands, and a brass band suddenly appeared with the strains of 'God Triumphant' played by an old chap on a *go-to-me-come-from-me*, and a sexton thumping a harmonium, and the row must have been heard down the Rhondda.

'Aha! And what have we here?' In size and majesty the preacher stood.

Six-foot-six if he was an inch, this one, with a spade beard on him like Abraham's son, and dressed in undertaker's black: a man and a half was this Tomos Traherne. Little did I know that he would affect my life.

'Welsh?' he asked, towering beside us.

'Aye, sir,' said I, and gave him some, and he turned a pair of piercing eyes on to Bendy.

'You?'

'English, sir.'

'Ah well, we can't have everything. Happy, are we, in the service of God?'

'Happy indeed, sir,' said I.

At this he bent to Bendy, saying: 'Hope in God, my son, and he will treat you better than mankind.'

We did not reply to this, so he put his ham hands upon our shoulders and steered us away.

'Come,' said he.

Over my shoulder, as he took us down to the Bridge Arches, I saw them carrying off the semi-conscious.

Nine

'Name?' asked Effyn Tasker, the overman of Hopkins Drift. His Christian name is Waldo; why they call him Effyn do beat me, said Bendy.

'Hywel Mortymer.'

'Your'n?'

'Bendy Oldroyd.'

'Ages?' Out came his little book: a square, blue chin on this one, shoulders like an elephant, size-twelve boots.

'I'm sixteen, he's twelve,' said I.

The morning was cold and with a hint of frost in him, terrible for July, and I reckon it was ten degrees colder up here at Pwll-du. But the crows were still discussing the summer in squawks and squarks, rising above us in the sun like handfuls of burnt feathers.

'Takin' you on 'cause Pastor Traherne asked, got it?' said Tasker.

'Got it.'

'Bugger Selwyn ap Pringle. One foot wrong, me lads, and my boot's under your arse, have you got that, too?'

'Aye,' answered Bendy, who knew about overmen. 'How about bait tins and Tommy?'

'Tins you supply yourselves, bait ye'll get off Ma Corrigan. And nothin' in Hopkins comes free.'

'You could have fooled me,' said Bendy, and Tasker eyed him, saying, 'You know about coal working?'

'Aye.'

'The lower galleries?'

'Since Jesus were a baby,' said Bendy.

It was a long drift, this Hopkins, three-quarters of a mile into the mountain from Pwll-du to Blaenafon, and where it emerged there it crossed a deep declivity by means of a nine-arch covered bridge, the narrow gauge tram-road ending in a hoist to the Stack Square Balance Tower.

Into the maws of the North Street furnaces was fed the products of Pwll-du – limestone, ironstone worked from the 'patches', and coal. And, since workers' housing was in short supply with the rush of incoming immigrants, Mr Hopkins bricked up the bridge arches and turned them into homes: secure against all weathers, whole families were raised in this accommodation: folks like Mrs Ten Beynon's Irish mother, who raised fifteen children. In Number One Bridge Arches, which was ruled by Ma Corrigan, lived some of the labouring children, including me, the eldest.

In contrast, the mansion of Old Sam and his sister, Sarah, was being built at the bottom of North Street – a most elegant establishment for the entertainment of visiting dignitaries, such as Archdeacon Coxe and his artistic companion, Sir Richard Colt Hoare.

The working conditions in the Hopkins Drift were anything but elegant.

For a start, the roof of this drift was no more than two feet high in places, which was hard on Bendy, but harder still on me. It was usually boy and girl tramming; the girl in front with a chain between her legs, the lad pushing up behind.

'I'll take the haul.'

'You'll be sorry,' said Bendy, and we got behind the three-hundredweight tram and pushed her off to the face.

Time was when skips on skids were used in Hopkins, like those in Pumsaint, but a railway tram-road had been laid here, so our trams went on wheels. On all fours I rode the towing chain, bracing my toes on the stone sleepers for a purchase, and Bendy, his body as rigid as a bar, pushed behind. We hadn't got a hundred yards when I hit my head against a halted tram in front.

'Hey up, lads,' said a girl, coming round with a candle and sitting on the line for a breather. 'You just come in?'

'Ay, ay,' answered Bendy. 'Or you'd have seen us down by 'ere before. Get your old tub movin'.'

For answer the girl eased off the chain and rolled down her petticoats, 'Ach, take it slow, lads. You don't get a bonus for speed,' and her pusher joined us, his eyes like stars in the candle glow; I judged their ages at ten or eleven. 'That right, Elija? You get filled too soon, boys, and you'll give old Effyn a heart attack.'

'How far's the face?' I asked.

She lay back on the line and cocked up her boots and wiped her cheeky little face with her sweat rag. 'Two hundred yards, about. And it's Ben Thomas's shift this mornin', and he don't baste the childer much. Like old Conky-Bum when he were cutting. A right good fella was Conky. You watch them boots, mun,' and she kicked one of mine. 'It do come hard on the old toes when the boots wear out – ay, ay, it plays hell with the poor old bacon hooks,' and she took off a boot two sizes too big for her and wiggled her toes, and her toenails were like her fingernails, broken and cracked. 'Last night shift Effyn did his nut and made me take 'em off. You Irish? – you don't talk a lot for Welsh.'

'The chance'd be a fine thing,' said Bendy.

'I'm a Scot,' said she. 'Me name's Beth Ponty.' She jerked a thumb at the lad. 'He's my marrer, but he be deaf and dumb,' and she chucked him under the chin and yelled, 'Deaf and dumb, b'aint you, Elija. What's your names?'

'Hywel – he's Bendy,' I replied.

'Jesus, I can see that. Down the bottom galleries, is it?'

'My business,' said Bendy. 'How long you been down here?'

She put a dusty finger between her rose-bud lips and her eyes shone in the wavering light. 'Don't know, really. About three-year, I think – actual, I was down the Abraham Harry first; afore then I was a door-keeper at Sirhowy.' She held her candle higher and peered at Bendy. 'You been burned?'

77

'Some time.'

'They burned us down in Sirhowy – that fookin' old Fothergill and Parson Monkhouse – they brought in gas-flashers while the shift were still down. I lost a trammer, and he was a right good foal; his name was Luke.'

And Bendy said, rising off the line: 'If you'll stop bloody gassin', we can get along. We're askin' for stripes hanging round by here.'

'Ay, ay,' replied Beth Ponty. 'No offence. See you tonight in Corrigan's, eh?'

'Not if we see you first,' said Bendy, and she squirmed around to the hook of her tram, shackled herself up on the chain and hauled it away, with Elija's boots scrabbling on the sleepers behind it.

'Some girl,' I called to him.

'Ach, no! *Diawch!* Give her an inch and she'd take a yard. Like the rest of 'em, she talks too much.'

Now he was singing his words; more Welsh every minute since he'd been with me. He added, as we hauled the empty tub, 'Don't make friends easy, Gent – don't pay. They'll take your bait and steal your sweat. You got a marrer like me, all right? Just you and me, Gent, sod the others.' And he added fiercely. 'And them's dirty old girls down here. Next thing you know, they've got your trousers off.'

'That'll be the day!'

'Don't you worry, I've seen 'em.'

At the face, when we drew up, the colliers were at it: every one in a birthday suit, save for their hobnails in which they clattered about, shovelling, picking, hewing in an orchestra of squeaks, rasps and gasps.

Women colliers were working among them, stripped to the waist; of brawny arms and bulging strength.

Women took their place with men in 1800; later they were banned from underground by Parliamentary Acts which most employers ignored; it was the same with the employment of children in the mines. Nobody, not even the

78

children, knew their ages in many cases, since there was no official registration of birth; a girl of five could say she was ten if her parents needed the money. The employers took advantage of this; two children aged ten could do the work of a man and take home a quarter of his money. Hopkins and Hill were about the best employers on the mountains, but they weren't behind the door when it came to fiddling.

'I'm never working naked,' I said, straightening in the higher stall.

'Say you don't know,' came the reply. 'Those women wear tops when it's cold, of course. They wouldn't wear skirts in summer neither, if it weren't for ladies' sickness.'

'What's that?'

'Don't you know?'

'Don't know a lot about ladies.'

'You and me'd better 'ave a talk some time,' said Bendy.

It was a joy to see those colliers at work; the sex didn't matter, for they worked in comradeship. I've heard say that no collier passes a level or a drift without comradely thoughts, for folks up in the sun don't know a collier's mind. Fine and strong were this lot, their backs inlaid with dirt, for they never washed these lest it washed away their strength. They punctuated the music of their shovels and picks with an untidy orchestra of shouts and banter:

'Dear Christ, blutty fagged out, I am!'

'Aw, sad, ye'll be *cwtched* up fancy when your old man gets you.'

'Not worth much, he is – gone all *didoreth* lately.'

'So would I, sleepin' wi' you.'

'Ain't up to it much at all, poor old dab. Like Nana Dorney's goat, always bloody grizzling.'

'Proper 'alf-soaked, is my Ifor – too sick to catch a cold.'

'What you doin' tonight, Sam?'

'You, if your old man don't catch me.'

Our tram filled now, Bendy and I stood in the candle's swirling dust; in your hair, your mouth, your soul: the top was heaped high with black nuggets: on to the turntable; a grunt, skidding boots . . . the tram swings round.

'Right you, lads, next one up!' bawled Ben Thomas, and we were off to Blaenafon. Looking back at the first turn-out, I saw the pygmy colliers, their bodies white against the coal, labouring like a cluster of fiends within a small, personal hell. In darkness, my candle out, I barged on . . . and hit my head again on another tram stopped on the line.

'Oh Jesus, no!' cried Bendy, as Beth Ponty crawled out from beneath it. 'Not you again!'

Now another gallery and another stall; oil lamps were glowing: a longstall, and the colliers were wearing stiff caps, for this was a plug-fall area: on the caps they'd stuck stubs of candles, and the coal was fairly pouring down from this face. Men were hammering wooden props; a small army labouring in flashes of sweat; rivers of sweat that streamed down their hairy chests and clung in shining patches to their buttocks.

There were fat men and skinnies; young bodies hardened already – farm labourers turned colliers overnight. Stomachs of many varieties were there; the eight-muscled midriffs of the young, thin-flanked and strong; ale-swilling bellies of roly-poly hair. And as these laboured they raised a chant that was beset at times with the high descant of women sopranos: a harmonious sound like a hymn: bright gleamed the seams laden with quartz and Fool's Gold: incrustations of mother-of pearl and cockle shell garnered the candlelight in beams and flashes; the beauty stilled me.

Two women were lazing against a tram, while two more filled it in a storm of dust, and their eyes blinked from the red sockets of their faces; one in the family way – she looks near dropping it, said Bendy, and if she does on this shift that'll be fifteen I've watched born underground: fifteen born, it will be, said he, and never saw one go up in a box, for colliers, male or female, make good midwives.

One of the lounging girls cried: 'Come on, Ned Taters, ye

anna digging spuds. I got to get back and do me old man's dinner.' Her name, they said, was Annie Oh-No.

'When you've done him ye can do mine, girl.'

'And me in this state?'

She was seventeen, but I took her for older.

'I've seen her before today,' said Bendy. 'Folks say she's a brickworks girl. When she has this one out it'll be her second.'

Afterwards they told me about her first.

She had come from Bream in the Forest of Dean, when she was aged thirteen, and a forester had taken her in legal concubinage on a lease of six years, properly drawn up by a Lydney lawyer; a form of marriage for folks who didn't believe in Church. The man had brought her to Blaenafon, taught her to read and write, then put her in the brickyards. When she came to child he left her and she gave birth to a son outside Bunker's Row in December.

Not knowing about umbilical cords, she arrived at Big House with it holding up her dress in front; in her arms she carried her baby.

Later, the deacons had her out of Chapel. Now she was in child again and didn't know the father. Aware, perhaps, that I was watching her, she came up to me with a fine swagger, one hand on her hips like a gentry filly, and she was a Negress, not a white girl, being painted black by coal. Beautiful, her skin glowed ebony in the light of the rush flares. As she smiled now, her white teeth appeared like magic.

'Dear me, Idris, what have we here?' She sounded quite educated.

Idris, an overman, came from the back; he was small and tubby, his belly sagging over his belt; he said, 'New trammers, likely so – come for filling to Blaenafon?'

'That's it,' said I, and the girl came closer, saying:

'We've turned up a handsome fella in this dump at last. Dear me, I'd like to fall over you in the dark. What's your name?'

'Hywel Mortymer.'

The workers lowered their tools and gathered about us, curious. Later still I learned their names. Big Rhys Jenkins was one, a lad a bit older than me; the marks of fighting were borne upon his blunted features: twin boys, Owen and Griff Howells from the Bridge Houses, were behind him. There was Abraham Harris, who was a butcher part-time, but later died of the cholera, and Albert, who later died in the press – Meg Laundry's chap.

Afron Madoc was there, a collier's butty who cut spoons for girls; he cut one for Sian Lewis, but never married her: also Will Tafarn, a little weasel who lived in Aaron Brute's Row, and beat his wife.

Some looked ill, their faces riven with hunger and endemic fevers; others had the bulbous countenances of heavy drinking, like big Barney Kerrigan who went to live in Nantyglo. All were possessed of coal's tattoos, even two lads aged ten, Dai and Dodo Jones, another pair of twins. Among them were oldies; bald men and shawled crones who held the tattered dignity of dead who wouldn't die. They looked like a mob from the French Revolution, and smelled as such.

The girl said, coming close: 'My name's Annie Oh-No.'

'Oh, no,' said Bendy, turning away; Bendy, clearly, didn't like women.

An Irish voice bawled: 'Ach, leave 'em be, Annie. 'Tis the organ-grinder and his monkey – be your age.'

'It's the organ-grinder who appeals to me,' said she.

Idris Foreman shouldered his way to the front then and banged his fist on our tram. 'Get going, here, there's too much chat. Now come on, the lot of ye, come on!'

As Annie Oh-No went she winked over her shoulder.

'*Diawch!*' ejaculated Bendy as we heaved our tram away. 'I'll be sorry I picked you off the road. When women are about, you mean trouble.'

'Don't blame me, I didn't give her the eye.'

I did not know as I hauled that tram up to Blaenafon that I

had met people who would influence my life. Annie Oh-No, for one.

One man there, however, did not.

His name was John Evans, and he left the Hopkins Drift two years later and became a collier in the Pentre Fron pit near Wrexham. There, with ten other colliers he was trapped underground by flood water, and a fortnight later men went down with a shroud to recover his body, only to discover he had kept himself alive by eating candles. So, the legend of John Evans stayed in the Hopkins, but the candles, said John, were pretty hard to get down; they'd have been much more enjoyable with a sprinkle of salt.

Thereafter no collier ever went down the Hopkins without a little packet of salt, for luck.

But John Evans had nothing on me in terms of hardship; within an hour of ending the shift, I was in agony.

'The chain?' asked Bendy, watching me walking bandy.

'Dear Jesus!' I said.

'There's only one way for a trammer to learn, Gent, and that's the hard way,' said he. 'Let's look.'

'You'll be lucky!'

'Come on, don't be daft, get your trews down.'

'What's wrong?' asked Annie Oh-no, coming into the entrance.

'He's had the chain,' said Bendy.

'Is the skin broken?' She bent to me and I fought to get my trousers up, and she said: 'Look, boyo, your set isn't any different from the others. Just lie back and enjoy it,' and I lay back on the tumps and turned away my face and she prodded and peered, and I saw her profile clear against the dying sunset. 'Go and fetch a cow-pat, Bendy Oldroyd,' she commanded.

'You the doctor round these parts, then?' I asked her, and she patted her stomach.

'While I'm not otherwise employed, for it keeps me on the books. You've just got this in time, before you cut.'

'It's bad?'

'I've seen worse for a first-time trammer. If you get cut with the chain on the inside of the thigh you're abed, and there's nothing more for it. If it skins you, you'll miss six shifts. But if you only graze, like you've done, a night on the cow-pat will harden you off – you'll be right as rain in the morning.

'I've seen chain cuts so bad that men had blood on their knees, but they had to keep tramming because the family was waiting for their pay. And men cut worse than women, which you can understand, but you must have skin like a rhino,' and she looked up when Bendy came back with a cow-pat. This she flattened off, and plastered it between my thighs. I could have screamed with pain.

Cow-pat on a skin chafe is like branding by hot iron.

'Some kind of butty you've got,' said Annie, and took from her girdle a flannel bandage with which she tied the cow-pat into place.

'I'm obliged to you, missus,' I said, walking with my legs so splayed I'd not have stopped a pig in a passage.

'She's some woman,' said Bendy, looking back.

'You can say that again.'

'Ych-a-fi, you don't half stink,' said he, holding his nose.

'You're a rotten little bugger. You knew this would happen!'

'Aye, but the sooner ye chafe, the sooner you ride the chain. When you've learned how to splay your knees, you'll make a trammer.'

In this fashion, hanging on to Bendy, I made my way down to the Bridge Houses, to meet Ma Corrigan.

This wasn't going to last, I thought: I'm not having this. I'd stick it for a bit until I'd proved it to myself that whatever they called me, Gent or otherwise, anything they could take, I could, too. I'd work like a horse if there was no alternative; I'd even have a girl plaster cow-pats between my legs without so much as asking my permission – but only for

84

so long. No Mortymer in the world, spelt how they liked, was going to put up with this bloody lot.

I gave myself a grin; I was even using Bendy's language.

Ten

'What's wrong with him?' demanded Ma Corrigan, seeing me walking bandy.

'He got caught on the shovels and chains,' explained Bendy.

'Oh aye? That's what comes of having the Quality workin' for the first time in their lives – I've heard about you,' said she to me.

She was a queer old girl, this Ma Corrigan. Rumour had it that the chap responsible for making males and females was dozing on a cloud when Ma Corrigan came up for selection; the poor old thing was turned out in between.

On the man side she was six feet up and as brawny as Atlas; on the female side she wore skirts right down to her feet, plus a mass of flaming red hair in curlers. Come Sundays, Annie Oh-No told us, Ma would band her chest with hessian to prevent injury to the womanly parts, then knock hell out of the local pugilists on the Blorenge Punch-bowl. As Bo'sun Corrigan she had fought at the Battle of the Nile, and lost an eye at the Battle of Calvi: fifty years old, she looked like ninety.

'What's your name, my lovely?'

'Hywel Mortymer, ma'am.'

'And this wee charmer?' She stooped to Bendy, and when he told her she hauled him up and smacked him a kiss. 'What they been doin' to ye, me darling?'

'They got me down Durham way, Haswell Hole, mainly – two foot seams,' chirped Bendy, and Ma cried, falsetto:

'Sure to God, I'd burn the tabs off every coalmaster from here to Ponty for what they're doin' to the rising generation,' and she went wet in the eyes and bent to another new entry; this one was three feet high and blacker than the Ace of Spades.

'And you, my pidge?' asked Ma, and little Blackie Garn, a blackamoor, shivered to lay his bones out, his eyes like bed sheets in his tear-stained face.

'Will Blaenafon found him wandering down the Garn,' explained Annie Oh-No, coming up, 'so they've called him Blackie Garn.'

'But that ain't your real name, lad?' whispered Ma, holding the black boy's hands.

'Don't know me real name, lady,' said the lad. 'They just called me Blackamoor.'

'Run away, have ye?' asked Bendy.

At which Blackie sobbed to break the heart of a county slaughterer, and it did the trick on Ma Corrigan, for she cried, lifting him, 'Away, the bloody lot of ye. Don't you worry now Ma's got you, me little black pidge.'

The floor of Number One Bridge Arches was covered with stamped cinders, and from time to time the Cinder Girls from the coke ovens would bring in fresh supplies, for I do insist on a decent floor for the children, said Ma.

Four Cinder Girls in all: there was Jenny Loom who had come down from Bradford; Dot Popkin, her mate; Iris Gold, the Jewess who had run from the hiring fairs; and Charity Chiano, the Italian who carried a picture of Pope Pius VII – though he didn't do a lot of Charity, who was orphaned when she was three, adopted by Mr Conky-Bum, the pew-collector in Chapel, and was a door-keeper down Abraham Harry's levels before she was six.

Day and night you could see the cinderers at it on twelve-hour shifts at a ha'penny an hour. With wet rags around their faces against sulphur fumes, and their kerchiefs and bodices burned to holes, they'd haul the glowing slag from North Street to Pwll-du, and come to Annie Oh-No with terrible burns.

They had come in now; cold cinders for the floor, with Jenny and Dot shovelling it out of the tram and Charity and Iris stamping it firm and level.

'There we are, girls,' said Ma. 'You won't lose by it, neither will you gain a lot, but it's Christian, ain't it, to keep the childer clean!' And they gulped down water from Ma's dip and barrel, and pushed off into the dusk. Charity, I noticed, was wearing a little black crucifix.

'Don't they talk?' asked Bendy.

'Not a lot,' said Ma.

After this Harry Ostler arrived with Enid Donkey and her cart and brought in a load of straw, and this we helped spread to renew the beds, for fresh cinders do discourage the rats, said Ma, and new straw keeps down fleas. 'You got fleas?'

'Not so far,' replied Bendy.

'Tell me when you do and I'll call in the Inspector of Nuisances – he'll wash you down with a bottle of carbolic.'

So we settled into Number One, the three of us – Bendy, Blackie and me in a corner, and about twenty others, their ages ranging from six to sixteen, coming in or going out on shift. And above us the trams rumbled along the line from Pwll-du to the tower in a thundering on the rails above us. Ma Corrigan, immense in her apron, stirred the contents of a big cast iron pot over a fire; a witch's brew of meat and vegetables, our one square meal of the day.

Through the wide entrance where she worked I saw red and golden light flashing on the cloud layer above the Usk Valley, and the distant peak of Pen-y-fal was tinged with rosy light. For the furnace bungs of Blaenafon were being tapped, and the night pulsated in rainbow colours. Behind the balance tower in the Works compound, there came a roar of labour; the clanging of rails, the hissing of sand moulds as the iron ran in firey streams.

'Right, children, here it comes!'

Ma Corrigan rose from the bubbling pot like a triumphant ghost. Scarecrowed against the glare, stark black I saw her.

The children, obeying her, raced from the straw. Elbowing one another for room, shouting, gesticulating, they banged on their bait tins while Ma, in her element, ladled out the steaming 'lobscouse'. The children blew at the steam and sucked up the food in noisy relish.

I tell you this, I've eaten in some places; from ribs of beef in the Abergavenny Angel to salmon and cucumber down in Jackson's with the Quality of London looking on. But never in my life have I tasted a stew like this, the Welsh name for which is *cawl*. We ate until we were as full as eggs, Bendy, Blackie and me, and then crawled into straw to sleep the sleep of the just.

But I did not sleep.

Kept awake by the pain of my chafed thighs, I eventually sat up and listened to the night-shift trams rumbling over-head: within the vacuum of sleep and wakefulness, I sat, and looked at the faces of the sleeping children about me; the features of the prematurely aged, for coal ages the young quicker than the travail of years. And I recall thinking that, unknown to me within the splendour of my life at Tregaron, with servants to attend to my every whim, those about me were the outcasts of my generation.

Years later, William Lloyd, the Works Manager at Blaen-afon, claimed that his total child labour was less than forty; this might have been accurate then, but it wasn't true now. Today, the beginning of the nineteenth century, before Victoria came to the throne, famished children were lan-guishing in thousands.

All the Top Towns of Wales, from the Crawshays of Cyfarthfa to the Reverend Monkhouse of Sirhowy, were small armies of children; even animals took preference to the battalions of urchin young who, driven by hunger, besieged the iron towns: here they were cornered, given a shilling for the bait tin, and taken on in droves.

Mines, iron compounds, drifts and levels opened and engulfed them in a score of trades, from rag-cleaners to mule-skinners, ore-scrabblers to tub-trammers: and the normal shift was of twelve hours, at a ha'penny an hour. Some of these children never saw daylight, but worked underground, ate underground and slept in conditions where no decent master would have kept his pigs.

They were run over by trams in darkness when they fell asleep at the brattice doors; crushed by runaway journeys, trapped in foul air pockets (we didn't know it was gas in those days). They were thrashed for eating in employers' time or dozing on the job.

Earlier, when Ma was doling out the *cawl*, I had talked to Blackie, and he told me: 'I was brought into Bristol on the slaver and got sold with ten other blacks on the wharf,' and he stared at me in the glow of the furnaces, his eyes like orbs in a face of watered coal. 'Most were sold in a batch and went to the factory, but a lady in a carriage saw me, paid six guineas to the slave merchant, took me home, bathed me and dressed me up in silk. Gawd, you never seen anything like me, mister: I 'ad a cloth o' gold wrapped round my head, and she called me the Star of Africa.'

'What's he on about?' asked Bendy, turning over.

'Heisht, you, let him talk!' I said, and Blackie continued, though I cannot find his words, which were broken, black velvet words from the cotton plantations: 'The old girl was all right, for she'd cuddle me up in bed in the mornings and put wool on me when I was shiverin' cold, and take me out dressed like an Indian prince to show me off to her friends.'

I lay back in the straw and listened to his music; Blackie said: 'But her old chap got tired of havin' me around, and every time he saw me he kicked my backside without the lady knowing, and after a while the lady got tired, too, and put me down the cellar with the skivvies, and there was a fat old cook down there who used to stripe me terrible with a jenny she kept over the mantel. So one night I up and run for it. I got on a sailer-coaster for a stowaway, and went up north to a place called Bootle, and they sent me down Tinker's Day

Hole, which was a coal drift, and I used to hurry with the belt and chain, pulling the corves.'

Bendy was listening now, and other children gathered about us, lying or kneeling, and Blackie talked and waved in the air with his white-palmed hands.

'He's an old sod for tellin' a tale, mind,' mentioned Bendy.

'You shut up,' cried Gwen Lewis. 'He's the same as us, really speaking, but white inside, ain't you, Blackie?'

'That's right, same as King George,' he replied. 'Down Tinker's I did sixteen runs a day with the corves, uphill and down, and she were a drift to soak your bum. I had a young fella to help me on the slopes, and his name was Togo Walley, and he was five. I was on the chain and he pushed at back – you know, foal and marrer – but he were that skinny on the starve I had to thrash him to keep him awake lest the overman saw him dozing – mind, I didn't hurt him much, just enough to keep him going, and sometimes lugged him on by the hair.'

'Did they stripe the girls down Tinker's, too?' asked Gwen, her eyes like saucers.

'Not much. But they did other things to girls.'

'Like what?'

'Like taking down their drawers and sleeping them out if they was more than ten years old.'

'What did they take their drawers off for?' asked somebody.

'Search me,' said Blackie.

'Don't you know, Hywel Mortymer?' asked another.

'I do,' announced Bendy, 'but I anna tellin' you.' And he added to me, 'You want to watch that black fella, mun. He do tell a bloody good yarn – next thing you'll know he'll be into your bait tin.'

'I never did!' protested Blackie. 'I never did stole.'

And Gwen Lewis elbowed Beth Ponty, whispering, 'You got any ideas about those drawers?'

'You two don't speak so much,' cried Bendy, 'you'm dirty old buggers.'

91

After a bit Blackie dozed off and I lay back and examined their faces again – one by one; this my generation.

Vaguely, I wondered if my father, who once had financial interests here, knew of these things . . .

Eleven

Two years we worked down Hopkins and it seemed like ten: another October came in with threats of freeze and driving rain, but it was warm down the drift, for the ash-tipper girls like Jenny Loom and Dot Popkin were ordered by Effyn Tasker to dump their hot slag right on top of us, filling in the declivity of Tonno. This warmed us up no end, but it do also warm up the Foul below, said Bendy, so watch out from now on.

'What do you mean?' I asked him, but he didn't reply.

We were stopped on the line between Stalls Fifteen and Twelve, which was worked by women colliers, mainly: folks like Gin Trimm and Ada Cader who had given their husbands the sailor's farewell and struck out on their own: massive women, these two; talk had it that Ada had once given Dai Swipo, the Waunavon boxer, something to go on with, and time was when young Ada acted as a bouncer in the Lamb, but that was before my time.

'What ye gassin' around for, you two?' demanded Ada, and Gin let two notches in her leather lifting belt and took a pace towards us.

'No offence,' said Bendy. 'Just lookin', ladies.'

'Right, you've had your look. Now piss off!'

Rumour had it that Ada and Gin had something in common, but I never really understood it.

Now, in greater safety, six stalls up, Bendy said in deep confidence: 'Things were safe down Haswell Hole up Durham way, till Gaffer started slag-laying over us: it warmed us up come winter, aye, but it loosed off the Foul an' all; it pocketed all over the stalls, it did, and my overman, old Owen Steffan, knew it, see?'

'Knew what?'

'Christ, don't you listen?' demanded Bendy. 'I just told you. Our Gaffer covered the drift wi' hot furnace slag and the lads beneath it in the roadway got all warmed up, and so did the air.'

About us was the song of the shovels. Soon the twins, Dai and Dodo, would come up behind us with their tram, and behind them, laying well into it, would come Gwen Lewis and Beth Ponty, for Gwen's deaf and dumb lad was off with toe chafes. When they arrived there'd be a lot of pushing and shoving and a quarrel for right of way, so I said to Bendy: 'Go on, then, if you're tellin' the yarn.'

'Well, there was a fall down that Haswell Hole and me and my Gaffer was shut . . .'

'Shut up?'

'Entombed, the managers call it.'

I stared at him in the light of the candles, but his face portrayed no emotion; he added, simply, 'It were a roof plug – big 'un, and we had a roadway nag with us, and it took her an' all, with her back legs up to the hocks in our hole and the rest of her buried, and she took more'n three hours to die. My Gaffer said, "If she takes that long to snuff it, there can't be foul air; all we do, lucky lad, is to sit it out till the boys come burrowing. You hurt?"'

'"No, Gaffer," I told him, and after six hours o' sitting there, he said, "You'm a good little lad, Bendy Oldroyd. You don't make fuss nor fart. You'm a good lad, but I tell you this, wi' that top foreman loading us with hot slag, this old drift's a'comin' warm, and soon we'll have the Foul."'

There was a silence. 'What happened?' I asked.

Bendy said, 'He were right, weren't he? We listened and listened and tapped and sang, and didn't hear nothin' – like the rescue party had gone off shift, and forgotten us. And after a bit my eyes began to smart and my throat began to

94

choke and my lungs began a strangling in the chest, and Gaffer felt for me in the dark.'

'"Gas," he said. "You feel it, Oldroyd?"

"Yes," I told him, and I asked:

'But surely you could smell it, too?'

'Can't smell it, can't see it – just plain air, it is, but foul.'

Later, but not then, we had a name for it – methane. Bendy said: 'Then my Gaffer said, "I don't know about you, lovely lad, but I anna goin' to choke alive for any fookin' employer. Here, give me your hand," and I did, and touched the tinder box and flint he had taken out of his pocket. He said to me, "Feel that tinder box? Do ye want to die slow on the choke, boy, or go out quick with a bang?"

'"Out quick, Gaffer." He were a right good lad, that overman. I heard him open the tinder box and take out the striker; and I knew that one strike spark would blow us to St Peter, because by now that hole was chock full o' Foul, and we couldn't breathe. You know what happened then?'

'Tell me!'

'There comes one almighty bang from the roadway outside that lifted that dead mare straight up so she took the shock, the wall went down and we saw the rescue gang with their sweating old faces.

'"You all right in there?" asked a rescue chap.

'"Couldn't be better," said my Gaffer.

'"Is that right? Jesus, we heard ye singing and yelling – you were making enough palaver for breech-birth twins."

'"You got your stalls twisted. That weren't us, were it, Bendy?"

'"Weren't us, Gaffer," said I, and the lads hauled us out, and that poor old mare she farted all up the roadway, chock full of the Foul. Queer, ain't it?'

I didn't reply, but looked at his small, wizened face, and knew him better. He said, with finality, taking from his pocket a little tinder box and striker, 'So now I always carry a flash-match just in case. If I'm goin' out, Gent, I'm goin' civil. You choke to death, you can't talk to God when you stand there, the old colliers say. You ever thought of that?'

I watched him, shaking my head. 'No, I never thought of that.'

'We'd best get moving,' said Bendy. 'There's someone coming up behind.'

Someone was; I could hear the grinding of tram wheels, the grunts and the gasps, and thought it was either Gwen Lewis and Beth Ponty or Dai and Dodo, the twins: it was neither. I lit my candle tack as the tram came looming up in the glow of lanthorns.

'Hello there,' said Bimbo, and he saw me on the line and grinned, with his milk teeth missing in the front, and behind him came Rhian, his sister.

'Ach, dear me!' ejaculated Bendy. 'Here comes that old girl again – let's get going!'

'No wait,' said I.

'I reckon she's following you around.'

I'll say one thing for Rhian Evans, which was her full name, she looked like a woman but she pushed like a proper half-marrow: with her hair tied back with string and her skirts tied up like a pair of trews, she worked horizontal to the loads and on the chain now, with Bimbo heaving behind.

Down at the faces the colliers took note of her, one especially, and this was Big Rhys Jenkins, who was six-feet-two and four feet wide. Even then, at nineteen, he was coming up for a mountain fighter, and had twice taken on Bill Noakes. And, though rumour had it that Big Rhys was chancing his arm with Selwyn ap Pringle's daughter over at the Royal Oak, he do go real goof, every time he sees that woman of yours, said Bendy a week later.

'She's not my woman – she's not anyone's woman.'

'Oh aye? Yesterday she put a bit of her dinner on your plate, didn't she?'

'That's because she wasn't hungry.'

'She's hungry all right,' he replied. 'She could eat you as well as her dinner.'

'Aw, get off!'

'Lest Big Rhys Jenkins eats you first.'

Early winter had got into us after Rhian and Bimbo had been with us a few months, and the spit-gob spiders of autumn had long since spun their webs of iced gossamer on the hedge-rows. Even the dandies had withered and died, and the winds of the mountains had needles of sleet in them, hissing and singing into the fires of the vagrant Irish.

Down the road to Abergavenny the windows of the new Puddler's Arms and the Gardener's were all iced up, and the customers within were crouched over the fires. Ginger from China was soaked in hot water to keep out the chills; red-hot pokers were plunged into the ale to warm up the cockles of the heart; red-faced colliers' wives tied themselves up with belly bands and flannel petticoats.

Staffordshire Row for the Midland iron specialists, and Shepherd's Square for the puddlers and refiners, were com-pleted that year, I remember: Stack Square, warmer than most, being near by the furnaces, had underground tunnels dug for cottage heating, and they were the cosiest rooms in town – the furnace gases, hot from the engine blast, first circulated in the tunnels before going up the stack. And this I promised myself – if I ever took a woman for wife, I'd settle her into one of Stack Square's cottages – though the rent was two shillings a week, enough to break a normal family.

For there was growing in me a shine for Rhian Evans, the dark Welsh; with a wish in me to take her to bed and bring out sons, such was her beauty. Some, though, thought her too small for sons, being only four-foot-ten in her boots; lavish at the top, she's skinny on the bottom, said Ma Corrigan: 'If you want lusty sons, Hywel Mortymer, you need 'em wider. How old are you, lad?'

'Eighteen, Ma.'

'You'll 'ave a thin old time with a family born on

tramming, you know, especially if you're after a cottage in Stack Square. But you can always put your name down – mind, they do give preference to ironworkers.'

'That's what I'm after – improving myself.'

'Puddling's what you should go for.'

'Aye.'

'With a size like yours, they'd take you on. But you'll 'ave to wait a while, I reckon, now the troubles are on us,' said Ma. 'Sweet Jesus, I leave the Navy for a quiet time and here I am landed with mountain riots.'

'The troubles won't last long, though.'

Ma rose up, looking belligerent. 'And I should hope not. If they'd seen mainmast floggings like I done, they'd 'ave something to riot about. Sure to God, in the name of the Mother, what's wrong with folks today?'

I didn't answer. It was the same old argument all over the Top Towns these days; the old generation beating its breast and standing to attention for 'God Save the King'; the younger generation joining marching gangs and carrying banners saying 'More Pigs and Less Parsons'.

'If ye want to puddle, why don't ye send a letter to Mr Hopkins – he ain't such a bad fella, you know. You can write, can't you?'

'Yes, Ma.'

'Then get going. Or do ye want to be a tram-haulier all your life?'

What she didn't understand was this – if I left the tramming at Hopkins Drift, I'd have to leave Rhian.

A new spring, bright and hot, came dancing over the mountains, and while the shifts were filled with the thunder of the trams and the bawling of Effyn Tasker, the days off were alive with bee-hum, warm winds and mountain flowers. The fields in our valley shone like square sovereigns; the old Usk flowed like white honey in the sultry heat.

Coloured birds winged over hills topped with sunlight and burning hot like cottage loaves straight from the baker's dozen. Herons waded in the river down at Llanellen; wood sorrel and late bluebells dozed in the woods around Pigloo Farmer's Arms; early honeysuckle entwined the trees; wild strawberry was free for the taking.

And, as spring and summer flowered into ripeness, so did Rhian Evans. Tram-hauling might have calloused her hands and knees, but she grew that year from miniature girlhood into a lovely, pleasurable woman.

Her hair was blue-black and parted in the middle, falling in ringlets about her shoulders: and if the dress she wore was ragged, it enhanced her fragile beauty. Her skin was transparent; its olive sheen a contrast with her eyes, which were as blue as an Irish girl's: her voice possessed the depths of the lower clef contralto.

How to tell of her, with only words to use?

'She be a queer-looking little bugger, mind you,' commented Bendy.

I sighed and tried to change the subject, but he went on: 'All right, you're a stately old gent and you're after a woman, but ye'll need one to fill a pint pot, mun – this old girl's got duck's disease.'

'She suits me!'

'*Diawch*, ye could lose her under a stall in Ponty market – she only comes up to your elbow!' and he went huffy and cocked up his legs on the gob, and made no eyes to speak of.

Twelve

'Be on your best behaviour, you kids,' shouted Effyn Tasker.
'There's an archdeacon and a baronet coming round.'

'A who?' asked Bendy.

'A servant of God and a Knight of the Realm,' said I, and
Rhian gave me a winning smile.

'That's different,' said Bendy.

It was the time Big Rhys Jenkins laid a good one on Effyn
Tasker's whiskers.

Now, I was six foot up, but Rhys Jenkins had two inches on
me and a couple of stone; and he wandered up in Five Stall
when Bendy and I came up with our tram, followed by Rhian
and Bimbo with theirs.

With his thumbs in his belt came Big Rhys, and looked me
up and down. The flares were playing shadows on his face,
which looked as if it had been cut from granite: he called the
tune in Hopkins Drift, and nobody had taken exception to
this until now. Stripped to the belt, he looked like Atlas.

'This your woman, Mortymer?' His voice was thick with
Welsh.

'I reckon,' I replied, and got up from the haul and tossed
off the chain, since if a woman's worth having she's worth
fighting for, once said my father.

Rhian whispered behind me: 'Don't fight, Hywel, not
over me . . .'

Will Blaenafon, Big Rhys's butty, came up behind him; he
wasn't as big as Rhys, but a bit older – about twenty. This
didn't worry me; he wouldn't interfere: mountain fighters
had their own brand of honour.

Big Rhys said, looking ugly: 'Listen, boyo, everything down in Hopkins belongs to me; when I whistle the women come running.'

'Not this one, son.' I slipped off my coat.

'Oh, dear me,' said Rhys, and turned to his mate. 'Hark at it. You're more his weight, Will. Will you save me the trouble?'

And Bendy, coming out into the roadway, struck a fighting pose, his little fists up, and cried: 'Come on, ye pair of dumb nuts, let's be 'aving ye! My gent'll take the pair of you in under ten seconds. A minute back I'd 'ave given you the woman, but now you've got a scrap on!'

'Right you!' cried Big Rhys, and swung a right that would have dropped a donkey; I ducked, and it got Bendy on the ear and turned up his hobnails. Bedlam now, with Bimbo biting Big Rhys's legs and Rhian on his back tearing out his hair, and Dodo and Dai Jones came up from one direction and Blackie and Elija Deaf Mute from another, and in the mêlée I caught Will Blaenafon the prettiest left hook I've ever thrown, and he tripped over Rhys in the dark, his boots waving goodbye.

'Listen!' shrieked Rhian, and she stood above us waving a rush torch above our heads. 'Listen, listen!'

Her hair was down and her face was sweating; the commotion subsiding, we listened, all except Bendy, who was out to the wide.

'*Listen!*'

'Sweet Jesus,' whispered Bendy, waking up. 'Somebody's gettin' it proper.'

From the direction of Ten Stall, further down the line, came the swishing strokes of a cane and the screams of a child.

Big Rhys shook himself beside me; Rhian raised the torch higher. 'That's the brattice door on Ten Stall,' said Rhian. 'And that's Beth Ponty!'

The fight forgotten, we all went up to Ten Stall, which was practically next door to Ten Arches, and nearly above us as the rats preened themselves in the light of the niche lamps, we could hear the drop-hammers of the North Street forge. At first we thought the stall was empty, but a jinny-boy I hadn't seen before came into the light.

The drift of Ten Stall was so steep that they used two jinny-boys with a block-and-pulley tackle to haul the trams up the incline from the working face, for coal's a queer commodity. Men mine it and follow its trail in Mother Earth; sometimes it goes up, sometimes down, and you have to go after the seam whatever it does; this drift delved. It was a foul-air stall, too, so they had a brattice door to seal it off from the roadway.

Beth Ponty was on this door; Effyn Tasker had recently taken her off the trams.

'Mind, he don't half give her a going-over,' said the jinny-boy.

'What did she do?' rumbled Big Rhys.

'Fell asleep on the line,' said another, the jinny-boy's butty, and they called him Boyo Drifter.

'Where is she?' asked Rhian.

'Over by here,' said a voice, and Rhian lifted her torch: Beth Ponty, it was, huddled in a corner with her sack dress pulled up round her ears and her face wet with tears.

Rhian gave the torch to me, knelt, and held her, and Beth said, 'By Christ, missus, he do stripe me, look at me poor old shoulders.'

I held the torch higher and Rhian lifted Beth's dress and the weals were red-bright upon her, standing proud on the flesh: down further, too, said Rhian, pulling down the child's drawers.

'He be keen on that, is Effyn Tasker,' said Big Rhys, and Beth Ponty said against Rhian's chest:

'It's a steep old stall in here, see, and the rats get down the sump-hole in the black, and when the colliers change shift the buggers come up the pitch and whip my singin' hinni, look,' and she held out her empty bait tin.

'Singin' hinni?' I asked.

'She's a Scot,' said Bendy. 'Like bakestone – they do sing on the griddle when cooking. I told you, Gent – remember?'

'Why did Tasker baste ye?' asked Will Blaenafon.

'Fell asleep on the line, I did.'

'Mind, we've been down the twelve-hour shift,' added Drifter. 'We only had another ten minutes to go. I was down the sump knocking out the rats, for the colliers had packed them and they were squealing out of the gob. Tasker came up and Beth was asleep on the line – her candle had gone out.'

'I'm scared of the dark when the rats are squealing,' said Beth, tearful. 'And if me candle goes out I always drop off; for you ain't here, really speakin', are you, when you're asleep in the dark.'

And Drifter cried, falsetto: 'She do ask for it, you know! Like Tasker said when he was striping her – it's for your own good, my girl, he said, next tram up in the dark will cut your legs off.'

'He didn't need to stripe her so bad,' mumbled Big Rhys. 'He's always bastin' the girls; first chance going I'm having that bastard.'

'You'll go out feet first if you do.'

'Good an' all, who cares?'

Beth turned her stained face to the light, and said: 'That's right, Big Rhys, you do him for me. I dunna mind being striped for somethin', but I ain't being done for nowt.' Her Scots accent was pretty against the squealing of the rats; Drifter grinned and jerked his thumb.

'They're enjoying it, any road. It's a hell of a drift, this, for rats and black pats. I knew a collier up North. He reckoned his missus got his cheese out o' the mouse-trap, so he used to eat black-pat sandwiches – very tasty, he reckoned.'

'It stinks in this stall,' I said.

'It stinks and it must stop,' said Will Blaenafon. 'To think that our kids work in this hell – look at the walls.'

The walls were alive with armies of black-pats; waddling black beetles, the staple food of the rats. Rhian lifted young

Beth and sat her on the road, and said to her: 'Listen, Beth Ponty. Listen to what Ma Corrigan told me . . .'

Beth cried, bubbling tears, 'Ay, ay, and I'm tellin' on old Tasker when I see Ma Corrigan, and she'll land him one for striping my poor old bum . . .'

'Listen, girl, listen to me,' whispered Rhian, holding her. 'You know Sue Reece, the Welsh girl who sleeps two down from you in Corrigan's? You know what happened to her little brother when he went to sleep on the line?'

We all stood silently, wondering what was coming. Rhian said: 'Sue had this little brother, four years old: there was no kick nor push in him for the tramming, so down Sirhowy they put him on the doors, and he fell asleep. Sue was with the jinny-boys and his pa was shot-firing over in Tredegar, and through the dark comes a big farming lad with his tram heaped high, and he pushed his tram through the brattice and cut the little lad's feet off.'

'Eh, dear me,' whispered Beth Ponty. 'I dunna want me feet cut off.'

'So you won't go to sleep again on the brattice, eh? Better have a basting from Tasker than that.'

Big Rhys was on his knees. 'Maybe so,' said he, and got up, and his eyes were shining under his beetled brow, as an ape's eyes shine when they are turned to the light. 'But that Tasker's stripin' the kids no more,' and he looked at our faces one by one. 'No more, you hear me? Give me a day or two, lovely girl, and I'll have that Effyn Tasker.'

'Leave it, Rhys Jenkins,' I told him. 'Leave it to Ma.'

'Leave it, bloody leave it. You gentry are all the same. I'm tellin' you, fancy lad, I ain't leaving it no more, I'm seeing to Tasker.'

I suppose I should have lined myself up with Big Rhys that day: had I done so he might not have been suspended. But it seemed enough that he should turn his attention to Effyn Tasker, and forget about Rhian and me.

Bendy had taken Bimbo as his foal, and Rhian was now with me; I used to push my guts out to make it light for her; this was underground, during the day, in darkness. In the same darkness of the night, off shift, I would lie in Ma Corrigan's, nearly beside her, for Rhian always made sure that Bimbo was between us, and I used to wish him to the devil and back.

Aye, at night I would lie there and listen to her breathing. And if I looked past the snub profile of Bimbo's sleeping face, I could see Rhian as a pale outline, with the blackness of her hair like a wreath on her pillow. She always slept white; clean vest, clean stockings, clean pillow, said Rhian, and everything else comes white inside, which was what her mother had taught her.

This damned old Bimbo competed with Bendy for grunts and snorts like a pair of pigs getting off to market. But, despite this, I would lie contained by fancy; devising kisses for a mouth so near and yet so far; spinning dreams of escape from this hell into a land of beauty; from nightmare visions of mutilation to a place of gentleness. Aye, I promised myself, one day it would be like this – a cottage in Stack Square, perhaps, with the old chimney blowing heat into the cellars: a kitchen with a tablecloth prim and white, and a merry fire burning in the grate.

I awoke one night, put a board on my knee, licked the stub of pencil, and on a white sheet of paper wrote in a round, clear hand:

Bridge Arches,
Blaenafon

Dear Sir,
My name is Mortymer and I am a trammer down Hopkins Drift, and I wish for a chance to improve myself. Be good enough to consider this my application for training as a puddler. I would be happy to give you further details regarding myself if you wish it.

Yours obediently,
Hywel Mortymer

16th October, 1803

Then I turned once more to Rhian and found her eyes full upon my face.

Soon, I thought, will come the dawn, and Ma Corrigan will be up and doing, swiping the children into wakefulness, bawling, 'Come on, show a leg, me lucky girls and boys – out of ye hammocks, me darlin's. Full and by, full and by! Up the mainmast wi' you, me little powder monkeys,' for she spoke the language of the Navy. And all would be confusion and shouts as we fought to start another day.

But now, in this quiet time before the dawn, all was peace; Number One Bridge Arches was a sea of mist from sleeping faces; a dreamlike place of sighs, snores and ethereal visions, save for the blasts coming up from Ma Corrigan among the first straw bales behind the door. With her legs crossed and her bare arms folded on her chest, Ma snored in bass triumphant; with pictures in her brain of the broadsides of the big three-deckers; the snap-shots of the rigging muskets and the clash of the grappling irons as they got to windward for boarders. And she grimaced and bucked in a flash of cutlass steel, did Ma, and expired in one long-drawn sigh in the first red flush of the Pwll-du dawn where Nelson's blood-soaked pennants were streaming over the sky.

Forty children – no, more, with the new intakes the day before yesterday – slept in that unquiet dawn; but Rhian and I, our eyes meeting above the baby profile of Bimbo's face, did not sleep.

Because we were no longer children.

Soon, I thought, I would put a lace pillow under this woman's head, and go into her and bring forth sons.

Thirteen

Rhian seemed to have taken over from Annie Oh-No when it came to surgery down Hopkins, for since Annie's baby had arrived (she was living down Hush Silence Street, which was handy for the single colliers) she couldn't carry on with her work.

Unless we had amputations and suchlike, Dr Steel, who lived in a house at the top of North Street, was never called in, and the Company liked having Rhian as an unofficial nurse.

Sprains she cured with compresses of hessian towels and spring water, which she collected from the cellar of the Royal Oak. For minor chafes on the hauling chain or raws like colliers' elbows, a snail broken out of its shell, rubbed well in and then eaten, did a world of good; the pain being forgotten while chewing the snail, said Bendy. Even the cracks in pit-props Rhian used, for these exuded a sort of gum – it's the wood weeping in the dark for sunlight, she used to say. This was unsurpassed when it came to hardening knees before the callouses came: heartburn was cured by sucking chalk; cobwebs gathered in her little boxes stopped light bleeding; and every night she made new trammers harden off their knees and toes by washing them in pee.

She was a cure for everything, was Rhian Evans; now fast becoming famous in Pwll-du for home cures; she was as good as a witch-doctor, they said in the Puddler's Arms.

The only thing she didn't have was a remedy for love.

Autumn caught bronchitis round about November; she hung on late that third year in Pwll-du; tempering the threat of the winter gales, sweeping up storms of brown leaves from the bosom of the Blorenge and dusting them golden over the great Van Rocks of the Beacons.

Winter showed her fist at us from the top of the Sugar Loaf, then skidded on her backside down into the valley and froze the Usk, and the children of the vagrant Irish began to die again; a sure sign winter was here.

Evans the Death, flourishing in a galaxy of provision-box wood for paupers and mahogany for gentry, rubbed boot blacking into the hides of his funeral mares to add a little more sadness, and their ostrich feathers waved death up and down the valleys.

Tad Stewart's two lads (Tad was the top refiner over at Clydach Vale) died, but not with the cold: the pair of them hadn't been down Abraham Harry's drift a week when a pit-prop got a wane and snapped, and the vicar of St Peter's crawled on his hands and knees under the plug and gave them last rites: God, as is widely known, sees every sparrow fall. A couple of brickyard girls were drowned in their mixing pond when it trapped them in a sump, but nobody took a lot of notice of that; a few years later it got fourteen of them. Also, there was a lot of talk about cholera coming, for it was always knocking around Merthyr and Dowlais where the masters collared all the best water for their Works.

Then came the snows of December and January, and we were waist-deep in it down Heol-ust-tewi, later called King Street. Even the sheep were slipping on their rears down Heol-y-nant, which was afterwards called Broad Street. Indeed, we got so iced up that February that the Bridge Level colliery was closed to heat the turnouts, and the whole population was coughing rheumatic, with blue noses sticking out of their mufflers and their mittened hands under their arms.

A couple of other things happened, too, like Big Rhys Jenkins bouncing Effyn Tasker again – this time in full sight of Tom Leadbetter and John Williams, the officially appointed town Special Constables, and spent three days in the stocks at the top of North Street, which didn't do a lot for Effyn's eye and did less for Beth Ponty, who passed on with the chest that March. But the greatest calamity of all was the disappearance of a baron of beef on its way from the Angel Hotel, Abergavenny to Big House, where Old Sam Hopkins was giving an official banquet.

Apparently Archdeacon Coxe and his mate Sir Richard Colt Hoare were in the vicinity again, so a pony and trap was commissioned to carry the pre-cooked joint up the coach road via Gilwern and Pwll-du, which was the first mistake – it was along this road that the starving Irish lived.

Peak-faced, clutching their bony children, they would also sit with their backs against the walls from Heol Garegog to the Royal Oak, and every night begin their keening under the round winter moon which hung like a beacon.

Later, they would throng the lime-kilns up by Bunker's Hill and the heat of the brickworks above River Row, and seek their beds there, many to die from breathing sulphur. I've never understood why God paid so little tribute to the poor Irish, for they paid enough to Him in prayers and prostrations. It could well be, of course, that He gave them a thought on the night that the baron of beef went missing on its way up from Abergavenny.

Everything was set up for the banquet, apparently: toasts had been drunk, speeches given, and the Hopkins table laid with best silver. But back in the kitchen Mrs Amelia Peabody, the cook, was doing a war dance because the sirloin hadn't arrived, while guests with their knives and forks at the ready, and napkins tucked in, were becoming edgy.

Outside Big House violent scenes were occurring; respectable citizens were being pushed up against the walls by Tom Leadbetter and searched, for it's coming to something when a twenty-pound baron of beef goes missing; as Tomos said, it reflects very badly on the community.

More, there was a lot of ferreting around in hedgerows and a disturbing of local lovers, for Blaenafon inhabitants are known to be ardent in any climate. Up by Cae White, for instance, Selwyn ap Pringle came across a bare leg and pulled it, and out came Dai Paternity and Mrs Dulcie Bigg.

Nobody could think where the succulent joint had got to, but while the guests up in Big House were on faggots and peas, there was a gorgeous perfume wafting over Pwll-du: which is a scandal, said Tomos Traherne; a gentry dinner is entitled to travel without Irish interference.

It is astonishing to me how popular God becomes when cholera and typhoid arrive in a community; even more amazed am I by the antics of people who like God best when He sends the sun.

April!

I saw a doormouse in a hedge; his beady little eye winked at me, and I whispered, grabbing Rhian and hauling her to me.

'Hush and look, girl! Oh, he's beautiful!'

For now a garlanded woman was dancing over the mountains, and her drapes of gossamer floated on warm winds: the sun arrived, melting the polar ice-caps of the mountains, bartering them for wild hyacinth and cuckoo-pint, also early forget-me-not and daffies with their seas of waving heads that dance in sunlight.

Perhaps our world of coal blackness claimed us by night, but our days were filled with sun. The sky was cobalt, the wind like wine; the turf of the hills springy beneath our feet.

'Please don't do that,' said Rhian.

'Ach, come on, girl!'

'Somebody might come.'

How beautiful is the world when you are lying on your back on a mountain with the one you love beside you: all about you is the sighing of the wind in secret places and the symphony of the grasses. And far below you, in the Golden Valley, the old Usk, who doesn't give a damn for what humans get up to, dances like a capricious Welsh maid through the paradise called Gwent.

'Should know better, you being a gentleman,' said Rhian.

No gentleman could conceive the thoughts I had in mind. 'Besides . . .'

'Besides what?' I was up on an elbow and looking into her face, and such was the purity of her eyes, cornflower blue, that they seemed not to be of this earth. Red ribbons were in her hair (sometimes, though, they were yellow) and the neck of her old black dress was drooped with grandma lace, which I had bought from Flannel Street, Abergavenny: lithe and quick was Rhian in my arms now, her red lips seeking mine in gasps, until in a sudden movement of rejection she pushed me away, and got up and stood above me: her face was flushed; her twisting fingers spoke words she could not find.

'What's wrong?' I asked.

She closed her eyes and shook her head. 'It do not matter!'

I turned her into my arms again. 'Oh, but it does. What did I do that was so terrible?'

'Please . . .' On tiptoe now, for she scarcely came up to my shoulder, she stroked my face; her hand, I remember, was calloused in the touch.

Some woman's secret, I reckoned, for they can be queer old beggars at times, said Bendy, who appeared an expert. So I let it ride this time, and said, drawing her down to the grass again, 'Tell you what – I've got something precious belonging to you!'

Boy and girl again; she pushed me, laughing, head back. 'No, you have not!'

'Give you three guesses.' And I took the little coloured purse from my pocket and secreted it in my cupped hands and held it before her and her eyes danced at my hands and she bent, kissing them.

'Something in here – something you've lost, remember?'

Prettily she looked at me, her head on one side: it is her mouth that is beautiful, I thought, full and expressive;

she said: 'How can that be? I do not possess anything to lose!'

Her speech, too, was quaint; the cadent, sing-song music of the West.

I opened my hands and her eyes widened with surprise: lifting the purse, she held it up to the sun like a child in wonder. 'My purse!'

I nodded. 'That day you came to the lake, remember? You saw me at the fire and Bendy chased you off. I followed, but lost you, so I went back to the place where you were bathing.'

'You saw me bathing?'

'No, earlier. That time I saw only the purse, and all this time it has been lying at the bottom of my bag, forgotten.

'You saw me naked?'

I smiled at her, and the redness flew to her cheeks and she lowered her face. 'Skinny old thing, eh?'

'I thought you were beautiful.'

We sat side by side and there were no words between us, and I thought: this is purity. In a world where lust transgresses against love, this is how it is meant to be.

Pay a shilling, I'd heard say, and you could have a night with Annie Oh-No who never said No. Pay twopence and you could ferret in a hedge with Pru Knock-Twice, while down in Cockroad Row you couldn't go wrong with sixpence in your hand on pay night: a handful of gravel would bring down Duckie Droopy-Drawers all aboard for Japanese dreams.

My father knew it all, of course, for he once said to me, 'Do not forget, Hywel, that you fornicate with a woman but make love to a wife,' and now I said with business: 'Come, *cariad*, what does it matter if I love you?' and Rhian clung to me, whispering:

'And I love you, too, and one day will be your girl. Oh, my precious! But not yet, Hywel. Please, not yet.'

And so, with one hand pressing the purse to her breast and the other arm round me, we went over the old Coity back to Pwll-du Chapel, because it was Sunday.

❧

Stiff and starched sit the congregation in the Horeb Chapel; in rank according to social status, they sit: agents like Mr Ebenezer Orpington (who succeeded Sod-O Digby) in his black alpaca suit, his stock arching proudly under his big spade beard and his boots polished to shave in . . . he sat in the front pew beside the glory of Mrs Mercy Orpington, her frills and fancies enveloping Orpingtons Major and Minor, both so called since being accepted for private education, aged six. Behind these came Mr Effyn Tasker, his eye back to normal following the second attention of Big Rhys; and Mrs Siwan Tasker, with Ben Thomas and his missus on the other side of the aisle.

In the rear of these, strictly in social rank, sat the Midland specialists of Staffordshire Row; these were flanked by the Special Constables, Tom Leadbetter and John Williams, and behind these came the publicans, such as Mr and Mrs Selwyn ap Pringle of the Royal Oak and Billy Handy of the Drum and Monkey, who always worshipped at Pwll-du.

With two rows of pews kept vacant lest the gentry in the front should catch something, then came the labouring riff-raff; the refuse of industry such as trammers, cinder girls, brickwork labourers, lime-kiln burners and, at the very back pew of all, engine-oilers and rag-cleaners.

A few vagrant Irish, of unspecified denomination, stood aloof and unrecorded; uninvited, unaccepted. Their heads bowed suitably to denote their humility, they neither sang the hymns nor mouthed the prayers lest it drew attention to their presence. Behind these, mainly on their knees, doubtful characters like Annie Oh-No worshipped; beside her Pru Knock-Twice, Duckie Droopy-Drawers and another very dubious character (her aunt kept a disorderly house in Cardiff) hid their faces from the Big Seat and a God who, thank God, couldn't see beyond his nose.

In this situation, with the Elders polished and bewhiskered in terrifying authority, Tomos Traherne, immense in funeral black, brought down his fist on to the pulpit and cried in a voice to shake the earth: 'For a fire is kindled in mine anger, and shall burn unto the lowest hell, and shall consume the earth with her increase, and set on fire the foundations of the mountains . . .' And he took a great breath.

'I will heap mischiefs upon them; I will spend mine arrows upon them. They shall be burnt with hunger and devoured with burning heat, and bitter destruction: I will also send the teeth of beasts upon them, with the poison of serpents of the dust. The sword without and terror within, shall destroy both the young man and the virgin, the suckling also with the man of grey hairs!'

Panting, he glared down at us, and feeling Rhian trembling beside me, I knew his wizardry: about him was wailing, the hissing of fires and lamentations. And Tomos, arms upraised so that the black-blood veins of his hands stood out like snakes, bawled at us: 'I tell you this – you who sit there and contemplate the mercy of the Lord – that you hope in vain. For His judgement shall be instant and unpitying. Yea, unto the harlot shall be paid the fruits of harlotry, and to her customer shall be given the fruits of his custom, which is a withering of the stones. Aye – even unto the high and mighty shall this be, also.'

With this his voice sank so low that you had to strain to hear it, for it crept like a serpent among the buttoned boots and up the bombazine skirts: it entered the pages of Bibles and hymn-books; it slid up the curly candles of Duckie Droopy-Drawers's wig, and she shivered with fright. For it's a devil of a thing to come in hope of Absolution only to collect the likes of Tomos, and he cried now, full to the teeth with *hwyl*.

'For the fornicators shall be reserved the hottest fires of Satan's palace – into his white-hot caverns he will draw them like an incandescent flame!' and there was a clatter and a shriek as Mrs Dulcie Bigg went over backwards in a dead faint, and her grape assembly hat came off and her hair came down, and Selwyn ap Pringle went as white as a sheet.

'Behold the tabernacle of cooling streams' it was then,

done in full harmony with Miss Modesty Doherty, the spinster, on the harmonium, and it was marvellous to get away from the heat for a bit, and everybody let rip in soprano, contralto, tenor and bass. I chanced a look down at Rhian; with Bimbo's hand in hers she was singing in a beautiful contralto, her eyes lowered, and I wanted to shout to everybody there that this woman was mine.

I wanted to walk the aisle and declaim it to their astonished faces – that however poor we were, whatever the labour, one day I would call her my own. She glanced up then as if aware, and our eyes met and I saw the acquiesence to share her life with me, however poor the future. The colour sped to her cheeks, as it does when a woman knows she is being watched by her lover. Aye, like I said before – she is gone now, my Rhian; she lies in the Horeb graveyard, her pale, sad beauty going to dust. But always will I remember her; my lover and my wife.

Out in the sunset now, with the sun going down over the hills and the valley bathed red and the Usk running ripples of blood: aye, out in smells of hot cloth and lavender, with Tomos at the door, glaring in bespectacled wrath at the miscreants, and shaking hands with those more fortunate.

'Mind, you do wonderful, Pastor, if I may say!' Beautific and comely is Mrs Di Eynon, putting her elbow into her chap to keep him upright. 'Give it to 'em straight we say, don't we? Right on the button where it hurts, eh?'

'Yes, my love.' Stretched on the rack of her bitter archery is Albert Eynon, loveworn and as thin as a plasterer's lath.

'Oh, Mr Traherne, you do give a lovely sermon!' This from Miss Modesty Doherty, who has snapped down her harmonium and rushed out to press the pastor's hand: and no tabernacle of cooling streams can quench the ardour of Miss Doherty's erotic dreams in the harem of her heart where Pastor Traherne flies, braces dangling, across the faded counterpane of her virgin bed. 'Oh, Pastor!'

'Good evening to you, Miss Doherty.' The rumble is in his

chest and not his heart, and he dispenses with her fidgety hopes for conversation. Ianto Idler, who hasn't done a stroke since his Doris died, raises his eyes to the beauty of the Heavens, the only one there, save the sheep, with a soul as white as a bedsheet cloud.

Clustered about the pastor like a clutch of famished crows, they sigh and simper, begging for recognition from this, their passport to Heaven: old men with the hunger of their labour, lined and dripping; fat men furnished with brewer's goitres; old shinbones in stays; cuddly small girls who have not been underground; scarecrowed lads who have, but now ardent in Sunday collars and vivid lusts. Elders in pomposity, trammers like us in rags; Duckie Droopy-Drawers in her new boa, escaping from Tomos's gimlet eye, with Pru Knock-Twice in hot pursuit: both admonished and cleansed by close proximity with the Lord. Annie Oh-no, the baby-maker, collecting her two kids (one in long clothes) from Gran Fat Beti who lived in Twenty-one Long Row, goes off into the sunset, alone with her sins.

'Mind, a sermon like that do make them think twice, I always say, eh, Pastor?' said someone.

'That, ma'am, is my intention.'

'They got a door key down the back o' Mrs Dulcie Bigg, though. Thought she was dead, they did.'

'I trust not.'

Now, alone at the back of the woodshed behind the Prince of Wales, I put my arms around Rhian, but she fended me off, whispering: 'All right, just kisses. But don't you ever do that awful thing again, Hywel Mortymer!'

Through a rift in her hair I saw the sun going down; it sank my hopes.

One thing was certain. If I was going to get anywhere with this particular lover, I'd have to change the preacher.

Over in the graveyard Ianto Idler kneels by the flowers of Doris, who died, and raises his face to the pale April moon.

'Good night, my lovely.'

Fourteen

'Hey, you, come here!' commanded Ma Corrigan, and Rhian and I moved sharp, which was advisable when Ma did the calling. 'I got news for you, Hywel Mortymer.'

I stood before her in the Arches. But for Rhian and me the place was empty, all the others being on shift. Ma said, 'I bumped into Mrs Peabody the Hopkins's cook down Abergavenny market today. Did you write a letter to improve yourself?'

'Aye.' I'd long since given up hope on this score, having heard nothing for months.

'Old man Samuel's goin' to send for you, me son, so you need smartening up.'

'No!'

'There now,' cried Rhian, proudly. 'What did I tell you?'

In fact she'd told me nothing. But now she put Ma's flat Navy hat on at a rakish angle, a hand on her hip, and strutted around in the straw. 'How's this for a Gentleman Puddler?'

'Ach, take it off, it'll be years yet!'

'You gotta start somewhere, son,' said Ma. 'And I say we start on you – Rhian, girl, the fella needs mending and trimming – look at his hair!'

So, for the next two days Rhian and Ma Corrigan stitched up my tunic and mended the tears in my trews. They put me on a chair and cut my hair to a reasonable length, for it was now down to my shoulders; by the time they'd finished I was fit for a palace.

Rhian said: 'Oh, *cariad*, just think!' and she held me,

117

whispering: 'Just to get out of this hole! And married!' She danced around me in the sun. 'A cottage in Stack Square!'

'Don't be stupid! One's the Company Office and the others are for master puddlers.'

'You could apply!'

'Anyway, who's talking about marriage?'

She went soft and batted her eyes, and the mountain lying on his shoulder in the sun raised the relish in me; I put my arm round her waist and swung her down on to the grass, and she took off Annie Oh-No's valley talk: 'I ain't goin' to let you lest I get a ring, Hywel Mortymer . . .'

Trouble was coming again on the mountains; furnaces had been blown out in Merthyr, Dowlais and Tredegar; talk had it that marching gangs were on their way here.

The trouble was the French wars; the price of wheat was going up, the price of iron sliding down. This brought wage reductions, and the workers were fighting it in nightly meetings.

New leaders were arising; men like Big Rhys Jenkins, who were defying the Yeomanry Militia patrolling the iron towns. One mob, led by a woman so starved that she had to be carried on a litter, had ambushed a mule-train of wheat carts being taken out of the county, comandeered and distributed it to hungry labourers all over Monmouthshire and to the verderers of the Forest of Dean, always our comrades. Only last month, a detachment of soldiers from Brecon had taken barracks at the top of High Street in Town. And night and day now, galloping patrols of the hated Militia, the sons of gentry, were pledged to bring the Welsh Unwashed to heel; clip-clopping around the iron towns with their sabres at the ready.

Things were becoming worse economically.

With a surplus of iron being manufactured, the iron-masters were now selling to friend and foe alike; profit knowing no patriotism or loyalty. Also, as the profit in iron went down, then prices in their Company Shops went higher.

Flour was up to thirty-five shillings a bushel, salt had peaked at ninepence a pound; mutton and beef was selling at the fantastic price of sixpence. These price rises immediately put us on vegetable stew in Bridge Arches, with the prospect of meat once a fortnight.

Mass meetings were being held all over The Top; torch-light processions met at the square outside the Lion and at Big Stone, the traditional centre of rebellion to authority. The heroes of my generation, men like Sam Hill and Aaron Williams who were hanged for their role in the 1800 Riots, were being replaced by younger militants.

The troubles spread again like fire over the mountains: secret meetings were being held in the Pigloo Farmer's Arms down on the Llanfoist coach road: magistrates' homes were being attacked, Agents being ducked like witches or carried on poles. Meanwhile, the wheat crop, summer after summer, was a failure: oatmeal and barley were in such short supply that only the rich could buy them, and workers were condemned to work for food. Poverty and famine stalked the land.

Things were hard enough when Mr Hopkins sent for me to attend Big House for an interview, without Effyn Tasker taking a hand.

Above the Afon Llwyd, in the basin of Cwm, lies Old Coal Drift, which was chock full of foul air; a good seam of coal was here, and was in commission when Abraham Harry was a baby. According to legend, ghosts roam here; from its deep inclines strange sounds are heard; the barking of dogs that never lived, the crying of children who were never born, the sobbing of women who never existed.

'I want you to open up Old Coal Drift,' announced Effyn Tasker, and he came into Bridge Arches as if he owned the place, shouldering Ma aside. It was dawn, and Rhian and I were coming on shift.

'Old Coalie?' said Ma. 'That's been closed for years.'

'That's why it's time it was opened,' said Tasker, 'You, you, you and you,' and he indicated Rhian, Bendy, Bimbo and me.

'It's full of Foul to the roof!' cried Ma.

'It isn't, it's been flashed,' replied Tasker. 'All right, you lot, follow me,' and he led the way from Pwll-du along the tram-road, then struck out across country when he reached the river. Here he paused, looking back for Bendy and Bimbo.

'Where have the other two got to?' he demanded.

'I sent them down Hopkins,' I answered. 'If it's fouled we don't need kids, and Sam Hopkins doesn't agree with children down the old drifts.'

Tasker weighed me for size, then thought better of it, saying, 'Up to you, but you won't get anyone else,' and he came to the rock entrance of Coalie Drift, went down on his belly and squeezed under the roof entrance; there, on his knees, with Rhian and I beside him under a roof three feet high, he lit a rush: the dark was banished; grotesque, dancing shadows lit up his face like a fiend.

'See, I told you, it's been flashed.'

'It's one way of finding out,' I replied, and as he stumbled forward into the darkness, I took Rhian's hand and followed.

Tasker stopped in a narrow place, took an old niche lanthorn down from the roof, and lit it.

'You and her – I need colliers,' said he.

'Then why don't you bring colliers in?'

'Because they're scared to death of the fairies. Christ, the things I have to put up with. Two old chaps started last night. They wouldn't take lodgings up on Bunker's Hill – seen 'em with our own eyes, they said – "Sitting on the chimney-pots of Toll Bar cottage, combing out their long fair hair," they said.' Tasker spat. 'And I'm supposed to run Pwll-du.' He gestured at the roadway about him. 'Must be a hundred years since this old place was worked, for it's older than Blaenafon. Chock full o' Foul? Rubbish! Chock full o' ghosties, weirdies and hobgoblins – the old ones have more suspicions than teeth. But, the younger generation . . ."

'Don't believe in such nonsense,' said Rhian.

'Then now's your chance to prove it. Three ha'pence an hour each, and you can name your shift. How about it?'

I replied, 'A six-hour shift, two shillings for the two of us.'

'Christ, you'll break me!'

He pondered it; the outlay was tremendous; twelve shillings a week! A month of this and we could marry.

'Tell us what you want,' I asked him, and Tasker answered.

'Clear the roadway up to the face; get the rubbish back to the entrance; re-cut the niches for candles, widen narrow places, for I'm bringing ponies in; flatten off the bottom for rails.'

We watched him waving his flare right down to the entrance, and we were alone with the ghosts of Old Coalie; and generations of colliers who had worked this drift mine before Blaenafon was born.

It is astonishing to me how women can read thoughts.

After Tasker had gone Rhian and I stood together in the light of the lanthorn, and the very silence murmured between us the need for fulfilment.

Until this moment we had not known the isolation necessary to lovers; even in the loneliness of the mountain there existed the possibility of a spy and wagging tongues.

But here, in this ancient place where ghosts were said to walk, no eyes or tongues existed: the small ecstasy of our nearness grew like a bond between us, the silence betraying every drawn breath; the wavering light enhanced the shadows of Rhian's face, as candlelight unveils with soft accord all beauty. She was, I thought, a complete and lovely human despite her rags and callouses; beautifully put together, from the mass of her tumbling hair to her ungainly boots.

'Best get on,' said she.

But she did not move immediately, and we faced each

other within a concord of togetherness: as ebony statues we stood, moulded in coal. And then Rhian lowered her face and said, 'No, Hywel! It is not right. Best . . . best get on.'

I thought: I am in love with you. My heart beats because of you; my eyes see because yours see also, for you are of me and I am of you. I would give the fingers of my hand for a minute of joy in you.

'No, Hywel. Come!'

Picking up our picks and shovels, I followed her down the tunnel. As we went I held my cap candle so that it shone on the roof, and from time to time struck up with the pick handle at suspected plugs, for bell-stone plugs are the worst danger of all. Concentrated in weight like lead, they slice down through the mountain; down, down, knifing through bog and rock, splintering up the shale until they reach a cavern. And down they crash, bringing with them boulder falls to kill or maim colliers.

Now, about a hundred yards down the roadway, we reached the seam; it slanted up from floor to roof, thickening from nine inches to two feet wide above our heads. Primitive workers had laboured to get this seam, until it had disappeared upwards in a rich-black jagged wedge of first-rate coal: Tasker, I reflected, had known what he was doing when he decided to reopen Old Coalie; this seam was better quality than anything I had seen down Hopkins.

Stripping off my coat and tightening my crow-belt, I began to work, and so did Rhian. For an hour we worked, never together, but always within reach. It was hot in the roadway and the sweat streamed, bathing us in a shining wetness. Looking up for a breather, I saw that Rhian was naked to the waist, like me. She straightened, too, wiping away sweat: gasping, she awaited me.

It was like a transfiguration; a step back in Time.

No longer was she Rhian, but a being out of another age. The veil of centuries had been swept aside by this simple togetherness; we, the living tokens of that age, seemed to be the only people in the world.

By that small abandonment all was simplified: all the fusty ethics crumbled with every step I took towards her. She had only removed her coat because she was hot; in Bridge Arches, when washing, I had seen her so a hundred times, as down in the lake of Tal-y-Bont, but this was strangely different: women mark their need not only with the tongue.

'I love you, Hywel. We have both waited too long.'

I held her, then swept her up into my arms and carried her to a place beyond the road: here a stall swept downwards into a little sump where water plopped and swirled; here, too, the coal had been cut by ancient and forgotten tools.

How many lovers, I wondered as I set Rhian down, had known this splendid isolation? How many kisses had been given and taken in this sunless world below Cwm Afon? I heard within our gusty breathing the distant river flowing; reaching up, I snuffed out the niche candle, bringing us to total blackness, and there was no sight in us; no sounds were real to us save the gasped words of lovers.

This was no coquetry; neither advance nor formal accept-ance was made, but a union of marriage that would live in time. As a wife Rhian received me, being lithe and quick beneath me; gasping once only . . . to a pain that was not virginity as I entered her body. A man is great in the loins then. With the petal smoothness of her body against mine and her kisses upon my mouth, her breath was sweet to me. And when the fervour of that love-making faded, so was another born in us, transcending what had gone before. And even when I drew away from her, I was yet within her enchantment.

How beautiful is this joining together of lovers! If this mating is devised by God, how can it be sinful?

'What is that?' whispered Rhian.

'I heard nothing!'

But she clung to me, tensed, for her head was upon the earth, and mine was not; and then in the stinging silence, I heard it, too, in disbelief.

Faint, as if coming to us from a crack in the earth's soul, was the sound of a woman sobbing.

In the blackness we struggled up: I lit the lanthorn, and yellow light glowed around us like a pool of gold; quartz and Fool's Gold glinted and shone; the exotic crustaceans born of a million years gleamed bright in seams of useless silver.

Again the sobbing.

'Oh, listen to it!'

Upon her feet now, Rhian clung to me. 'What is it, for God's sake?' She stared about her. 'We are cursed for this! What is it?'

Her trembling, which began in her hands, was now enveloping her; she shook as with an ague.

'It is the river,' I said.

'The what?' Terrified, she stared at me.

'The Afon Llwyd. It is only a few yards from here. Calm yourself. When you were lying you heard it running underground.' And as I said this there came from a fissure in the roof a foot above my head a thin trickle of earth; like a silver strand in the candlelight, it fell between us. I heard, also, a distant rumbling. Rhian's eyes were wide and startled.

'Pounce thunder,' I said. 'It is nothing.'

'Look, Hywel – *the roof*!'

The roof above me was trembling as if the mountain above us had turned upon his shoulder in the sun. Now the stomach of the earth began to rumble, and the rumbling grew, shaking our world so that debris and dust showered down upon us. And in the moment before the roof went down I grasped Rhian and swung her into the shelter of the stall; pushed her on to the gob and there held her. I saw through swirling dust a tiny hole appear above the zig-zag seam of the coal; this widened, as a crevice is levered aside by a collier to find the seam. As it widened and I stared upwards past Rhian's sweltering face, I felt upon my lips a cold kiss of air. Now, as the gap in the crevice spread, the rumbling died and I smelt in new air a stink of rottenness.

Again the sobbing of a woman. Quite clearly I heard this; no error in this, no echo coming from the earth, but the sound of a woman in tears: in the eye of my mind I saw her with her sack apron up to her face, as I have seen women cry when the accident stretchers come down North Street.

Now I left Rhian and rose from where I was sheltering her, and climbed to my knees. Leaning forward, I took the niche candle and held it high; the dancing flame spluttered on grease, and the flame leaped higher.

I looked through the crevice into a cavern beyond.

What I saw was the enactment of something long past: a reincarnation of a primitive time when Man first dug in the bowels of the earth for coal.

Fifteen

Now there grew in me the instinct of self-preservation, and I tensed my muscles to run; yet fear held me rooted beside Rhian. I moved the candle nearer to the crevice, illuminating the little cavern before us.

Five people, perfect in form, sat round a little pile of stones, and on this stood a rusted lanthorn, of a design unknown to me. Three of the group were children; the remaining two the parents, perhaps, of what was once a family.

The adults were facing me: indeed, the man was staring in our direction, and we saw his features in detail; the sunken cheeks from which peered two dull eyes. He was fair; his spade beard hung upon his chest and rested on his thighs, grown to this length long after death had claimed him, and the draught in the cavern stirred it, as a live man's beard stirs in the wind. Not a hair upon his head had he, giving him the appearance of an old biblical character.

The woman beside him was young; her long black dress, which Rhian later said was homespun, was in tatters, the neck hanging in rags about her wasted chest: yet her up-turned face, slanted as if death had struck her in the middle of a prayer, was, like the man's, incredibly alive. I saw and traced in my mind – and the vision stays with me still – every feature; the high cheekbones of the Celt, the flared nostrils of some ancient tribe; there was about her, even in her decay, an almost noble arrogance: it was as if in death she was defying the passing of the generations.

The children – and one was a child in arms – had their backs to us; the man was propped against the cavern wall; the woman squatted. The children lay in desultory bundles, their shape indefinable, save for one skeletal arm that projected from a sleeve. The candle-tack flickered and flared, one moment lighting the scene, then dousing it. And I heard, as before, a faint but unmistakable sobbing.

Rhian whispered something, gripped my arm and pointed into the cavern. I raised the candle, which was threatening to expire.

The face of the man was beginning to crumble; Rhian bowed her head, but, riveted, I went on staring at the phenomenon. In a flash of the candlelight his eyes glazed and died in his face: the sunken cheeks, momentarily bloating, sagged and withered, exposing the bones that held them: then, as if by an obscene phantasm, his entire form began to shrivel, the tatters about it crumbling. Suddenly, the whole contraption of his being collapsed, and he was no longer there.

White dust arose in the place where he once sat, leaving behind the spectre of his skeleton. Another few moments, and the body of the woman did likewise: one moment there as if embalmed by the oil of centuries, the mummy of her corpse disintegrated; even the outstretched arm of the child, once rigid, now sagged, leaving the bones of spread fingers clearly defined.

The air moved within the cavern again, and spread to our nostrils in a stink of putrefaction.

I thought at first that Rhian had fainted, for now the candle had gone out; we were in darkness and I could no longer see her face.

As I turned to drag her away from the crevice, a bellstone fell somewhere down the gallery, and I heard the roof crashing.

I held Rhian in my arms, protecting her from stones and dirt that showered upon us, awaiting the engulfing fall, but it did not come. She, still half clothed, was shaking with fear and cold: suddenly she said, her voice calm and clear: 'We are going to die, aren't we?'

'We are not going to die.'

'In a hundred years someone will come down here and find us, as we found them.'

'Don't be ridiculous!'

'What has happened?'

'It was an earth tremor. The land gets sick of us, the old ones say, and sometimes the Mother shakes in anger. A plug has fallen and we'll have to clear it.'

'And what we have just seen?'

'Exposed by the tremor. It is nothing. Old Betsy Small-Coal says there are a hundred scenes like this under Wales.'

'They were ghosts?'

'They were not ghosts. Once they were living people.'

I struck the tinder flint and re-lit a niche candle: strangely, in that savaging moment of fear she appeared more beautiful than ever; I saw the dark mass of her hair, the subtle geometry of her breasts. The candle's kind glow made her appearance ethereal. I held her against me again, whispering, 'Now pull yourself together. It is all explainable . . .'

'But the sobbing?'

'That was new air rushing into the cavern.'

'And those people? One moment there, then gone!'

'There was an air-lock within the cave: when fresh air touched them, they fell to nothing.' I looked about me. 'Now follow me, and we'll try to clear that fall – it's somewhere down at the entrance.'

Groping back to the entrance in the light of the lanthorn, we found a bellstone fall that almost blocked the light; one ray of sunlight shafting through on to our faces as we worked, giving us hope. But I was becoming aware, as I picked and shovelled at the obstruction, that my breath was coming in staccato gasps, as was Rhian's.

'This needs flashing,' said she, resting on her shovel.

'Aye, when we get back we'll tell Tasker. It's madness opening up this old drift, she's chock full of something waiting to happen.'

We made a crawl-hole in the fall, and we emerged on all fours into the blinding sunlight of midday. Birds were singing, the sun high in molten splendour.

Rhian touched me, 'Look who's coming!'

It was Mr Leadbetter, the manager of the North Street furnaces.

'Don't tell me he's after us.' We held our shovels and picks in front of us in the customary manner of a labourer's respect.

Tom Leadbetter, according to Billy Handy, was a pie-faced northerner: rosy-cheeked and cold, with a long nose cocking up, he envinced a stuffy disregard for Welsh Taffs. He had a cackling rooster of a wife, who used to claw at him with the savagery of an alley-cat. So he took it out on us. Strange indeed are the ways of God who makes vultures from the same moulds as swallows. Tom's first wife was a duster-and-pie woman who could stitch a yard of homespun a day, while Effie Leadbetter spent her time mainly in church, arranging flowers.

'Your name Mortymer?' Tom asked belligerently. Big in the belly and pompous, he strolled around us.

'Yes.'

'You applied to the Owner for puddling rates?'

'I applied to be trained as a puddler.'

He was already walking away, saying, 'The Bridge Arches woman said I'd find you here. Mr Tasker, your overman, is down in Abergavenny for tools. Come. The Master wants to see you.'

First we went to Number One Stack Square, which was the official company office, to check it was me who was wanted. Here were weighbridge clerks in shiny suits, red noses and starched collars: shillings jingled here in the hands of the lofty paymaster; an enormous safe in a corner had KEEP OUT written on the door.

Here were produced the tally-cards and receipts; how much coal, iron and limestone had poured into the furnaces since a week last Monday. Here, too, was fiddled the prices in the Company Shops in Stack Square, up at Pwll-du, and behind the Drum and Monkey.

'Hywel Mortymer, trammer, up before Mr Samuel Hopkins,' said somebody: it sounded like a sentence of death.

Samuel Hopkins and Thomas Hill, his partner, the masters of Blaenafon, had little to do with the clerical staff, apparently. Interviews of significance, such as the reception of Archdeacon Coxe, took place in Big House, the fine new mansion in the Company Park. This surprised me, for an application for training as a furnaceman was scarcely a world-shaking event. Tom Leadbetter led the way into the holy portals, but he suddenly thought better about Rhian.

'You wait here,' he commanded.

With my bare feet a satin slither on the cold mosaic, I followed the manager to a great door of gilded oak.

'And you wait here,' and I obeyed, standing black-faced, filthy, and in my rags. So much, I thought, for Rhian's sprucing me up for this interview.

Bewigged servants preceded by trays clopped past me, their eyes downcast in disdain at such impoverishment, for there are no snobs like the working class.

Waddling matrons in creaking stays and boots came and went with pails, brooms and businesslike authority. And then, to my concern, I heard a clatter of military horsemen, and saw through a window beside me a troop of Yeoman Militia arrive; six troopers, a red-sashed sergeant and an officer. Dismounting, they tethered their horses. The sergeant saluted and the officer turned and faced my window; sunlight flashed upon his ceremonial cap, his spurs rattled as he walked: instantly I recognized him –

Kent Mortimer.

A moment later they called my name, and I was happy to make myself scarce.

Sixteen

Samuel Hopkins, an anglicized Welshman although Welsh-speaking, allying himself with Thomas Hill, an Englishman to whom money was a god, brought to the town the gift of centuries – Sarah, his gentle sister: it was Sarah who poured oil on our town's troubled waters.

Sarah Hopkins it was who built the school, and taught in it long before the millionaires of Dowlais, Merthyr and another dozen English ironmasters gave a thought to the education of their Welsh near-slaves.

It was Sarah Hopkins, sitting in her Bath chair beside her brother's massive oak desk, who smiled up at me as I entered.

'Your name is Mortymer?' Samuel's little bald head was exchanged for his small, ferrety face; he adjusted his pebble spectacles and peered up at me.

'Yes, sir.'

'Spelled with a "y", I notice.'

I nodded, and he said, 'We are not aloof to the name at the moment. The yeoman captain who has just taken charge in town also has this name.' Samuel Hopkins looked bored. 'Indeed, he tells me that it is derived from Morte Mer, the Dead Sea in Palestine where his ancestors fought in the Crusades – to my mind a palpable waste of time and money. You are not of this ancestry, apparently.'

'No, sir.'

This was astonishing and frightening.

'Your hand is such, young Mortymer, your English so educated, that one could be forgiven for assuming that you were.' A thin smile ghosted upon his florid little face, then vanished. 'Indeed, Miss Hopkins has heard that you are beautifully educated. Where?'

'Privately, sir, in Canterbury.'

'Do we know of private schools in Canterbury?'

Miss Sarah gave an angelic smile, and shook her head, and her brother, his tone changed, snapped a question at Mr Leadbetter. 'How do we employ him?'

'Head trammer, sir, Hopkins Drift.'

'For how long?'

'Two years,' I said.

'This, you know, is absolutely scandalous,' interjected Miss Sarah quietly, and asked me, 'You read and write in English and Welsh?'

'In Welsh and English, ma'am. Welsh is my mother tongue,' and she clapped her hands together in a little joy, saying, in Welsh:

'How wonderful it would be to conduct a school in our language!'

'Marvellous,' I replied, also in Welsh, and the manager sighed.

Her brother looked faintly amused. 'But we will conduct this interview in English for the sake of the furnace manager. You wish to improve yourself, it seems.'

'Yes.'

'As a puddler's apprentice?'

'To be trained, sir.'

Samuel Hopkins sat back in his chair. 'Attend to it, Mr Leadbetter. It would appear that the change is overdue. On all sides we are crying out for furnacemen, puddlers in particular. But now Miss Hopkins has a question for you, Mortymer.'

And his sister wheeled her chair closer to me, saying: 'It is not often that we employ trammers of such education. Is that not so, Mr Leadbetter?'

'That is certainly so, ma'am.' He bowed to her.

'And so I ask, Mortymer, since I am thinking of opening a

school for the education of children – would you consider the post of a teacher there?'

'Certainly, ma'am.'

'The stipend would be small, but it would be a beginning. I have strong views as to the benefits of keeping our Welsh . . .' Her voice trailed into silence like one exhausted by the effort. 'Eventually, I hope to build a school of some proportions, when . . . when the money allows, of course.' She sighed.

Samuel Hopkins was now showing signs of disinterest; it was a precise example, I remember reflecting, of the Welsh nationalist and the anglicized brother.

'Right,' he snapped with finality. 'Your application is approved; Mr Leadbetter will take it on from here. You may go.'

I bowed to them, and left.

But I do not remember that summer day for the brief triumph of my application's acceptance; nor for the kindness of Miss Sarah's reception of me. I do not recall it as a moment of magical entry into a world long past – the dead workers of Old Coalie; not even for the the first time I had made love to Rhian.

I remember it only as the day Bendy and Bimbo died.

There was a crass and bitter impudence about the day as I went back with Rhian to continue our shift in Old Coalie. The sky was an ocean of white petticoats; a consuming by heat. The sun-fed giant of the Blorenge Mountain lay quiet and still upon his back enjoying the errant winds of summer. But the innocence was besmirched by betrayal, for under his breast Bendy and Bimbo were sentenced.

Rhian and I went back to the entrance of Old Coalie and found it blocked.

So we went up to Garndyrus to report the fall in Old Coalie.

Ma Corrigan said, 'After you two left for the interview,

Tasker called up Bendy and Bimbo. "Take their shift down Old Coalie," he said, "the other two will join you there soon,"' and Rhian put her hands to her face and went ashen.

'You mean the boys aren't here?'

'No,' answered Ma. 'I just told you. Tasker sent them down Old Coalie.'

'God in heaven!' whispered Rhian, and I shouted:

'Then they're trapped down there. Ma, get hold of Tasker –' and Blackie came running up and I seized him, crying: 'Run to the Royal Oak and fetch Tasker.' I shook Ma Corrigan. 'You get as many colliers as you can. The entrance is blocked in Old Coalie!'

She cried back: 'You won't get no collier sailing his pick down Old Coalie, mun. Too many ghosties and ghoulies . . . !'

'Tell them there's kids down there.' And we ran full pelt back to the drift, and began to pick and hew and tear at the fall with our hands.

Come nightfall, we were still at it.

Tread softly down the roadway of Old Coalie where the ghosts of ancient people walk: behind you the entrance is blocked fifty yards long from floor to roof, and Bendy knows it.

'Don't you cry, my son,' he said to Bimbo. 'Give 'em a coupla hours – they'll have us out.'

'What happened, mun?' asked Bimbo, tearful in the dark.

'The bloody old roof's come down.'

'That all?'

'Aye, but it's only a bellstone – lucky we wasn't under it. You all right, kid?'

'Aye, but I've only got one leg . . . ? And me bloody linnet's flown off.'

'Jesus,' said Bendy, feeling in the blackness. 'Aw, come off it, here's the other one.'

'It feels like it's off, mind.'

'Hold on, son, and I'll lift this boulder off it,' and Bendy added, 'That better?' His fingers were webbed with Bimbo's blood.

'Like I say, though, it feels like I ain't got it, you know.' He felt for Bendy in the dark, found him, and said, 'It's awful dark in 'ere, marrer, can't we light a candle?'

And Bendy patted the candle-stub upon his cap, and answered: 'Bugger me. I got the tinder-box; I only put a new flint in this mornin', but I forgot to bring the candle.'

'Weren't there one on your cap?' and Bendy took it off and dropped it into his pocket. Then he heard a faint twittering, and said:

'There was, but it must 'ave fell off.'

There was a silence. Bimbo said, 'Oh, good, me linnet's come back!'

'Sod old Tasker for sending us down here!' Bendy said, after a while. 'Never mind, Hywel and your sister'll be back soon,' and Bimbo began to cry again.

'Christ, will you dry up?'

'Me leg hurts.' Then Bimbo said, 'I got me bird cupped in me hands, Bendy, and he ain't movin' . . . D'ye know somethin'? I reckon he's dead,' and he listened. 'What's that trickling?'

'A little bit of water – drain sump. Here, hold on and I'll take the pain away better'n Annie Oh-No and your sister rolled into one.' And, kneeling, Bendy took off his jacket and tore out the sleeve. In his teeth he ripped it and bound it above Bimbo's knee where the leg was off; found a stone and twisted it in a tourniquet, and the trickling stopped.

Bimbo said: 'My Rhian and Hywel are somewhere down here, did ye say?'

Bendy laid down beside him, squirmed in the dark and pulled Bimbo across his shoulders. 'That's right, me son, and we're going off to find 'em.' He paused. 'Is your linnet dead, you say?'

In this manner, upon his knees and with Bimbo on his back, Bendy hauled him away from the fall.

And he remembered as he went, did Bendy, the first time

he had been entombed, down Haswell Hole, and the hind leg of the mare that projected out of the fall into the hole where he and Gaffer were sitting. He were a good gaffer, that one, for he never striped nor basted the lads or felt the girls: also, he knew when to die.

Go quieter still up to the leaded window of the Royal Oak: a little while ago Effyn Tasker was in here, boozing with Selwyn ap Pringle, but some kids are trapped down Old Coalie, according to Mrs Dulcie Bigg, whose chap is on night shift.

'Watch when you turn over, girl,' says Selwyn, 'for a bed like this can wake the Devil, never mind my missus.'

In a shaft of moonlight sits Selwyn, his sleeping-cap awry, and Dulcie Bigg very formal beside him done up in her new black nightie, and for God's sake keep it off the ground at twopence a yard, said the seamstress.

'What was you sayin' just now, my poppet?' asks Selwyn.

'About them two kids being trapped down Old Coalie. I keep tellin' you, Sel, but you ain't listening!'

'Two kids? Where?'

'Old Coalie! Old Coalie! How many more times?'

'Wanton! Harlot! Why didn't you say?' And Selwyn fell out of bed, caught his big toe in the sheet and upended Mrs Dulcie Bigg. 'I been a collier, you realize? Who's trapped? *Where?*'

She stood by the window in her new lace nightie, did Dulcie, and watched him in the moonlight, running upto Pwll-du, crying, 'Wait for me lads – I'm comin' – Wait for me!'

Mr Jess Conky-bum, sidesman at the Horeb – so called since he got the wrong side of a collier's pick down Hopkins and ever since walked sideways – knelt at the grave of Beth Ponty, put out his hand in the moonlight and caressed the earth.

Earlier, old Meg Laundry, who took in high-grade

washing, had come up with ox-eye daisies; Conky, for his part, had brought golden rod, which Beth always wore in the month of July on her way to Sunday School.

'Mind, they do go happy together, daisies and golden rod,' said Mrs Laundry, coming up behind him. 'You come here often, Conky?'

Stiff and starched is he, a string-bean man with a sunflower head. Round and comely is Meg Laundry; snow-white in her world of blue-bags and carbolic soap, pegs and washboards.

'It was the two children down Old Coalie, in fact,' says Conky.

'Me, too, at this time o' night. "Suffer little children," sort of, innit?' She peered with frightening intimacy. 'You heard anythin' more?'

For answer he left her, collected his pick and shovel, which were leaning against the lych-gate, and went in a crab-like, swaying run towards Pwll-du.

In the attic of the Drum and Monkey, Billy Handy lies flat on his back in the goose-down, snoring, while his Belinda, bereft of sleep beside him, pulls down her lace cap over her ears. Billy Handy, official pig-killer of Blaenafon, smiles and dreams in an official capacity, for if it is hating live pigs that makes me unpopular, says he, then find me guilty.

It be pathological, mind, says his Belinda.

Talk had it that years back Billy spawned a little son; aged three, he was, and coming into boots. Indeed, Billy took his little lad over to King Crispin, the Nantyglo cobbler, especially for a fitting: then, returning, carried his baby over to Grandfer Shams-y-Coed to collect honey, and while this was happening the boy waded about in the farm shippon.

'Right you,' said Billy, 'you've messed up those new boots, 'aven't ye? Behave like a little grunt and you can live with the grunters,' and he locked the lad in with Grandfer's prize porker, a pig by the name of Betsy, while he tipped up a bottle of ale with Grandfer.

After an hour or so Billy came back to collect his son, and there was nothing in the pig's cot but the Nantyglo boots, and old Betsy licking her chops and thanks for the meat course.

Ever since then, having learned the trade of pig-sticker, Billy Handy sat in judgement while pig after pig was arraigned before him: sentence after sentence he declared with clerical impartiality – that the jugular vein be severed and the criminal bled to death, with sacks tied over their snouts to avoid inconvenience to the neighbours.

Mind you, he did the job well, did Billy Handy: he always had the black cap on when pronouncing sentence on a pig, and read a little from the Bible with all the family present. And now . . .

Bang bang on the back of the Drum and Monkey.

'At this time of night?' cried Belinda Handy. 'Wake up, wake up, Mr Handy!'

And Billy, waking from a pleasurable dream of cutting a throat, saw not the fair vision of his beloved Belinda, but that of a live pig leering from the darkness; and he got her by the neck, did Billy, and lifted his Belinda on to the killing-board of the bolster. With the pillows beneath her head, his hand searched the bedside table for the knife while she shrieked blue murder, and they heard her all the way down North Street and as far as the Whistle Inn up the road to Brynmawr.

'*Diawch!* Hold still, ye bastard! Hey, you, grab that back leg!'

'*Nefoeddwen!*' shrieks his Belinda, nearly undone. 'Oh, Billy!'

Bang bang bang on the front door. Now a handful of gravel at the bedroom window, spraying thunder.

'Good grief! What the hell's that?'

Billy's head out of the window now, shouting down, and

his Belinda behind him wailing to wake the churchyard; and Ianto Idler, his cupped hands to his mouth, shouts up in the moonlight: 'Trouble down Old Coalie, Billy – volunteers wanted – a fall!'

'You ain't getting me down that bloody place, son – sod off.'

'Two little kids trapped.'

'What's that?'

'Young Bendy Oldroyd and Bimbo Evans.'

'Why didn't you bloody say, mun? Hold it, I'm comin'!'

Which is strange, you come to think of it, says Belinda. For I heard tell that human flesh do taste much the same as a pig's, and really, there ain't a lot to choose between 'em.

Now, reaching the crevice which Hywel and Rhian had discovered, Bendy put down the load of Bimbo and listened to distant sobbing, and saw in his mind a woman with an apron up to her face. But it was a sound he had heard before down Haswell Hole, and he knew it was air coming in from an old working.

'What's that?' whispered Bimbo.

'Forget it, it's nothin'.'

'Has Rhian come for me yet?'

'Don't you worry, my son, she's on her way.'

'She'll get me out when she comes, Bendy?'

'Like yesterday. She don't hang around, your sister,' and he thought: you can say that twice, Bendy Oldroyd – she don't hang around at all, for she took my friend. One moment he was there, then he wasn't. Sod women, and sod Rhian Evans in particular. You find a mate and make him a butty, and along comes a skirt and he goes dafto: Dai bloody Daftos, the pair of 'em. He put his hands over his face.

He had first learned of the companionship of men when he was entombed down Haswell; for ten hours cut off in the bowels of the earth. He had seen the rottenness of it all: little lads of six coughing up black dust and blood. He'd watched women give birth at the coal face, their feet drumming on the roof in the pushing; he'd seen another drown in the sump and they pulled her out by the hair. So life and death, for Bendy Oldroyd, were inextricably linked.

They'd taken his name and sent him down into the two-foot roofs to deform his back while his spine was growing, and paid him a ha'penny over the odds for work which nobody else could reach, the richer seams of profit. Perhaps, Bendy thought now, this was all he was born for; to work and die in coal. The thought brought almost a sanctity, and it gave him a little release from the fear of death, for he knew now that he was going to die: in any case, poor old Bimbo was close to snuffing it. The child's voice brought him back to their predicament.

'Mister, I can't breathe.'

'Of course ye can – now you hold on, Bimbo, for Rhian will be here any minute. I thought I heard her comin' now just.'

'My throat's hurting bad, too,' said Bendy, and laid his head in Bendy's lap.

'Pastor! *Pastor!*'

The Reverend Tomos Traherne up in Pwll-du heard this in his prayer, but did not answer the knocking on his door, for he already knew the reason: lowering his head, he searched his spade beard with thick, hairy fingers, and said in bass voice: 'O Lord God of Israel, hear this prayer, and save these children. With Thy kindly arms cherish them in Thy bosom. Cast Thy judgement upon me for my iniquities; draw me down into the pit of my defilement and reject me. But save these children, I beseech Thee!'

'Pastor! *Pastor!*'

Tomos Traherne rose from his knees, threw off his night-shirt and drew upon him the torn vest of the pit: pulled up his fat legs the coal-starched trews of the collier; candle-tack and cap he put on, also the crow-belt, which he fastened into the last notch round his large stomach. From out the back he fetched his pick and shovel; these he laid upon his shoulders as he went out into the road. In this manner, with the people of Long Row running behind him, he made his way over the top of Pwll-du and down the tram-road that led to Old Coalie.

After a little while the Foul in the roadway became worse; this seemed to increase Bimbo's pain, and he began to moan with his shattered leg: later, he knew the nerve agony and shouted and threw himself about, so that Bendy once could not find him in the dark.

It was then that Bendy remembered the name of the gaffer who was entombed with others down Haswell Hole, and this was Johnny Duff, and this overman had said, 'Listen, lads. If the Foul comes I anna going down choking, for I've seen men choke on the Foul. So, if it comes, let's go out quick, eh?'

The other men nodded, so Bendy nodded, too: he had not seen them nod because of the blackness of the entombment; nor could he see them licking their white lips and the way their eyes shone in the candle's flame earlier. But he knew what they were doing, and copied them.

'All agreed, then?' asked Johnny Duff.

All had grunted assent, but then one said, 'What about the kid, Overman? He ain't even begun to live . . .'

'How about it, Bendy Oldroyd?'

'Anything you say, Overman,' said Bendy, like a man.

But the Foul did not get worse; indeed, it was swept away on a rush of air. For the rescue party got the fall down and the haft of a collier's pick came through a hole, and the first they lifted through was Bendy Oldroyd.

But that, thought Bendy, was a lifetime ago; and this was now.

'Please!' cried Bimbo. 'Please light the candle, for I'm scared in this dark!'

Bendy said, 'Bimbo, dark is light, really speakin': like when the sun goes behind the clouds: like sleep, too, only cold, see, with the blanket slipped off.'

But it was then that he sensed the Foul.

It came from the crevice of the dead generation; it crossed the floor of the stall where he was cradling Bimbo; it snitched up between his knees, and Bendy smelled it, not with his nostrils, but with his soul.

Knowing this, the slow death by choking, Bendy rummaged in his pockets and brought out the tinder-box, and this he set upon a stone, opening it in the darkness.

'There now, my son,' said he. 'I've found the candle and we'll have a bit o' light until your sister and my butty come,' and he struck the flint and their world of entombment momentarily glowed: the blaze was small at first before the sympathetic detonation when the bowels of the mountain flashed and flashed in vivid light up and down the gallery. Now the firedamp ignited and went roaring around the face, blowing to pieces the crevice, the roof and the floor. Their world of coal exploded in strickening light and thunder, as if it was the ending of the world.

How to describe the empty, hungering loss?

Only those who have lost loved ones can truly understand; the knife is too sharp, the wound too deep.

The weeks down Hopkins Drift passed in a fervour of loneliness. In dark places, with trams, hauliers and donkeys passing within inches of us, I comforted Rhian's sobbing. And, by a twist of love's coquetry, the loss we suffered bound us closer than any passionate kiss. Even her tears were precious to me as I smoothed them away with my hands. And this comforting confirmed in me the love I held for her; therefore I resolved, with the loving down Old Coalie deep in my heart, to take Rhian Evans to the Big Seat in the Horeb, and make her one with me in the sight of God.

In later years a fine metalled road was built linking Blaenafon and Abergavenny, but in our time this was only a stony track beaten flat by Pwll-du and Blaenafon housewives trudging down to Aber market.

Upon this track stood Selwyn ap Pringle's Royal Oak; at the bottom of the hill was the Puddler's Arms; near Llanfoist was the Gardener's, with water troughs outside each, and thank God for that, said the mules, donkeys and horses.

This track was a living hell for draught animals. I would lie in Bridge Arches of a night and listen to the cracking of whips as the mule and horse trains rumbled up the mountains. Hooves skidding and sparking on the stone road, their hides bathed in sweat and blood, they hauled their loads under heartless drivers who tipped their whips with blackthorn for an extra journey a day.

The Indians say that it doesn't matter how many legs an animal possesses, he is still your brother. If that is so, then Man's inhumanity is fratricide: I have seen his victims dying under the loads. More than all, I remember the donkeys tiptoeing along, shivering in expectation of the next brutal beating.

The ancient coach road which brought our mail ran from Llanover to Llanellen and up the side of the Blorenge: serving Blaenafon, it then descended Gilwern Hill, to fall down to Clydach and return to the Usk; bridging on this journey countless brooks and streams. One of these streams, like white blood spewing from a wound in the mountain, ran through the valley of Llanwennarth in a torrent to the mothering river. On its way, in a paradise as yet untainted by the hand of man, it forms deep pools where trout and dace and little minnows lie.

Herons stand here in statuesque silence, contemplating the earth; coloured birds hunt the shouting water: it is a poetic frenzy of unspoiled Nature. Here little white farmsteads stand in splendid isolation.

To this place, seeking the pools cut into the rock by rushing water, Rhia and I often came to wash.

For it was *Rhia* now; which was not her name but the name by which I called her: the maiden having now become the mistress.

Later, but a little further down the valley at Llanellen, my son came to bathe; in another generation and with one almost as beautiful. This, my son, came to bathe with his lover. But he was not of Rhia's womb.

Such is the impudence of Time. All our happenings, all our loves are swept away; as the wind of the mountain sweeps up the refuse of autumns. But not this autumn – the crown of my year – one of blazing colour, sun and warmth; when Rhia, my first love, was wife to me.

How strange the coinage of the mind that brings silence amid the shout of rushing water.

No hand had ever moved here, it seemed, but ours; no foot had trod our land of fantasy. It was like living while everything else was dying. Time here, in Llanwennarth, snatched from exacting masters, was like a rhapsodic dream.

A dream that was rudely awakened.

I was lying outstretched on a grassy bank: Rhia was waist-deep in the stream, soaped up, washing. I recall thinking that she was like some wood sprite . . . in an afternoon drowsy with bee-hum.

Through heavy-lidded eyes I saw her: lathered white, her hair comically tufted and plastered upon her shoulders. And there suddenly appeared at my feet a pair of outsize boots: these I traced upwards to a brewer's belly sagging upon a buckled belt. Above this was the massive figure, fists on hips, of Tomos Traherne.

'*Duw!*' I exclaimed, and sat up.

Rhia cried from the pool, washing away soap from her eyes: 'Come on, give a hand – dry me off!'

In novels the earth opens and swallows you; in life it stays solid. Tomos, trembling with suppressed fury, sweetened and, bowing low, said: 'I beg you, Mortymer, do as the lady commands.'

Rhia, receiving no reply, tiptoed gracefully out of the water, her hands running in sunlight as she smoothed her hair out of her eyes. Seeing Tomos, she froze.

'Come, my child,' said he. Taking her hand, he led her to a seat beside me. 'Sit,' he said, and we sat. The river sang to the heated day. My heart was pounding against my chest; I dared not look at Rhia in case she had died. It was so quiet that I heard fish sipping.

And Tomos Traherne, now calmed and in full possession of the situation, threw his coat tails before him and, grunting, eased his great shining backside on to the nearest boulder.

'The surroundings, of course,' said he, 'are quite idyllic. In my youth – and I have been coming here since my childhood – I named this place Havilah. Declare, one of you, the book, chapter and verse to which I refer.'

His small, black eyes riveted upon us.

Rhia said, her face low: 'Genesis Two, verse eleven, Pastor.'

Tremendous in authority, he answered, 'Let your sin be absolved by the shame of your nakedness, woman.' In Welsh he said this. 'And hearken now to me, the pair of you.' He swept an arm about him. 'Is not this a second Eden? Are you not Adam and Eve, to whom God has given this beauty that you may enjoy it?' His voice rose to the working of an inner fury. 'And have you not despoiled it? You have known your nakedness, one to the other!'

At this I raised my face.

'Do what you like! We are husband and wife in the sight of God!'

'Oho, the cockerel crows, eh? How dare you compound your behaviour by defiance of the laws of God! How dare you dispute with me the ethics of my community, which demands that fornicators should know public abuse! Shame upon you both, shame indeed!'

And he pointed a shaking finger at Rhia's face and raised his voice, and she wept in her hands, rocking herself, as he shouted: 'Yours is the responsibility, woman. You have tempted this man and he has fallen into your snare. "Now shall the Lord God multiply thy sorrow" – Genesis Three, sixteen,' and he rose to his feet and pointed. 'Go! Go before I publicly condemn you and leave you to the will of the people!'

'We are leaving here, anyway,' I said, and rose, too, drawing Rhia to her feet and giving her clothes to her.

Tomos Traherne, as if touched by some unknown magic, then put out his hand and said gently: 'No, do not go, my children. Instead, dress yourselves, and listen to what I have to say.'

'We have listened already, and you've said too much!' I fought my way into my shirt.

'I beg you, stay,' said Tomos. 'For what you have just heard is the voice of my mouth, and not my heart. I have condemned you under the law, now I console you in compassion.' He raised his eyes.

'You have listened to your pastor, but now you hear the man, and the man grieves for you. He grieves that your youth is wasted in dark places for the profits of others; he grieves that you hunger for ease and comfort; for while God made the world, the devil made coal and hid it in the innermost recesses of the earth, that he might drive men mad going in search of it. Who am I to condemn the young who go in search of love?'

There came a silence, then he added, 'I can never know the treasures of love; the joining together of a man and a woman is beyond my comprehension, for I am beyond the charms of such women,' and he touched Rhia. 'You have known each other, you say?'

'I have told you,' I replied. 'We are man and wife in the sight of God. And nothing can alter it, even if your deacons drive us out of the Horeb.'

'Then give your pastor ease and allow him a victory over the incarnate fiend – let me marry you in the sight of God, and win your souls? So few of these have come my way of late.'

We looked at each other, Rhia and me, and she put out her hand and smiled: always will I remember that smile; her

146

hair was straggled upon her breasts; water glistened and shone upon her skin.

And Tomos Traherne, as if with an inner pain, bowed his head.

There may have been stranger pronouncements of love than on that autumn day at Llanwennarth, but I very much doubt it.

'I will leave you now,' announced Tomos, getting up in grunts and groans.

Seventeen

And so, on a bright morning in the month of August, 1804, while the old Blorenge was putting away her summer clothes and decking herself in brown, I married Rhia Evans in the little chapel of Horeb and made myself a hostage to fortune.

A fortune indeed, for we were both barefooted – my boots had long since snapped their soles in the hauling, and Rhia's last pair of shoes had been stolen in Bridge Arches; we even had to borrow Gran Fat Beti's wedding ring. Later, Selwyn ap Pringle gave us a curtain ring off his kitchen window.

Then there was a lot of sniffing and wiping, and doesn't she look lovely, and Mrs Dulcie Bigg broke down in the back pews of the Horeb, and a few of the vagrant Irish begging down North Street came up and watched.

Within a week we left Pwll-du as man and wife. No point in staying; neither the puddling job nor the school had materialized; besides, we could see the wraiths of Bendy and Bimbo round every corner.

The day we left was seraphic; the sun got up and shaved early, beaming his radiance on the alapaca suits and the women's coloured shawls.

There was a nip in the air, too, but the grans and granchers were on their chairs at the front doors of Long Row as we picked up our few belongings and bowed to Jenny Loom and Dot Popkin, Dai and Dodo, the twins; Iris Gold and Mrs Ten Beynon and about fifty others were there, including Ma Corrigan, who wished us good sailing, and away we went hand in hand along the terraced rows to say goodbye.

So, we took our leave respectfully of our neighbours, which was the custom.

Albert Laundry was helping Meg to peg out; Mrs Di Eynon was having Mrs Dulcie Bigg over with Gran Fat Beti; Duckie Droopy-Drawers and Pru Knock-Twice came up from town especially; even Half-Pint Jove arrived with Ned Taters, the vegetable man who did half-shifts down Hopkins, and Mr Conky-Bum, walking sideways, came up from the grave of Beth Ponty.

No chance of graves for Bendy and Bimbo: every inch we searched Old Coalie – no sign of them.

We visited each door; side by side we bowed to our elders: cackling roosters of old girls, maybe – but good neighbours. Ben Thomas, the under-Overman of Stall Ten, was there, square and squat, drunk with strength; his eyes, I recall, were incredibly blue in his brown face. A lot of whispers and elbowing as Selwyn ap Pringle came up from the Royal Oak with Mrs Dulcie Bigg, and quite by chance I did meet this lady on the road, said he, and Dulcie with her blinds down at the back, showing six inches of black lace.

'That's her nightie underneath her coat, ye know.'

'One day the pastor will catch 'em at it.'

'Very sorry you are going, though,' said Dulcie, and her tears were real.

'Take this little gift, Hywel Mortymer,' said Ianto Idler with flowers, and up to us came Elija Deaf-Mute with some pennies in his cap. 'The folks in Pwll-du do want you to have it. Elija went round the doors last night, didn't you, son?'

'Oh, no,' protested Rhia, 'they can't afford it!'

Eightpence in that hat.

'Take it!' boomed Tomos, coming up behind us, and from somewhere at the back appeared Idris Foreman, who conducted the Pwll-du brass band, which so far was Dai Swipo on the melodeon and Idris on his come-to-me-go-from-me: and I tell you this – no sweeter music ever came from that trombone. The people gathered around us, and sang: 'Iesu, cyfaill f'enaid i, gâd i'm ffoi i'th fynwes grêf . . .'

149

The trombone flashed in the sun, the melodeon hummed: the people had their faces upturned; the champing jaws of burnt-out colliers, the milk-teeth countenances of children; the youthful vigour of off-shift colliers, their hands cupped to their ears for the harmony . . . as I later saw the broken-booted miners sing along the gutters of Swansea. Nellie Washboard arrived from the Puddler's to give Meg Laundry a hand, being a Monday. It is friends you need, mind, when the day is heavy, said she.

Now a prayer from Tomos, and we stood in the sun with bowed heads like the Angelus, while his bass voice floated over us.

'Grant, Lord, bounty and peace to our young friends leaving us today: receive the souls of the loved ones they are leaving behind.

Hand in hand we left them, and turned but once to wave.

The villagers of Pwll-du were tiny figures against the sky, and Meg Laundry's washing was blowing in the wind. The trombone and melodeon played on: 'Jesus, lover of my soul; let me to Thy bosom fly . . .'

'Life is all goodbyes, innit . . . ?' said Ianto Idler. 'It do sound daft, mind, but I reckon I only said "Hello" to my Doris once.'

Rhia was crying when we met Annie Oh-No down North Street.

'Ach, no, me little love,' whispered Annie, holding her. 'Cry when they're born, not when they die . . . Look, come home with me and have a cup of tea?' She looked at me. 'You, too?'

'No,' I replied. 'I've got a spare penny and fancy a pint. Pick you up later, eh?'

Through the window of the Drum and Monkey I had noticed Effyn Tasker, laughing with his mates.

'No trouble with Tasker, remember,' whispered Annie.

'Good gracious, girl, do you think I'm daft? He'd coffin me.'

Giving the girls a minute or so to get clear, I shouldered

the door of the Drum and Monkey and put it back on to its hinges.

'Right, you bastard,' I said to Effyn Tasker, and Belinda Handy, as pale as a corpse with a painted smile, got a touch of the vapours, while Billy jumped up on to the flap with a barrel-tapper in his hand and yelled: 'Hywel Mortymer, if you want to hammer the fella, take him outside!'

There were some good men there – people like Barney Kerrigan, the Irishman from Nantyglo – but Tasker's cronies were there as well: Afron Madoc, the horse-goader; Harry Ostler, whom I tangled with later; and little Will Tafarn, who lived in Aaron Brute's Row and beat his wife. But, as I approached them across the floor, they backed away and left Tasker alone.

He seemed to have grown since I'd seen him last; wide in the shoulders, deep-chested; his chin was square and blue; I'd seen the like of him before – in a zoo – no neck, and his knuckles dragging backwards on the floor.

'You reckon you can take me, lad?' he asked, grinning.

'I'll have a bloody try.'

And Billy Handy cried, 'You daft nut, Tasker'll kill ye.'

'Like he killed Bendy Oldroyd?' I slipped my coat down and tied the sleeves round my waist, and Tasker shouted:

'I had no hand in it! The silly young buggers ducked the shift: before I knew where they was, they'd gone down Coalie!'

'Ay, ay. Will you have it in here or outside?'

Tasker backed away.

Will Tafarn turned up his peaky face and said, 'And you take that, Effyn? Jesus, it's an intellectual leap for the likes of you to lift a pint, mun. But the fellas are watching – you call yourself foreman?'

Afron Madoc said, 'In my time I saw you take Caradoc Owen, Tasker. Gi' us a pint of your blood to water the garden – where's the spunk in ye these days?'

Another said, and I think it was Harry Ostler, 'He be only a young cock, me old son. A boot in the right place would turn him into a rooster,' and as he said it Tasker turned as if to take a glass, an old trick I'd seen before, so I went in low, feinted, and caught him with a right that would have floored a rhino. But he only staggered, straightened, and ran at me, his big fists flailing; I side-stepped, and he ran through the open door and clattered head first down the steps into North Street.

'Right, lads, outside everybody!' cried Billy Handy, and Belinda took the chance to faint right off.

I can't remember where the dusk had gone, but now the moon was out, sliding down the broken lance of sunset; the sky a muslin of pale stars.

Tasker rose from the ground against the glow of the North Street furnaces, for the night shift had just come on and the cauldrons were tipping the molten iron.

'God forgive me, Mortymer, but you've asked for it,' said Tasker, gathered himself and came in hooking to have my head off, but I had a left in his eye and another on his nose when he blinked; I circled him, shooting left hands through his flailing guard. Mind you, this is the benefit of taking on big ones, you can hit them at will, for they're muscle-bound and cumbersome. On the other hand, if they do land you one, they knock you into the middle of next week. But, fighting Tasker meant controlling something else – a hatred born of seething anger – the face of Bendy kept rising before me.

Now a crowd was gathering round us as news of the fight spread. Men dropped tools in the furnace compound, overmen simmered the fires; refiners came running out of the puddling shed and came bawling through into North Street.

'A fight! A fight!'

One moment peace, next moment bedlam, with doors flying open, windows shooting up and ancient grandfers easing out of their beds.

All down Staffordshire Row the neighbours peered out of their windows; it don't pay to get involved, mind you, us being Midland specialists – it's the mad Irish again, fighting in the street: 'Alfie, come back in here this minute!'

'It anna the Irish, Delicia, it's the Welsh!'

'And they're as bad.'

'The Drum and Monkey, is it?'

'A man and a lad, and he's handing him a shellacking.'

I was. For as fast as Tasker came stumbling in, I caught him with corkers that were shifting his uncle up in Wrexham; and his boots weren't helping him much, for he was slipping and sliding on the metalled road while, I barefooted, lambasted him. The crowd had made a ring; pressing in upon us, the circle became smaller. With Tasker's face swaying before me, I was hitting him with everything but ladles; ducking, weaving, feinting, remembering everything old Dai Bando had taught me in Canterbury.

Until this point I'd done everything right, for although Tasker had six inches on me and a couple of stone, speed was giving me the advantage. But, with the ring becoming smaller, his grasping lunges were more difficult to avoid; once in his bear-hug, I knew I'd be finished.

Now the publics downtown were getting wind of it. As far away as the Boot and Britannia, the White Lion and the Winning Horse, landlords were draping tea-cloths over their jugs, and their clients, the peace-makers, were making for North Street in large numbers.

People I later loved, such as Shanco Mathews and his missus, came (she who later delivered my son); also Twm-y-Beddau, later to be my neighbour in Shepherds' Square. Some whom I despised came also, such as Mrs Dafydd Phillips whose son wasted under her domination; and they had much to say, such people, like, 'Isn't it a damned scandal, the riff-raff of our town fighting on the street like animals,' and I smiled at her and hit old Tasker a fourpenny that turned up his toes. Up he got, raging, and I steadied my hands and hit him another that nearly took his head off.

'That's for Bimbo,' I said.

Bets were being laid now, fists going in, eyes becoming shut and boots being applied to backsides; then Johnny Williams, the Assistant Special Constable, got his chin in the way of one of Tasker's swings and was laid out like a man embalmed. Now there's a palaver and who the hell did that, with tidy old girls in pinafores kneeling on the cobbles fanning him back to life.

Everybody was fighting now, with Belinda Handy flattening combatants with a bottle of home-brew, and just when the situation looked like getting out of hand, I saw Rhia and Annie Oh-No arrive with Tomos Traherne. He came like an avenging angel, grabbing collars and lifting pugilists aside: reaching the middle of the ring, he roared –

'*Animals!* Desecrating the town with your drinking and fighting!' and he got me by the scruff and shook me like a rat, bawling, 'Proverbs Four, seventeen. Can't you read, you alley-cats? "For thy violence against thy brother shame shall cover thee!"' and out shot his hairy fist, and he landed a pile-driver on Tasker's ear and dropped him like a sack; then he stooped and whispered into mine: 'Away, ye numbskull! God will attend to the wickedness of the Philistines,' and he shook me to rattle. 'Away out of here – the militia is coming.'

They were; at a gallop down North Street, with war cries and sabres.

'The militia! The militia!'

The old cry went up, and those still in one piece were patting each other and bathing cuts, and those that were standing took away sharp, while those that were horizontal became vertical. It is amazing to me how quick the dead become in Blaenafon when sabres and stallions get among them.

As for us – Rhia, Annie Oh-No and me, we went down North Street full pelt just as the militia reached the Drum and Monkey, raced across the square to Mr Afel Hughes, who was holding his door open, and straight through his kitchen where he was bathing his missus – out the back and away up the mountain.

Eighteen

About a century before my time the famous Hanbury family of Pontypool, now richer than a gaggle of Indian maharajas, had built the Llanelly furnace in Clydach Vale; they made their fortune in japanware, and a few years ago sold out to the incoming Clydach Ironworks company.

It was then that the serious vandalizing of the Vale began.

God must have been in a good mood when He created Clydach. First, said old Tomos, He pressed his forefinger into the breast of Gildwern Hill and in the gorge so formed He poured a foaming torrent to cool the passions of men. Then, with a dextrous hand He painted in rainbow colours of mist and haze; planted a million trees and flowers of every hue.

Below the great pavilions of the night He offered for our benediction this new paradise, rivalling that of His earlier Eden; tending this new garden as a collier nurtures his allotment. Then He called forth the words of Moses, saying 'Let there be light', and light came with the sun. Therefore collected all the mountain streams and foamed down the gorge where God had pressed his finger, and it was light, because He had flung His right eye into space and made the sun. Then, knowing men must sleep, He called his left eye to make the moon, and it was so.

Said Tomos, God blessed Clydach and called it His garden; bade it bring forth all that He had planned: the little fishes who make their spawn above the waterfalls; the kingfishers to flash their colours over the brooks, and the gnat-flies upon which they feed. Then commanded He that trees should take root, and this they did; great were the forests that decked the hills of Clydach – great oaks and towering pines; the elm and the ash; birch and poplar came, too; also the yew, the magnolia and the tulip tree.

Now the brooks and streams were shouting down Clydach Vale from the riven wounds of Gilwern and Llanelly Hills, and the Gorge was filled with life and sound. The sun shone. In a haze of heat and summer-snow boiled waterfalls. Primitive man came and marvelled at what he saw.

But millions of years later a traveller came and saw the greed of men, and wrote: 'Farewell, beautiful Clydach Vale; welcome, to wealth, dreariness and filth.'

In the year that Rhia and I came, Clydach had already been vandalized by incoming industrialists who, discovering its mineral wealth, saw not beauty, but a source of profit.

They stripped the forests of trees to make charcoal for their furnaces: they felled the great pines to make coffins for their workers, who, by drinking Clydach's now polluted waters, died of typhoid, scarlet fever and cholera. While the Hanburys initiated the Vale's violation, it was the Freres who tolled its death knell. Iron-making demands ironstone, fuel and limestone, and Clydach possessed these in plenty. To facilitate their removal, tram-roads began to criss-cross the fair land like bleeding veins; viaducts spanned the ravines, tunnels were bored into the hills, streams dammed and broken on the wheel.

Taverns and alehouses sprang up – the Prince, an iniquitous inn on Black Rock; the Forgehammer and the Navigation Inn down on the new canal. Into these the workers crowded to escape in tipsy dreams the sweated labour and the stink of sulphur. Revelry, whoring and bawdy singing replaced the hymns of the Nonconformist Welsh: hamlets and new villages mushroomed their drinking parlours and festering rooms where foreign immigrants lived fifty to a hovel; shift-work mattresses never grew cold.

Easy ladies arrived, flouting their carmine lips like painted corpses, and an immorality yet unknown to Clydach flourished like a rampant penis. Illegitimacy rose and invaded the Bands of Hope and Penny Readings. On one side of the road, as in Blaenafon, the tavern boozies staggered home, jeering at the stately Welsh on the other side . . . with their brass-bound Bibles on their way to Chapel.

This was the future facing Rhia and me as we made our way across Gilwern Hill, eastward for Clydach; soon to come to a lonely place in the moonlight called *Bedd Gwr Hir*, which, being translated from the Welsh, means 'the Long Man's Grave'; that of an ancient chieftain who was over ten feet tall. Killed in battle nine centuries before, he was being carried by his comrades for burial at Llanwennarth, but, overcome by his great weight, they were forced to bury him here. At his head and feet they placed a standing stone marking his length; his ghost, says legend, roams in search of holy ground.

'You believe the tale?' asked Rhia, shivering.

Resting against the stones we seemed to be the only people in the world: some bread and dripping in our eating-tins, one-and-eightpence and the Cyfarthfa blanket were our sole possessions. I answered, 'Well, I've never seen a ghost yet, but we'll strike a few live ones before we're finished, I expect.'

'You are afraid?' Rhia's face was pale.

'No.'

'Are you afraid of anything?'

'Yes. That you may regret that you met me.'

The common land about us was merciless in its brooding silence; a tambourine moon was playing his cymbals to the star-laden orchards of the Milky Way; fear assailed me like a finger on my grave.

Rhia said: 'How can you say that? I love you better than life. My only fear is that I may lose you.'

'You are strange and beautiful,' I replied, but thought: be careful – this is robber country; it could be dangerous for a

woman up here in the hills. I said: 'Come, it's getting cold –
we're off.'

'Where to?'

'To a place I know which will enchant you. I have people
who are my friends around here.'

And she went coy, saying archly, 'In the Prince Tavern,
the Rock and Fountain, or the Forgehammer? Cushy
Cuddlecome and Poll Plenty? I've heard a bit about you
lately.'

'But they'll find us a bed,' and I rose, but Rhia did
not.

Her cheeks were high, of the Celtic Welsh; her eyes bright
with expectation. Then I knew of another emotion in her,
which was not grief, and it stilled me.

Now was not the time. Sitting above the skeleton of *Bedd
Gwr Hir*, I felt the goose-pimple glances of the dead.

It could well be that he would not approve of such
behaviour.

'Not here,' I said, and drew Rhia to her feet.

It was as well I did, because other ghosts were walking.

There came upon the wind a distant sound; the hoarse
shouts of men, the soprano shrieks of women.

The sounds grew closer and we peered through the dim-
ness, for the moon had repented behind silver-lined clouds,
and it was owl-time, one of hoots and squawks. Then I heard
a faint creaking; the slithering of bare feet in the grass.
Nearer, nearer this came. I knelt to hide behind a standing
stone of the giant's grave; Rhia hid behind the other, but
then had to race away to a furrow in the land, since the cover
was too slight.

There, on our stomachs, we saw a little procession of
people come through the night mist. Of the people coming,
eight women ranged themselves in a circle round the stones:
another four, all men, entered, and they were carrying a
ladder.

Upon the ladder, naked and bound back to back, sat a
man and a woman, their legs dangling through the ladder's

rungs; they were chattering, and their bodies were blue with cold.

'In the name of God!' breathed Rhia.

'*Heisht*, or they will have us, too!'

Like monumental wraiths the people stood, with the victims in the middle of them; the ladder that carried them was hoisted on to the stones so that their legs dangled. And there came from the people a tiny old man with his body twisted awry; he came into the circle and, with his stick raised, he cried: 'I say by Leviticus, so hearken unto me, for I say by the word of God.'

Rhia shrank against me. 'It is Eli Rodent!'

'Who?'

'Eli Rodent, which is not his name, but the name by which they call him in Sirhowy.'

'You know him?'

'All in Sirhowy know him. He comes from the west, the counties of the *ceffyl pren*.'

'The Wooden Horse?'

Rhia did not reply; Eli Rodent cried: 'Chapter Twenty, verse ten; I read, "And the man that committeth adultery . . . even adultery with his neighbour's wife, so shall the adulterer and the adulteress surely be put to death." You hear me?' He raised a little monkey's face up to the moon.

'We hear you!' shouted the people.

Eli cried: '"Sanctify yourselves therefore and be holy: for I am the Lord thy God,"' and he turned, waving his stick at the two on the ladder.

'Thus are we met to discuss the punishment of Sarah Woods and Mathew Grant, who have been discovered in adultery. Name the punishment!'

'Kill them. Kill them with stones!'

Now an old crone ran into the middle, shouting, 'Thou shalt not kill – murder is against the law. I say cut off his little John Thomas!' She waved her drumstick arms akimbo.

'Stone them, Eli, but do not kill them!' shouted a man, and he came into the middle and did a little dance.

A woman, joining him, armed him around to the music of a fiddle now, crying at the woman on the ladder: 'Stuck up conceited, ain't you, Sarah Woods! Don't give a glance to me and mine, do ye?' She slapped her face. 'Walk her around Clydach, I say, and fetch folks out with their jinnies!'

The people shouted laughter.

'Twenty apiece on their backsides'll learn 'em!'

'Walk 'em round the village till they're wanged out.'

'Duck them in the Balance!'

Now the crowd walked in a circle round the ladder, pelting the pair with rubbish. The man sat with bowed head; the woman was in a flood of tears. Jigging, jogging, the people danced, and in the middle of them was Eli.

Young men hoisted the ladder upon their shoulders, and in the ensuing clamour, Rhia suddenly left the cover of the stone, and ran, weeping. Instantly the commotion ceased. Heads turned in our direction. A voice said: 'What was that?'

'I don't hear nothin' . . .'

'Someone's about.'

'Ye think so? Up here, mun? Don't be daft!'

I sank lower into the furrow; I could hear Rhia's retreating footsteps. Then the woman on the ladder began to wail as the men carried her. Somebody shouted: 'Down to the village. Come on, we'll give ye something to wail about, girl!'

The procession went off. The man and the woman, exhausted, were lolling obscenely. I lay until all was quiet, then ran in search of Rhia.

I found her, knelt and lifted her against me.

'All right, all right, they're gone,' I said. 'For God's sake, if they'd heard you go, they'd have had us, too!'

Rhia didn't reply, and I think I knew, by some faint premonition, that there was more to this than fear.

I asked, 'You know this Eli Rodent?'

She nodded violently.

'Where?'

'Sirhowy, I told you before, remember?'

'I didn't even know you'd been to Sirhowy.'

A small defiance grew in her face, and she gently pushed herself away.

'There's a lot you don't know about me, Hywel.' She smiled at the moon, and in that smile I knew a stranger. She said, distantly: 'Later, after they've walked them round the village, they'll pay a sin-eater to eat the sin of fornication. In this manner, says old Eli, the sin is absolved, the sinners purified.' Then she seized my hands and held them against her. 'See now, I am all right. Why so glum? Oh, what a long face! They didn't catch us, did they?' She laughed, her voice high-pitched.

I said: 'But you'll tell me about Sirhowy?'

'One day.'

We wandered again hand in hand, but it was like being with a stranger.

For the first time since I'd met Rhia Evans, I realized that I knew almost nothing about her.

Nineteen

The trees were creaking rheumatic on the early October day when Rhia and I started work in Clydach Ironworks. Up to then it had been an Indian summer. Then November tore in with her dew-drops and sneezes, showed her fist at the Sugar Loaf, skidded down the slopes of Little Skirrid, and painted up the Blorenge as white as an English bride.

Talk had it that a Church of England bishop passed on with water troubles up on the slopes of the Ysgyryd Fawr, but the undertaker couldn't pronounce the name, so he finished up in Hereford. The lads had to bring him down on a sledge for speed, since bishops tend to go off song, just like normal people. The driver fell off on the ice, and they reckon that bishop was doing eighty miles an hour before the rector of Llantilio Pertholey got him with a twelve-bore as he went past the vicarage window.

Mind you, some funny things have happened in Llantilio Pertholey, but nothing so queer as the things happening down in Clydach. And while we might have got rid of Effyn Tasker, it appeared we'd collected another eccentric in the form of Mr Ephraim Davies.

Perhaps there's something wrong with me, but I always seemed to bring out the worst in overmen and foremen. Certainly, I'll never forget the interview we had with this one when Rhia and I asked him for work.

'Names?'

'Hywel Mortymer. This is Rhia, my wife.'

Not more than five feet tall, Mr Ephraim Davies regarded us with small, dark eyes.

He was the first and only Welshman I've met who had

risen to a controlling post, for this was not the policy of our English masters: English overmen, English agents, English profits; to put Welshmen in charge of anything could dilute the foreign control. This man was an exception. His small, round face, wealed with furnace burns, regarded us.

'Do you know the owner, Mr Frere?' he asked, and I shook my head.

'Frere knows you. Sarah Hopkins's schoolteacher, is it?

'It was suggested, but we never got round to it.'

'But you can read and write in Welsh?'

'Certainly.'

'And you know your country's history?'

'Passably.'

He made a wry face. 'There's a large surprise. Half the Welsh round here reckon this is an English county. Listen, lad. One day we may need a schoolteacher, but until then I'm after a furnace top-filler. But with a school in mind – and I'm after this, too – tell me where our prince was murdered.

'At Irfon's Bridge, outside Builth.'

'And the name of the English knight who killed him?'

'Adam de Francton.'

'Dear me, there's education for you!' Ephraim peered up at me, a terrible apparition in the sun.

Only in Wales could this happen, I thought: education at this time was at a premium, the only schooling for the workers being dame classes run by spinsters in the cellars of somebody's hovel. If they could afford it, which was rare, the pupils paid the teacher a penny a week.

Luckier centres sometimes possessed a minister of the church or chapel as a teacher, but this was rarer, because the ironmasters resisted education on the grounds that it would make the workers competent to bargain.

However, they supported totally the licensing of private houses as beer- and gin-houses, adding to the swarms that abounded in the iron towns, and invested heavily in the supply of ale. And from what I'd heard of the Freres, if

Ephraim Davies got a school going in this place, he'd be lucky.

'You now,' said he to Rhia. 'Who interceded to save our prince being buried in unconsecrated ground?'

'Lady Matilda Langspec,' answered Rhia, and I was surprised at her alacrity: every day I was learning more about her. But it was a trap question, and Ephraim's little eyes danced when she added: 'But the English general refused her request. Llewellyn's head was cut off and sent to London. There it was crowned with false silver and nailed to a pillory, and the people of Cheapside threw refuse at it, to ridicule our country.'

I added, 'Another legend says that his headless body is buried in Abbey Cwmhir.'

'Good God,' ejaculated Ephraim Davies. 'And the other legend?' He turned back to Rhia. 'There is also another legend, is there not?'

'Yes, the prediction of a soothsayer. That one day our prince will be crowned with real silver in a Welsh castle and ride in state through the streets of London.'

'*Duw!*' He seized our hands. 'Consider yourselves employed, the pair of you. I tell you this, children. Being of Welsh blood, I'm having every man jack here a Celt of some device before I'm finished with these bloody Freres,' and he put our names down on the books of Clydach, then went fluffed up and strolled around the cinders like an adjutant bird, crowing like a cockerel on a dunghill.

'If that fella's sane, I'm *didoreth*,' said Rhia.

It was a start, but not one to boast about. I was made a top-filler on the furnaces, the most dangerous job in iron-making; Rhia joined three other women as a cinder girl, a guarantee to destroy the lungs.

So much for education.

But we got a roof as well, which was next door to a miracle; one worked by Ephraim, the Sorcerer of Gilwern Hill.

Number One Forge Row was on the end of twenty terraced cottages situated between Clydach River and the road, near the new tin works and the furnace compound.

The cottage was two up and two down, with male lodgers crammed in downstairs and four families upstairs, but it was said that Number One possessed the best upstairs for decoration in Clydach Vale. In the upstairs back were the Bert Hanmans and the Davie Half-Moon family, and if Ephraim Davies wasn't quite the ticket, neither was Davie Half-Moon. The Hanmans weren't much better, for Mave suffered from religious mania: she didn't have children, nor did she intend to; she confided to our neighbour, Mrs Mo O'Hara, who was Irish, that she couldn't bring herself to do so rude a thing even with her Bert.

Mo O'Hara, however, was a woman of a different calibre, as her biological performance proved.

Said Mo: 'Look, I've got seven; another in the shawl and a ninth in the stomach, for my Pa's a pesterin' fella when it comes to the passion. And I don't stint him none – I mean, ye can't, can ye? They're all the same, ye know, these lovely Irish fellas.'

So we took the front-room-east-upstairs in Number One Forge Side and looked down on to Tramroadside, where the trammers pushed their loads uphill and down, day and night, seven days a week.

Only half the room we owned, to be precise – a blanket down the middle sheltering us from the activities of Mo, Pa, and eight plus another; a dog as big as Rhia and two cats for stalking the rats; the mice having long ago given up when Mo got after them with the copperstick.

There were other disadvantages; the farmhouse noises coming from the other side of the Walls of Jericho did nothing for our appetites. Mind you, to have puddlers as neighbours was going up in the social world. Pa O'Hara was a top puddler in Clydach, Mo was his 'second hand' – nothing unusual in these early days of iron-making. Any day shift at

Llanelly Forge you could see Pa, gigantic in size and strength, puddling up the balls. Stripped to the belt he'd be, and so was Mo, and that was some sight, for she'd sweat like a Spanish bull; carrying enough milk for the starvers of Blaenafon. Pa would 'duff up' the incandescent ball on the end of his firing tongs, swing it high (and this took a Hercules) and yell: 'Right you, me little darlin' – into it!' and Mo would 'chuck in' with her dolly, balance it on the stand, poising and counterpoising her weight, taking it in and out of the fire while Pa worked it up.

'Next one – *setters!* Let's be 'aving ye!'

And the setters would run in. Working the blazing ball under the drop-hammers, they'd run it through the rollers.

Now Rhia said to Ephraim, looking round the little room: 'The rent, mun – how much?'

'Search me, woman – I ain't the rent man – go to the bloody office.'

A shilling a *week!*

Enough to break us.

Twenty

In front of Forge Row was the Clydach River that turned the giant waterwheel for the Llanelly mill, and tripped the drop-hammers. Just over the way were the stables, and the farriers kept us awake with their shoeing and hammering: a branch tram-road connected us with the Office. So, what with the roaring of the furnaces under blast, the hammering in the tin works, and the ringing of the anvils, trying to get to sleep was a major occupation.

It was even more difficult trying to keep Mo O'Hara on the other side of the Walls of Jericho.

'God reward ye, me throat's parched. Do ye happen to have a spoon of tea, me darlings, if I provide the water?'

We had just moved in and I was knocking up a bed to keep us off the floor. Sean, aged two, had got my hammer and Sonner and Sam, Bridget and Milly were trying to eat the nails, and I didn't know if I was on my ear or my elbow.

Fat and jolly was Mo, with her hair down her back and flourishing her three-chinned obesity, and I wished her to the devil and back, for it was worse than Kibby's Looney.

'Now, ye can see the size of it, can't you?' cried Mo, and she had one in her arms, another on her back and two more swinging on her skirt. 'The fella got me on an off day and I'm pestered in the breast and loins. But he's lovely when ye get to know him.'

We were off-shift from the furnace compound; Rhia had a night shift with the cinder girls; I was top-filling on Two furnace.

'Mind,' cried Mo, 'he's a bugger when the hops are in him,' and she landed Sean one that sagged his knees. 'Will ye give the foine gentleman back his hammer, or I'll beat the ass's reins off you, so I will. Is it Welsh ye are?'

'Beg pardon?'

'Ach, I heard talk that you're as Welsh as leeks, the pair of ye, which makes us cousins, for we're all Celts under the skin, isn't it?' And she took the tea and scalded the pot, crying as she went, 'Praise be for the good kind souls that ye are, the pair of ye. Will ye take a jar o' tea with me if you have the milk?'

'No milk, Mrs O'Hara,' I said, getting the hammer off Sean, and he aimed a kick at my rear as I went.

'Mind, you're welcome,' said Mo, disappearing behind the dividing blanket. 'Good neighbours are always welcome – share and share alike. Anything ye need settlin' in, don't be afraid to ask.'

We said we wouldn't.

'Good God, this is terrible,' whispered Rhia.

I hauled the bed upright and hammered the legs. 'It won't be for ever,' and there came such a commotion from the other side of the blanket, with skin and hair flying, that even old Steffan Fetchit came out of Number Ten to see what was up, and he was ninety.

Forge Row in Clydach was not where we had consummated our marriage, but despite its shortcomings it was precious, being our first home; with a little flock-mattress bed, narrow enough to keep us in close proximity.

For sixpence I'd bought a table and two chairs from the outgoing tenants; from scrap firewood I'd knocked up a corner to hang our clothes, and Rhia gathered winter leaves from the bank of the Clydach. These she put in jam jars, and I tell you this – that room looked like a little palace. The Company Shop was at the end of the Row, and we went into debt for new boots, another blanket to help out the Cyfarthfa, warm socks and red flannel from Abergavenny market, and we cocked a snook at January.

Some were not so lucky. That winter the poor Irish

vagrants died like flies. Shivering, they would cluster round the glowing furnaces with their wailing children; scorched one side, frozen on the other, and the little black processions of County Mayo and Limerick, Wexford and Connacht, preceded by coffins, went keening to church.

They died of starvation mainly, their constitution stricken by the homeland famines: wasting away, they flooded down the roads from Fishguard, dying in their scores on the way. Arriving in the Top Towns, they beseeched alms to feed their skeletal children by day and scavenged in the bins for scraps at night. The Quakers succoured them: one could always see a little Quaker boiler with its donkey rumbling along in the dusk. And the black-garbed saints, aloof but kindly, would be doling out mealy soup and vegetables before facing a shivering night.

February came with her long red nose and icicles; hand in hand with March she set a frozen moon rolling on the rim of the mountains, and froze the Usk solid on Castle Meadows, Abergavenny. Clydach River, right up to Devil's Gorge, was one gigantic palace of ice. And then, when we least expected it, a little wind breathed over Gilwern Hill which was the wind of heaven, and spoke of spring. Snowdrops appeared on the greening banks; wood anemones painted up the copses, sending lovely stems of folded leaves and drooping buds; buttercup and lesser celandine burnished their gold stars along the roads: early columbine made love to the sun, and the heart-shaped leaves decorated the lilac of lady's smock.

But this was not the only decoration going on in Clydach.

Come over by here to the corner where I am sitting; pretend to be looking out of the window; *watch*.

A woman dressing can be an education.

Like the Queen of Nepal, straight-backed and proud, sits Rhia before the little cracked mirror. With her black hair down to her waist she sits, humming a little tune to the hairpins as she puts them in one by one. Turn the face this way and that, screw up one eye against the sun; lean forward and grin at the glass, smooth a finger over the lips; tie back the hair with red and white ribbon.

On with the stays now; tighten the laces in the front; take a deep breath and swing them round the back; a bit of a scratch under the arms, a tug on the bodice; pull up the breastplates, for the girl has turned into a woman – there's a lot more there this spring. Stand now, wiggle the hips. Wave long white arms into the new blue dress; lace at the bosom, cuffs and hem. On with the little pink bonnet bought from the Indian packman: take the shawl off its peg; fasten it round the neck; turn.

'Am I all right?'

In all the sacred journeyings of the sun I'd never seen the like of her, for she turned every head in Clydach.

'You'll do,' I said.

But I did not know if she was all right, or not.

Dot Popkin and Jenny Loom, the cinder girls up in Pwll-du, had signed on to the Clydach workforce, and joined Rhia under Ephraim Davies. Sometimes I'd see them working together when I was off-shift.

This was when I saw the scarecrow working, a Rhia removed from the blue dress and pink bonnet for walking out. Now her hair was scragged back and tied with yarn; the sack shift she wore barely covered her nakedness; torn away at the top so her breasts could cool. From her thighs down to the ugly hob-nailed boots she wore, she was bare; her arms were bound with hessian to protect her from tram burns, for the ash within the iron sides was red and seething; piled so high that following ash-urchins had to clear it off the line.

With Dot and Jenny, the Bradford girls, hauling on front chains, the ash was removed from the furnace fire-boxes; Rhia pushed behind, the most dangerous position. I met them once on Smart's bridge. With her hair hanging over her face, wild-eyed, she went; her small body as straight as a bar. Dot and Jenny chanted a labourer's song, but Rhia did not sing.

Here, beyond the little bridge, the rail sloped upwards. In passing, I flung my weight against the tram to ease it on, and stared into the face of the creature I called wife. She had just been burnt, and the weal of it lay across her cheek; ash had spilled and burnt holes into the protective hessian around her arms. I saw her through a cloud of steamy vapour, for it was raining; the raindrops hissed, spitting off the tram's sides; the wheels grated as Rhia jammed the sprag and brought it to a stop. Straightening, she shrieked unintelligibly at me.

I saw in her eyes something of madness.

'Sorry,' I said, 'I thought I'd give you a pound.'

'Well don't! We're the cinderers – sod off!' And she cleared her throat and spat like a cinder girl.

Later, as I was down in the Vale furnace compound, top-filling with Guto Snapkin, Dot and Jenny, Rhia's tram-butties, came to me.

'You got a minute, Hywel Mortymer?'

Built like a man, this Dot, and Jenny was no different; broad-backed, flat-chested, their breasts had long disappeared into the muscles of the towing; their shoulders, naked beneath the rags, were scarred by years of the chain. Guto, eager to be off, walked on, shouting: 'Come on, come on, what is this? We don't need the Streams of Loveliness up by 'ere – I got mine waiting on the mountain,' but I ignored him, and Jenny said:

'Your Rhia's getting the sulphur – you noticed, Mortymer?'

'The sulphur?'

'Too much pushin' at the back,' said Dot.

I stared from one to the other; this was new to me, then cried, 'Christ! Put her on the chain, then – you go on the back!'

'Anna that easy, she won't come.'

The bedlam of the Works beat about us; the stokers were

going off, having raked the fire-boxes; the puddlers were coming on in a rattling of firing-irons with their usual vulgar banter.

I shouted as they went past us. 'The sulphur?' and Dot said:

'She's took it early. They gets light up top – like seein' things, you know . . . ?'

'I don't know. What are you saying?'

'Sod you, Mortymer, it ain't up to us,' cried Jenny belligerently. 'We knows the game, so we books up the chain, see? We knows what it's like on the back.'

'The fumes, you mean?'

'It do choke you no end after a bit.'

I shouted, 'Then take your fair turns!'

'You bloody try her, then. Day 'fore yesterday she ups with her boot and kicks old Dot right in the crotch. She's sugar in the attic, mun – we ain't standin' for it.' Jenny peered at me with her red-rimmed eyes, and I saw upon her cheeks the old scars of the ash burns when the wind took it red and flicked it off and it burned through the water-rags over her mouth. I felt hostile and angry. Two old pros, these; they knew the ropes, and I was furious at my own uncaring. It had been hard enough staying alive on the top-filling without giving a lot of thought to Rhia.

Anyway, I went to see Ephraim and he talked a lot about opening a school and putting the pair of us in as teachers, and that he was going to see Mr Frere about it. But Ephraim Davies was one of those men who promised a lot and never came up with anything.

He came up with something for Rhia, though; he put her on rag-cleaning and dropped her ninepence a week, which didn't help her temper, and she didn't speak to me for a fortnight.

Twenty-one

Came summer bright and hot, and Clydach Vale thrived, sending its iron down the canal to Newport. With the third furnace now at work and the compound loaded with trammers, barrow-men, butties, puddlers and refiners, there was more commotion than at a Connemara pig-fight. Shock waves of heat and light were blasting up from the valley; the vale now sent its own rainbow colours to join the Top Town night.

The Great Wheel, competing with Merthyr's wheel of later years, whirred above the pouring leet that spun it; then roared the work-out water down the Gorge to the foaming Cascader and the tripping bellows of the wooden launder. Some said they could hear its thundering down in Abergavenny.

Twenty feet above the great compound the charging house was mobbed with filler-gangs; the barrow-handlers scampering like pygmies against the glow. We worked silently, leaving to the furnaces their bellowing as we stuffed their hot bellies with ore, lime and coal.

And the shed about our long-handled barrows swirled with smoke and light as the fire-boxes belched and flashed: now choking us, the air filled with sulphurous smoke; this to vanish as the fires below got a hold, and the upshot flames drove us back. I saw the grimed cheeks of comrades – first barrow up, tip, and away; up floods the smoke, smothering us.

'Come on, come on, for Christ's sake – keep her movin'!' and this is Ephraim, hard at the morning shift.

The wealed, sweating faces I saw; the bandaged arms of

those who got too close; the opaque eyeballs of one who nearly fell in. And along comes Guto bloody Snapkin, all six foot of him, charging along beside me, his body braced to the wheelbarrow-load. Head bumps and belligerence, this was Guto; his face riven by years of coal. He cried: 'Right you, Hywel – in we go!' and he steadied the three hundredweight load as I positioned it on the charging platform: steadied it with his great strength, and the barrow slanted as we tipped it.

'Hold on, *hold on!*' I bawled, for the barrowers in front of us were scarcely clear. Our barrow was still easing forward, so I trapped it on the ledge, shouting above the roar of the furnace: 'What's the hurry? Wait, you fool!'

'I got a date,' said Guto Snapkin.

'Aye, what's the hurry?' shouted Ephraim, and he was below us in the compound now, cupping his hands, yelling up. 'Wait till the last fella goes, mun! Are ye daft up there? Keep in line!'

God knows what was wrong with Snapkin that morning; I thought he was drunk. And, as the last barrow slid away in front, he flung himself at our load like a man demented. The barrow slanted again, the coal tipped and slid. And I saw the molten furnace bubbling its iron below as it took the mouthful and flung it up to us in flame. Just for a moment the sun appeared, as if waving goodbye, then vanished in gouts of smoke.

When we got back to the tram-road and the hurriers filled our barrow like madmen, I said to Guto, 'What the hell's wrong with you? Are you catching the midday coach?'

'Got a date, like I said,' said Guto.

'Jesus, she'll wait five minutes, won't she?'

He cocked a smile and rolled a wicked eye at me, and I added, 'Keep her in the heather, mun; if you take her up there with us she'll put you in head first.'

I thought I'd said nothing out of the ordinary.

Rhia was awaiting me at the door of our room. 'Are you ready, love?' she asked.

It was the way she asked it. Then she sat in front of her bit of a mirror and put perfume behind her ears.

My heart began to thud against my shirt, for this was a time of an unspoken tryst.

Let this be understood: it wasn't easy for married people in the towns of the Industrial Revolution. Because, if it wasn't half a dozen lodgers sitting around at home it was Dai getting into the bed while Sean was coming out of it. Most rooms housed half a dozen people with blankets down the middle for privacy, and folks standing in queues for their turn on the seat. It may sound vulgar, but it's worse when it happens to you. And when it came to soil buckets, the women got it worst, as usual; trying to cover themselves with strangers in the room.

More, it beat me how we managed to keep up the birth-rate in those days, for the Welsh are prim in public and amorous in private. Of course, people had their own peculiar ways of getting around things, and Clydach Vale was no exception.

Take Tom Meadows, for instance. Now Tom had an unspoken agreement with Bill Balder, who was a top-filler down Benjamin's shift. They, like us, lived in Forge Row, their families divided by a hanging blanket. So, if Tom was on day shift, Bill took nights; and if Tom was on nights, Bill took days. If all else failed, of course, you could always go for a walk up the mountain with your wife. It just wasn't possible to bill and coo in the feathers in the iron towns; only the gentry were entitled to that, people said. Few of the workers were conceived on mattresses.

But Rhia and I didn't go up the mountain. When the fancy took my lover – and I always left it to her – we walked up the hill to Clydach Gorge. Even in winter, with rime on our hair and our kisses steaming with frost, we still went up to Clydach, with assistance from the Cyfarthfa blanket. Soon after our marriage, I had saved up and bought Lily Scotch perfume from the Brynmawr's Lady Stall in the market, and this Rhia used as an unspoken signal.

When she put this behind her ears, my blood would quicken.

Strangely, my love-making was never achieved without Rhia's initial rejection. It was as if any advance must be met with a rebuff, so that she had constantly to be wooed; cajoled, then dominated.

At first I could not understand this. Even more strange, on this June night Rhia did not lead me up to Clydach for love-making: instead, we sat together on the little iron bridge over the gorge and watched the moon playing his phosphorescence on the roaring water. Taking my hands in hers, she said: 'Not for love-making, Hywel, but to tell you a secret. I am with child.'

Later, in the bed of Forge Row I held her, for the O'Haras were out drinking at the Forgehammer.

We talked until the O'Haras came back at midnight.

The moon, I remember, was grinning like a pumpkin in the window of the little room; the sky was a calico of stars.

Then the night shift got going, tapping a great valedictory flame that lit the Vale. White ash fell, drifting past the window like snow, and I lay in the belly of the bed, holding Rhia's hand. The crashing of the drop-hammers I heard then, and the crying of animals under the whips: all this I heard, yet, strangely, did not hear.

For there was growing in the eye of my mind a star of exceptional brightness: brighter, brighter it grew upon the smudged window of the room, and its light seemed to shine upon us as we lay there hand in hand. And I think I knew that in this mesmerism lay a star-born; that deep in her womb was Rhia's gift to me – a son. For a man without a son is like a meteor flashing across the sky.

Later, we heard the accident bell ringing somewhere in

177

the Vale; it was like a fatal message being handed down to us through the years.

Guto Snapkin was on form next morning: talk had it that he was sparking a little widow from Abergavenny: she had big sons, the tale went, and Guto was frowned upon when calling at her cottage – two six-foot chaps within kicking distance. So she and Guto met on Llanelly Hill. While I didn't blame Guto for courting, I did so for not keeping his mind on the job.

Rhia said in her sleep on the night before Guto was killed: 'Old Mo O'Hara is at it again, dear me!'

It awakened me; turning over, I heard her say:

'Why do we have to have her, Hywel? Can't she sleep in her own bed?'

This brought me up on to an elbow. 'Rhia, you're talking in your sleep!'

'Bimbo always used to sleep with me, you know . . .'

'*Heisht!*'

'After he was born I used to take him to bed to feed him, then he'd stay all night.'

The Vale was quiet, as if the Devil slept; somewhere on a hill a night-jar was calling to its mate.

Rhia said: 'I had no money and the milk left me, so I took him down to the Parish and the vicar put him on a wet-nurse. He was a good old boy, that Church of England vicar.'

I frowned in the darkness: she was floating in the vacuum between truth and reality, I concluded, but now she said: 'I was only thirteen when I had him, you know, and the milk comes poor at that age, the surgeon said. "Put him on old Biddy Allan for a bit, Vicar," and they did, and Bimbo growed.'

I looked into her face and Rhia turned and smiled at me. I said, 'Darling . . . it's gibberish!'

'You awake, Hywel lad?' Her voice was firm and strong.

'I was,' I replied, 'until you started talking rubbish. And she whispered: 'Oh, Bimbo, my little Bimbo!'

I took her into my arms. After a little while, she slept.

Now I knew that something was wrong with her.

Guto, as I said, was on form next morning, keen for the shift to end and to get after his widow.

'Right, Hywel, me son, here we go!' and he gripped the side of the charging barrow and we ran it, balancing it at speed until we caught up the others in the line.

The charging shed was full that morning – double shift working – new tram-road rails on contract somewhere over in Spain, and the furnaces were roaring.

'Make way, make way!' cried Guto, and we eased forward in our turn as the barrow-lads before us wheeled up, tipped and clattered out of it. In a flurry of smoke we found the furnace lip and I saw the tumult of the molten iron below me. Heat and vapour shot up, enveloping us; Ephraim shouted from the compound: 'Hold that one, Mortymer, *hold it!* Firemen up, lads – come on, rake her, she's needin' air!' And I saw past Guto's crouched body by the barrow wheel two firemen come running; the furnace belched fire and smoke as the raking irons went in. He made good iron, did Ephraim. Talk had it that he got the secret off Betsy Williams down in the Forgehammer tap. Now he bawled: 'Right, now plug her, let her fire up! And ease that coal back, Mortymer, she needs to quieten. Limestone up, come on, where's the bloody limestone?'

The furnace was farting and belching like a cow in labour: the top-fillers, including me, were scurrying like ants, which always happened when Foreman changed his mind. There wasn't much room to move in the charging-house when the coal went back and stone was barrowed up, and Guto complained, 'This'll lengthen the bloody shift, poor cow.'

I laughed, 'If she wants it bad enough, she'll wait,' and just then a coke barrow came wheeling out of the charging-house, but I couldn't see the barrow-man for smoke.

'You called for coke?' I shouted this down to Ephraim. 'She wants stone, you said!'

'I'll do the mixing, Mortymer, you do the loading,' he cried back at me. 'Right you, stranger, bring it up!' and he blew his whistle.

I saw the stretched biceps of a big man at the barrow as he wheeled it past me; a great deep chest on him; whoever he was, this was a two-man load and he was taking it in one.

'Stand clear, stand clear!'

We stepped out of the smoke, Guto and me, wiping with our sweat rags, and I thought the stranger with the barrow was clear, for I heard the tip and the slide of his coke; then I saw the barrow's handles slanted upwards and heard him shout a warning as he fought to control it. 'Hey up, give a hand!'

The barrow swayed about. I leaped towards him, but Guto was quicker: reaching the wobbling barrow, he tipped it high; flame and smoke shot up, enveloping both him and the stranger. And in the instant before the bright light died, I saw this man's face, and it was a face I had seen before: one scarred by a vivid slash like an old sabre cut: a face that rose to me during the attack on our coach near Tregaron, and the name of this man was Musker. In the moment of this recognition the furnace roared; I saw Guto's boots go up as he slipped under the load, and fell head-first into the boiling iron. The molten bubbling sprayed up white arms, as if to catch him. In a two-second fuzz he blazed, did Guto; the blaze shut off his shriek as the steam of him wisped up past me. When I looked again the barrow was still there, precariously tipping, but the stranger had gone.

And so had Guto.

We never did find out who that stranger was: why he was on coke-tipping that morning; why he was there at all, said Ephraim, though if ever I find him I'll give him a piece of my mind, he added.

We always get pieces of mind from people unable to afford it.

So Musker, my uncle's man, was in the vicinity! I couldn't help thinking that he had come for me, and got Guto Snapkin.

I might have known that men like Sir John and Kent wouldn't give up so easily.

In the course of a life everybody, they say, makes one fatal mistake; I realized now that I had made mine.

Despite the insistence of my father, who swore that a man should never change his name, if I'd had a modicum of sense when I first started in the Top Towns, I would have changed mine. Instead, defiant, I had actually flaunted the name of Mortymer.

Now they were on to me again, I realized that they would never give up until they had destroyed me.

Twenty-two

Rhia was becoming even prettier round about September, which women tend to do when making babies. Nature, in compensation for bulging bellies, paints up cheeks, brightens eyes and reddens lips; also strengthens the back muscles and widens the hips. And sometimes, when she wasn't looking, I'd glance at my wife and see her smile.

'The baby has moved?'

'Hywel! At three months?'

Nevertheless I think she sometimes knew a fluttering within her, which was not the child, but a grafting of another sinew upon my son.

A son, a son! The thought brought delight to me. How beautiful he would be! I am not a great one for religion, but I believe in the Man, and my heart sometimes went out to Him that He might grant me this tremendous gift.

I would have been even more grateful had He calmed the turbulence of Rhia's mind.

'Your missus all right, Hywel Mortymer?' This from Mo O'Hara.

You had to be careful with Mo; she was better than a travelling newspaper. A word in the wrong place would put it around the Cambrian up on Gilwern Hill. Enormous in girth, Mo surveyed me; I replied: 'Rhia's fine, couldn't be better.'

'Mind you,' she went on, 'some women get vexed when carryin'. Me mither went off her rocker – thought she were Lady Godiva.'

I went on lacing my boots, but Mo was after me the

moment she had parted the Walls of Jericho, saying, 'She don't give much away though, do she?'

'She minds her own business, and so should you.'

'But, ye cannot get a decent answer out of her, mun – folks like a bit o' the gossip, ye know – only natural.'

'If they gossip about us, I'll have a hand in it.' I got up.

'Now, that's just what I told Pa. I ain't tangling wi' that Welshman next door, I says. But it's that Eli Rodent, see?'

'Eli Rodent?'

'The manager of the Forgehammer. He reckons he knew your girl back in Sirhowy, when he were working for Mr Justice Williams. Though he's a lay preacher, he's got a flagon o' piss for a heart, that one – employed over at Llanfoist House he is now.'

'Where?'

'Llanfoist, workin' for Sir John Mortimer – same name as you.'

'What doing?'

'Gardening spare time, like he did in Sirhowy. And he's putting it around that your Rhia had a baby outta wedlock.' We stared at one another and I fought to keep my temper.

'This Eli Rodent – he works for Sir John Mortimer, and he's in Llanfoist, you say?'

'Aye, mun, but that ain't important, is it? It's him saying that she had this little lad – the trammer killed over in Pwll-du.'

'Bimbo?'

'Ay ay, that's his name – is it true he's her son?'

'It's a lie,' I retorted. 'What folks round here don't know they make up, and the first chance I get I'm seeing to this Eli Rodent.'

This came as no great shock. Until now I had put down Bimbo's facial likeness to Rhia as brotherhood; now, quite suddenly, the evidence was clear; I knew him to be her son. In retrospect I realized that her every word to him, the way she soothed, comforted and tended him, told of this relationship, and I hated my foolishness. Worse, I hated

Rhia's lie. It savoured of betrayal, and burned deep in me.

One thing I'd always known – hers was a woman's body, not a girl's. The suspicions I had nurtured now grew like a cancer within me: often I had wondered if I was her first lover; now I knew that I was not.

How many others had she known? I wondered.

Love is trust, I told myself. For her own reasons Rhia had kept this secret. Perhaps, in her good time, she would tell me . . . ?

Meanwhile, I was now filled with foreboding on another score. This Eli Rodent, once the gardener of Mr Justice Williams of Sirhowy, worked spare time for my uncle: a new and dangerous link had been forged down the hill at Llanfoist.

Apart from the usual village gossip, few important things occurred in Clydach Vale that summer. Cushy Cuddlecome, one-time landlady of the old Cothi Inn, took up residence in the Rock and Fountain, bringing with her her two minders, Ham Bone and Swillickin' Jock, plus Grandfer in his wheel-chair, whom she kept in the parlour; the clients being given to think he was alive and kicking.

A woman jumped off the top of Clydach Quarry to her death; some said she was sparking one of our top-fillers who had promised her matrimony; I hadn't got the facts of it, but thought it could have been Guto; who proved a most unusual case when it came to burial.

Ephraim Davies, our gaffer, was known as undependable.

He was dependable all right after Guto Snapkin stopped it, though.

'Right you, lads,' he told our shift when Guto died, 'we're not tapping pig iron on Number Two today; this is holy iron, so start the furnace simmering and dig a little hole.'

'My dear man,' complained our agent. 'Whatever are you doing?'

'You bugger off, sir,' cried Ephraim, 'you'd never understand,' which delighted me, and he cried to the sand-moulders: 'I want a little pit dug, sized two by two. Guto Snapkin ain't going to end up as a tram-road rail in the bloody Argentine.'

So they dug a square hole in the ground and Ephraim himself knocked out the bung and the part-iron and part-Guto Snapkin, poured into the mould: they sealed the furnace, and we all knelt around in prayer.

'My God, what's happening?' asked the agent, falsetto.

'"Ashes to ashes, dust to dust,"' said Ephraim. 'Please God have mercy on the soul of our butty, Guto Snapkin.' And called up the hauliers, crying: 'When Guto cools, dig him out. Nobody's going up in smoke on my compound. Legs and arms can go, if they like, but this iron isn't taking their souls.'

The following Sunday we put the iron cube on to a funeral cart. It was done properly, with deference and respect; with fifty mourners walking behind, we took Guto up to the Calfaria and put him down six feet. But he had the last word, did Guto Snapkin; in life he weighed normal; in death half a ton. When the pallbearers were lowering him, he broke the ropes and took five down into the hole with him.

Rhia and I, having taken flowers up to Guto's grave, were walking back to Tramroadside, down Gilwern Hill.

Earlier, it had rained; a rich downpouring that had quenched the cobalt blue of the sky. But now the sun was making love to September and the valley spread out before us in a vast panorama; the farmsteads glittered with light, the fair country danced in hues of topaz, green and gold.

Things were a mite better for us on Tramroadside: we had a few shillings in the tea caddy for the baby coming: indeed, the things blowing on Rhia's wash line were as good as anything you'd see in Clydach, and we weren't in debt to the Shop, like some I could mention.

Not that we tried to outdo neighbours, or anything like that – I hope we were above such thoughts, but if you keep yourself decent, like stitching up the tears in curtains and polishing a bit of brass, it does wonders for your status. I don't mean we were snobs; just that we kept ourselves to ourselves, and people took note of it.

The sight of Rhia as I saw her that evening stays in my mind.

She had on her new white dress, and this reached to her ankles; her breast, full and robust, she had covered with grandma lace – Annie Oh-No turned this out (she was now making shrouds for a living up in Blaenafon). Rhia's bodice was lilac, dyed butcher's muslin she had stitched up herself, and nobody could tell it from gentry cotton. Upon her head she wore her little pink bonnet; her long black hair was down her back. Her pink shawl was a perfection that would have delighted Lady Grace.

Her arms were bare to the elbows; she looked like an Arabian princess, steeped in sun. Only the gentle curve of her stomach told that there were three of us. Hand in hand we walked on that glorious September evening.

'What shall we call him?' I asked.

'My son?' and Rhia made a pretty clasp of her hands and smiled at the sky. 'Why not Bimbo?'

It was only when we talked of the coming baby that things went wrong.

I laughed. 'Oh no, Bimbo is a nickname!'

'He is my son and I shall call him what I like. His name will be Bimbo!'

This she shouted, and I recoiled before her, for I had again seen in her eyes the hint of madness.

We sat in silence then; the evening sun beat hot upon us. Behind us reared up the wall ramparts of Clydach Quarry where Guto's sweetheart had died; a tomb-like structure that seemed to foretell our destiny. Church bells were ringing in the valley, coming up to us in gentle flushes of the wind.

'Chapel time,' I said, and drew Rhia to her feet.

She smiled brilliantly, her face lifted, I remember.

We arrived early in Calfaria; few rear pews were occupied as we took our seats at the back, mainly reserved for the labouring classes. And I noticed, as other worshippers entered and took their places, that Rhia and I were slowly becoming isolated; that stares of open disapproval were being levelled in her direction.

Tall-hatted matrons came, severe in their hugged black shawls and cheek-frilled lace: in Sunday-suit dignity their husbands came with stately tread. Amid disdainful eyes we sat, as people rejected. Then the pastor entered, sallow of face and bent with age; his mutton-chop whiskers bristled at the sight of us. Slowly I realized that this was a rejection by one's community.

Children tried to enter our pew, only to be ushered away by embarrassed parents. And, as the service began, I became aware of sly stares; of unheard whispers behind hands.

We sat alone, isolated by our neighbours' absolute ostracism, and I could not understand it. Suddenly Rhia put her hands to her face, burst into tears, and ran out of the place. Even as I followed her into the road, I saw the smiles of general satisfaction.

This is what some call religion.

In the middle of the road I caught Rhia, and held her.

'What is wrong? For God's sake, tell me, what's wrong?'

Later, lying hand in hand in the bed at Tramroadside; white-faced, her lips trembling on the verge of tears, she told me.

Rhia said, 'Years ago, when my father was alive, we had a little farm near Ammanford; times were hard, but we made a living. But then the Land Enclosures began, and the landowner near by fenced us off, and evicted us. At least, he tried to, failed, and brought in the military to enforce it; I was about twelve.

'My mother led me to safety, but my father would not leave. The bailiffs put a chain around our cottage and with two horses pulled it down, and he was killed. My mother and

I left west Wales and came to Abergavenny, where we were hired at the spring fair. After a year working in the fields, we heard of Sirhowy iron, where money was paid for good women, so we went there.'

The night was silent save for the simmering of the furnaces; a single shaft of moonlight lighted the room.

'But, it was a time of the marching gangs. Armies of workers were on the march in the mountains, seeking food; the price of iron was low and wage cuts meant starvation. Had wheat been there people couldn't afford to buy it because of the war; furnaces were blown out, Company Shops raided, property destroyed –'

'I know all this,' I said impatiently.

'Samuel Hill, Aaron Williams and many others were hanged for grain-raiding.' She raised a pale face. 'We starved, me and my mother. At night we foraged in refuse bins; that winter my mother died.'

I thought she was going to cry.

'Then one night an agent saw me begging in Sirhowy. I was in rags in the middle of January, and he took me in. His name was Ben Williams and his cousin was Mr Justice Williams. And, when Ben was killed down Dukestown Pit, the cousin took me into his house as a scullery maid . . .' Rhia hesitated.

'Tell me.'

'You will not like it.'

'Now you've started, tell me everything.'

'This cousin – Justice Paul Williams – was a very different man, and he was hated in Sirhowy. No woman was safe with him. He would always appear when I was doing the fires in the morning. He told me that unless I did it, he would put me out again. Other girls working in the house had to do it, there was no other way to eat. One girl drowned herself in the balance pond up near the furnaces . . .' She faltered.

'Tell me,' I said again.

'He . . . he was drunk, even at that time of the morning. After an assizes when he had sentenced people, he'd drink all

188

night. I tried to get up, but he pushed me down. He was shouting and falling all over me. I had not been used before, and I was terrified. The other girls said it wasn't so bad – only the first time . . . so I went on raking out the ashes, and while he was doing it he was throwing pennies into the grate.'

I closed my eyes.

'That night he took me to his bed. I stayed for the winter, eating as never before. When spring came, I had conceived.'

'Bimbo?'

'Aye, Bimbo – my son – not my brother . . . I lied to you, Hywel. Forgive me – I'll never lie to you again.'

I held her, kissing her face. She continued.

'The wife of the Reverend Monkhouse, Fothergill's partner, took me in. This family was good to me, but when bad times got worse they said I'd have to go. Bimbo was beginning to walk, so I left Sirhowy and took to the road with a caravan of gypsy folk. But there was a man in Sirhowy who recognized me and put the tale around. His name is Eli Rodent – remember? – which is not his name but the one by which folks call him. Now he is the new landlord of the Forgehammer Inn. Soon he will come for me, he says, and carry me on the ladder – Pa O'Hara says he has vowed this – to come, perhaps tonight.'

'Let him come!'

She wept, her fingers forming a cage over her mouth to stifle the indignity. 'Perhaps it would be better if I died?'

'Don't talk like that!'

'You saw the faces of the people in Chapel. Even now, says Mo, there's a meeting about me going on down at the Forgehammer . . . This is why I had to tell you.' She tensed in my arms. 'Remember that night at *Bedd Gwr Hir? Listen!*' The wind buffeted the eaves.

I said: 'It is nothing – you are imagining things. Sleep now.'

'Listen, you!' She sat up beside me.

Faintly on the wind came the sounds of a marching mob.

Hobnailed boots were hammering the flinted road to Clydach; a sudden rosy tinge painted up the window beside us – the torches.

Next moment footsteps hammered the stairs of the cottage and Mo O'Hara tore back the dividing blanket and yelled: 'Quick, you two – for God's sake! Me man and me tried to stop them, but they're all mad drunk and coming with a ladder, and Eli Rodent's leading 'em!' Taking a grip on me, she hauled me out on to the floor. 'Run, the pair of you – *run!*'

'We're not running anywhere,' I said, and I'd just got my clothes on when a mob with flaring torches came tramping into Tramroadside, and the occupants of Forge Row – for the word had spread – were awaiting them.

Well!

To this day I don't know how the Cambrian clients up on the hill got to hear of it, but they turned out their best pugs to defend the Welsh girl, and there was no love lost between the Cambrian boozers and the Forgehammer God-botherers.

Led by Big Rhys Jenkins and Will Blaenafon, who happened to be up there sheltering behind a pint, they came pell-mell, shouting war cries. I locked Rhia in Mo's bedroom and went through the front door and into battle.

'Come on, mun, where you been?' shouted Big Rhys, and he caught a Forgehammer specialist the prettiest right hook I've ever seen and got another one by the whiskers. Copper sticks were going up, pick handles coming down, and Mo was in the middle of it, delighted: soon the road was littered with apparent dead and dying; comrades wiping cuts and patting bruises, and we'll hit them with everything but the bucket, said Will, until they get back to where they came from, plus their ladder.

Then up came Pa O'Hara with a band of Irish heroes and took them in the rear like Father John Murphy did at the '98 Wexford, and you've never heard such a bloody palaver since the Romans got Caerleon, with kids crawling among the halt and lame, kicking their legs from under them and tapping out the semi-conscious. Then, apparently, Ephraim Davies got hold of it over in Clydach House, and he turned out with a gang of outsize top-fillers, and it was all over bar the shouting, with Big Rhys and Will Blaenafon, being Blacklist outlaws, making for the hills.

'What the hell's happenin' here?' bellowed Ephraim, and he got into the middle of us with a puddler's ladle. 'Are ye mad? Do ye want the militia in?' And then we got it in Welsh as well, and stood looking sheepish while the Forgehammer specialists took flight.

Nobody spoke.

'Is your girl all right?' demanded Ephraim, glaring.

'Yes, sir,' I said.

There was a strange, perfidious quiet about the night: men shifted their feet uncertainly; women tied back their hair. Good neighbours, every one; I wouldn't have exchanged them for gold, Welsh, English or Irish.

'But I can't have this – ye'll have to get her from here, you realize?'

'Yes, Mr Davies.'

In the Middle Ages we burnt to death eight million witches. In terms of Man's inhumanity to Man, what chance had Rhia got?

For among the mob Eli Rodent had led up from the Forgehammer Inn, I had recognized a face I knew – it had the scarred features of the man I'd seen once before.

'Aye,' I said to Rhia. 'Ephraim's right – it is best we go from here.'

Twenty-three

There was a peasant sadness on the evening we left Clydach. Usually, whatever the misery, God does his best to spin our bawdy Welsh exuberance. For life in our valleys, Rhia used to say, is a sort of cannibal stew: Heaven fills a pot with spring water, throws in all the elements of living – love, envy, hate, greed, joy and laughter – and boils it all up. And the steam that comes off that human stew is humour; if you haven't got that, said she, you might as well pack up.

Earlier, desperate for a new start, I'd tried the Top Towns from Blaina to Sirhowy; true, they were quarrying hard on the Rassau tram-road and Llangattock caves, but quarrymen were only labourers, ten a penny, and the Irish did that job on twelve-hour shifts for a bag of potatoes. We hadn't got anywhere to put our heads until I remembered Cushy Cuddlecome in the Rock and Fountain.

'All me rooms are filled with payers,' said she. 'But you can have straw bales in the barn, till ye find something better.'

By this time I was frantic, for autumn, grim and cold, had caught an early coach from the Beacons, and was peering at me with icicles. Winter threatened; come November on the starve and a woman in child, anything could happen. And I was terrified of the Blacklist.

The masters blacklisted trouble-makers. They who were denying us the right to form Combinations, themselves formed a Union of Owners.

A man, his wife and children could be turned out in winter and wander, starving, from town to town seeking work . . . in a gentry age of elegance.

'Mind,' said Poll Plenty, recently arrived from the Grouse Inn at Abergwysen to work as a barmaid for Cushy, 'only last night I were talkin' in the bar to a gent and he reckoned you were on it already.'

'On what?' I asked.

'The Blacklist.'

The drovers of the Grouse had mistreated Polly; her young fresh beauty had died in the arms of men, and Cushy said with a sniff: 'Don't heed her, Hywel. What she don't know she makes up.' And she fluffed up her hair and painted up her carmine lips, making faces in the mirror. 'You bring your little woman here.'

'As long as we don't have to sleep with Grancher,' said I.

And she giggled and tipped Grancher under the chin.

There he sat in a corner of the bar, with his embalming plate removed lest it caught the eye of the Inspector of Nuisances. Very popular with the customers was Grancher; every time I saw him he had a pint in his hand, his dead eyes staring across the spit and sawdust.

'I know it ain't hygienic, like,' said Cushy, 'but I just can't part with the poor old sod. You bring your little missus in, Hywel Mortymer's son, and welcome.'

When I got to the door of the Rock and Fountain, Cushy followed me out to the stars: the wind had a terrier's nip in him; the clouds were putting a chemise on a winter moon. Cushy's eyes, usually bright blue, were as shadowed as an undertaker's corpse, and she whispered in a fearful contralto: 'Sir John's livin' round here, did ye know?'

I knew, of course, but didn't let on. She said: 'Took over all your pa's ironworks assets, didn't he? Sleeping director in Blaina iron and a lot of canal shares. Time was your feyther was in deep round here, till Jackson's Rooms and the gaming got him.'

'So the Mortimers have moved from Tregaron?'

'Sold up your place lock, stock, barrel. Dai Swipo, one of Big Rhys's pugs, says he's got a mansion on the canal, but I ain't been invited there as yet.'

Cushy caught my hands in old friendship, saying, 'Stay here for a bit, then get off – you'd best be where the Mortimers ain't, lad. Besides . . .' and she wrinkled her nose at the moon. 'Young Poll's always had a shine for you, and now you're hitched . . . our Poll's got a tongue . . .'

Cushy was right.

Now the Mortimers were in Gwent – ironically to prosper on money that was rightly mine – it was time I moved out.

'After all,' added Cushy. 'To this day they're swearing that you killed their Tom.'

It would have been better had I moved out of the district then, but, by the time we'd settled the little debt at the Company Shop, we only had shillings between us.

Rhia was squatting on a hay bale in the Rock and Fountain barn. Earlier, Mo O'Hara, Pa, Dot and Jenny had heaved our few possessions down to Cushy's, with the help of Enid donkey, a friend of Cushy's.

Now, wrapped in the Cyfarthfa blanket, Rhia opened her little green purse which held our accounts, and counted out our money.

'Four and eightpence,' she announced, shivering.

It was as cold as a miser's heart in that barn; even the rats were chattering: preening away their dew-drops, they were squatting on the tie beams above us, their little beady eyes shining in the lamp.

Cushy had lent us a big fat tom-cat called Joe, who was wanted in the county for murder. He slept in Rhia's arms to keep the rats away after I awoke to find one snoring between my legs, which can be very disconcerting. But five monsters, taking umbrage at Joe's presence, chased him up Gilwern Hill, and nobody had seen him since.

The second night in Cushy's barn was one of bitter cold; as we shivered in each other's arms, Rhia whispered against my throat: 'Do you remember saying – that time we stopped at the grave of *Bedd Gwr Hir* – that one day I may regret having met you?'

I nodded, and she went on, 'And now I have brought you to this by lying about Bimbo. Do you now regret?'

'I love you better than life – my only fear is that I may lose you,' I said again.

'I have no perfume to put behind my ears. But I still have my little pink hat, so I will put it on,' and she did so and paraded around the barn like an Egyptian princess, with one hand on her hip, making eyes at me.

I drew her down into my warmth, and beneath the Cyfarthfa blanket which I wrapped about her I touched her and knew her sweetness, also the soft swell of her where she was carrying my son.

Of time and place we were not aware; it was enough that we were together. Gently I divided her body, seeking her kisses.

'I can see the moon in a rift of your hair,' said she.

It began to snow outside and the snowflakes swirled down upon us through tears in the roof above us; it mantled Rhia's hair; settled like confetti upon the blanket, turning Rhia into a Church of England bride.

'This is a terrible thing to do to a girl, mind,' said she.

No love-making could have been kinder or sweeter than this reaffirmation of our love when all seemed lost to us; when cold and hunger faced us like ghosts pointing the way to death.

But this was life: the low-minded call it sex, but sex is a nonentity without the gift of love. And when the bright explosion of our youth called to us, I cried her name, and Rhia called mine. We lay together, the cold forgotten, in a warm and summery drowse.

It was the last time I made love to her.

Twenty-four

I had to have money, and quickly. To be unemployed, homeless and penniless in the Top Towns in winter was suicidal; and the nearer we came to Rhia's time, the worse our situation would become.

I had left to me only one resource.

Often, walking in the Usk valley at dusk, I had seen a ring of lights burning on the slopes of the Punchbowl on the Blorenge mountain; a prize-fight would be in progress, and this would herald the Special Constables and Militia from the Red Lion Inn at Abergavenny, for prize-fighting was illegal: it was up on the mountain that men like Big Rhys, Will Blaenafon and Dai Swipo earned good money.

It was a Saturday night. Leaving Rhia asleep in the Rock and Fountain barn, I turned out to make a quick sovereign. Up to my elbows in my trews and with my coat collar turned against the biting wind, I set out for the mountain. Climbing Gilwern Hill, I went through Pwll-du in the dark. Above the old Tumble-down-Dic, I saw a galaxy of lights, then further on, a small square of flaming torches.

Slipping, sliding down the mountain, I reached the prize ring.

About a hundred men were gathered here round a square of a single rope and sagging posts, and within this two old mountain fighters, grizzled with age, were having a Grandpa Fight; one always sought by the dandies of the day. These, in finely creased trews, were crying their wagers as the two old men battered each other: stripped to the belt the pair of them, their wrinkled bodies streaming blood, they pummelled and wrestled and gouged.

Top hats and riding-crops jostled with the flat-hats of the ironworkers and colliers: I saw the aristocratic faces of the young fops, and the hawk-like visages of the puffed-up gentry, they who had never shed blood in their lives except at the hunt. With their finely bred horses tethered by their grooms, they lined the ring, bawling encouragement to the ancient contestants, the two old pugilists whose faces were scarred by a hundred fights; now they were battering at each other for a gentry sovereign, wildly swinging their broken fists. One, his right eye-socket bloody with a gaping wound, collapsed soon after I arrived: doused with a bucket of water, he was dragged to his corner.

'*Duw!*' said a voice behind me. 'What you doin' here?'

It was Big Rhys.

'I'm after a fight,' I answered.

Will Blaenafon, coming up, said: 'You that short, mun? All right, you took Effyn Tasker, but this anna compound overmen, you know, we're pros.'

Two others arrived, Bill Noakes, the son of Selwyn ap Pringle of the Royal Oak, and Dai Swipo. And they peered at me in the red torchlight with their flattened noses and cauliflower ears.

They were big men, all four cast in the same mould, heavy with strength; yet possessed of the easy grace of men of fists.

'You need it that bad, Hywel?' Big Rhys now, inches above me.

'Worse than that.'

'I heard as how you was down in Cushy's barn,' said Dai Swipo, and he looked at me with his crossed eyes; the glazed, uncomprehending smile of the mentally ill. Bill Noakes was young and not yet injured, but old Dai, they said, was addled in the head through fighting pugilists two stones larger. The sight of him brought me memories of Jackson's Rooms and the thick-eared fraternity of Canterbury, where, in better days, I'd received lessons in the Noble Art from Welsh Dai Bando: there, men like the dim-witted Dai rubbed mufflers with the aristocracy: were fed on raw vegetables, red meat and the chicken legs of game-cocks.

Two classes of society made what was called the Fancy: the rich, lavish with wealth, who kept horses for racing, men for pugilism, and both for wagers; and the poor, giants of strength and courage. Kept like a horse in a barn, a pug would be beaten by his owner if he displeased: made to vomit if constipated, and purged.

A master would bleed his pugilist regularly with leeches, run him for thirty miles a day tied to a horse: half a gallon of ale was his every day, drunk with the raw yoke of eggs. He would eat nothing in the way of fish, which his master thought insipid. Looked upon as an animal bred for conflict, he was his master's property; acclaimed and spoilt when he won a contest, he could be reviled and horse-whipped if he lost his master's money.

Such men were the descendants of the Roman gladiatorial combats, when contestants first fought to the death with lead bands round their fists: but such contests were over so quickly that the *amphotides* was invented to lengthen them; this was a leather apparatus made to encase the fighters' heads. The 'sport' continued down to the present day: in many aspects it was no less brutal, for it attracted the effete in society who followed the smell of blood. And these had now arrived, for all heads turned to a new party approaching – that of the Marquis of Abergavenny come up with his young bloods from a Neville Hall ball. Led by the Marquis, they came on horseback; most already tipsy from drinking and revelry with their paramours.

'They're after blood tonight with the Marquis here,' said Big Rhys. 'Best make off back to Rhia, lad.'

'For Christ's sake, Rhys – I told you – I need the loot.'

'Wait here,' said Will Blaenafon, and went to the match-maker, a small, fat man in a loud suit.

'I've got a shilling you can have, butty,' said Bill Noakes:

he was little older than me, his head black curls, his eyes bright.

'And I've got a woman in child, so I'm after sovereigns.'

The men were pressing about us in smells of dandy perfume, sweat and whisky: the torches flared, painting red light on the half-naked bodies of waiting pugilists, and the Marquis had brought in another; a wide-shouldered youngster with the white scars of fighting over his eyes. His hair was fair, falling in thick waves to his neck, and he moved with the grace and sinewy strength of a young tiger.

'Dear me, where did they shoot 'im?' asked Big Rhys.

'The White Celt,' said Bill Noakes, bass-voiced. 'I do know him.'

'Are they calling on him?'

'Calling?' I asked, and old Dai Swipo explained:

'No opponent; the Marquis brings him and he takes pot luck. You reckon I could handle him, Noakesy?'

'One time, old man. But if he misses you now you'd die of pneumonia.'

'Oh aye? I'll try you for size any time, young 'un!' said Swipo.

Bill Noakes chuckled with surly contempt. 'Leave him for Big Rhys, mun, he'll bloody tame him.'

The young pug stripped off his coat; his muscles rippled and shone.

'Mind, he do show off some, don't he!'

'He do fancy himself, that one.'

'White Celt, is he? Call me black bastard, son,' and Old Dai put his fingers into his mouth and gave a collier's whistle, waving a pansy hand to the youngster, who scowled.

'Come up and see my sister, lad.'

'Poor little bugger.'

'The thing is to get his dandy up,' whispered Noakesy. 'Fair-head Welshman don't do a lot, mind, and the blood do show, don't it, Nance?' He shouted the last sentence, did Noakesy, dancing lightly on the balls of his feet, and I knew I was with the professionals. Then Will Blaenafon came back with Rhys, looking glum.

'Matchmaker won't have us,' he announced. 'He wants a carver first.'

'A carver?'

'The marquis wants to make a good impression,' Dai Swipo said, thickly. 'If the Celt can spill some blood first fight, the odds go up next week up in Blaina.'

'That sounds like me,' I said, and pushed into the ring. 'How much?' I asked the matchmaker. Tubby, wide-legged was he.

'How much what?' He tipped his hat over his eyes, regarding me; the crowd went quiet and the marquis strolled up, pressing a little lace handkerchief against his nostrils, asking, 'We have an amateur?'

'Yes, sir,' I said.

'And you think you can take my man?' The air moved and it was perfumed.

'I can try.'

The marquis drew an eye-spy from his waistcoat pocket and looked me up and down. The matchmaker waited upon his pleasure.

'By God, I do believe it – the man's educated.' The marquis peered up at me.

'No odds to that. I need the money.'

'Odds indeed, young man. As a carver? I vow my man will kill you.'

'How much?' I asked.

The marquis turned to his friends; there was no sound but the crackle of the torches and the mountain wind buffeting in dark places. He cried, his hand up, 'Gentlemen, I do declare we've got a fighting cock. A young buck fallen on hard times. Do you entertain the idea?'

They cheered, swaying; some raised flasks, others bottles, guzzling at the red wine.

The marquis cried: '"How much?" he asks. Gentlemen, I like this. Are ye game?' and his guests roared assent.

'You want your brains looked at, boy,' whispered Big Rhys, beside me.

'He'll 'ave none after this,' mumbled Will Blaenafon.

The marquis turned and left the ring. 'Put him on,' he said over his shoulder. 'Win or lose, pay him two guineas.'

'What's your name, lad?' asked the matchmaker.

'Dear God,' said Dai Swipo. 'He'll hit you sick.'

'What's that?' asked the matchmaker now with a megaphone.

'Call him The Amateur Gent,' said Big Rhys, and went to a corner, and knelt; I followed. After stripping to the waist I sat on his knee; behind me Will Blaenafon waited with a rag and a bucket of water.

'Don't die on us, for God's sake,' said Bill Noakes. 'Just bleed freely. This fella gave me a right old shellacking down Carmarthen a week last Monday.'

The bell tolled like the gong of doom; with my fists held high as Dai Bando had taught me, I went out to meet the White Celt.

He was quick. I knew it with the first blow of the fight, a swinging right that grazed my chin, and I slipped on the damp grass and went headlong. Instantly he was on top of me, his elbow sinking into the pit of my stomach, but I threw him off and came upright. Ducking and weaving, he came storming in with hooks to have my head off.

With his fair-skinned body cobbled with muscle, he followed me round the ring now, and I saw past his broad, flat features the drink-stained faces of the ringside charlatans; the fancy fops, their lace cravats sopping with drink, their eyes puddles of wetness, for now it had begun to rain.

As the White Celt rushed again I stood him off with a stiff left to the face. Astonished, he dropped his guard, and I hit him a one-two, over the top and underneath: the last, a hook, took him full, and he dropped at my feet.

The crowd was roaring. I heard Big Rhys's voice and Dai Swipo's throat-punch soprano ringing above the cheering of the dandies. Money was chinked as new bets were laid: the body of my opponent was shining with sweat and his expression changed from surprise to pain as I circled him, shooting straight lefts through his guard, snapping his head back.

Suddenly all was silent. A night bird was singing plaintively, as if availing himself of the stinging quiet, and in that silence, the man rushed. Stepping inside his arms, I got him with an uppercut and he took it full weight: this stopped his forward rush; his flailing arms dropped and his chin was unguarded.

'Now!' roared Big Rhys, and I got up on my toes and hooked him flush to the jaw; the White Celt staggered, suddenly tottered on the balls of his feet, and fell face down. I thought it was the end of him as they dragged him to his corner to revive him, but then I knew the truth; I was fighting a professional.

Within seconds he had regained his senses; seconds later he was on his feet and into me, his fists coming at me in widening hooks and swings. One of these caught me high on the forehead, and the stars swung over the sky. Hooks and uppercuts came now as I wilted before him; I stood within a daze of pain as his fists thumped into my face and body. The crowd went silent, watching the execution. It was the same old tale, the amateur against the professional, a man rock-hard and inured to heavy punishment and I was not.

I fell under an avalanche of punches as he hit me with everything but the bucket. Then the ground thumped me.

Through puffy eyes I saw the sky aflame with stars; the rain had ceased; the moon rode on a chariot of gold.

Turning over, I got to one knee and into the arms of Big Rhys. Momentarily he held me under his coat while Will Blaenafon washed my face clean of the blood.

'That'll bloody teach ye,' said Dai Swipo.

'Here's your two guineas,' said Bill Noakes.

I never knew for how long I'd been unconscious, but the

marquis and the toffs had gone; even the ring had been dismantled.

'You all right?' asked someone.

'Aye.'

'Shall I see ye back to Rhia, lad?' asked Big Rhys.

'I can manage.' I peered about me through blackened slits of eyes.

With a sovereign in each hand in case they jumped out of my pocket, I went through a deserted Pwll-du and took the coach road over Gilwern Hill and back to the Rock and Fountain.

I had expected to find the lamp alight when I got to the barn, and Rhia awaiting me, but she was not there. Then I realized that she must be in the tap-room with Cushy, but the inn doors were locked, and through a leaded window I could see that the place was empty. In growing panic, for the moon said it was nearly midnight, I hammered on the back door, and down came Poll Plenty with her hair in crackers.

'Is Rhia in there with you?'

Momentarily, she stared, dazed with sleep, so I caught her by the shoulders and shook her.

'Where's Rhia? Have you seen Rhia?'

'Aye, this evening, sure . . .' She faltered.

'No – now, *now*. Have you seen her?'

Poll said at the moon, 'Just after you went she came into the tap – aye, she did come. The man said for her to meet you . . .'

'A man? What man?'

Cushy, frowzed with sleeping, said, coming into the tap-room: 'Not seen hide nor hair of him before, but he said he'd come from you, didn't he, Poll . . .?' and Poll added in a gush of words:

'Said for her to go because you was waitin', Hywel –'

'Waiting? Me waiting? Where?'

'Up in the gorge – where you and her used to meet –

remember you told us?' Poll paused, coming to her senses. 'Hey, I know him – he comes in here, don't he?'

I stared at Cushy. Her hair was straggling down, her eyes were wild in the shadowed hollows of her face, her cheeks were blanched. And she said, like a woman coming out of a dream, 'That's right. I have seen him before – the man with the scar . . .'

'Jesus God!' breathed Poll. 'That were hours back, weren't it? You sure she ain't in the barn?'

The bile rose in my throat and I swallowed it down. Turning, I raced back up the hill on the Brynmawr road, dived through the bushes and floundered down the track that led to Devil's Bridge in Clydach Gorge, where we used to make love.

Now, racing up and down Devil's Bridge, I called her name: 'Rhia! Rhia!'

Flooded with rain, the little brooks and rivulets were gushing like white blood, the arteries of the Vale; the waterfall, pounding in the misted moonlight, thundered below me.

'*Rhia!*'

My cries were drowned in the din of falling water. Slipping, sliding down the Gilwern bank, I reached the mossy arbour of overhanging branches where we used to meet for love-making, but it was empty. Running upstream, I took the snake track beyond the bridge towards the whirlpool. I was hoarse with shouting.

Panic had seized me now, and I skidded and hobbled through calf-deep mud, fell and scrambled up, to fall again in my headlong rush, hauling myself on by overhanging branches, for here the torrent had overflowed the bank.

The ravine that emptied Gilwern slope was a cascade of water, and I recall thinking, even as I plunged thigh-deep through it, that Rhia never could have come this way. But the whirlpool, through some magnetic attraction, was calling me towards it.

It was raining again, pelting down through the canopy of trees; only shafts of moonlight guided me now; the under-growth was thinner as I neared the pool. And I heard, long before I saw it, the water-spout of resurgent flood water that drained the distant Llangattock caves: these, the honey-combing tunnels and cathedrals of emptiness born when the world was ice.

The thundering of chained water now beat about me; after the October rains the gorge was in full spate.

'Rhia! *Rhia!*'

The whirlpool, regurgitating, rose to its rim in a threat to engulf me, then sank low into its pit of blackness. The siphoning shrieked; the gravitation gurgled.

'Rhia . . .' I said, and stared at the throat of the gorge as it sank and sucked, to rise again into a bulging pool of silence.

And I saw, in that silence, something flashing a colour in the centre of the vortex. Higher, higher it rose; now circling out into the lazier swims of suction, before being snatched back and tossed, drowning, into the gush. Now it momen-tarily appeared again, and I saw it clearly before it finally sank.

It was Rhia's little pink hat.

I stood with my hands over my face.

The whirlpool hungered and sucked.

Book II

1810–1818

Twenty-five

North Street, Blaenafon was for me the fulcrum of the world, and Blind Olwen, later the proprietor of the most eminent bundling house in Newport, was the blessing of my life.

Shepherds' Square, the home of the craft trades of iron – refiners, puddlers, ballers and suchlike – had just been finished following the construction of Staffordshire Row, erected to house incoming specialists.

Blaenafon, about then, was a tipsy harlot of a frontier town where pavement girls walked one side of the street: on the other side walked chapel adherents with their Bibles under their arms and God on their faces; the men of stately tread, their souls uplifted, the women with splendid bosoms and the carriage of queens. Frilly daughters of lavender, their chins so high they'd have drowned in a downpour – they took to church or chapel their godly graces – ignoring the maimed beggars calling for alms.

Two classes, two towns; indeed, two nations, rich and poor. While in Big House you could eat a three-course breakfast, in Aaron Brute's Row you could starve to death on Christmas morning.

As a puddler in Blaenafon Ironworks, I chose Blind Olwen's top front room in Staffordshire Row, not because she was the best cook in the street, but because I was a bachelor, and what the eye doesn't see the heart doesn't grieve for. I could sit in the tin bath in front of the fire while Olwen prepared supper with no hint of scandalizing, which had always been a generous commodity in North Street. And since Staffordshire Row possessed half-door stabling, I was able to house my donkey and trap.

During the five years since the death of Rhia it had proved a gay and successful bachelor's existence; for, as is widely accepted, the Welsh female of the species is not only beautiful, but expectant.

One of the most expectant of these was the landlady of the Prince of Wales up at Pwll-du, now a seamstress of shrouds, and before that a trammer who went under the name of Annie Oh-No. And Pwll-du, accessible from any point of the compass in the dark, was geographically convenient when it came to privacy. Also, Blind Olwen never questioned a lodger's activities.

History had it that Olwen was blinded in a brickworks accident when a kiln exploded, yet her eyes, bright blue in her unscarred face, were her best feature. Her husband had left her a week after the accident for a woman who possessed two eyes, but couldn't boil water.

Blind Olwen, who had all her marbles about her, began to thrive. First she took in a lodger, then agents' washing, and supplemented this by running the bedroom next to mine as a bundling establishment for passionate creatures. Never have I seen a business run better. And respectfully, too; not even Tomos Traherne could take exception.

The courtship bed possessed a duck-down mattress, one far superior to the usual horsehair: the board down the middle was of mahogany, the window curtains were of pink muslin, the counterpane yellow.

More, at a ha'penny an hour, Olwen's charges were reasonable, with no bundling on Sundays and nothing after dusk. Pledged couples, many arriving with parental notes, were among Olwen's clientele; shrouds tied at the neck were optional.

'You off out, Mr Mortymer?' Olwen asked now.

'Merthyr Horse Fair,' I said. 'To buy a cob.'

'You don't need a horse, Hywel Mortymer, you need a wife. I may be blind, but I've got me ear to the ground, you know.'

'Don't tell me.'

'Accordin' to reports, there's some shenanigans going on up at the Prince of Wales after dark, but don't tell Annie Oh-No I said so.'

Aye, I thought; lovers are plentiful. But, I'd already got a wife . . . lying under the flowers I took up to the Horeb at Pwll-du, and her name was Rhia.

The June morning was bright with sun, the wind sweet with wild flowers, as if greeting the better times coming to Blaenafon. Folks on the Top didn't have to die to go to Heaven that year, they were having it now.

With the riots of 1800 forgotten and the starving of 1815 yet to come, people in town were eating again. And if you were eating, it was Heaven.

The demand for iron on world markets began slowly to improve. Church of England soup kitchens were out, always a sign that the workers were being wooed by the Establishment, and the masters began their roistering again in the Three Salmons at Usk, and ticking up six-course dinners in the Abergavenny Angel.

But the refuse of iron was still crowding down North Street: the cripples of the furnaces holding up their spindly children for the inspection of passing carriages; rattling their begging tins with their amputated stumps and sticking up their bone-white feet – molten iron having got into their boots.

It was said that Crawshay's Merthyr held the world record for amputees; there being more maimed there than any other place on earth: but Blaenafon, I reckon, came a close second, both in this and political disquiet.

On one hand we had the managerial class competing with Lady Charlotte Guest for ostentatious parties; on the other hand the working population was drinking itself silly from the Royal George to the Miner's Arms and forty ale parlours in between: those not working either begged outside the public houses, or went hungry.

Half the town was reasonably dressed, the other was in tatters; one lot was eating, the rest were famished. Two nations thronged our streets; one of brisk professionalism, the other beseeching it crusts of bread. This, to their credit, brought in the chapels and churches, mainly Nonconformist and Roman Catholic, for Church of England ministers were largely landowners, magistrates, or both. When God tots it all up, he'll have a good word for priests. If one was seen washing the face of a woman in labour or feeding a beggar, he'd either be High Church or a dissenter.

Catholics and Quakers, for my money, earned their passports to St Peter.

Now, up North Street I went with my jack donkey and trap, and along the Works wall where Beef O'Shea caught the fizz last month.

When the molten iron sprayed him he ran in a circle, all twenty stones of him, and tore off with an agent and two puddlers after him until he reached the wall I was passing now: this he cleared at a single bound, said the inquest, and died smoking: six foot up was that wall – a Welsh high-jump record, said the coroner.

Little Spinster Tooley was hanging out her napkins outside the Drum and Monkey, with her twin rag dolls in her arms; never wooed, never breached, was Miss Tooley, and thin in the head for a baby, 'But, never mind, me lovelies,' she used to tell her dolls, 'perhaps I'll 'ave one on the change.' 'You all right, Hywel Mortymer?'

'Good morning, Miss Tooley!' I waved my whip at her.

Joe Codger was in the stocks outside Stock Square, and urchins throwing clods at him; heading them off was Joe, still drunk, for the on-shift lads had given him a bottle to help pass the day. Young Sian, Pop Lewis's daughter, was feeding her baby on the pavement: pretty she looked in the sun, one hand shielding her breast. Only the good girls get caught, but her pa didn't agree.

'Not allowed home yet, Sian?' I called to her.

'"Tis a week now, Mr Mortymer,' cried she, showing me the baby. 'But Mr Traherne will speak for me, he says.'

'Your pa's a good man, girl, he'll come round to it.'

On, on, lifting my top hat to friends and neighbours, for when you're a top puddler folks show respect, but a gentleman puddler takes some handling.

God, I thought, my girl would have been proud!

Now up to the Brynmawr corner, and here comes Peg Cuddle of the Whistle Inn near the Garn, and plenty to spare has she, with the wind under her skirts and her bonnet streamers flourishing. Talk had it that Will Blaenafon was dying the death further down in Broad Street, and off his food, too, but I didn't have the proof of it. I raised my hat and down she went in a curtsy.

'You want a lift, lady?' I called.

'Well, I never did, Hywel Mortymer!'

I slowed the donkey. 'Come on, here's a hand,' and I hauled her aboard, since it pays to keep in with the local layer-out in case you ever need her. Swept up at the bosom and undone at the knee, was Peg, and her moral intentions packed like shrimps in a casket. But good otherwise, mind you. Placid in black bombazine she sat: I'm fourteen stones, yet the trap had a list to starboard. We clip-clopped along, Peg and me, with the old donkey looking over his shoulder to see what the hell he'd got.

'I've just been laying out Chinko Yang,' Peg explained.

'I heard he'd passed on.'

'They do things different up in Peking, ye know.'

'Different?'

'Sort of. You gotta plug the nine orifices as well, ye know.'

'Beg pardon?'

The day glittered with sun and heat; the track before us wavered in mirages of light. Peg said, 'He's Chinese, see? – so I'm off to Brynmawr for a Taoist monk. Got to plug his orifices, or the devils get in. Queer, ain't it?'

'The monk, you mean?'

213

'Jesus,' said Peg Cuddle, 'you do make things difficult – of course not – Chinko Yang.'

'Well, I never,' I said, shaking the reins.

'That's what I said, but I still got to plug 'im. Mind, they pays a bit extra, of course.'

'I should think so, too,' I answered, counting up the orifices. 'Ten, did you say?'

'Nine,' replied Peg with a glare. 'Chinko Yang, the laundryman, I told you. 'Tis him who's snuffed it, not his missus.'

'Sorry,' I said.

She was a good old girl was Peg Cuddle, and we stopped at the Whistle Inn for a pail of spring water for Donkey and a pint for me. But she gave me a watery come-hither, did Peg Cuddle, and I went off the boil, for ladies with come-hithers and no husbands can raise problems for a bachelor chap. On, on again; the June sky dripped naked in a sea of flame; the wide, green breast of the sleeping mountain rose and fell in the sun.

Twice a year Merthyr Tydfil, the home of the Saint, made merry in her churchyard, and the fair went on from dawn until dusk.

Stalls and booths were erected for fortune-tellers and soothsayers; there were prize standings filled with marvellous gimcrackery, toss-penny for a piglet and bran tubs for lucky dips. Along the walls barrels of *craw da* were placed with cups and pewters, and most farm labourers were three sheets to the wind before the sun was up.

There was gambling for milking sows, who'd have their throats cut within the hour, horse-riding, hog-riding, dog trials and sheep-shearing, with goats turned inside out and crucified on doors, and hens upside down in a mad, clucking chorus.

Pigeons and sparrows roasted whole were two a penny; spiced sugar cane straight from the West Indies; escaped slaves were here, their sweating bodies as black as watered coal, with yellow-faced Chinese gobbling at bowls of rice and shovelling chopsticks. There was a Hottentot dancing to the music of a fife and an Aborigine in a trance conversing with his mother outside Perth.

The children of the hiring fair were here, standing like cattle with straw in their mouths, with a burly auctioneer shouting his wares: 'Now come on, lucky gentlemen, come on! Snatch the straw from his mouth and you've got a year's labour – two pounds a year will keep him in pig swill. Look, here's a pair – one for the kitchen and one for the bed,' and he pushed up a brother and sister from the Poorhouse.

With my hands deep in my pockets I wandered through the Fair crowd.

Wheels of Fortune were whirring, roundabouts circling to the strains of a hurdy-gurdy: there was wrestling and boxing, a fat lady, a thin man, and a dwarf handspringing on a dais. All was a medley of colour and gaiety, and there were urchins throwing refuse at a caged lunatic somewhere down on Glebeland, for I could hear the shrieks.

Boundaries were being beaten, too, the custom of the June Fair. Led by a Special Constable they came, the magistrates of Merthyr town, leading by the ears the children to be beaten, and I followed them over the streets to the Star Inn. From millstone to millstone we went, with the constable caning an orphan at each boundary, and the scene echoed to crying and laughter; each orphan being laid across the boundary stones; to this day I can hear their treble recitations, and sad lamentations.

'Remember the parish boundary line, for this is Pontyrhun', or 'Remember this boundary, for this is the millstone of the Taff', 'Aah, ooh, aah!'

Leaving the boundary-beaters, I returned to the horse show.

The auction ring stood a little apart, and the fairgoers were more genteel here. Experts in horseflesh abounded among throngs of gentlemen yeomanry in riding breeches and tunics of scarlet and gold; squireens, proliferating in

Gwent and Glamorgan under the Land Enclosure swindles, were in evidence, attended by their agents, frock-coated, fawn-bellied. Shagged out, nasal women were attended by consorts and lovers, men of blue jowls and barks, virile in bed and the hunt.

But there was also the true gentility here, and these stood apart, conversing in hushed tones.

Near by was a girl in a white summer dress under a lace parasol; her fragile charm, the way she held herself, took my eye.

No great beauty, this one, but so well did she carry herself that I continued to watch her; and, as one does when another's eyes are upon you, the girl sensed it.

The auction crowd moved between us, obliterating and then presenting her to my gaze, and she smiled, a flush coming to her cheeks. A big, sweaty bear of a man in a clerical collar bent to her, but received no reply: the man lifted his sight to me, then back to the girl again; smiling, he walked away. Curlews were shouting at the day, I remember; somewhere above us a lark was singing, his voice cadent on the still air.

The girl smiled again and her mouth was charitable; then she was momentarily lost among the people. When I saw her again it appeared that she had duplicated herself; her companion, identically dressed, was clearly her twin: they engaged in secret whispering, as women do in assignation. This constructed in me a small enchantment; within my head was a faint consolation for the grievous loss of Rhia.

Grooms and stable-lads pushed about me now, and a babble of excitement arose; champing jaws, the yellow teeth of the wicked aged amid the treble shouts of the stable-lads. One of these led a little brown cob into the ring, and the clerical gent beside the girl cried: 'Six sovereigns, Gamer!'

A stable-lad replied: 'Six? Would ye break me, Pastor? Sure to God, he's worth twice. Out of Chancer by Bampton, he is, and a finer worker ye'll never find!'

'Seven,' shouted another, and the auctioneer called:

'Dear soul, is there no money in Merthyr this fair day? I've a reserve on this boyo of eight, and I'm not taking a penny less for me master. Now then!'

'Nine,' I called.

'Nine, is it?' The man wheeled to me.

'Ten!' cried the girl, and shot me a whimsical smile, brushing aside the protests of the pastor.

'Ten and a jack donkey,' I cried, and the crowd laughed, pushing closer.

I felt a hand touch me and turned for a pickpocket: an urchin face, thin and grimy, stared up into mine; finding my hand he pressed it.

'Sirhowy,' he said. Glancing about me for a listener, I pushed him away.

'Is it a good jack donkey, sir?' The pastor raised a hand on the other side of the ring.

'Should be, Pastor,' I called back. 'He's covered half the jennies in Gwent.'

The people laughed and clapped as I led my donkey and trap into the ring.

'Done business,' said the auctioneer. ''Tis a reasonable jack donkey.' And they took him out of the trap shafts and put in the cob.

'What shall we call him?' I paid out the sovereigns and looked around the people.

'Why not Chancer?' cried the girl.

Removing my hat, I bowed low to her.

As she went the girl held her parasol at a wicked angle and smiled over her shoulder. Then my sleeve was tugged. It was the urchin again.

'Midnight,' he said, and scampered away.

Twenty-six

Sunday evening; with my mutton-chops combed and curled, hair parted in the middle, chest out, stomach in, boots to shave in and tight fawn trews, I left Blind Olwen's in Staffordshire Row and took young Chancer high-stepping down North Street. He was a dear little cob with bright eyes and filled with the joy of living, which was not the way Olwen looked when I left her.

'You'll be leaving soon, I suppose?' said she, dull.

'Only to church courting, Olly, I'm not at the altar yet,' and I hooked a leg over Chancer. 'Anyway, I thought you wanted me cut and carried?'

'Bring her for tea. I'll run an eye over her.'

Doors were coming open and curtains going back, and I fashioned the gossip, for Mrs Eynon and Duckie Droopy-Drawers were out hunting.

'Where's that fella off to?'

'They do say he's a livin' terror on Annie Oh-No.'

'Six foot up, I bet he's hard on a woman.'

'Let's hope so,' and the pair of them dropped curtsys, Duckie with her skirts outspread like a dying butterfly, and I gave her a wink that brought apricots to her cheeks.

'How's Romeo Antic?' I asked.

'Don't talk to me about Romeo Antic, Mr Mortymer,' and it fetched her upright, her dark eyes blazing. 'One worse than the Iolo Milk, he is – oh dear me, I'm sick of boys . . .'

'Off to church now, we are,' said Mrs Eynon, old enough to be her aunt.

'Turned over a new leaf, have we?' I winked.

'Aye, well St Peter's is convenient, ain't it? It were a good old step over to Capel Newydd, and dangerous for virgin women comin' back in the dark.'

Our church in Town, consecrated five years back on St Peter's day, had taken the place of Capel Newydd, where a church had stood for the past thousand years.

Ada Cader and Gin Trimm, massive in black shawls, capes and tall hats, went past arm in arm and ignored my greeting, males having been dispensed with in their female world: Miss Pantrych and skinny Miss Gwallter were leading Grandfer Trevor Lloyd, the blind puddler: Evans the Death, our undertaker was escorting Mrs Trimble, who had expectations in his direction: and Mr Snell, the seller of coloured Bibles, cringed by on his way to the Methodist. Little did I guess that his destiny was linked with mine.

Having seen half the population safely into St Peter's, I struck west off the road and began to climb the Coity Mountain where there was less chance of being seen.

I took Chancer slowly, for I had time to spare; not being due at the Quarryman's Arms, Sirhowy, until midnight.

With the sinking of the first downshaft pit in Wales three years before, Tredegar (*Tre-daear-dêg* in Welsh, meaning Town of Fair Land) had begun to thrive.

Ancient before the coming of the Romans, Tredegar held in her arms a sister town, Sirhowy, one of the earliest commercial ironworks in Wales. Two gentlemen of Brittany, fleeing their country and the war with England, built a furnace. 'What shall we call it?' they asked, and this was Pontygwaith. From this beginning they produced kitchen utensils, then, with patriotic impartiality, sold cannonballs to France and Britain; rich, they returned to France.

Then arrived Mr Kettle from Shropshire, an adventurer who built the Dukestown Furnace. With the aid of a waterwheel and cold blast, he produced twelve tons of pig iron weekly: this he sent by pack mule to Newport and the world.

Next came the Reverend Monkhouse and his partner Fothergill. Mrs Monkhouse might have succoured Rhia in her need, but her husband did nothing for Sirhowy, and Fothergill did less. As the Freres outraged Clydach Vale, so these two violated Tredegar. Beautiful Sirhowy of the silvan glades and bright river, was doomed.

As the production rate of pig iron increased and the foreign immigrants poured in, so the ironmasters cornered them, flinging up terraced houses for them, putting them to work in honeycombing the hills for coal and ore: they excavated the river for clay for furnace bricks, built beehive lime kilns and drop-hammers.

Fothergill, as his workers rebelled against his low wages and filthy social conditions, built his infamous Folly; a Round House in which to face a siege until the military came to his aid.

When mass violence flared; when starving marching gangs were streaming over the mountains, much of this originated from the secret meetings held in the taverns of the Monkhouse and Fothergill Works. And one of these taverns was the Quarryman's Arms on the Rassau stony road at Trefil.

This is what brought me to Sirhowy on that Sunday evening, having made the alibi that I was riding to Merthyr for Chapel. As I got clear of the wayside cottages in the dark, I pulled a knitted black stocking over my head: slits for eyes, this stocking, stolen off Olwen's wash line.

Tethering Chancer in a little quarry near by, I went to the tavern door. Here a man was standing, his hands in his pockets.

'Password?'

'Fothergill's Folly,' I said.

About fifteen men were sitting in the cellar of the tavern, all hooded, so that none could recognize his neighbour. No records were kept at such meetings, nobody knew where a man had come from; the password, always changing, was the protection.

The spokesman at such meetings always came from the complaining area. With unionism banned by the employers and benefit clubs like the Ivorites and Oddfellows frowned upon, there was left no access to Works agents or the owners. Immediately a man expressed complaint, he was put on the Blacklist and his name circulated to other employers. It was said that a Newport lawyer organized these secret meetings, selected the complaints and the remedy to be taken.

Inspired with the success of the French Revolution and Tom Paine's *The Rights of Man*, emissaries of the New Republic were ranging over Europe, and the unrest of Wales's new frontier towns was attracting organized revolt. The riots of ten years before were now being reborn in the failure of harvest after harvest. And, while owners were basking in the rush for armaments, the price of wheat went up again. The hanging of Samuel Hill, Aaron Williams, and others who inspired the 1800 marching gangs, had temporarily halted the revolutionary fervour. But now even the King was worried: the government sent spies into Wales to track down the sources of this new anarchy.

Discussion at these secret meetings, for security reasons, was always limited to a leader; he was the spokesman who gave the commands, and instructed each man in his appointed role.

The leader this night was small, insignificant in manner; his voice might have been disguised, for he spoke in a low, toneless croak, saying: 'The instructions tonight will be brief; there is no need to complicate what is a simple issue. Three prisoners in Brecon Barracks are being escorted from there to Chepstow for transport to Portsmouth and the convict ship.

In Welsh he spoke now, saying, 'Do all understand me?'

All hands went up. He continued: 'The prisoners and an escort of six dragoons are due to leave Brecon at dawn – five hours from now. Your ambush of the prison van in which the prisoners will be carried will take place on the Usk bridge at Crickhowell. Understand this – if violence occurs it will not come from us. The captives are Sirhowy men. All three are manacled – leg irons and chains. Will the blacksmith show?'

A man raised his hand.

'Blacksmith, while the dragoons are being engaged, you will enter the prison van and strike off the men's fetters. The cart will be on the move, so this will be difficult. Is the van driver here?'

Another raised an arm.

'After the van has been captured and the blacksmith is at work, you will drive the van to the Llangattock caves; there you will abandon it, first directing the prisoners to the cave guide who will be waiting at the *Maen Eglwys* entrance. Is the shot-firer here?'

A man stood up. The leader continued: 'Your charges are laid on the Crickhowell bridge approach?' and the man nodded assent. 'Right, these will be detonated when the dragoons are packed on the bridge: the horses will panic, and townspeople will herd on the bridge to prevent pursuit. Is food for the prisoners here?'

Another stood up, holding a bag.

'And two shillings each in money?'

The same man jingled it in his hand. The speaker said, 'Finally, is the cave guide present?'

I nodded at him, and he said: 'When the prisoners arrive at the entrance you will signal with a light, then lead them deep into the *Maen Eglwys* cavern. You know these caves intimately?'

I nodded again.

'No heroics. Take them in quickly and keep them quiet – no lights after your first signal from the entrance. Stay hidden while the soldiers search; only after you are certain they are gone will you bring the three men out. After that they take their chances. Any questions?' He glanced about him; the room was silent. 'Right,' said he. 'Meeting closed.'

Owls were hooting on the slopes of Mynydd Llangynidr, right music, I thought, for a dawn attack upon the Fifth Horse from Brecon Barracks, the best soldiers in the county.

I took Chancer at a gallop across the open moors; he was sprightly, loving the sense of freedom. If things went wrong, I reflected, he might well be on the gallop again before the night was out. Soon we reached the Llangattock caves; the moon was bathing the mountain in a blue, eerie light. The sky burned candlefire stars.

These caves, home of Neolithic tribes, had been cut from solid rock when the world was ice: underground streams rush here; caverns abound, some as big as cathedrals: stalactites and stalagmites form gigantic pillars, decorating towering shelves and grottoes.

Here, in later years, was born the fund of the Chartist Rebellion; in this secret place, where a man can be lost in time and space, arms were manufactured. Men of military precision have guarded the entrance, *Maen Eglwys*; down deep lie underground lakes; the resurgent waters that come flooding up through miles of tunnels into Clydach Gorge. There, in its head waters, the whirlpool, my Rhia had lost her life. Many said that I would find her within this honeycomb; search parties hoped to find her body in Shakespeare Cave near the Rock and Fountain, but she was found within yards of the pool in which she was murdered.

For me these caves held a grieving fascination.

Now, at the *Maen Eglwys* entrance, looking down into the valley, I heard distant explosions, and knew that the dragoons were being ambushed on Crickhowell bridge.

The road was a ribbon of moonlight over the rock-strewn

hills. The prison van came along it madly, with the horses under the whip. Reaching a bend, it skidded and struck the hedgerow; sparks flew from its iron-shod wheels and the galloping hooves. I watched it clatter to a stop; saw the back doors open and three men spill out: I saw them clearly; scarecrows of men, their arms and legs flailing as they vaulted from the van and raced for open country. Kneeling, I struck the instantaneous light box: dry leaves I had prepared glowed and flared. The escaping men instantly turned towards the fire; behind them the van driver scrambled off his perch, and ran.

Slipping, sliding over the rocks, the men approached.

I stamped out the signal fire when they neared me: breathing heavily, they sank down before me. Two were little more than lads, their faces bruised, evidence of beatings. The third man had an arm in a sling; he peered into the stocking mask I wore.

'Fothergill's Folly?' he gasped.

'Come,' I commanded.

Once within the shelter of the caves, I rested them, for they were weakened by starvation and the House of Correction. Squatting on the floor in the light of my taper, they ate like famished wolves, the two young ones tearing at the bread with their strong white teeth and gulping down cave water. I found the third man, now I could clearly see him, was much older; he ate delicately, and his voice was cultured: 'One thing we left undone – we should have killed that magistrate.' He drank from a cupped hand. 'Talk of Judge Jeffries and the Monmouth insurrection! We had a hanging judge all to ourselves.'

'Death – us two; and we wasn't anywhere near the Brynmawr riots!' added one of the others.

'I was, and proud of it,' said the older man. 'But he threw these lads in for good measure. Just kids, aren't they? They haven't begun to live.' He made a fist of his hand. 'I tell you this, friend. Get me out of this, and I'll be back. In the name of Aaron Williams and Sam Hill, I'll swing for Justice Williams.'

I asked, 'You a Sirhowy man?' and he nodded.

'Born and bred; back in the days of old man Kettle I was a toddler and saw it rise; under Fothergill I've watched it fall – him and his bloody lackeys. Listen, you. I've balled and refined, puddled and forged – I've done it all. But now I've a missus and five, and a ten-pound debt to the Truck Shop. I was down Dukestown pit when the rope broke and old Ben Williams died, and I broke this arm getting him out, and now it won't heal.'

His eyes were bright in the light of the taper, and he wiped his mouth with his good hand. 'Wombs spawn strange. One moment a saint like poor old Ben, then his blood cousin who hangs men when they riot to feed their children. I tell you, I'll swing for that Paul Williams.'

Up to now I had let him ramble on, but the name sparked in me a distant memory.

'Paul Williams? Of Sirhowy?

'Jesus, I just told you!'

'Paul Williams the lawyer, the cousin of Ben Williams who was killed down Dukestown?'

'The same. Now Judge Williams. Does the name mean something?'

All three peered at me: the shadows danced around the dripping walls; in the distance I could hear an underground stream babbling down to Clydach.

'Not a thing.' I adjusted the stocking mask closer about my face. 'Come, we'd better get moving.'

Later, with the taper out, we lay side by side in the dark and watched the redcoat oil lamps flashing within the entrance of *Maen Eglwys*, which, translated, means Church Stone. After the soldiers had gone, for they feared to enter, I led the way along well-known passages to an exit point. There we crept out into the cold night air and took a sheep track to Mynydd Llangynidr.

Down in the valley flares were burning on Crickhowell bridge, the point of the ambush: faint commands floated up.

'God go with you,' I said to the three men, and they melted into the night.

Twenty-seven

You could always get a breakfast at the Rock and Fountain, Cushy's place. Clean as a polished flea, it was, with the windows open and washed before breakfast and a shine you could shave in on Poll Plenty's loaves, which she cooked in the garden oven. So, I didn't go back to Blaenafon and Blind Olwen, but galloped down the coach road on Gilwern Hill.

Off-shift night colliers were tossing the pots in the tap-room; the walls stained by the usual burnt-out colliers who sat behind their pewters in staring desolation, eating their lungs and champing their walrus whiskers. Meg Laundry, fat and comely, was there at the counter on blue ruin, her mate being a new entry down from Wigan, Nellie Washboard. Beggars for gossip were these two; even the roses had changed to ghouls by the time they'd done with them, and they were having the place in fits.

'Mind, being in the laundry trade do make for fine philosophy,' announced Meg, and her bosomy bodice shook with mirth. 'We can tell ye who's in the family way when a petticoat starts going at the seams, can't we, Nell!'

The men roared, loving it; unnoticed, I entered, returned a wink from Poll, who made big eyes at the bread and cheese: I nodded, starving.

Then Nell Washboard cried in her northern lilt: 'Aye, there's nowt like a wash line to give ye knowledge of folks,' and she drew a pale, skeletal hand across her brow. 'Billy Handy of the Drum and Monkey's in trouble – Belinda's into belly bands and June ain't out.'

The colliers bawled vulgarities; the aged champed on toothless jaws, banging the spittoons, and Nell, the new woman, cried in her nasal dialect, 'Butcher Harris is dressing to the right again – a woman don't know where she is from minute to minute!'

The tap-room erupted, which suited me, for I had seen the flash of metal on the glass of the door, and rose, turning away.

An army captain and two dragoons came in; following them was the Lord Lieutenant of the County.

'I want a room for his lordship,' said the captain, and put his fist on the counter. 'And another for Justice Williams.'

Silence dropped on the room like the slam of a coffin.

'Of course, your worship,' said Cushy Cuddlecome, appearing from nowhere, and lowered a curtsy.

I was outside the door now and Poll, I noticed, closed it gently behind me. Going round to the front, I looked through a window into the tap-room where the captain was interrogating Cushy with violent gesticulations: soldiers had lined the old men up against the wall for searching.

The fourth man, Justice Williams, riveted my attention. He was portly; his florid cheeks, bloated with good living, sagged their purple jowls upon his lace cravat; his belly bulged under his pearl-buttoned waistcoat. His eyes, red-rimmed, peered from the folds of a face that had died: this, the father of Bimbo, by rape.

Hatred, deep and pure, welled up within me.

Soon, I thought, this one will leave here. With or without dragoon protection, he will take to the road. Probably, I reasoned, the dragoon escort was for the Lord Lieutenant, yet it was inconceivable that Williams would travel on horseback alone.

'That was quick,' said a voice. Poll was leaning against a wall behind me.

'I'm not hanging around with these buggers about,' I answered.

'Nor me, neither, I've left them to Cushy,' and she smiled and came closer. 'Safe enough, though, if you've nothing to hide.'

'What are they up to now?'

'Searching the old chaps; got 'em practically naked.'

'What are they after?'

Poll shrugged, looking beautiful.

Talk had it that she was giving Dai Swipo and Bill Noakes a couple these days, with a ladder up to her attic window on Tuesdays for Bill and another on Fridays for Dai. More, gossip was that she'd got her hand in Cushy's till, with delusions about taking over the Rock and Fountain, but she'd have to be up early in the morning to put one over Cushy. Now Poll made big eyes at me.

'What are they after? Don't you know? Last night someone ambushed a prison van. Three prisoners to transportation got away. They'll check every inn between here and the Abergavenny Angel.'

'They're staying here the night?'

Poll nodded. 'Nearer the iron towns,' and she followed me round to the back where Chancer was tethered. 'Don't you ever give a thought to me? It's years since your woman passed on. You and me were pretty close at the Grouse, remember?'

I gave her a smile; she said, 'Is that all I get?'

I swung up into the saddle. 'From what I hear you're doing all right, pretty Poll . . .'

'With mountain fighters? That pair? Christ! They're only slap, bang, wallop – have a heart!' And she reached up her face and pouted her lips for kissing.

Bending in the saddle, I kissed her. 'You're a good old girl,' I said. 'But I've got things on, and that's all I can spare right now.'

'*Diawl!* Mortymer, you don't give much away.'

Ynysgau Chapel, the old pile barring the entrance to Merthyr's 'China', was bathed in sun-go-down as I took Chancer and trap up to the entrance and tethered him for the evening service.

Loungers, pimps and procurers were thronging the Iron Bridge over the nearby Taff River, and there was a sweet song of fiddles and melodeons in the air, with Tory squires and suchlike taking their evening stroll in lorgnettes and powdered wigs, with pomanders of aromatic substances dangling at their waists: they hadn't taken a bath since the midwife by the smell of them. Harlots of rouged face and carmine mouth were touting the off-shift colliers under the naphtha flares, for it was the night of the illuminations in Merthyr.

The narrow streets and courts and yards were crowded with incoming immigrants; the alleys were gay with lumbering traps and high-stepping ponies. Watching every move, the toothless grans and granchers, the refuse of a lost generation, sat in their open doorways and watched the world go by: somewhere over in High Street was the sound of a Benefit band; soon tub-thumping agitators would be spouting their ideals of freedom and democracy to an uncaring shopocracy that opposed them in the name of profit.

Change would come, I reflected. What had happened in France, where the Revolution had lost its head and those of a thousand aristocrats, would be repeated in the face of parliamentary corruption that could no longer be tolerated.

Meanwhile, what I was after was a wife, not parliamentary reform.

The congregation was already seated as I entered Ynysgau Chapel.

The locals said that Elianor Jones, the youngest daughter of the Reverend John Jones of Ynysgau Methodist Chapel, was, like her sister Sioban, tied to her pa's religious fervour hook, line and sinker. But I'd had my doubts about this since our first meeting at Cyfarthfa Horse Fair, for she'd got a pert old eye.

The moment I took a pew on the other side of her aisle, she turned: momentarily, she stared; then her eyes opened like saucers, and she nudged her sister.

Inclining my head, I touched my cravat; bowed so you wouldn't notice it, and the flush sprang to her cheeks.

Outraged virtue now; chin up, shoulders set: in the frills and ribbons of her rosebud dress, Elianor Jones stared straight ahead . . . her eyes occasionally slanting across to see if I was still keen.

This is love-making done with the eyes; the flickering glance and casual air: a clever old business under the piercing stare of a sixteen-stone father up in the pulpit, and his voice rang out across the crowded heads.

'"But King Solomon loved many strange women, together with the daughter of Pharaoh, women of the Moabites, Ammonites, Edomites, Zidonians and Hittites . . . Solomon clave unto these in love. And he had seven hundred wives, princesses, and three hundred concubines . . ."' His eyes fixed upon mine and drilled to the back of my head: fierce and sweaty, this one, like a bear with a collar on. He'd make a queer old father-in-law, I reflected.

Yet it appeared, sitting there in the dust-mote silence, within the aura of mothballs, dubbinned boots, matrons and fresh young girls, that I was floating in a strange hypnotic dream . . . it was a mesmerism that banished time and space, one which possessed no time-interval, though much had happened in the two months in between, when autumn had turned into winter.

It was as if Time and Fate were eager to have me over and done with, and I awoke from that lost interval to find myself standing before the altar of Ynysgau Chapel with Big Rhys, my best man, on my right and Elianor, my young bride, on my left: and I looked into the face of the Reverend John Jones, her father, and heard him say: 'Do you take this woman, Elianor Jones, to be your lawful, wedded wife?'

Then I took my new bride away from Merthyr and her father's manse, with the old man humped and jagged at losing a daughter and Sioban weeping buckets at the loss of a sister; and installed her not in Blind Olwen's bundling house, for this was a wife, not a mistress. No, in Number Five Stack Square I installed my Elianor. As a gentleman puddler in the money, I spared nothing to do her proud. Solly Widdle Jew, the furniture man, I brought over from Nantyglo with gentry furniture; a table, two chairs, pink curtains at the window facing the furnaces; a good strong ball-topped bed with a horsehair mattress, and a rug for getting out on to a well-scrubbed floor, and Mrs Shanco Mathews came in and worked like a maniac at a penny an hour.

There was a pair of china dogs given by Big Rhys and Will Blaenafon; Tomos Traherne came down from Pwll-du with a brass-bound Bible, and Elianor's aunt landed us with a baby's mattress. Even Belinda Handy of the Drum and Monkey arrived with a two-gallon china, always a gift gratefully received, and Annie Oh-No suckled her new baby sitting on the threshold, a priceless lore that guaranteed sons.

'Your Rhia would be pleased, Hywel,' Annie whispered, and she gave me her son to hold. 'Just been up to her grave at Horeb, I have, and put on winter flowers.'

'I'll be up there myself directly,' I said.

'Pretty little woman you got, mind. Firm in the haunch and full in the breast – likely she'll milk well. Is it sons you're after?'

'Six like yours, Annie,' I said, and kissed her face.

This brought to her a redness, for it was the kiss of another's husband, and in our time I'd given her the kisses of a lover.

'You'll forget Rhia now, I suppose . . .' said Annie, low.

'Never will I forget Rhia. Nor will I ever forget you.'

She bowed to me. 'Got to go, Hywel Mortymer. God go with you and Elianor. I'll be around if ever ye need me, mind.'

The furnaces in the compound went into blast then, and I heard my new woman call me from the room upstairs. But I stayed for a moment or so watching Annie Oh-No leave: saw her with her shawled baby, his face pressed against hers to obliterate the thundering of the furnaces.

Elianor was awaiting me in the bedroom later, and the furnaces were simmering so that the night was quiet. Somewhere out on the unscarred hills a nightjar was singing to the moon.

I took Elianor to bed and went into her, and her eyes, I remember, were like a young fawn's in that black-red light, large and startled. Thinking I had hurt her, I drew away, but she clasped me close, whispering in Welsh to me words of love, but it was Gwynedd Welsh born of her fathers, and one I did not then fully understand.

So there was nothing but her foreign whispers and the song of a firer-man who was singing to himself in the compound: 'David of the White Rock' he sang, so this was our music; this, the nightjar, and the hissing furnaces.

Later we heard hobnails and the good nights of departing workers, for the Drum and Monkey was turning out and the shifts were changing, and I was one with Ellie, and she with me.

'You love me, Hywel?'

'Would I be here if I did not love you?' In English I said this, which was not our mother tongue.

'So soon after losing your Rhia?'

'Rhia is dead, you are alive.'

Marriage being a battlefield with lovers as the casualties, a man has to adapt his technique according to the opposition.

Making love to Elianor Jones, for instance, was chalk and cheese to courting Rhia, who was likely to get a giggling fit in the middle of things, which can be very disconcerting. Is there anything more comical, she used to say, than two grown people lying face to face, billing and cooing during such funny antics; and she refused to take it seriously. In some respects, therefore, Rhia Evans was more like Annie Oh-No – never so much a wife as Ellie, who was with me now.

It is the difference, perhaps, between mature women and young lovers.

Strangely, in this loving I knew a shyness; it had never happened before: and when it did Ellie only smiled, drawing me down to her in whispered consolation. Quiet and submissive was she, yet relentless in her call, so that there came to my loins a need of her, and our world stopped on the clock of joy: that need, too, was for a son, not mere gratification. Now there was no sound in the room but the rush of our breathing. And in that unifying I made my child within her womb in a great outpouring of the body and spirit. I called her name: '*Elianor!*'

So was Elianor born to me as wife, and Rhia, my old love, went back to her grave.

Mind you, he don't waste a lot of time, that Mortymer chap, they said in Blaenafon. Within nine months to the day that pastor's daughter was signed for, sealed, and had delivered her first in Five Stack Square. He's after a son, they do say – but you wait a bit, girl – when a woman carries high she'll likely birth a daughter.

In quiet moments I used to pray. A son, *a son*!

But it was not to be.

Twenty-eight

A new phenomenon began to stalk the mountains.

Scotch Cattle.

With the growth of the secret Benefit Clubs and the rise of the embryonic unions, the workers teetered on the edge of indecision. For, while the threats of the treadmills and the Blacklist were real, better half a wage than no wage at all. Better the hunger and debt of the Truck Shops with their prices going higher every month, than wander homeless in the winds of winter, people said. And so the fire of their bellies left them, and they worked on their masters' terms. They rejected their Benefit Clubs and outlawed their unions, and the Scotch Cattle struck to enforce their membership.

Living in secret caves and gullies on the hillsides, they roved in gangs. Led by the fiercest among them, they dressed themselves up in the skins of beasts, taking for their head-dress the horns of cattle; strapping these to their foreheads, they blackened their faces and bayed in chorus, as a cow who has lost her calf bays at the moon. The sound struck terror into the kitchens of men who worked on when the Cattle said 'stop'.

'Have you heard of the new Company regulation about children?' asked Elianor in the kitchen of Five Stack Square.

Morfydd, now aged four months, was at her breast, and rays of spring sunlight were flooding the room: the place was pretty with new spring flowers; every evening Elianor climbed the Blorenge in search of flowers, and the sight of an unusual variety would delight her. I had heard of the new

235

Company cage regulation, but a woman suckling a child has enough to think about.

Elianor said, raising her face to mine: 'Two more little ones were killed yesterday in Rhymney. Six were going down Duke's Pit on top of the cage and the handholds broke. One was eight, the other twelve. Both girls. Why can't they travel inside the cage with the colliers?'

'It is the new Company rule,' I replied, lacing boots.

'But why?'

'Because the Company forbids children travelling in the same cage as workmen.'

'I know that, but why?'

'The Company own the pits, they make the regulations.'

'Interference with children? Grown men? What a slander on our colliers!' She took Morfydd off one and settled her on the other and the baby fisted her and noisily sucked. 'Find me the collier who would interfere with a child, and we women would see to him.'

'There's an old fighting cock,' I said, knocking out my clay.

'Aye, and I'll tell you something else, Hywel Mortymer,' and her face was flushed with anger. 'There's talk about that Effyn Tasker up at Pwll-du – and him a pew collector in the Horeb? But I'll not believe any of it until I get the proof.' She levelled a finger at me, then poked it at the baby. 'If I found George III lifting the skirt of this one, I'd hit him out of Windsor Castle.'

I said, drearily, 'I doubt if George III would interfere with our Morfydd.'

'He won't get the chance. When this child's six years old she's not going down a dirty old pit to work like an animal!' Glancing at the clock, she added, 'What time will you be back tonight?'

These days Ellie's nerves were strained. Initially I'd put this down to birth depression, but it was linked, of course, to my night meanderings. Ellie was no fool, but if she knew what I was doing, she made no outward sign of it.

'Could be late again,' I said.

Taking Morfydd off the breast, she put the baby on her shoulder and began hitting her for wind.

'Late shift?'

'Ay, ay – another three o'clock.'

'That's funny. Tomos was here earlier and reckoned late shift finished just after midnight.'

'Is he staying here again tonight?' I asked, changing the subject.

'He is, and I don't like it. Welcome he may be, but we don't want him to take the house over.'

'Look, it's only until they finish the rebuilding of his cottage. He'll be away from here any day now.'

'That's what you said last week.'

When things went wrong for the pastor, people took him in on a shift basis. When his cottage roof fell in, he lodged with Billy Handy, then went with Rhys Jenkins for a week; so far he'd been with us a month.

Ellie said, 'Apart from anything else, he eats like a horse – I'd rather keep him a week than a fortnight.'

I asked with innocence.

'And his interest in you?'

On odd occasions Ellie left the cloth of the manse and reverted to her childhood peasantry, and I found it charming. She said, her head moving petulantly, 'He do fancy a look when I'm on the feed.'

I gave her a grin. 'He do fancy more than the feeding, girl – ach, be a sport – he's an old bachelor – give the lad a treat!'

'Nothing to laugh at, mind. Only my husband should see when I am feeding my baby.'

She looked like a little girl sitting there with Morfydd now belly-down on her lap. It is funny, I think, that the woman you'd give the world for always happens to live in the next town, or somewhere down the street. I could have searched the world and not found another like this one.

Bending, I kissed them both, kisses flavoured by the

warm, sweet smell of milk, and I pitied Tomos Traherne . . . and blessed his presence in the house. I had another week or so of grain-raiding; with luck I hoped to spin out the pastor's stay; no harm would come to these two while Tomos was about. The way he looked at Ellie, this man would die for her – I'd not had the services of such a friend when they drowned my Rhia.

Ellie said now, 'Be careful, Hywel.'

Before I closed the door, I winked at her.

'Don't bring us trouble.'

I said, 'I puddle by the book. The people who break the rules catch it at the furnaces.'

But she didn't mean that, and she knew that I knew it: yet, despite her strained face, I had to go. Something had to be done; there were things happening in Wales that one could scarcely believe.

'Prisoner at the bar,' said Mr Justice Williams at the spring Assizes, 'you have been found guilty of taking a salmon weighing seven pounds from the waters of Fothergill's, such being the property of Squire John de Kenton, from whom the water is under lease. An act of common poaching, and it must be stopped. Have you anything to say before sentence is passed upon you?'

The prisoner appeared nonplussed. The Clerk of the Court rose and said, 'If it please your worship, the prisoner does not understand English.'

'Then for God's sake explain it in Welsh,' cried Justice Williams, and this the Clerk did.

The prisoner said, in Welsh: 'Nothing. It is of no use to say anything.'

'He has nothing to say, he says,' the Clerk translated, and Justice Williams cried:

'Let this be understood by all right-thinking people, that such acts of theft will not be tolerated while I am a Justice of these Assizes during His Majesty's pleasure. The subject of the theft, the salmon. Has it been weighed and recorded?'

'Six pounds and five ounces, your worship,' replied the Clerk.

'Then, for every pound or part of a pound, my sentence is one year – seven years transportation to Botany Bay,' said Justice Williams. 'Therefore the prisoner, John Evan, will be taken from here to the bridewell at Usk, there to be chained; from Usk he will be taken to Chepstow and put aboard the packet *May Sall*, which will convey him to Portsmouth and the transportation ship the *Welsh Patriot*; this sails for Australia within the month. Next case.'

There is a light in the window of Justice Williams's mansion in Sirhowy, which is unusual when the judge is on the circuit and his wife away with relatives.

A sad case of female depreciation is Mrs Joy Williams, his wife. Born on ermine was she, in fierce Italian sunlight, but her husband's perfidy had aged her into a crone. Once tall and with the carriage of a queen, the years of his excesses had thumped her into skin and bone.

'You there, my lovely?' calls Susie Obligato from his bed.

'Just coming, my precious,' replies his worship.

Susie, no better than she should be until later taken in hand by Bad Boy Gold, stretches and sighs in the duck-down and her eyes are like stars after all the legal promises.

'Mind you, your honour,' says Susie, 'it don't look too good if your missus comes back sudden, like, do it?'

'My missus, Baggage, is in Verona.'

'Strike me dead,' says Susie. 'I can't duck out now, in any case, you being a legal gent an' all that. Do ye love me?'

'My paramour, my love-pearl, I shall love you for ever and ever,' says Justice Williams, and pads in bare-footed in his nightshirt and sleeping-cap.

'I mean, we ain't goin' to do nothin', are we, your excellency? Only passing the night together, like, until the morning, ain't it? Me missing the last coach home . . .'

In a rush of breathing from deep down in the arson of his

soul, Justice Williams adds to his list of conquests – forty under the age of sixteen and fifty under twelve – one book for the single births, another for the twins.

'Oh . . . oh, your honour, that don't 'alf hurt. Oh, please, your worship . . . Ooh!'

'Lie still, Baggage,' says Mr Justice Williams.

It also happened, in that same month before summer swept over the mountains, that a certain ironmaster, sojourning in the vicinity of Dowlais, saw a child on the street near Iron Lane: seeing her, he sent for his paymaster, and said: 'There is one who lives in Iron Lane, a child of great beauty. You know her?'

The paymaster replied: 'It is Carla Mordecai, the daughter of Joby Canal, the lock-keeper.'

'The new man with the amputated leg? The one we appointed recently.'

'It is he.'

'And the daughter?'

'Carla, the child? She is aged thirteen.'

'Send her to me,' said the ironmaster.

'It is against the law of the priests. She is under age.'

'Send her to me.'

'For payment?'

'For the price of a sovereign.'

So it was that after the paymaster had visited the lock-keeper's cottage, the girl Mordecai, who was the old man's adopted daughter, listened to his instructions and dressed in her Sunday clothes and came to the house of the ironmaster.

The sun was setting when she arrived at the gates of Big House, and Carla waited for a little while until dusk and bats were dropping over the Company park, but when lights shone from the great windows, she entered and went there, keeping to the shadows.

But another was walking in the parkland, and this was the master's wife: they met face to face on a path amid the rhododendrons, which had yet to come to bloom; she and

240

the child Carla Mordecai, they met, and neither knew the other. The ironmaster's wife asked: 'At this hour you walk in our park, child?'

'As I have been told,' answered Carla.

'By whom?'

'By the paymaster.'

'He bade you come? What for?'

'To meet with the ironmaster, and earn a sovereign.'

'In what manner?'

'I do not know. But if I wait for him outside the window that faces to the park, he will open the door for me.'

'This,' said the mistress, 'is the *droit de seigneur*. You have heard of that?'

'I have not, for I have never been to school. In the day I work as a scrubbing-maid in the house of the paymaster; he and his wife are good to my adopted father.' She pointed. 'Joby Canal is his name, and he keeps the lock on the canal.'

'How old are you?'

'Thirteen in two months.'

'You are a virgin?'

'Yes, ma'am.'

'My husband intends to have carnal knowledge of you, child. You understand this?'

'I have heard the other girls talking, but I do not really understand it. Will it hurt?'

'It will hurt you more than me,' said the mistress. 'Take off your clothes.'

Carla Mordecai, who was not yet a woman, had the plump curves of the adolescent: the ironmaster's wife, being comely, but small, was near to her shape and size. And so, in the rhododendron bushes the two changed clothes: now the child stood in the finery of the ironmaster's wife; her mistress stood in Carla's Sunday dress: Carla wore silk stockings and buckled shoes and about her was draped a silk gown. The legs and feet of the lady were bare.

'Wait here,' said she, and the girl dropped a curtsy, and waited.

Within the shaded lights of the ironmaster's bedroom also waited the man: he who had summoned a child to his bed. And because she had not arrived on time, he was pensive and disturbed. Pulling on his cigar, bearded and stately in his scarlet dressing-gown, the ironmaster awaited the coming of Carla Mordecai, the daughter of the lock-keeper, and in his hand he gripped a sovereign.

Peering through the window that faced the park, he watched for her coming and his body was impatient.

In his time he had pleasured, without affront, the wives of gentlemen and the harlots of the taverns. But it is for the sullying of virtue that such men pay most. So his heart beat faster when he saw a movement beyond the window that faced the park: and, to ensure that the tryst be unobserved, he snuffed out the candles and waited in the dark.

His eyes, straining in the moonlight, found the shape of the woman; his senses flushed when he saw the simple dress, the flowing hair and the bare legs of the one he sought. Fumbling in the dark, he opened the door leading to the garden; a vein in his temple was beating violently as the woman he thought was the child Mordecai walked into his arms.

Closing and locking the door, the ironmaster led her to the bed. There, in great strength, he stripped her of her clothes in gasping haste: and was surprised, when he had knowledge of her, that the child did not, like others, cry for gentleness. So he knew her in violent strength, which was the manner in which he used his wife.

Later, he knew her again and yet again, for he was a man terrified that his virility was leaving him, living as he was within a year of his final copulation. Then, sweating and dishevelled, he rolled off the bed, leaving the woman as one transfixed on the counterpane. Lifting a bottle now, he guzzled at the wine in the dark, and the woman spoke from the bed.

'A sovereign, remember?'

Approaching, he tossed the coin on to the bed. 'Now be off with you.'

He opened the french door leading to the park.

Carla Mordecai was watching the moon when the iron-master's wife returned. The woman said: 'You know who I am, for I told you, remember?'

Carla straightened. 'You are the ironmaster's wife.'

'Then bear that in mind,' said the woman as she stripped off her clothes. Carla took off her clothes also; pulled over her head her Sunday dress and stood with bare feet and legs, and straightened her hair so that it flowed down her back.

The lady asked her: 'What is your name, you say?'

'Carla Mordecai.'

'The daughter adopted by Joby Canal, the man who keeps the lock? I want to be quite sure.'

'The same, missus.'

The wife drew closer. 'Here is the sovereign. I pay this to you in pity that you could so slander my husband. I pay it to you with the promise that, should you speak foul of him again, I will visit the wrath of God upon you, Carla Mordecai. If you speak my husband's name even, except with pious respect, I will find you. For it is hateful that you should accuse him thus – he who loves children. Go now . . . !'

'But ma'am . . .'

The lady pointed with a trembling arm. 'Go, and may God forgive you.' Her voice rose. 'Tell what I have said to Joby Canal and the Paymaster. Go, *go!*'

After Carla Mordecai had gone, the lady, unseen, sank down to the ground. And, sobbing, saw the boots of a man appear before her; looking up, she perceived her husband.

His shirt, rumpled and stained with wine, was open to the waist: in one hand he held a bottle; his face, bulbous-nosed, was flushed and swollen.

'So,' said he, swaying, 'it was you! Damn this bottle, for *it was you!*' Bending, he caught her by the hair and turned up her face to his, and she saw his bloodshot eyes and the stink of him swept over her.

'I've had whores who were more enjoyable. Bitch, *bitch!*'

Twenty-nine

The night was flashing June when Tomos came down from Pwll-du for his weekly visit to Five Stack Square. As usual, Elianor was in a fury of activity, running her fingers around the furniture for dust and hitting the furnace grit from one corner to another. Morfydd, now aged three, was sticking herself up with a jam sandwich fit for a navvy.

'With Tomos Traherne for supper, you'll be staying in, of course?' said Elianor.

'Sorry, got a lodge meeting, girl.' We'd had a hard day at the furnaces, working to get a new rail order out to Spain by the end of the month.

'Why don't you say you don't like Tomos, and have done with it?' said Elianor, with a sniff.

Morfydd had got hold of my knee, so I lifted her, ducking her swipes with the jam sandwich.

'I've got a meeting with the Faithful Friends Benefit Club.'

Ellie's mouth was a little red button; always a sign she'd got something under her apron that was bound to come out.

'Lodges, benefit clubs! We never had them in Merthyr and we seemed to get by without a penny a week from the sick, lame and lazy.'

'Your family got by. Some didn't. I seem to remember a Merthyr in rags, with more crippled and maimed on the streets than any other town in Britain. The theme of the Benefits is self-help; I don't see anything wrong in that.'

'You will one day,' said she. 'Next it'll be the Union, and when that happens they'll bring in dragoons.'

'That's right. Meanwhile, old Joey Samuel got a pauper's grave last Monday – a penny a week for burial would have given him a decent put-you-down – so count me in to support the Benefits.'

'Tomos Traherne doesn't agree with them, mind.'

I slammed the door to warm its hinges.

Most families had started quarrelling about now, with Benefit bands thumping *ooompa, ooompa* in round-town processions and waving flags and making rude signs at the soldiers.

Every industrial town was under military occupation these days, with spies lying under floorboards and peeping through keyholes, and colliers storing shot-firing gun powder.

When I went up the mountain that night Tomos Traherne came to visit, I did so expecting a meeting about benefit clubs and self-help.

It was self-help, right enough, but not the kind I had expected.

The Hide was a favourite meeting place; a cavern on the side of the Coity mountain, with outpost sentries placed on higher ground to give warning of dragoons, for they broke up such meetings with cutlasses.

The meeting was already in progress when I arrived, pulling my stocking over my face like the others. A leader was speaking. About fifty men, all disguised, sat around in a half-circle. Some I recognized by their size – Will Blaenafon and Big Rhys Jenkins, for instance, and Isaac Thomas, the Merthyr revolutionary, for he was only five-foot-two – but all the rest were strangers. Short, squat, powerfully built, the leader cried: '. . . As I said, and I say it again for the sake of late-comers – this is a special meeting, but not to discuss social benefits: we are here to talk about social ills. Not hunger, not the cost of Tommy Shop groceries, not the exploitation and oppression which we daily suffer. We are here to talk of the condition of our children –'

He looked about him, his eyes bright gleams behind the slitted mask.

'And I do not mean the filthy conditions that take our

children down the pits to work within a yard of the Devil; nor do I mean the accident rate that takes or shortens their lives, for the safety rules in coal-getting and iron-making are non-existent.'

His voice rose. 'You and I, my friends, contribute to another evil by tolerating it: do not we ourselves take babies down the pits because another head means another tram, for money to pay our debts? Do not we stand by and watch our sons and daughters thrashed for falling asleep at the tunnel doors? And turn away when an agent boasts that he defiles a woman a week? And Welsh women at that!

'Listen – the time is coming when it will stop. The time is near when we'll put an end to the misery we've spawned in these mountains. Perhaps not in my time, or yours. Perhaps it will be decades before we uproot the cancer we have nourished – the rule of England which despoils everything it touches, from France to the Americas. So, was it not likely that we, her immediate neighbours, would be the first to fall? – we who are sitting on fortunes of coal, iron and limestone, and cheap Welsh labour.'

He paused for breath; the men about him sat transfixed by his oratory. He was not one of us, this we knew: some said he was a barrister from Carmarthen, the town that later spawned the secret Rebecca, Hugh Williams; some said he was a Scot; others that he used a Scottish accent to confuse his listeners, for we knew that there were men among us who would sell their souls for a quart of ale.

Now the leader cried, and this time we had to strain to hear his words: 'There is a new dirt arrived. It has come about through the working of children with adults. In every barrel there is a rotten apple, and we Welsh are not without them. We of the old days know that where adults work naked in hot pits, vulgarity and fornication will ensue, for we have seen it. It has been witnessed and reported; in the case of some masters, it has been dealt with – the guilty discharged and sent over the mountains. But now the disease has spread, this time to the young.' He raised a fist. 'It needs but one perverted man to outrage a child: but one murderer to kill another before it makes complaint.

'Last year five children were found dead in shallow graves: God knows how many more lie in deeper ones. This year so far two have been murdered, and June is not yet out. Not a single murderer brought to book, remember, although the English military have helped us search – pay them credit.

'But the horror is not confined to killing – though a child beneath a tram will put an end to most complaints – the cruelty occurs in high places, too. And if there be spies among us, I hope my words reach those I accuse – and give offence.

'The *droit de seigneur* stalks this land; it has arrived as a gift from France where the people have flung off the yoke of the aristocracy. You don't know what it means? I'll tell you. It is the procurement of the daughters of the poor for the sexual perversions of the rich: it is the spending of the first night with the bride – the master instructing the peasant wife in the elemental rites with which to entertain her husband. You are sickened? I can feel your anger, yet for long you have known this and thanked God that your own wives and daughters were safe. So what have you done about it? *Nothing.*'

The leader's voice rose again. 'But we're going to do something now. Christ, we may be under the yoke of a foreign land and we can't do much about it, but from now on we are going to protect our women and kids . . .'

His voice stopped; the leader turned.

About fifty half-naked men, wearing cattle horns and skins, rose on an incline to the south.

Led by an immense man, they came in fours; this, Joe Probert, destined to lead the Union enforcers until his son took over – he who was later to die in the Chartist Rebellion. And while his small army of followers squatted on their hunkers at a distance, Probert walked arrogantly into our meeting. Towering above our leader, he spoke in a bass voice: 'Outrage and cruelty, is it? And what are you going to

248

do about it? – sit on your backsides and whine while we do your fighting?'

'Away back to Blackwood, Probert. We'll handle our own affairs.'

'With petitions for higher wages and "God bless the squire"?' Probert laughed, and rubbed his bearded chin. 'By Christ, you lot, I give you credit! You don't beg from a tiger, mun, you shoot the bloody thing.' Now he strolled among us. 'Benefit clubs, eh? A penny a week for the starving and a sixpenny coffin for burial. Jesus alive and reigning! A lot of ale-soaked landlords like Billy Handy holding the money and marches around Blaenafon with gazooters and a big bass drum?'

He raised a huge bare arm to his fellows. 'You hear it, lads?' and he seized our leader by his lapels. 'Property is theft, ye bloody idiot, and there's masters in this county stealing souls. Today we hauled three blacklegs up to the pit wheels – upside down to clear their heads. Yesterday we broke the legs of another and burned the furniture of two more.' And as our men rose to their feet and the Scotch Cattle men faced them, their bull cried:

'Give it a year or so and you'll change your bloody tune. Come winter, with the price of corn up and queueing at the soup kitchens, you'll be smuggling arms, like us. And while you're running the risk of the Usk treadmill and singing "God Save the King", they're crucifying us on army tables with bayonets. But our families will be eating while your lot starve, and when that happens, remember this – Force the Union, fight for it and die for it, and when the history of our time is told, it will be the Union, one for all and all for one, that will bring you the freedom you shout for. *Moc!*'

A brutal-looking youngster with a cudgel came out of the ruck of the Cattle, and Probert clapped him on the shoulder, crying, 'Get me away from here before I go loose among them. Christ Almighty, with these apologies for Welshmen it's hard to know a friend from an enemy.'

Now on our feet, in some measure out of respect for them –

they who were later called the heroes of the Unions – we watched them go back to their caves in the mountains.

So a new era of respect for labouring children broke out over the mountains: 'Suffer little children' was the new theme of the pulpits where the bearded proponents of the New Society trembled with the indignation of their faith: Bibles were hammered on every side, posters went up denouncing the exploitation of children; masters rubbed their chins in vexed concern, wondering if this meant a drop in profits.

Meanwhile, children used to squat in droves down North Street and High, rattling their begging tins. Hundreds were occupying the stinking cellars of Pontmorlais, in Merthyr, living as thieves and pickpockets and as dirty as rats in a sewer: scores formed into gangs that infested the lanes and coach roads.

In winter, when icy winds blew over the mountains, they huddled together round their little fires, and in the icy mornings many would be found stiff and blue with the cold. Then it was transport to the Poor House at Goitre, or a one-way journey on a pauper's gambo to the cemetery.

And so, a new enlightenment was called for by public concern, and granted, to some effect . . . until the concern wore off, as always. But it never burnt to a brighter flame when little Stella, aged five, the daughter of Dot Popkin, was found dead in Cwm Streams one Sunday morning.

This was the autumn when the women, sick of it, took a hand.

'You seen Dot Popkin's girl?'

'Young Stella? Down at Pwll-du under Tasker, isn't she?'

'She was,' said Tasker. 'Come whistle-up she was on Two Door, I saw her there meself.'

'Two Door or Six Door, mate,' said Ephraim Davies, come over from Clydach on the search, 'she ain't there now,' and he grabbed a passing lad and shook him. 'You say you saw her, when?'

'An hour after shift, Overman.'

'Six o'clock on Saturday,' I said, arriving late. 'Where?'

The little lad's nose was running and his face smudged with tears.

'Nobody's goin' to beat your brains out, flower,' said Ephraim. 'Where did you see her?'

'Going down Cwm Streams, sir.'

'Alone?'

'No, sir. I just said – she was with a fella.'

'What fella?' asked Belinda Handy, coming up. Her arms were bulging to the shoulders and she was carrying a pig knife: three other women were behind her, and if anybody was around Cwm Streams without a good reason, God help him, I thought.

'Too far away, missus, couldn't tell,' answered the boy.

Tomos Traherne had his feet under my table again when I got back home after searching with the others. He was into jam tarts which Elianor cooked special for me.

As I came in the front door, Elianor went out through the back, but I caught her outside the Drum and Monkey with about twenty other females, all armed to the teeth.

'Where do you think you're off to?' I asked her.

'Looking for young Stella. The women are in this now,' said she. She had my moleskin cap on her ears and one of my coats reaching down to her ankles.

'Now come on, Ellie, leave it to us!'

'That's what we've done to date, Hywel Mortymer,' cried Annie Oh-No, and she was carrying a bit of her mangle.

'Look where it's landed us,' added Mrs Rhys Jenkins, ugly.

About fifteen more were there: folks like Dot Popkin, Stella's mam, and Gran Fat Beti, plus Dulcie Bigg and her mate Duckie Droopy-Drawers, come down from Pwll-du, and you're not getting me alone with that lot, shouted Selwyn ap Pringle, they're worse than a pack of whirling dervishes.

'God help any man who's done that little darlin' harm,'

cried Mrs Mo O'Hara over from Clydach. 'We'll chop him into accidents.'

'I tell you again,' said Tomos severely, when I returned to Stack Square. 'You'd be safer in here eating jam tarts with me than getting mixed up with those female savages.'

I replied reflectively: 'Perhaps that's what we should do to men who harm children – hand them over to the women.'

'No murderer deserves such a fate,' said Tomos, picking up another jam tart.

Thirty

An eye of moonlight is fingering the gulches of Cwm Streams, the place where I made love to Rhia: it moves with infinite beauty above the rushing stream; threads a path of light through the massed boulders where Tomos Traherne discovered our secret, so many loves ago. It glows and lightens the caverns of the bank; etches into sharpness the hawthorn where the petals blow in spring: here, in summer, Stella, the child of Dot Popkin, played; on Easter Sundays she came down here with the Sunday School.

Come closer.

Step from stone to stone across the stream that glides its silken depth of fauna; here the trout play, iris-eyed in tail-flipping darts of silver; here wag the minnows the children catch in jam-jars; a water-beetle is walking on the shallows of the Blorenge bank; there the stream swims and eddies.

Dot Popkin once sat here on her haunches and saw her reflection in the shining water: bright-haired was Dot Popkin, her eyes cornflower-blue; no teeth in front on Dot Popkin, having no time for milk teeth; grown up before she was young.

Later, Stella Popkin, the daughter of Dot Popkin, she also played here, with the lads; wading in the stream up to her drawers, flinging up the water in gay laughter, netting up the tadpoles for the wishy-washy jam-jar journey home.

And a man, watching from the bushes, saw this, and made play in his mind of her: made play that one day he would lay her bare and possess her in shrieks. The thought brought heat to him so that his eyes bulged and his cheeks shone red: the nakedness of a child fulfilling a desire that wilted before the eyes of women.

Fear struck him then like a contracting muscle and he knew an animal panic, for he remembered the fury of the colliers. The child playing in the stream was seraphic, and had the tiny unfilled breasts of a woman not yet made; seeing this, there spawned in the man a new virility. Amid sweet-sour earth smells and flowering convolvulus he knelt, and his mind stripped her . . . he who had a child of this age at home.

And Stella Popkin, aged five, played on oblivious to danger; splashing with the lads of Pwll-du, who were as naked as her.

Later, they squatted on their hunkers in the swim of Cwm Streams, and shared out their minnows into jam-jars.

Now, Carla Mordecai, the adopted daughter of Joby Canal, had no blood relative to whom she could confide trouble. But it happened that she met Poll Plenty at Cyfarthfa Fair that June.

The sickness being upon her, she told Poll Plenty.

'You know the father?' asked Poll.

'I know him,' answered Carla. 'But dare not tell his name or Joby will go on the Blacklist.'

'Will you tell his name to my landlady?' asked Poll. 'She's an expert when it comes to unwanted babies. How long is it?'

'It is the second month,' said Carla.

'If you are lucky, she will take you for a ride on Enid donkey, who understands such things. She did this for me once, when I lived in the Grouse Inn at Abergwysen. Come–' and Poll put her arm round Carla Mordecai and took her to see Cushy Cuddlecome over at the Rock and Fountain.

The master having got her at the second time of asking . . .

✿

Susie Obligato, on the other hand, had no fear in her. Being in the same predicament as Carla Mordecai, but with as yet no sickness, she waited upon Justice Williams outside the door of the Three Salmons at Usk where he was roistering with ironmasters; this being an occasion when they met to celebrate their Union of Iron and Coalmasters, a privilege of unionism which they forbade to their workers.

'Get about your business,' said the coachman, and pulled Susie away from the horse's bridle.

'You get buggered,' said Susie Obligato, and climbed into the coach. As fast as the coachman came in one side, Susie came out of the other, and the game was still on when Justice Williams emerged with a trollop on each arm, both showing enough bosom for harlots in gin.

'What is happening here?' the judge demanded.

'I am with child,' said Susie.

'So am I,' cried one of the harpies.

'By him,' said Susie, pointing at the judge.

'And me,' said the second harpy. 'It's the circuit, see – hanging and bunking – you don't 'alf get around, don't you, darling?'

'Away with you,' bawled the coachman, and raised his whip.

'How much?' asked Justice Williams, for he was known in the county as a generous man; one who reimbursed his ladies, with entries in his paymaster's birth-book; one page for the single births, another for the twins.

'Go on, your worship, give her a bob,' cried the first harpy.

'Make it a guinea, your honour,' said the second.

'She be probably pullin' your leg, Justice,' cried the coachman, 'begging ye pardon, sir. Let me give her a leatherin', and then we'll be off.'

After the horsewhipping, Susie sat in the gutter outside the Three Salmons at Usk and watched the coach drive off to the hoarse commands of the coachman, the cracking of his whip and the shrieks of the harpies, and she fingered a weal on her face where the whip had struck her.

'Right,' said Susie.

When the Pwll-du lads ran off to see the barges down on the Monmouthshire canal, they went with cries: for Llanfoist Wharf was where the barges were loaded with iron for Newport; others for Brecon with coal, some with burnt lime ready for the fields of Hereford. And when they went, Stella Popkin was alone. Nor did the boys return soon, for they were marvelling at the new Incline being built down the middle of the Blorenge to counterbalance the trams upon her breast.

And so, in the dusk, with a storm wind-staining the sky, Stella wandered home, picking daisies for a flower-chain to give to her mam, Dot Popkin.

Since the lads ran off the man had been watching Stella; now he awaited her coming in the first faint glimmer of the moon.

Selwyn ap Pringle, the landlord of the Royal Oak, was swilling down his counter for opening time when he heard a scream. At the coroner's inquest on Stella's death, he said he thought it was the shrieking of a small thing in the jaws of a stoat.

'The analogy,' commented the coroner, 'is more or less correct. What is the name of this child again?'

'Stella, sir,' said Dot Popkin, weeping. 'Stella Popkin.'

'You bastard,' said Will Blaenafon.

That coroner, said Tomos Traherne, possessed the eyes of a man who conversed with stones.

The night was hoarding up moonlight in a cupboard of shadows when an ironmaster and his wife rode out in their coach and four for dinner at Dowlais House.

Strangely, since the area at this point was well inhabited, no workers were on the streets: the only living things about – at a time when the alleys and courts should have been crowded – were cats and dogs nosing at the garbage of the living and the cholera coffins of the dead.

'Where has everybody got to?' asked the ironmaster, peering out of the coach window; this he asked of his wife, who sat beside him in a dress of satin; she did not reply. Indeed, she had no intention of replying, but sat rigidly, with the air of a woman who is not to be tampered with. So the ironmaster rapped on the woodwork, and cried: 'Faster, coachman – faster! I don't like it, I tell you!'

'Neither does I,' said the coachman.

'Faster. *Faster!*'

The four horses started a gallop, then reared up as the driver hauled on the reins, for people were blocking the road.

'What the devil's happening?' shouted the ironmaster as the door beside him was flung open. And he saw the women of the town, all of whom had blackened faces.

The ironmaster shouted commands as the women seized him; appealed to his wife to intercede, but she did not: haughty in her prideful isolation, she lifted her chin as the women dragged her husband out. Nor did she look right or left as he was frog-marched, shrieking, down to the canal outside the cottage of Joby Mordecai. The women of Merthyr flung him into the lock where the slime was thickest, and he floundered about among garbage and dead cats while Joby and Carla came running out with distressed cries, and boat-hooks.

And Cushy Cuddlecome, who had come from Clydach to lead this deputation, stood before the open door of the coach and bowed to the wife of the ironmaster.

'Go in peace, lady,' said she.

Still the ironmaster's wife sat in removed aloofness, as a woman who was not there.

'We're deeply obliged to ye,' added Cushy.

Stella Popkin began to run when the man came out of the bushes.

As she ran, slipping and sliding in the mud of the stream, she heard, above her own screams, the thudding boots of her pursuer, whom she feared as one who earlier had beaten her. It was because she feared another beating that she ran, not because the man had exposed himself to her; he had done this many times, and it meant nothing.

The bodies of men, to Stella Popkin, aged five, were no more unusual than that of the man who washed himself in the tin bath before the kitchen fire; no different from the naked men with whom she worked seven days a week down Hopkins.

Now she tripped on a stone, and fell. Momentarily she lay panting, then clambered up and ran on, sobbing.

In her panic she turned away from the stream, along a rock face where a boulder reared high; reaching an entrance in the rock face, she ran within, to find herself in a quarry: trapped, she sank to her knees; shrieked as the bulk of the man filled the entrance, obliterating the moon. Momentarily, Stella beseeched him, her hands clasped, then fell back as he approached her; full length now, she lay paralysed with fear while he knelt before her, unbuckling his belt. Her hands outstretched in mute appeal, now clawed at the rock floor; entwined in her fingers were the remnants of the daisy chain.

`She screamed once more; the night was scalped into silence.

Mr Justice Williams, sandwiched between his harpies, caroused in his coach on the road to Pwll-du. And at a deserted place on the sloping road above the Cambrian public, pulled in his horses, there to renew the wine: while the women guzzled at empty bottles, he came down the hill to the inn, jingling silver.

A hand reached out, gripped his cravat, twisted it to shut off his breath, and drew him bodily into the shadows of a wayside barn. There, on his buckled knees, Justice Williams knew the strangulation of the hangman's rope: saw in the red blood that flashed before his brain the purpling cheeks of a score of men whom he had sentenced during His Majesty's pleasure: heard in his ears the thump of garrotting death, and in his throat the gurgle that precedes a blocking of blood to the heart. And, as his bulging eyes surveyed the quicklime of the autumn moon, his captor walked him, dying, around the hay-strewn floor.

Justice Williams, within the final paroxysm of his dancing brain, saw in the mirror of his soul a thousand faces; scullery maids, chamber maids, parlour maids and table maids; and the faces of orphans fashioning toys with withered fingers. He saw rooms where old men yearned and wept; the bars that pinned young men from youthful escapades; the chain gangs of Botany Bay, the sagging paps of hungry widows. And when the stars swung over the sky with his last breath, he saw the Plough cleaving into the wide legs of Pleiades, and he peddled his last snore as a beggar peddles his groans, and died with purpling veins as his neck snapped in the hands of his executioner.

The fish were lively, tail-flipping darts of phosphorescence near the arbour where Stella lay; in spring, and I have seen this myself, there is a shower of white hawthorn in this place.

Now the moon is in tears with soft-falling rain, and a small, white arm, outstretched, beckons from the leaves. Upon the arm move two ants in whiskered conversation, while Stella Popkin sleeps. The stream flows on to the mothering Usk.

'Would she have come this way, think you?' asked Meg Laundry, wet up to her waist in the dark.

'That's what the lad told Ephraim Davies, remember?'

'Ephraim who?'

'*Nefoedd!*' ejaculated Meg. 'Ephraim Clydach Vale – you were there – wake up girl!'

'Saw her with a man down Cwm Streams, said the boy.'

'And before that with Tasker at whistle-up, on Door Two down Hopkins.'

'Don't talk to me about Effyn Tasker,' complained Belinda Handy, wading in two feet of water. 'He's always flicking up the skirts.'

'That's a dreadful thing to say,' said Pru Knock-Twice.

'Oh aye?' said Sue Reece. 'She's right. I wouldn't trust that bugger farther than I could throw his auntie.'

Mamie Goldie and Billa Jam Tart were there, too; young women from the West, recently come to Blaenafon for the brickworks. Belinda Handy with Billy's pig-killer was in the lead on the search, with Duckie Droopy-Drawers and Modesty Doherty, the chapel organist, following behind, carrying hammers. Annie Oh-No and Elianor Mortymer came next, the latter now with two pokers, and Mrs Rhys Jenkins, whose first husband died against Napoleon, shouldered her old man's sword. There was Cushy Cuddlecome and Poll Plenty and Gran Fat Beti in the rear, all looking belligerent, and I don't give a lot for a child abductor if that lot catches him, said Tomos Traherne.

Midnight, and the search is still on, with gangs of men beating the heather up on the Coity, and strings of torches winding down the valleys. From Nantyglo down to the Puddler's on the road to Abergavenny they searched, and did not find her. But, when the first red streaks of dawn razored the sky, a figure moved in the back of Aaron Brute's Row, which was next door to the cottage where Will Tafarn, the wife-beater, lived. Here a man came out with a spade, and took the road up to the keeper's cottage . . . and over the Top and down the sheep track leading to Cwm Streams.

Reaching the spot where the body of Stella Popkin lay, he began to dig.

But the new girl, Mamie Goldie, had ears to hear brown grass growing, and she heard the chinking of the spade, and a little bit of the bass shovelling that comes when a man is working; she listened down by the Puddler's Arms, her finger up in a lull of the wind.

'*Heisht!*' said Mamie, her eyes switching about her.

The women, exhausted, making for home up the Fiddler's Elbow, crowded about her like anarchists over a bomb.

'*Listen!*' whispered Mamie.

'What is it?'

'Someone digging. Hush!'

'She's got good drums, mind,' said Billa Jam Tart. 'She can hear a nit in a wig-sack . . .'

'What you heard, girl?' asked Cushy.

'Someone digging. Come on!'

With renewed strength, soaked with the rain now sheeting down with the dawn, the women trudged over the fields and into the vale of Cwm Streams. And with every step they took the sounds of digging came closer.

The man had got the body of Stella Popkin in a shallow grave and was covering her in when he heard gasped breathing, and straightened on the spade.

As the women closed in a circle round him, he fled.

He fled this way, and his path was barred by women; another way, and he came face to face with Cushy Cuddle-come. Shouting with fear, he scrambled away to the quarry, the place where he had raped and strangled the child; there turned, an animal at bay: with the spade high as a weapon, he backed into the shadows.

'You're goin' nowhere, me son,' said Cushy.

'Go and get the men! I'll give up if you fetch the men!' cried Effyn Tasker.

'This is a job for a pig-killer,' said Gran Fat Beti. 'Call up Belinda Handy. Ye can eat everything but the whistle, ye know.'

Tasker gibbered; the contortions of his terror changed the malevolence of his countenance. He dropped the spade and turned his face to the sky and screamed.

'*Rush him,*' commanded Cushy, and the young ones dived at his legs and brought him down. And in the confusion of the struggle, ten against one, Dot Popkin arrived in the quarry with her dead girl in her arms. Weeping, she turned her face up to the rain.

'Where's Belinda? Where's Belinda Handy?' the cry went up.

'I'm here,' said she, and knelt by the pinned body of Effyn Tasker, the overman at Pwll-du. 'Give him to the men and you know what will happen,' said she. 'An eye for an eye, the Good Book says; pigs do hang from ceilings, Effyn Tasker, and so shall you.' And she raised the knife.

'Again, about dawn,' said Selwyn ap Pringle, 'more screams came up from Cwm Streams, but dear me, that sounded like a man.'

'It were,' said Duckie Droopy-Drawers. 'Fellas ain't all that keen about losing their fourpennies, ye know.'

'Deuteronomy Twenty-three,' said Mrs Dot Popkin.

See them next morning in Chapel; the weaker sex, done up in best hats, ribbons and bows; smiling benignly, one to the other, patting the heads of their adoring children, and butter wouldn't melt in their mouths.

'I said it once and I'll say it again,' said Selwyn ap Pringle. 'When they get their ganders up they're a pack of whirling dervishes.'

Now, it happened that on the night Justice Williams died near the Cambrian, I was putting wild flowers on the grave of Rhia at the Horeb. Down upon my knees I was arranging them, when a light shone from the chapel, and Tomos Traherne came.

'You are happy with Elianor, Hywel?' said Tomos, gigantic in his cassock of black.

'No man is happier.'

'She is the kind of wife I pray for. Yet still you come, year after year, to put flowers on the grave of another love?'

'Of course.'

Tomos looked at the moon. 'These are terrible times. Tonight a child has been lost and the search is on for her. Earlier, I was told, the body of Justice Williams of Sirhowy, had been found on the coach road up near the Cambrian.'

'Yes, and it is tragic,' said I.

262

Tomos paused, measuring his words. 'Did Rhia not once work for him – years back, when he was a magistrate in Sirhowy?'

'If she did I am unaware of it.'

'Strange. Eli Rodent was a Sirhowy man – it was he who mentioned it. You did not know this?'

'It is the first I've heard of it.'

Tomos put a big arm around my shoulder and led me to his cottage.

'Hywel,' said he, 'you delight me. For one terrible moment I'd suspected that you had been in some unaccountable way involved.'

'How dreadful!'

'For the future lies in what is to come, my son, not in the past. Soon a second child will be born to you, and I pray God it will be a son. Meanwhile, Ellie is alive, remember, and Rhia is dead. May she rest in peace from now on.'

My presence up on the coach road on the night of the murder of Justice Williams was coincidental, of course.

Similarly, when Effyn Tasker disappeared, some saying that he had sickened of Pwll-du, this could scarcely be laid at the doors of the women of Blaenafon.

Thirty-one

The days of my life were passing with startling haste. Many things had happened in the last three years in Blaenafon.

Mr Conky-Bum, kneeling at Beth Ponty's grave, put out a hand to Meg Laundry, who was kneeling on the other side, and love was born, her Albert having swum the River Jordan.

Mrs Ten Beynon had two more, making twelve.

Poll Plenty, having acquired the majority of the profits of the Rock and Fountain with the help of Bill Noakes and Dai Swipo, eased Cushy Cuddlecome out of the ownership, and sent her and Grancher down to the Vale of Neath.

Ada Cader and Gin Trimm appeared to marry.

Annie Oh-No had another baby which died; Selwyn ap Pringle sent his missus back to her mother and took in Mrs Dulcie Bigg on a platonic basis, and on the tenth day of July, with summer in full bloom, a *tylwyth têg* was seen sitting on the chimney of our cottage in Stack Square.

This was a fearful omen. All the time I lived in Blaenafon these Little People had pestered us.

'For God's sake, don't tell Elianor,' I said to Meg Laundry and Mrs Shanco Mathews, who had come in for the labour; and old Meg sniffed.

'Mind, it ain't fair. We build 'em their own little place over at Elgham Farm, and they won't live in it. You ever seen 'em, Shanco?'

'Not lest I've had a tot o' blue ruin.'

'Gran Fat Beti did. Lots o' times she's seen them – remember last year's harvest? – and the ice-time in the middle of December? Hundreds of them, she says – skating up on the Pwll-du pond, playing touch-me-last – their lips stained black through eatin' windberries. Windberries in the middle of December – it's enough to frighten folks to death.'

I said, 'Well, keep these tales to yourself. If Elianor gets hold of it she'll have a rag baby.'

Old wives' tales, perhaps, but you can't dispense with lore entirely.

Colliers living in Bunker's Row, for instance, always walked in pairs: Widower Wilkes, who lived alone in Brick House at the bottom of the town, had his washing-up and sweeping done for months after his wife passed on . . . two little pairs of hands handling brooms and cups and saucers; they even made him tea in the morning.

Yes, I know, you can shut your eyes to these things, but they happen. Two feet high they were, naked and sexless, with long golden hair and silver fingernails. Good and bad ones, just like people. And God help you if you got on the wrong side of them. Most frightening of all, they were baby-stealers. More than one mother in Blaenafon has awakened to find her baby gone and another in the cot like something jumped in from Africa.

I spent a sleepless night pacing around the kitchen with Annie Oh-No in tow; when things went wrong she always turned up.

'It's a bad labour, isn't it?'

Annie shrugged. 'Strangely enough, she had an easier time with Morfydd.' She looked at the mantel clock that seemed to be ticking away Elianor's life in the room upstairs. Her cries drifted down to me, and most of the other women in Stack Square were up as well, holding their stomachs and having it with her.

'It's a boy this time, that's the trouble,' said Annie.

And then a silence came, and the crying upstairs ceased and a new crying came down to us. I swung open the kitchen door.

'No, wait, that's bad luck. Have the baby brought to you!'

Old Meg Laundry came within minutes; in her arms she carried the baby, and stood there in the doorway, her eyes splashing tears.

'It's a girl, Hywel Mortymer,' said she, and laid the baby against me. Trembling, I took her.

The child's hair was white; her eyes held in their depths a strange pinkish light, her fingernails and toenails were the colour of silver; as if come from the egg of a dove and blackbird mating.

'A white child,' said Old Meg.

'Don't be daft,' whispered Annie Oh-No, taking the baby from me.

''Tis bad for you, Mr Mortymer,' said Mrs Shanco, arriving. 'Gran Fat Beti anna so wrong, you know, when she do see one o' the Little People sitting on a chimney-pot. Right from the start this house was cursed. Best you put that baby on the doorstep for an hour and hope for an exchange – they usually come back for their own.'

I wept, but Annie did not: she opened the door of the back and shouted, 'Out, you old crows! You'll have your labour shillings tomorrow, but right now – *out!*' and very fast went Old Meg and Shanco.

Then Annie put Edwina back into my arms, saying, 'She's yours. She's white, pure and lovely. Don't take on so, Hywel Mortymer,' and she kissed me.

Time passed; skinny old years for us, starving times for many. Everything was short as the French war drew to a close, and more wage cuts came all over the valleys.

On the night events came to a head for me, Morfydd, now nearly six, sat at the kitchen table and her great dark eyes, orbs in her high-boned face, drifted around the room: at the black marble clock from Solly Three-Balls, price sixpence; at two more china dogs from Merthyr, now Ellie's father had passed on; at the black-leaded grate I could have shaved in, for Ellie kept us spic and span, with a candlestick ready for bedtime, underclothes airing on the fireguard, and a red-toothed fire grinning at the window that faced the yard.

And beside Morfydd in her high-backed chair sat Edwina, coming up for three years old.

Time has taken us by the neck and flung us to the winds of heaven since then, but I can see them now with vivid clarity: a wife and mother, comely and well corseted: the two children of her womb – one a blackbird, the other a dove . . . white, *white* . . . People crossed the road in town when I took my little albino walking.

Bang bang on the back door, and Rhys Jenkins and Will Blaenafon stand there; thirty stones of beef between them, and stinking of Allsopps to peel the paint off pulpits.

'Evenin', Mrs Mortymer . . .' Big Rhys, apprehensive of a welcome, touches his hat: Will bows low, sweeping up the doorstep with his collier's cap, and Elianor looks daggers: not too impressed with mountain fighters was my Ellie, being twice to chapel come Sunday and God Bless the Prince of Wales.

'Uncle Rhys, Uncle Rhys!' Morfydd had no such inhibitions: scrambling down from the table, she threw herself into his arms and he lifted her high in a gale of laughter: Rhys knew about girls; Dathyl, his beloved and eldest, was leading him a dance with the lads.

'How's Mrs Jenkins?' asked Ellie, formal.

'Tidy, missus, thanks, tidy.'

I raised an eye at Will; he was shivering to have his bones out, his eyes on Edwina: her strange, light eyes seemed to pierce him to the soul – not much good with fairies around, was Will Blaenafon.

'I'll leave you men to it,' announced Elianor, and she lifted Edwina on to her hip and towed Morfydd away.

'What's happening?' I asked, when I heard her feet upstairs.

'They're blowing out the furnaces,' whispered Will, sweating cobs.

'Where?'

Rhys replied, 'It began in Tredegar and has spread to Dowlais; a riot is on there. They've attacked Dowlais House and the Guest militia fired on the mob – one of our lads killed, two wounded. I tell ye, there'll be a right old shandibang here when they get here.'

'How many of them?'

'About ten thousand.'

'God Almighty.'

With the abdication and exile of Napoleon, victory was ours, but with it came starvation: the demand for iron had fallen flat now. And, as usual, when the profits went down, the prices in the masters' Tommy Shops went up; men would now work for bread rather than face the winter with bare larders.

With the coming of the spring of 1815 the funds of most Friendly Societies were decimated. While the Faithful Friends Society, Newtown were still paying out sickness benefits of six shillings a week and half that for old-age members, most Friendlys in Blaenafon had been wound up. I mentioned this. Big Rhys said, 'Aye, but the Ebbw Vale United and the Beaufort Union are still on the go.'

Will Blaenafon added, 'That's because they're sponsored by the Harfords, the best masters in the mountains. But we'll come thin in Blaenafon under Hopkins and Hill.'

'Old man Hopkins isn't so bad,' I answered. 'The town will stand by its people.'

'You blow out Sam Hopkins's furnaces, Hywel, and he won't stand by anyone – and the men are coming.'

'From Tredegar? Christ, there'll be thousands!'

'If they march via Nanty, Blaina and Brynmawr it'll be the whole of the Eastern Valley. Are you with us or against us, Hywel?'

I got up from the table. 'You've got a bloody cheek!'

'Then come to the Lodge tonight, and say so.'

'I've got better things to do.'

'Like sitting at home, and watching which way the wind blows?'

I'd like to have trusted them, but dared not. For all their belligerence and talk of violence, the pair of them could be bought for pints. These were not betrayers, but they moved in the taverns of the Thick Ear Brigade, and their intelligence was limited. Also, I could not take the risk of openly supporting their Lodge.

Spies in their scores were coming over from London; the marching gangs and violence of fifteen years ago would soon be repeated; this time on a wider and more vicious scale. And the government in London was seeking any excuse to send in the army to break Welsh heads.

One day, I knew, an organized and country-wide revolution would come to these mountains; but the biggest mistake the Welsh could make would be to move too soon.

Big Rhys said, his hand on the door, 'If you're not with us, you're against us.'

'God Almighty, what do you want from me?'

'Lead us. Come down to the meeting of the Lodge at the Goose and Cuckoo tonight – the old Farmer's Arms. You're the only man in town with a pound of brains.'

'We need you, Hywel,' said Will.

'To organize a marching gang and join that Tredegar rabble? No, it's a mistake.'

'Bloody hell, mun,' Rhys said to Will. 'What are we doing here?'

I said, 'That's what you'll ask when they send in the dragoons.'

They slammed the door to bring down the plaster, and Elianor appeared at the other door as if on an actor's cue.

I turned to her: 'Congratulations, you're sharper than I took you for. Listening, eh?'

'Outside the door,' said she. 'When it comes to my kids I'm even sharper. We're in this, too, you know.' She came to me. 'Don't go when the marching gangs come, Hywel. For the sake of Morfydd and Edwina . . . please?'

Thunder was muttering and slamming on the rim of the night when I left them; some lights were still burning in the windows of Staffordshire Row.

Mrs Twelve Beynon was getting her lot into the tin bath by the fire, the babies first. Standing in line were the older ones, their arms up ready for 'skinning the rabbit'. Every time one came out of the suds, Mrs Twelve put in another kettle of water, and by the time her chap came out and she went in, she was sitting in six inches of coal dust. But she was a good mother, with everybody at the kitchen table for afters; eating bread and turning up the dripping bowl for the thick, brown gravy.

Further down the hill in Six Shepherds' Square, Mamie Goldie and Billa Jam Tart were getting into their nighties without pulling the curtains: the long and the short of it, these two, with Mamie sporting sailor's delights, but you could tap a kettle drum on Billa's ribs.

Late-shift kids were playing hoopla among the wash lines, their shrill cries following me down to Big House, where I heard the clatter of dragoons.

I stood for a little while watching and listening to the noises of my town.

What is there, I wonder, in the sagging bricks and mortar of a little town that clutches at the heart? Like the Waun Mary Gunter, the Hill Pits cottages near Garn-y-erw; Stable Row where the farriers and ostlers lived, Engine Row where lived the engineers, and lovely St Peter's, the first real school on the mountains.

Ty-Fry, the gamekeeper's cottage up on Keeper's; the Pwcas over on Milfraen Moor, Elgham Farm where the Little People lived. The Ironworks Company Shop beside the Drum and Monkey, where shawled women ate bread through the glass in strike time; Dr Steel's surgery where Blackie Garn, the sin-eater, had his leg off twice. Regal St Peter's Church, where my son was later married; he who was as yet a quickening in Elianor's womb.

Aye, what is there in a town that enmeshes the soul? One

thing was certain; this town was worth fighting for, dying for if needs be; no, not the sagging walls, but the people within those walls. I smiled at her roofs and chimneys outlined against the summer moon. I looked once more at Blaenafon. Up to my elbows in my trews, I gave her a wink.

'*Ie siŵr, fy nhrêf, y Cymro perffaith,*' I said, and walked swiftly down the hill and over the mountain to the Whistle Inn at Garn-y-erw. 'Yes indeed,' I said in English to the moon. 'My town, the perfect Welshman.'

But for how much longer would she stay that way, I wondered, when the Revolution came?

Safe houses make cowards of us all, I thought: empty bellies, and weeping wives, can change politics.

And I knew, standing there outside the Whistle Inn before going in for a pint, that the most stubborn resistance has its limits in the face of family ties: that you can rape the stomach of a working man's wife and he will still resist oppression . . . all the time he has comrades.

But, to date, although comrades abounded, they were not welded into a cohesive whole; we had no Union of Brothers in a cause. Even our Friendly Societies had been dissipated, their funds lost or stolen. The tap-room politicians might rant and rave, but speeches would achieve nothing in the face of English violence.

Although I hated the Scotch Cattle, I supported their ideal. Only through organized unionism could we make Wales free. This I knew, yet could not accept: loyalty to the master was a potent force in me.

Laying a curse on the soul of George III or whoever was sitting on the throne these days, I decided on a pint – the answer to, and cause of, most economic problems.

Thirty-two

The Whistle Inn, which later sported more colliers' lamps than any pub on the Top, was crammed to the doors with secrecy that night; the only people not stocking-masked were Peg Cuddle, the landlady, and Spinster Tooley, her barmaid.

Holding court was Peg, her fat arms outspread on the counter, and poor little Tooley, with two rag dolls shawled on her back, was rushing her tabs off serving the customers. Still short in the attic was she – she must have been, folks said, to work for Peg Cuddle.

It beat me where the lads got the money for Allsopps these days; someone at home went short, no doubt; more than one woman in town kept her purse down the leg of her drawers, the best hiding-place in the home. When things went thin in the iron towns, it was the women who took the hammering.

Pushing through the packed bodies, I slammed down a penny, and Peg Cuddle, layered with obesity, eyed me like a motivated corpse. Behind her I saw a big man carrying a cask; Will Blaenafon, without a doubt. Got his feet under Peg's table at last. Mountain fighters were doing sizeably well these days, I reflected. The only one with honourable intentions being Big Rhys Jenkins, with a charming daughter, and expectations of another three by the size of Mrs Rhys Jenkins. He was more scared of his missus, was Rhys, than any man on the mountains; she'd think nothing of doing him over with the copperstick.

I had just got my teeth into my pewter when a man I sensed I'd seen before pushed up beside me and tossed a guinea to Peg. Snatching it with a podgy hand, she prised it between her teeth – big money these times. The man, masked like the rest there, pointed at a cask of whisky and put two fingers up. Peg filled a small glass and put down the change. Opening a purse, the man dropped in the coins and snapped it shut, but not before I'd seen it.

Rhia's little embroidered purse; now old and worn, but *Rhia's*.

I'd have known that purse anywhere.

During the night meeting, held in a field outside the Whistle, I couldn't take my eyes off the man with the purse. Among hundred, he yet moved in the dim recesses of my memory: I'd seen him before and couldn't think where. One thing was certain – the purse had been in Rhia's possession on the night of her death.

His face was masked, but I knew I'd seen before the easy pace of his bulky strength.

The leader cried, 'The masters have reduced our wages because of the slump in trade. But did they increase them when their profits were up?' He raised a fist before us. 'The cost of imported wheat, by a Parliamentary Act this year, has fixed eighty shillings for a quarter; for barley thirty-three, and for oats twenty-two a quarter; this means hunger for our families and animals. Even to maintain some food level, cattle on the hoof are being imported from starving Ireland!'

He glared around him. 'The wet harvests and the ending of the war are producing destitution. Floods of Erin immigrants are growing, and they are undercutting our wages. And what's Blaenafon doing about it? Nothing! For the past three days there's been rioting in Tredegar: Company Shops there have been ransacked, Sirhowy tram-road's been attacked. The rioters last night marched on Merthyr – several were killed and wounded in an attack on Dowlais House, the home of the ironmaster. Furnaces have been blown out in Cyfarthfa, and pits damaged in the River of Fire. This afternoon three thousand marched on Nantyglo, and five thousand are on their way here now!'

Wild cheering broke out.

'Over ten thousand are in Crumlin, Abercarn and Newbridge! We shall not sit down and wait for starvation!'

'Here they come, here they come!' bawled another voice, and I saw a column of blazing torches streaming down the mountain.

Ten abreast, they were coming along the Brynmawr road; a great black stream of illuminated ants in the moonlight, and the thunder of their marching boots, the clamour of their songs was growing on the wind. But my mind was not upon the marchers; it was fixed upon the man with Rhia's purse, whom I'd seen in the inn. He had now moved away from the main body of the watchers: seeking the cover of nearby bushes, he ran through the men, but I followed, keeping my eyes on his darting figure.

Nearer, nearer came the marchers, and in the van, guiding them to Blaenafon, were Probert's half-naked Scotch Cattle armed with furnace ladles and cudgels.

Momentarily eluding me, the man I was following slipped away, and I sank into the cover of the road berm as the marching army came abreast; and saw him again, running swiftly over the moors towards the foot of the Coity. I followed, leaping ditches and scrambling through the marshy land that was the drain of the hills. Now he was etched against the flow of the moonlit sky; now a jet shadow floundering through boulders: relentlessly I followed, and came to a crest of a hill; gasping, I sank down behind it, and watched.

As if snatched away by an unseen hand, the man had disappeared.

Then I saw a faint glow; it vanished, then glowed again: crouching low, I approached it with care; and saw, within an outcrop of rock where the moonlight beamed, a man kneeling beside a little fire: this sparked and glowed, then died;

sparked and darkened again as he smothered it with his coat. He was signalling.

As if on this signal came hoof-beats.

Crouching out of sight, I listened and heard them clearly, drumming on the hair of the moors.

Nearer they came; the drum-roll of the hooves now a gallop that rose above the chanting song of the marching men on the road behind me. And I saw emerge from the darkness the ragged outline of a horse and rider; straight for the signal fire came that rider, the horse taking the boulders and crevices at speed; the rider professionally flattened along its mane in an unmistakable clanking of spur and sabre.

A dragoon. Reaching the fire, the rider reined hard and his horse reared, prancing: dismounting with easy skill, he approached the fire.

Straining my ears, I listened; inwardly cursing the chanting of the column on the road. The rider said: 'Blaenafon men, Musker?' I could see him clearly now – yes, a dragoon.

'Blaenafon, sir, and some Waunafon, too. Colliers, mainly, and they're after joining them.'

Musker. *Musker* . . . The name echoed in my head.

'How many, do you think?' asked the soldier.

The man replied: 'They say ten thousand, but I reckon nearer five, Captain Kent. But there's another few thousand knocking up Crumlin and Newbridge – the men are out all over the Top between here and Swansea.' And he pulled the stocking mask off his face.

Captain Kent. These two were down to Christian names – this was Kent Mortimer. And the man he addressed was Musker, one of the group who attacked our coach on the Llandovery road.

A hatred arose in me.

I swallowed down a sickness born of anger. It was all I could do to stop myself racing down upon them. Then, suddenly, Kent Mortimer remounted, and galloped away in the direction of Nantyglo.

I rose from my hiding place and went down to the fire.

Musker had entered a little alcove behind the now smoking fire. I drew close, and, hearing my step, he swung round. In the light of the moon I saw that unmistakable face; parched white, with a grapeshot burn on one side where the ball had taken it, ripping away the cheekbone in a purple scar. In surprise, he ejaculated something unintelligible, and his hand went to a knife in his belt; I leapt and kicked, and the knife went spinning away. Crying aloud with pain and rage, Musker came slowly out of the alcove. There, crouched, he faced me.

The wind moved between us in a bitter tang of burning peat.

'Mortymer, eh?'

Strangely, now that I had confronted him some of my anger seeped into a cold pity, and I never knew why.

'What you want?'

'The purse,' I said.

I was there beside him, yet I was not: my mind was up in Clydach Vale, and the whirlpool, evil, sucked and swirled; Rhia's little pink hat made narrowing circles in the eddies of the vortex.

'Purse? What purse?' His fists momentarily unclenched, and Musker stared at me in disbelief. 'Yours? A purse, you say?'

'The one you stole from my wife before you drowned her.'

My own statement banished my strange apathy: so much had happened since then. The long years since Rhia's death, my marriage and the birth of two daughters had stifled the searing loss. Had Musker dropped to his knees and begged my forgiveness then, I'd have had to fan my rage to keep it hot. Instead, cornered and guilty, he attacked me, driving me before him and bearing me down. Up first, all my compassion stripped away; and as he scrambled up and attacked again I caught him with a right-hand smash to the face that dropped him. Groaning, he rolled over, and I knelt, searching his pockets for the purse; found it, and held it before his drooping eyes.

'This purse. Now tell me where you got it!'

His words floated unintelligibly, his brain stunned by the blow.

Gripping him by the throat, I pulled him to a sitting position.

'Tell me, Musker. *Tell me!*'

Fetching the knife, I held it against his throat, and his eyes rolled at me. I whispered, 'You killed her, Musker, and now you'll die for it.'

His senses returning, he moaned. 'I didn't kill her. I took the purse off her after bringing her to Clydach, but I didn't kill her!'

'Then who did?' The knife pricked him, bringing blood; the sight of it moved in me a sudden lust to kill him and have done with it, but I kept seeing Rhia's face in the vortex.

'Kent Mortimer,' said Musker.

'When?'

'He threw her in. He told me to fetch her from the inn, and I did.'

'But why? *Why?*'

'Because she was carrying, and he thought she might breed a son.'

'He killed her because she was in child?' I stared down at him.

'In child by you, a Mortymer bastard, he said. No true Mortimer could live side by side with bastardy, he said. Wherever they met you, they would stamp you out – you, your son and his son.'

Sensing my perplexity and disbelief, Musker struck, and I went headlong: when I saw him next, he had the knife again: crouched now, he suddenly sprang, sweeping the weapon so that I had to arch my stomach to avoid the slash. As he went off-balance, I caught his leg and upended him; stamped upon his hand and freed the knife again. He rose and I was into him, hitting him with hooks to go through him; he fell, crashing against a boulder; like a crucified doll, he slipped slowly down to the grass, and lay still.

'Kent Mortimer swore it – you'll never wean a son,' whispered Musker; sighed, and lay still. I bent to him.

Blood was upon my hands.

The back of his head was crushed.

Thirty-three

Blaenafon was filled with bad-tempered men. The great mob of marchers, cramming into Lion Square, were like herrings in a barrel. To lose myself after the killing of Musker, I pushed my way through them.

Scotch Cattle were here – their disguises abandoned – and I saw Big Rhys and Will Blaenafon lifted up on to the shoulders of others, and Rhys cried: 'Lads, all over the Top they've reduced our wages. From the Eastern Valley down to Swansea the boys are on the march. We've ransacked the Company Shops and eaten our fill, put the owners under beds and the parsons under their pulpits. If we all stick together, we'll come out of this well.'

A roar went up that must have shaken the gentry down in Cardiff.

Big Rhys bawled: 'Now the masters are buying wheat and tossing it at us like feeding bloody chickens. Fothergill has a soup kitchen going in his mansion, Richard Crawshay is cornering corn at bargain prices. But who gave us free rations when we didn't go on strike, eh? Who gave us anything but kicks and the Blacklist before we blew out their furnaces?'

Wild cheering now, with men looting the Lion, later the headquarters of the Tories, and carrying out bread and cheese; casks of ale were hauled up on a brewer's dray, but Will Blaenafon sent it away. Big Rhys cried: 'Is it fair, I ask – is it fair?'

'No, no, no!' The men began to chant.

'Already you're committed, so go the whole hog. And if the town militia want to come with sabres, let them try it!'

and he flung up his arms in challenge. But almost immediately he was pulled down, and another, a man of good looks and slim build, was lifted up on to a chair. His cultured voice rang out, bringing the men to instant quiet.

'He is right, for all his ignorant bawling. Now is the time to make a stand, in the name of Samuel Hill and Aaron Williams who were hanged in our name fifteen years back – remember? England called it riot then and they'll call this rebellion now. So, what have you got to lose?

'The wealth of England, my friends, is not based on her maritime fleet, her great banking houses – not even on her iniquitous slave trade which still flourishes.' His fist was swinging an inch from their faces. 'It is built, Welshmen, on the labour of four hundred thousand little children, English mostly – for capitalists don't give a sod where they make their profits – who labour for the price of bread, like you. A ten-hour day, you cry? Impossible, say they – or English gentry starves. A share of those profits, you ask? Listen! You can insult their daughters and rape their wives, but touch a penny of their profits and they'll burn you alive. The torch and the bloodstained rack, that's how England made her laws!'

Bedlam now, with hats going up and sticks being waved, but suddenly, as if cut with a knife, the shouting and stamping stopped. I heard Big Rhys cry: 'Wait! Give way there – the Master comes!'

Men pulled off their hats; others, near the chair, made way as old Sam Hopkins, now a shadow of the man he was, reined in his pony and trap among us.

Taking his time, the old man rose upon the footboard: top-hatted, dapper with mutton-chop whiskers, he surveyed the thousands before him, for they were packed like sardines down High, Lion Street and Broad: and he cried, shrill: 'Men, if you have grievances, why not talk with me? Have I ever shut you out? You march in and take my town, all you who come from foreign parts. But you at home here, have I not always treated with you? Who built St Peter's, where you worship? Who opens soup kitchens when times are hard? Who buys up corn to minimize your distress and pays you a bonus in time of war?'

The old man, he who was so soon to die, pointed down the hill. 'Even now my sister, your beloved Sarah, is building you the first official school on these mountains – while other masters keep you ignorant and base.' His thin voice rose. 'What do you want of me? I give you wheat and you blow out my furnaces. I give you pay rises . . .'

'Come off it, old man, you never done that!'

'I'm about to restore your working wage . . . !'

'Ay, ay, that's better. Don't let's have lies, Master. We've had enough o' them from Crawshay, Monkhouse, Fothergill and Bacon, the slave owner!'

And it was here that Hopkins made his mistake, for he shouted: 'Did I not see a brewer's dray with ale just now? Come, lads, come! A pint apiece will make us sociable . . .'

A silence came, and in it Will Blaenafon shouted: 'Aye, that's the sum of it – keep 'em drugged! But not this time, Sam Hopkins. No man here is drinking on an empty stomach. You feed our kids proper, give us back our wages, then we'll talk.'

'Get away, old master!'

The mob began to rumble like bulls at empty mangers; somebody climbed up beside old Sam and took the pony's reins; the crowd opened, the trap went off.

Cheering now, with barrels of ale being rolled down the hill, and the guest speaker again climbed upon the chair.

It began to snow, I remember, in great wavering flakes that mantled the hats of the men; shawled women, rocking babies, stared up at the sullen sky. The wind howled about us, the snow swirled. After listening for a while, the memory of Musker's death gripped me with icy hands. After a little longer, cold to the bone, I pushed my way out of the crowd.

Desolate in the face of Musker's death, I made my way home.

281

Never will I forget that winter.

My town, up to its waist in snow, down to its elbows in its trews, began to starve.

Gone was the chattering firelight of the black-leaded grates; ice was on the boards of the houses, including Five Stack Square. Company clerks, skinny and dew-dropped, blew on their mittened fingers, adding up profits no longer there.

Only those who starve in winter know the pain that drags at the guts; the billious, heady swims that blind you into collisions; the retching that brings up nothing. Yet, compared with many, we were lucky; having a bit put away in the tea-caddie.

Morfydd, aged seven now, once plump and gay with wickedness (even at that age she had an eye for the lads), was now as skinny as a plasterer's lath: Edwina, four years younger, moved in Tomos's arms like a child approaching death.

We sat, all five of us, beside an empty grate and watched the moon sliding down an icy window, listening to the do-re-mi of the wind: Tomos, snuffling with a heavy cold, said in his beard: '"O God, thou art my God; early will I seek thee; my soul thirsteth for thee, my flesh longeth for thee in a dry and thirsty land, where no water is . . ."'

He closed the Book.

Tread softly in the snow outside Six Heol-ust-tewi; bend beside the cracked window; rub the frost from the glass; peep.

The room is empty. Old Soldier sleeps.

But he does not sleep in our town: he sleeps among the French dead in a field near Charleroi; amid the piled redcoats of the British grenadiers, he sleeps where the upturned muzzles of shattered cannon spear the June sky. With eyes wide open, Old Soldier sleeps, considering in the buzz of fly-blown flies the argument at Quatre Bras that brought him thus last June; with torn ligaments and blood-smeared hands gripping the live bones that jut from his mutilated thigh. La Haye Sainte, did you say? Blücher's bloody Prussians at Ligny, and Ney's French Imperial Guard attacking into the sun?

Old Soldier, outraged, bawled: 'Fookin' hell, mun, here I am back home on a minimum discharge, a Taff unwanted in England's soddin' war. Bloody marvellous, ain't it? You got any grub-tack out there, comrade?'

Now, hauled up on his broom crutch; in his tattered uniform of the Third Grenadiers, with buttons to shave in and boots snapping at the snow, he stands to attention does Old Soldier, as the Fifth Dragoons ride by.

Swaying on the doorstep, munching his iced whiskers, 1869681, drummer boy in His Majesty's Guard, now a Grenadier, he stands stiffly to attention. With one trew-leg creased to shave with, the other blotched red about the shattered bone, he stands; drawing himself up stiffly as the dragoons approach. And salutes in his doorway on the snow-clad street; deserted save for curtains moving down Heol-ust-tewi. Like a ramrod he stands, and the dragoon captain reins in. Old Soldier, chest out, stomach in, swaying to his hunger, trembles to the salute.

He who had watched the Little Corporal leave for Elba . . . salutes the English horse.

The dragoon captain drew his sabre, presented it to the front, and sheathed it.

At Charleroi they was bloody marvellous, said Old Soldier.

'Dismiss the guard,' said the dragoon officer, and his men grinned at one another.

'Dismiss!' bawled Old Soldier.

Later, when the town was darkened, Old Soldier took his sword, polished it with a bit of four-by-two and, with sword waving at the sky, went on guard outside Bunker's Hill. Clearly, he reasoned, since enemy troops were about, it was necessary to prevent further infiltration: these bloody frogs are everywhere, the sods.

It was here that Dai and Dodo, the twins, found him in the dawn; a snow-man with a face of icicles.

'Are you alive in there, Old Soldier?' called Dai, rubbing away the frost.

Stiff to attention stands Old Soldier.

'He's as dead as a bloody doornail,' said Dodo, hushed. 'Best have a word with Evans the Death.'

'You're having me on, you two,' said Evans the Death. 'We heard last week. Old Soldier was killed at Charleroi – are you both daft?'

'We tell you we saw him – we spoke to him, didn't we, Dai?'

'Go on, bugger off, I got real stiffs to bury.'

Sian Lewis, Pop Lewis's daughter who gave birth to a bastard son, is still not under her pa's protective roof: weasel-thin is old Pop, skinnier than his compassion, with social inter-course preferable to the other kind.

'My little lad's so ill, Dada,' begs Sian. 'Please let me come home.'

And Pop Lewis bawls, fists up: 'Adulteress, prostitute, strumpet, tart! Harlot, whore, trollop, trull! Wanton and fornicator, away from my door!'

Within the room, with her sack apron up to her face, Mrs Pop Lewis weeps. And Sian, now down upon her knees, begs before the door.

'Just a bit o' *cawl*, then; he do need nourish', Dada, that thin and pale he is,' and she holds her breast. 'I got no loaf nor the makings, I got no milk in me. Oh, Jesus, Dada, we got no fire an' my little lad's shiverin' cold.'

He picked up a bucket of water, did Pop Lewis, which was melted snow for drinking, flung it over her and slammed the door.

Now, it happened that Bad Boy Gold (twice to church come Sunday, and recently married to Susie) was living with Susie

Obligato in Six Sheepshead Row, sometimes known as the Black Ranks, on the road to Brynmawr.

'He be inclined to Jesus, see,' said Poll Plenty.

Susie Obligato, now a respectable spouse, was quite a different woman; with ambitions to learn her Bible from Genesis to Malachi and Matthew to Revelation.

'Then you get started, lovely girl,' said Bad Boy Gold, the son of Iris, 'you got a lot o' things to make up for, darlin'. Tell ye what, I'll get you a Bible for Christmas.'

Borrowing his mam's fob watch, he took it down to Solly Three-Balls, the cripple in Lion Street, but Solly Jew hadn't got a Bible. Then Bad Boy visited many preachers, but none had a Bible to give or sell, until he came to the door of St Peter's church, and entered. And there on a pew before him as he knelt to pray, was a Bible; small, ancient, torn, perhaps; it was as if the Lord had offered it as a gift.

'Thanks very much, God,' said Bad Boy Gold, and put it into his pocket.

But a sidesman, who was also praying, saw this, and told the Special Constables. Within a month Susie's husband was arraigned at the Assizes.

After being sentenced for the theft, Bad Boy was escorted back home, which was the custom of the time; there to have his fetters struck on by the local blacksmith.

Now came the ringing hammer while Susie, beseeching and wailing, performed her obligato.

The neighbours, hearing this, came in wonder. In twos and threes they came at first; shawled women with babies on their backs; men who were once muscled and strong, now drooped before the flying sparks. More people came, and more: from Stack and Shepherds' and Staffordshire Row they came. And the more Susie wept and cried, the greater was their anger. So the dragoons were called out in force, and one, the captain who had saluted Old Soldier, drew his sabre, crying, 'Is it blood you want, you women?'

'Blood's nothin',' shouted Mrs Shanco Mathews. 'We see it every month, ye ninny!'

'This kind,' cried the captain, slashed down with his sabre and cut a passing dog in half: the front half of the dog tried to run and went in circles; the back half went off in leaps and bounds, trailing entrails, and the captain cried, 'Now, away with the lot of you, d'you hear me?' and he plunged his stallion among the people and began to beat them with the flat of his weapon, until Big Rhys pulled him off the horse.

Now there was a to-do, with dragoons coming off their horses and colliers hitting hell out of blue chins, and the women bonking them with anything handy. The Temperance Benefit Club came out of the Garn, the Women's League Against Child Labour came rushing up from Stable Row with shovels and pitchforks. And then the Irish, hearing of a fight, came pell-mell from as far away as Pwll-du. But the dragoons had eaten and the Celts had not, and a lot went rope-haltered by the neck to the cellars at the top of King Street, where they later built the barracks.

And Bad Boy Gold went to transportation just the same; in ten-pound leg irons and manacled, with two balls and chain. Seven years in Botany Bay, Australia. Susie was still hanging on to the prison cart as it went past Pwll-Du. They reckoned they heard her obligato right over in Waunavon.

There's a light in the attic window of the Rock and Fountain inn, once the possession of the landlady, Miss Cushy Cuddlecome. But now the deeds were owned collectively by Bill Noakes, Dai Swipo – mountain fighters by profession – and the delectable Poll Plenty, who had plenty to spare when it came to Noakes and Swipo.

Come up the ladder outside the barn; steady at the top, hold on to the gutter, and look through the window. See the big four-poster, with Noakesy on one side, Swipo on the other and Poll in the middle. *Listen!*

''Avin' settled the hash of Cushy Cuddlecome by matters of financial genius,' says Poll, 'now comes the business o' settlin' up.'

'Yes, Miss Poll.' Dai Swipo and Noakesy reply in chorus.

'You two 'aving done up her minders, Ham Bone and Swillickin' Jock, you're legally entitled to a fourth share each.'

'A fourth share?' questions Swipo, and in his brain, numbed by the head punches of men six inches taller, he saw the puckered images of a thousand opponents, including the bastards who hit him when he was down.

'A fourth share?' whispers Noakesy; he heard in the night silence the roar of the crowds and in the dousing buckets tasted blood.

'A fourth share, I said,' answered Poll. 'For it is my intention, after five years as a publican, to retire to the Midlands. Therefore . . .' and she took shillings out of the till in her lap. 'One for you, Swipo, one for you, Noaksey, one for me, your darlin' Poll, and one for Coventry . . . one for you two, three for me, and four for Coventry . . .'

'Anything you says, my beauty,' says Swipo. 'You knows best.'

'Anything you like, my flower,' says Noakesy.

'After which, you apes, there's a small contingency to be set aside for repairs to the roof, payments to the brewers, renewal of the furnishings and decorating the establishment.'

'*Diawch!*' says Noakesy. 'What's a fookin' contingency?'

'There's back rental of a hundred and twenty pounds to be paid, an outstanding debt to a money-lender which has to be met, and –'

'Mark, Mary and Joseph,' exclaims Swipo. 'Will there be anythin' left?'

'Not a lot, but since you both agree to continue with your profession of the Noble Art, our financial difficulties will soon be resolved. I want you both to look upon me as your own personal accountant. Trust yourselves to my foresight, comrades, and you can't go wrong.'

'But what does me and Noakesy get out of it, my charmer?' asks Swipo, his brow furrowed, fighting for intelligence.

'Dear me, I thought you'd never ask,' says Poll Plenty, and

snuggles deeper into the feathers. 'Hang on to this, Swipo,' and she hands him the till.

'Trouble is, we don't know when we're well off, really speakin', does we?' says Bill Noakes. 'We're a bit slow catchin' on, like ain't we?'

'You can say that again, comrade,' says Dai Swipo, holding the till.

Tap tap on the back door.

'Who can that be at this time of night?' said Elianor, and paused at the door leading to the stairs.

'Annie Oh-No,' said I, opening the back. 'Come you in, Annie.'

This was not the ghost of the woman to whom I once made love, now so long ago that I can scarce remember, but the ghost of a woman who never was. And Elianor said, taking Annie's hands: 'Here, sit down, *cariad*, you look ill.'

'Never felt better, Mrs Mortymer. No fire?' She was shivering.

'A bit tomorrow, if we're lucky. Tomos is fetching some from up the patches. The Hopkins guards will let the clergy pass, though it isn't a lot. What can we do for you, Annie?'

'Come to see Hywel, really speaking, Mrs Mortymer. Private talkin', like, you understand?'

'Of course. Anyway, I was on my way to bed.'

The door closed and we were alone, Annie Oh-No and me.

I lit a candle and put it between us and her eyes gleamed like diamonds in the flickering light. Somewhere down in Staffordshire Row a child was crying; the night was black in a sky of beaming stars.

'I'm goin' from here, Hywel,' said Annie. 'But couldn't go, see, without saying goodbye to you.'

'Back to Newcastle, mun?'

Annie nodded. 'Back up home wi' the old folks. Ain't fair, is it, them not seeing the childer growing up. Besides . . .' and she smiled at me. 'There ain't a lot for me here, is there?'

'Not a lot for any of us, Annie,' I answered.

With words steamed dry in the silence of loyalty, we sat, but the shine of her eyes told of the unspoken bond still between us. I said, going to the mantel, 'We've got a bit saved, if you're short . . .'

'Not money, Hywel, not from you.'

Getting up, she went to the door and opened it. The snow swirled in, riming her brows, painting up her hair; she said: 'Only you I want, boy. Only you I ever wanted, see?'

I bowed my head. She whispered, 'I called one o' my lads Hywel, but he ain't yours, ye know – nothin' to reproach yourself about, you understand . . .'

I nodded.

'Always loved you, *cariad* . . .'

The wind hit between us. She added, 'Every time I had a man I pretended it was you . . . but don't you grieve nor fret for me after I am gone,' and she put out a hand to me, saying: 'Kiss me, Hywel. Just once more . . . ?'

Pulling herself out of my arms, she ran. I watched her going past the stack and up to Cae White.

When she got to her kitchen, Annie lit the fire with the last of the coal and firewood. Then she took scissors to her big red pincushion which had flying cherubims and seraphims embroidered on it by her aunt; it was stuffed with porridge oats; these Annie emptied into a saucepan and boiled them up with water.

This done, she went to the old Pwll-du medical shelf and took down the last of the laudanum, then awoke her three sons, saying: 'Come on, you lot, if we eat proper now it'll save time in the mornin' when the stagecoach comes, for we've got to make an early start.'

'Newcastle, here we come!' They leapt about her, pulling at her.

'Good old Mam,' cried Alfie, aged six as he took the plate. 'Marvellous porridge – she always do feed us, don't she? – they ain't eatin' up in the Forgeside Stinchcombs, ye know.'

'Should be,' said Robin, aged thirteen. 'They met Jesus up at the Keeper's a week last Sunday, and he gave 'em five shillings!'

'You believe that, mun? Jesus ain't got five shilling.'

'This could 'ave done wi' a bit of sugar, Mam, don't let it happen again,' said Hywel, the one in the middle.

Bending, Annie kissed him.

'Where's your porridge, Mam?' he asked her.

'I'm having it later,' replied Annie.

With unshed tears she watched them eating like starved tigers at the kill; elbowing, oohing and aahing, blowing at the steam, and Annie turned her head to the window, listening.

Somewhere at the bottom of the town a choir was singing Tans'er's 'Bangor', Hywel Mortymer's favourite hymn, in full harmony, and it was beautiful. She wondered if it was coming from the Bethany Baptist, or down from the clouds.

'Now then,' said Annie, 'have a spoonful or two of this,' and she fed them the laudanum. 'It'll help you to sleep on the stagecoach.'

'Where's yours, then?' asked Robin.

'Don't worry, I've got mine coming.'

Now, standing by the iced window, she watched the stars beaming over Pwll-du and remembered the man who had left her when she was thirteen. If she'd had any sense she'd have done this then, she thought, and said softly at the ceiling while the children slept: 'Oh God, how long will you forget me? All this was never worth my mother's pain. Am I of no consequence to you? And if you do not consider me, how can you forget my sons?'

Momentarily, Annie paused, looking through the window, for the Quakers' soup kitchen was rumbling down the hill: either side of it, packed deep, came the Irish: doors were coming open all down Staffordshire Row, light was shooting from windows; the night was filled with the sounds of people.

Annie, turning away from the scarecrow clamour, picked up the pillow from her place on the bed.

'Goodbye, my darling,' she said, and smothered Hywel.

He was strong, like his father, even in the drowse of laudanum.

Exhausted by the effort, Annie regained her feet.

Next she smothered Robin.

The youngest, Alfie, she smothered last.

After kissing them in death, Annie Oh-No then took down from the shelf the bottle of caustic soda, which had been left last year by the Inspector of Nuisances.

Icicles are hanging from the ceiling, frost is shining on our boards; stiff as canvas are the blankets you pull up round your chin, even the mice are shivering at being out all night. And Tomos, always in his element when things were at their worst, said his favourite prayer; all of us knelt in a half-circle in the bare kitchen while the black kettle sweated on the hob, longing for summer.

Very hard on the knees is this business of faith, especially on an empty stomach.

'"Why art thou cast down, O my soul?"' asked Tomos, though I could have told him, '"and why art thou disquieted within me? Hope thou in God; for I shall yet praise Him for the help of His countenance. In God we boast all the day long, and praise Thy name for ever. *Selah!*"'

'Amen,' we said, all except Morfydd.

I raised my eyes to her at that moment and saw the fury of her face, aged eight.

Earlier, on my way down North Street, I had seen her feeding Blackie Garn, who used to tram with Rhia and me up at Pwll-du in the old days.

Fate had taken Blackie, broken him on its rack and sent him out to starve.

Losing his right leg below the knee in a tram, he worked on Two Furnace, and fell asleep near the steam saw; this sprung a bolt, shifted, and the saw came out and cut the same leg off above the knee. Blackie took to a broom, and began to starve in earnest.

Folks fed him, until the Big Strike, then he went short; in desperation he had taken to sin-eating . . . attending funerals and consuming the sins of the dear departed: it was standard fare – a leg of chicken, a loaf and a bottle of Allsopps – and Blackie Garn thrived, especially during the cholera. But now folks said he was black with sin, and kept clear of him; even the Quakers began looking at him sideways, until Morfydd came on the scene.

Not a meal passed that she didn't put aside a bit for Blackie on her plate. Four times her age, she had adopted him. 'No, don't interfere with the child,' said Elianor.

Blackie Garn wouldn't be alive if it hadn't been for Morfydd.

And now, Tomos's prayer over, Morfydd raised her great dark eyes to him – he who would not feed Blackie Garn because of sin-eating, and said, her voice low: 'May the starving die because of their iniquities, Pastor, and may the Man of the Lower Palace possess them. Judges Nineteen, chapter nineteen; *read!*'

'Upon my soul,' said Tomos, getting up in grunts and wheezes. 'The babies are from their long clothes, are they? What is all that supposed to mean?'

Morfydd, white-faced, ran out of the room.

Thirty-four

After a lot of argument, fighting and threats, the men got up off their hunkers all over the Top and said they'd organize a French Revolution in Wales, so the masters relented. Proclamations were issued at every ironworks and colliery saying that wage rates existing before the strike would be restored, whatever the cost to common sense and bankruptcy.

'The fact is they can see their bloody heads coming off,' said Big Rhys.

'But was it worth it?' asked Will Blaenafon.

'It means we can starve in comfort,' replied Pa O'Hara, who had just arrived with Mo and her brood and was living at Upper Rank, the Garn. 'But I'm tellin' you this. I'd rather be scratchin' a beggar's arse in this foreign place than grazing the fields like a beast in County Mayo,' and he was right, said the other Irish, for they were flooding in anew.

And as fast as the Irish arrived, the Welsh emigrated – Philadelphia, Pittsburgh, Boston – this was the cry: get out of this hell to the Land of Promise.

Cardiff, Swansea and Saundersfoot were packed with three-master coffin ships steering for the Atlantic. But, while we had masters like Crawshay and Fothergill, the Freres and the Baileys, America had her own land sharks waiting to exploit the incoming misery, men such as Andrew Carnegie and Clay Frick who came later.

One set of pigs in exchange for another.

But, at least the strike was over after fourteen months, and a new summer, bright and warm, blew her forgiving winds over the mountains: the dear land shone.

Elianor's new summer dress (twopence a yard from Flannel Street, Abergavenny) went up two inches to show her ankles; this supported Tomos's theory that peace was breaking out; women's skirts going up or down according to political harmony or discord – they foretell the fate of the world, said he. I decided to keep an eye on him; Elianor's ankles were my prerogative.

Romance now being in the air, Mrs Jenkins presented Big Rhys with a son he called Moesen, one who gave Mrs Shanco, the midwife, a shiner at the moment of birth. Pru Knock-Twice left Cinder House for Swansea, where the men had more life in them, said she, and Butcher Harris, having opened a milk and bakery department, took on two young rams known as Iolo Milk and Dai Paternity for home delivery, in which they amply succeeded.

Mamie Goldie and Billa Jam Tart went into the laundry business with Old Meg and Nellie Washboard, renting Blind Olwen's old place in Staffordshire Row.

Eli Rodent, the Methodist lay preacher, disapproving of Poll Plenty living in sin, started having prayer meetings outside the Rock and Fountain with exhortations forbidding entry on pain of Everlasting Fire; which put the skids under Poll's plans to retire to Coventry. More, Cushy Cuddlecome, hearing of the lock-out, arrived from Neath to take up the tenancy of the Prince opposite Clydach Gorge: in frills and fancies came Cushy in a coach and pair, with Ham Bone driving, Grancher on Swillickin' Jock's knee, and the wheelchair tied on behind.

More beneficial things happened in the three years following the Big Strike.

Pop Lewis passed on to the Lower Palace, and Sian, his daughter, took her son to live with her widowed mam, and a blessing that, said Elianor.

Some old bones were found buried on the slopes of the Coity; though I didn't inquire further, it could have been Musker.

The ghost of Old Soldier, usually howling down Hush

Silence Street on nights of storm, was seen drinking at the bar of the Rifleman's Arms up on the Green; nobody would believe the customers, until it lifted a pint.

Susie Obligato stopped dreaming about Bad Boy Gold and went to raise a family with him in Australia, and one of her lads became a magistrate in Perth.

Dot Popkin and Jenny Loom took the tenancy of the Quarrymen's Arms over on the new Rassau tram-road, and there was more talk about Jesus giving away five shillings a time up on the Keeper's road.

But best of all was the news Elianor gave me, which set Tomos back a bit. Sitting alone in the firelight, with the old red grate airing belly bands, she suddenly put out her hand to me.

'I have conceived,' said she. 'And this time, my love, I will give you a son – we will call him Iestyn, after my father.'

She did. One cold day in February, in the year 1818, my son, Iestyn, was born.

A blessing, true, but it was the beginning of new trouble.

'You'll never wean a son, you'll never wean a son . . .'

The words of Kent Mortimer beat in my head.

Stack Square was communally heated. The engineers knew what they were about in our time. By positioning the main smoke chimney within the three sides of a square and building the workers' cottages around it, there wasn't a room in those cottages unheated, except in strike time.

But now the furnaces were alight again; work was in full swing getting out a new consignment for a great viaduct somewhere in the Pyrenees, and shifts were on round the clock.

A favourite rendezvous for the occupation troops was Stack Square and the warmth of the chimney: day and night the redcoats would lounge here; away from the sight of their officers they would play cards and fetch in ale from the Drum and Monkey. No business of ours what they got up to, so long as they left us alone, though a Welsh girl fraternizing with one could lose her hair.

I was due on shift that midnight, I remember.

I recall looking at the clock on the mantel – two hours to go. Morfydd and Edwina were upstairs, abed; Elianor was feeding Iestyn by the fire: with him wrapped in the Cyfarthfa blanket, she was crooning to him some plaintive song in Welsh. She said: 'You'll be going to Nantyglo tomorrow?'

'I'm due there in Bailey's office after dinner.'

'Do you know what he wants you for?'

'According to the new manager, he's after a foreman puddler.'

'Does he have to get one from Hopkins and Hill?'

'We aren't ten a penny, you know.'

'Will it mean a move?'

'Probably. They transfer us around like chaff, but, when it comes to payment for the job, you don't see the owners for dust.'

She looked sad and apprehensive. Iestyn was suckling noisily, his tiny red fists hammering her, his puckered rosebud of a mouth running with milk. Elianor said, 'I don't want to move to Nanty, *cariad.*'

I got up, stretching. 'Why not? Blaenafon, Clydach, Pwll-du or Nantyglo. They're all the same, as long as we're together.' Bending, I kissed her: Iestyn, as if shocked by the sudden intimacy, stopped feeding and stared at me with clear annoyance.

'Plainly, you belong to him,' I said, and we laughed together.

Washing out the back now, I could still see them through the open door of the kitchen: I'd built on a little lean-to we called a scullery. It had a copper and wash lines to hang the clothes. No house-proud woman could hang her clothes outside; while the stack might dry them quickly, the furnace grit would burn them into holes.

Stripped now, I could still see her.

Maturity was lending to my Elianor a defined and easy grace: her brow was high, her black hair parted in the middle and gathered into a bun at the nape of her neck: pride and purity contended for expression upon her smooth, untainted features; her lips were cupid bows, blood-red. No woman, in my judgement, is truly formed until she has borne children. Motherhood, I thought, bears the true fruit of womanhood. And while Ellie was not the only pleasure I had known . . . a bachelor has the jump of a dozen beds before the grasp of manhood's decency . . . of all the women I had known and loved, this was the flower.

Later, Elianor put Iestyn into his cot and, sitting on the other side of the grate, rocked it with a finger, watching me as women do, with the eye of her soul. Smoking my clay, I saw the lamp burn low; the fire-grate took over, painting up her face with flickering redness. No genius of Brueghel, I thought, could capture the transparent loveliness of the face before me; the simple, rustic portrayal of the peasant manse; the clergyman's daughter who was now the puddler's wife.

'I love you . . . !' I said.

From the compound where the soldiers were lounging came the rough English banter of men at play: the vulgarity, the filthy language in some strange way sealed the bond of our togetherness. Never have I felt so close to her. Disturbed, Iestyn snuffled in sleep; milk-fed, he snored softly, the only other sound of the little room beyond the simmering furnaces. Then, suddenly, Number Two went into blast, lighting the compound, the room, the world with a great plume of fire, and the night was shattered into a nothingness: it beat upon the ears with insistent thunder.

'And I love you, *cariad*.'

I only saw her lips move, I did not hear her words.

Only Elianor's calm beauty diluted the suspended evil of that night. It was as if the suffering of the long months of the strike was a cancer on the body of the town, now threatening to burst: in retrospect I have never been able to explain the dread built up within me. Certainly my apprehension was not shared by Dai and Dodo Jones when they joined me on shift at One Furnace – they who were about to die.

Big Rhys was stoking One Furnace: Will Blaenafon was balling in the Forge House; Owen and Griff Howells, another pair of twins, were top-filling from the trams coming in from Pwll-du, and Ephraim Davies had come over from Clydach for a special project ordered by the Freres.

'It's the biggest base-plate I've ever known,' said Ephraim. 'How ye doing, Hywel?'

'Worse now you've arrived,' I said, and Big Rhys, already stripped for stoking, cried:

'What's up, Ephraim, can't you handle it in bloody old Clydach?'

Ephraim, old and grizzled, said, 'Your profits are down, mun, so me gaffer's givin' Blaenafon a lift.'

'You're down on good puddlers, boyo, tell the truth!' Will Blaenafon now, pulling the old chap's leg, but Ephraim had been good to me; I wouldn't let it go too far.

'What's it for, Gaffer?'

'A tramway turntable.' The old boy squinted at the moon. 'We pour better iron than you at Clydach, but we haven't got the quantity. Fifteen feet diameter.'

'Thickness?'

'Two inches,' answered Ephraim.

The summer wind beat about us; smells of heather perfumed the sulphuric fumes. I ejaculated, 'Fifteen feet? And two inches thick? She'll crack when she cools.'

'That's what I keep on bloody tellin' 'em,' growled Ephraim, 'but we've got clever-dick Freres over in the Vale, and they don't listen.'

'Pour it in quarters – we might get away with it.'

'Cast in one piece, boyo – start forming the mould.'

'They got rainbows in their heads over at bloody Clydach,' said Big Rhys.

'You heard what Gaffer said,' I called to Dai and Dodo, the formers. 'Form the mould.'

'We anna got forms that radius, Puddler,' cried Dai.

'Then cut some more.'

The dawn was coming up before we were ready to pour

that shift; Dai and Dodo piled in the sand, spreading it out to fifteen feet diameter. Old Ephraim cried: 'Flat, mind, flat, I want no warts. There's many a silk dress hides a dirty shift – do it proper.'

I gave Rhys a wink as he came up with his rodder.

'Tap her,' I said, and he stooped, narrowing his eyes to the molten glare, and knocked out the stone bung.

Until now the compound had been a cascade of noise; a cannonade of singing furnaces, thudding drop-hammers (for the Garndyrus mill was not yet working) and the buzz of steam saws cutting scrap iron into furnace lengths. The bawled commands, the cracking whips and shrieks of horses always grew into a festivity of noise . . . until this moment, when the iron was tapped. Then, in an instant, came silence, as if the Devil had put a smoking finger to his lips.

The people of the compound gathered round to see the furnace tapped; to see the phenomenon of the liquid iron, boiled into shape to last a thousand years, take its first wet breath of the mountain.

It was like watching a birth.

See the red blaze turn white at the flaring plug; the quick billow of sooted smoke, a black shroud over the fantastic heat.

We stood back, shielding our eyes from the incandescent glare as the molten iron hissed at the plug, sending waves of refracted light batting on the clouds: down, down, belching, sighing. Rhys, his body glistening sweat, guides it gently across the mould: down, down; the watchers back away in fear of a splash; now comes Will, creaming off the radiant mass; bubbling, moaning, it is a million little fiery darts now, almost translucent: now covered with lambent flames as its temper expires; searching with its hissing fingers the furthest reaches of the mould. Glittering now, it illumines all Blaenafon in one last despairing act to stay on fire.

The mould is filled. The furnace farts: then sits in sombre black with empty bowels.

Before us lay the great circle of cooling iron; changing to

purple in the glow of the naphtha flares. The people shifted nervously, waiting for the crack.

'Right, you, back to work!' I shouted, and they moved like sheep, staring over their shoulders.

'Come on, come on!'

'Any minute now,' whispered Will Blaenafon, 'it won't half blow up.'

'Keep clear,' commanded Ephraim, and at that moment the nearest naphtha flare went out, bringing us to darkness.

The lamp went out and someone behind me jostled; this sent me sprawling, and I arched my body as I was pushed upwards. Twisting in mid-air, I fell within a foot of the mould and felt on my face and hands the instant blaze of heat. Even as I fell on the edge, face down, I felt another stumble over me: saw as black clumps a pair of boots sail over the moon, and the body of a man go skidding on all fours over the surface of the purpling mould. Next moment Big Rhys and Ephraim hauled me clear.

On hands and knees I stared across the mould; saw the man kneeling in the middle of the steaming plate; saw his hands clasped as if in prayer; heard behind me a stamping and another collision of massed bodies. Then Dodo shrieked: 'Dai! *Dai!*' And dashed forward on to the tramway turntable and clasped his twin, trying to heave him off.

But the hot iron had got Dai in its arms, and he was stuck by the knees as bacon is stuck to a frying-pan. So they knelt there embraced like lovers; Dodo trying to tear away his brother; and, heaving, they fell, and their clothes caught alight and their bodies caught fire. In silhouette they knelt, and the flames leapt around them. They made no sound; not a sound they made in that burning alive and we, the watchers, could only stare. Then came a scream; a single, hollow cry and the fire, sparkling and resplendent in radiant colours of red and gold, consumed them in spitting, noisy flares.

I covered my face with my blistered hands.

'Where's that soldier?'

'What soldier?'

'The one standing here when the lamps went out.'

'Don't be daft, mun, look – they're over by the Stack.'

'One weren't – I tell ye, one was here.'

'Can't be, Rhys. They're not allowed in the compound.'

'He was, I tell you. Don't call me a liar, Will, I bloody saw him.'

I was cursing the pain of my blistered hands.

'Best get over to your missus with them, Hywel,' said Ephraim. 'God alive, I'll never forget those two lads dying.'

We got what was left of Dai and Dodo and laid them side by side.

Strangely, their faces were unburnt; they lay together, eyes open at the sky.

'Someone pushed at the back – did nobody see who?'

Nobody. The people looked from one to the other.

'Couldn't have been one of the soldiers,' said Elianor later. 'They were here all the time. I saw them – I tell you I saw them!'

But someone pushed; somebody who wanted me dead on the turntable.

Guto Snapkin first; now Dai and Dodo.

All right, I thought, they can have their tries at me. But if anyone touches my son, I'll do the burning alive.

Book III

1823–1826

Thirty-five

In our town the masters allowed us an annual holiday – one day a year. This took a variety of forms. Sometimes we would walk to Nantyglo and be escorted around the rhodie bushes of *Ty-Mawr*, Crawshay Bailey's new mansion; on this occasion we had a ride along the tram-road and a picnic in the mountains.

It happened that I had been associated with *Ty-Mawr*.

This new house, the pride of the Baileys' heart, was fronted by a colonnade of six cast-iron pillars. Lacking an ironworker of sufficient ability, the Baileys applied to Sam Hopkins for a gentleman puddler, and I was sent over there on loan. Thereafter, my name was entered on the Nantyglo books; this entailed me journeying there once a month to sign on; Bailey, the all-powerful, having decided that I would be paid by him in case he ever needed me.

It was an unenviable situation, to be held in esteem by the Pig of Nantyglo.

The Harvest Festival coincided with the annual Illuminations. We had no street lamps; so on such occasions the streets were lit up, providing the workers produced their own oil and candles. We paid for these in any case – stopped out of our wages at inflated prices. With a seven-day working week, the celebrations were times of great excitement.

It was up early for the Harvest Festival; trousers were hauled out from under mattresses, boots and shoes polished overnight; the men shaving extra close and the women ironing bonnet-streamers in a panic of activity, and for

God's sake keep that dress off the ground at threepence a yard.

Stack Square was a bustle, with neighbours coming in to show off the latest, and Mrs Twm-y-Beddau from next door arrived in a fruit-assembly hat and a crocheted pattern over the bosom, very daring, and she wants to watch that lot if she ties a boot-lace, said Morfydd.

A word about my eldest daughter while on the subject.

Beautiful enough to bring a sigh to Satan, this one, going in where she should and out where she shouldn't, and the lads were hanging on the garden wall like string-beans.

Tall and straight was she; at thirteen years a woman; the men were walking into lamp-posts. All in black she was today, with long hair in waves down her back and a waist pulled in to the size of a dog-collar.

'Another year or so and we're in trouble,' I mentioned to Elianor.

'Don't worry, we're in trouble already,' said she.

Edwina, my youngest daughter, was also an enigma, but in a different way.

Elianor dressed her in light colours, making a feature of her pale, sad beauty. At ten years old, she was tiny, her sight impaired within her eyes of pinkish depth. Calm in the face of Morfydd's belligerence, she also turned every head in the street, but for a different reason.

My son, Iestyn, I have little to say about; a man must be circumspect when speaking of his son.

Welsh dark was he, and broad, with a dent in his nose through fighting at the age of five. His black hair, contriving to wave, he straightened with water: rare with words, he was yet solicitous of the gabble of sisters; tempestuous in play, he was quick to anger.

'Am I tidy?'

In he came now, his starched chapel collar cutting his throat; bare knees, polished boots, his hair parted in the middle like Dan Mendoza, his fighting idol. God help them when he started school.

'You'll do,' said Morfydd, and looked behind his ears.

Elianor now, the next to arrive in the kitchen; the starched matron in black bombazine, with high-buttoned boots, the dress to her ankles and a cameo brooch of the Duke of Devonshire on her chest, and how he got there I never did know. Tall Welsh hat, a Welsh shawl over her shoulders, black mittens.

'Are we ready?'

'As we'll ever be,' said I.

'No chapel tonight, Dada?' asked Morfydd, hopefully.

'Not if I can help it.'

'That's a fine example to give to the children, I must say, and you a deacon!' said Ellie. And she took us up to the Horeb at Pwll-du.

This needs explaining.

Religion, at this time, was in bad repute among free-thinkers. But Elianor, her childhood ingrained by pews and sermons, opposed me on the subject.

While I am all for God in his place, I have little time for his self-appointed disciples; men such as Tomos Traherne who were powerful on their knees, but weak when it came to resisting social wrongs. With a few exceptions, our ministers of religion were in the pay of the masters; in supporting their employers' quest for law and order they were in conflict with the laws of God; their preached compassion didn't extend to justice.

Many ministers were landowners and magistrates. Take a trout from private water and it would be a vicar, perhaps, who would send you to the whipping-frame. Man-traps on the big estates, some of which would sever a leg for the price of a partridge egg, were often laid by the clergy. Not a year before, the vestry of Dolgelley publicly stated that no parish relief should be given to the starving if a 'clock or any other furniture be available for impounding'.

The harshness of the Poor Law was exploited by both Church and Chapel; all over the country these carried out

307

Dutch auctions of the parish poor – hiring them out to those who would keep them for the least amount. It was the clerics who insisted that all relieved persons should wear a pauper's badge. Six years back the poet Ap Vychan had indignantly protested when the vestry removed the mattress from beneath his dying father as a chattel of value to be sold in public.

And so, contrary to later popular belief, religion was at a low ebb in my time; the younger generation being particularly incensed by the unholy liaison between Church and State. And while the chapels were full at a time of emergency – God became very popular when the cholera came to town – the young lost no chance to drive home the lesson – local disapproval of organized religion.

Up to the night of the Illuminations I didn't realize that I had a dissident in my own house. I did now. It was a course of domestic re-education.

Daughters!

We were sitting as a family behind the deacons in the Horeb, all except Morfydd who had met a friend outside, and was delayed. Up in the Big Seat sat Tomos Traherne, immense in size and authority. A lot of shuffling of boots now and a clearing of throats as the congregation rose to sing the harvest hymn.

'Where's that girl got to?' whispered Elianor.

'Don't ask me,' I whispered back.

'I'll warm her backside when I get her home.'

'O, bounteous grace bestowed on all' it was then, with Modesty Doherty rolling her little fat behind on the harmonium seat, and folks started coming out of their pews with their fruits of the earth – a pair of swedes from Owen and Griff Howells, the Cockroad twins; a bag of tomatoes from Mr Afel Hughes, and I gave a thought to his wife, burnt to the lungs and now lying in straw. Big Rhys came with an egg, and Will Blaenafon with a bottle of parsnip wine donated by Peg Cuddle, and then we were out, Ellie leading, laying our gifts on the altar steps to Tomos's smiling approval.

Now the congregation was letting it rip in a marvellous harmony of soprano, contralto, tenor and bass: 'Such wonderful gifts of earth be given, to open all the doors of Heaven . . .' and right in the middle of it the chapel door opens and in comes Morfydd, leading skinny Blackie Garn the sin-eater in his rags and tatters; with one foot bare and his broom-crutch thumping the mosaic came Blackie, and Morfydd beside him like Beauty and the Beast.

The harmonium stopped; the singing died to a discord. Big hats went round in a creak of stays, and Ellie's eyes, like saucers, threatened to drop from her face.

'Oh God, *no!*' said she.

'You got your banana, Mr Blackie?' asked Morfydd, and she turned to the congregation and gave it a long, cold stare.

The terror was in Blackie's rolling bedsheet eyes when he saw the fury of Tomos's face.

'What is happening here?' Gigantic in anger, the preacher rose in the Big Seat, staring down at them, and Morfydd said:

'Harvest Festival, Mr Traherne. Blackie Garn's brought a banana.'

Consternation at this; men nudging each other, women whispering behind their hands, children giggling, and Tomos roared: 'You dare to bring this black creature into my house?'

'Not your house, Pastor,' replied Morfydd. 'You said it was God's.'

'But I am its keeper!' His voice rose to a shriek. 'This man's soul is decomposed by the eating of sin. As with Miriam, whose body was leprous, Numbers Twelve, ten, so his body is filthy and in rags. I cast him out of this tabernacle in the name of God. Out, black man! *Out!*' And he came with a giant's tread down the altar steps, but a hand went across the front of me and grasped his arm.

'No, Tomos, no,' said Elianor.

It stilled, and turned him. Momentarily, he stared at her.

'You, Elianor? You know of this?'

'I did not know, but I agree with it.'

The incredulity was upon his face: I could have told him. He'd come across one fighting-cock and now he'd landed its mother.

Ellie's voice rang out: 'You quote us Numbers – but what if I quote you Hebrews Five? – "Who can have compassion on the ignorant, and on them that are out of the way; for that he himself also is compassed with infirmity . . ."'

Perplexed, Tomos paused, then seized Blackie Garn, and bellowed: 'Deacons, elders! Remove this person. Remove him!'

Elianor shouted over the hubbub, 'Leprous, like Miriam, is he? Because he starves?' and she came out into the aisle. 'I tell you this. I would eat the garbage of pigs and feed it to my children before I'd let them starve. What kind of people are you? If the men won't stop this, where are the women of this chapel?'

'*Silence!*' roared Tomos, and his body was trembling to his anger. 'I command you, woman, stay silent!'

'Aye, silence, is it?' shouted a voice from the back, and out into the aisle came old Ephraim Davies, the Clydach overman. Approaching on his stick, he cried: 'Perhaps you'll dry her up, mun, but ye won't dry me. I say put this to God,' and he turned and faced the chattering people. 'Black or white, halt or whole, this beggar is a brother, and he brings his tribute. I shall not stand by and see him flung out. *Listen!* Sit tight all those who agree with Mr Traherne; away out of here all who call this beggar equal – I know who's side I'm on – I'm with Jesus,' and he lifted his stick high. 'Clear the way, lads, I'm off.'

One by one at first, then in couples, lastly in families, the people, tight-lipped, filed out of the Horeb while Tomos's voice bellowed his threats and deprecations.

Outside now, Ellie got hold of Morfydd and shook her to rattle her bones, whispering, 'Bad girl! I'll give you Blackie Garn and bananas. I'll warm your breeches when I get you

home!' Then she turned on me. 'Vandals and disbelievers –
it's your fault for encouraging them.'

'Mine? I haven't said a word!'

'Then it's high time you did. Where's Mr Blackie?'

'Here, Mam,' piped Iestyn, hauling him up.

'Back home now for a bite of supper, love – all six of us,'
said Ellie.

On our way down from Pwll-du I dropped into the stables
opposite Rifle Green, to see how Chancer, my old cob, was
getting on. He was earning his keep these days on the trams,
plus sixpence a week to the ostlers for stabling and oats.
Chancer whinnied with delight when I stroked his nose.

'Later, son,' I said.

Leaning on the toll-gate by Turnpike was Big Rhys.

'Ay, ay,' I said, and went to pass, for these days there was a
coldness between us that no words could bridge.

'Your girl did all right tonight,' said Rhys.

'The young ones are coming sick of the clergy,' I replied.

'Like I'm coming sick of you,' said he. 'One thing's sure,
she's got more spunk than the head of the family.'

I went to leave, but he barred the way, his hand on the
bar. 'Time was we called you Gent, remember? Time was,
Mortymer, we looked on you for a lead. What happened to
make you an employer's man?'

'My business, Rhys – what's it to you.'

He screwed up a fist and put it against his face. 'Just this.
There's good men risking their lives tonight over in
Nanty . . .'

'More fool them.'

'Good Christ, listen to that!' he breathed hard at the
moon. 'I told you once and I'll tell you again, Mortymer.
You're either with us or against us. Do ye realize there's
children starving to death for a mouthful of bread?'

I weighed him. Soon, I knew, it would be him or me, and I
knew the sadness of lost friendship. At the rate Rhys and

Will were going they'd end in transportation. I said: 'Grain-raiding, eh?'

'That's right. Are you with us?'

'I am not,' and I pushed him away from the toll-bar. 'Time was I might have been, but not now, for I've watched you and Will. You haven't time to wash off the soot before you're into the bloody ale; an hour later you haven't a leg under you. Do you call that rebellion?'

We faced each other like leashed terriers, hands clenched, and just then Will Blaenafon came up, and said: 'Don't waste your time, Rhys. Let him get back under Ellie's skirts, he's useless these days.'

One day, I knew, I'd have to try them for size.

Thirty-six

While we weren't starving to death in our town these days, nothing was plentiful, and famine stalked the valleys; especially down in West Wales, where its spectre pointed at us like a ghost with an empty sleeve.

But with the furnaces alight again, the iron industry, hastened by the advent of commercial coal, painted up our larders with food.

For years our band instruments had been in store in Big House: now they were brought out, dusted, polished and handed over to the Faithful Friends Benefit. And on the night of the Illuminations our band was at its best.

What is it, I wonder, that stirs the blood when a brass band comes marching up a hill: the very toes vibrate to the thump, thump, thumping. Everybody in town turned out when our band went by, with urchins doing cartwheels alongside Billy Handy, walking bandy with the big bass drum.

Here they come now, the Howell twins working the come-to-me-go-from-mes, and Mr Afel Hughes farting on the horn. Full to the ears, too, plaiting their knees, and behind them comes a crowd like the hags of the French Revolution, with Duckie Droopy-Drawers dancing a fandango and Billa Jam Tart and Mamie Goldie flourishing their petticoats.

On they came, nearer, nearer; all down North Street doors were coming open and windows going up to let out the light. From Dr Steel's residence down to Big House the road was a river of blazing light, with lamps cocked up on sticks outside Staffordshire Row. And as the town band came up the hill, the Irish came down it; to the shrill fiddles, the outside of a horse scraping the inside of a cat, Irishmen were arming round their ragged wives and tattered children were doing the Derry reels. Never will I forget the noise of the Illuminations.

Forming up on chairs in Shepherds' Square, the band got going in earnest on 'Llewelyn the Conqueror'. With Welsh chins well down into their collars in case of Irish confetti, cheeks livid, they boomed and blasted, and soon the square was alive with whirling skirts; scarves rising and falling, the lads spinning their girls in a medley of colour: Spaniards came from Ton-mawr; the men in national dress, tight waistcoats and flat hats; the girls in bright skirts and black mantillas. Of fierce Cordoba sunlight, these now took centre stage while the Welsh encircled them, clapping the time.

Everybody who was anybody was in Shepherds' Square that night, including Iolo Milk and Dai Paternity, just arrived from Brynmawr, and I saw one of them wink at Morfydd. Romeo Antic had got Carla Mordecai in a clinch in the doorway of Number Three, I noticed; Spinster Tooley and Peg Cuddle were dancing together on the cobbles; and no sign of Big Rhys and Will Blaenafon, I noticed – and Poll Plenty arrived with Noakes and Swipo, all three in rags. Very sad it was to see them come down in the world, with Noakes holding the begging-tin and Swipo accompanying Poll on a mouth organ; her singing 'Cherry Ripe' in a cracked soprano.

But now all noise was stilled, for Miss Sarah Hopkins arrived from Big House with prizes for the Children's Recitation: the women curtsied, the men pulled off their caps, for Miss Sarah was loved in Blaenafon. We had the best school on the mountains because of her, and she taught in it.

The Master of Ceremonies cried, his arms high: 'Now that Miss Sarah's here – all children up for the recitation prize' –

and I was glad when Iestyn was first out of the hat, because I needed to get going. Ellie patted and smoothed him and brushed back his quiff with spit, as fussy as an old hen. 'Win that sucking pig and you'll have bacon every day for tea.'

'*Diawch,*' ejaculated Morfydd, 'I'm off!' and Ellie cried:

'You stay! You ought to be ashamed – our Iestyn about to win the recitation prize and half the family absent.' And she kissed him. 'Up you go, my beautiful.'

Up went Iestyn on to the band platform, and there was a lot of barging and shoving by the organizers, and the band gave a long blast of introduction, and the MC cried: '"There once was a frog and he would a'wooing go" – to be recited by Master Iestyn Mortymer.'

'Oh no,' said Morfydd, 'I can't bear it!' and I was with her on this – we'd been having this bloody frog for breakfast, dinner and tea. Now he was wriggling his behind up on the platform, looking gormless, a finger in his mouth.

'"There once was a frog" – come on, *cariad*, come on . . .' urged Ellie, and Iestyn's face brightened and, to hurrahs and cheers, he was off, eyes shut tight, shoulders wagging.

'"There once was a frog and he would a'wooing go with another little frog he knew . . ." Christ, Mam, I've forgotten it!'

'"And he happened to stray . . ."' Ellie prompted, her eyes like stars.

'Oh aye! "And he happened to stray in a field one day where a dear little mushroom grew . . . That night he told his sweetheart what he had found – it's a model little home, said he. For the front's at the front of that pretty little shack – it'll just suit two, perhaps three . . ."' Now he was off you'd have to shoot him to stop him.

'Oh, Gawd!' ejaculated Morfydd, and was away.

'Ellie, I've got to go, too.' I tugged at her sleeve.

'Shame on you! And your son the centre of attraction!'

So he was, for this was a school song and all the kids in the Square bawled the chorus: '"Grow, grow, grow little

315

mushroom, grow. Grow, grow, somebody wants you so. I will call again tomorrow morn, you see, and if you grow bigger you will just suit me . . ."'

My son's eyes grew big in his face as he saw me leave, and his thin voice beat in my brain. By some unfathomable trick of consciousness the terror that I might lose him assailed me then: his piping voice became a drum-like accompaniment to Chancer's hooves on the mountain grass . . . 'Grow, grow, grow little mushroom, grow . . .'

I was aware of the danger he was in, but, with a living to earn, could do little about it. The lad was dying to leave school and start work, but I intended delaying this for as long as possible – it was at work that the convenient accident could happen.

On short shifts, if the weather was fine, I used to take him up the Keeper's Road and hand him over to Shant-y-Brain, the tough old game-keeper, and pick him up on my way back. He was safe up there with Old Shant, who was an ex-sailor and used to make ships in bottles. But . . . I couldn't watch Iestyn every moment of the day, and neither could Ellie.

Remembering that danger now, I screwed up my hands on the reins. God, I thought, I'd kill with red iron the man who took him away from me.

No illuminations for Nantyglo that night: nothing to relieve the pitch darkness of its squalid courts and alleys where the fevered Irish lived fifteen to a room among open drains and sewers: these, the victims of the Baileys' greed.

People were old at twenty here; the expectation of life, as at her sister, Merthyr, was often under sixteen years. Children were crippled here, men blinded; prostitution and child labour were at their worst. Here aged grandfathers ate their lungs and mothers died at the coal faces. A man with his leg off was carried to the bed of his wife. There was no hospital in Nantyglo.

Within these decaying walls rebellion was being spawned; the slums here being worse than the slums of India.

I reined Chancer in and took him carefully through the piled refuse scattered before the doors of Long Row where later, to my disgrace, my daughter, Morfydd, lived.

This was Crawshay Bailey's town; he who ate a sheep's head for his dinner; the tramping-boy who borrowed a thousand pounds and shared with Joseph, his brother, in Nantyglo's systematic crucifixion.

Earlier, I had signed on with the night clerks, as Bailey required. Now a distant hammering took my attention as I tethered the pony in shadows: seeing, in a sudden glow of molten iron, the Bailey's Roundtowers; two great battlements they were building to protect them from their workers. From one, talk had it, a tunnel was being constructed that linked it to *Ty-Mawr*, the mansion that dominated Trosnant Estate.

These fortifications, like Fothergill's Folly in Sirhowy and Cyfarthfa Castle (soon to be erected in Merthyr), were the masters' replies to local hatred. The riots of 1800, 1816 and last year threatened not only their profits at a time of their workers' distress, but also their lives. The Roundtowers here, for instance, were to be stocked with arms and provisions to resist siege until military protection arrived from Brecon Barracks.

Rickety children were rattling begging tins; shawled women, stamped with the pallor of hunger, were eating bread through the windows of the Company shop, as I waded through slush. And, as I approached the Bush Inn tap-room door, long-limbed spectres of hunger, their skeletal bodies fluttering with rags, rose up before me with hoarse pleas, their emaciated faces alight with furnace glare.

I turned away, pulled down my stocking mask and entered the inn. Immediately within the doorway a sentry was standing.

'Password?' he asked.

'Roundtowers.'

His rough hands moved over me for a weapon, and he grunted.

'Down the steps, the door on the right.'

Descending stone steps to a cellar, I waited there to accustom my eyes to the dark, for a single candle was the only light. Beyond the candle a man was sitting cross-legged, his form and features etched in blackness. The only bit I could see clearly were his boots.

'You have a horse?' he asked.

'Yes.'

'A barley meal convoy – mule train. It left the Eppynt farms yesterday for shipping from Newport. Tonight it is picking up an armed escort from Brecon Barracks . . .'

'How many soldiers?' I asked.

'Perhaps a dozen.'

'Dragoons?'

'None. The 5th is exercising around Senny.'

'What route?' I asked.

'The old redcoat road below Allt Ddu – you know it?'

'Like my hand.'

'At Pontsticill the mule-train will be joined by the Merthyr Militia – let them in and you're in trouble. The ambush will be made at Allt, and the convoy diverted east to the canal wharf at Tal-y-Bont.'

I said, 'I hope the bargees know.'

'Of course the bargees know – do ye think we're bloody idiots?'

'I've hit some of these capers. Where are the men?'

'Camped at Pen Milon.'

'How many?'

'Fifteen or so, if no backsliders.'

'Christ,' I said, 'what a country!'

He rose in anger. 'Aye? What do you expect of them? They're half starved, most of them. They've little to gain and plenty to lose. And the barley is coming to Nanty, remember

– most of them are Swansea and Hirwaun fellas – they won't see a bloody grain of it.'

'All right – keep your hair on. What happens when the barges get south.'

'My business.'

'Distribution?'

'You ambush the bloody stuff, mun, we'll distribute it and eat it tidy. This is a stink of a place – the Baileys have got us in rags at the height of winter – get off and do your job, that's all.' He peered at a watch. 'You'd best get along, the rendezvous at Milon is midnight. The man at the door will give you something. Use it if necessary.'

It was a farce, really: clearly, he knew who I was for he had selected me; and I knew his identity – King Crispin, friend of the later Zephaniah Williams of the Royal Oak at Coalbrookvale in the River of Fire. Aye, I had to grin – King Crispin the Brynmawr shoemaker – his boots, about the only thing of him visible to me – were the best I'd ever seen on a collier.

At the door, the sentry gave me a flintlock pistol, ball and powder.

'Perish the privilege orders,' said he.

The night was black with him and nipping cold as I went out to Chancer.

'Death to the aristocracy,' said I.

Thirty-seven

In later years, at the height of the Irish famines when a million Irish peasants died after failure of the potato crop, the English government was shipping cattle on the hoof out of County Galway to the tables of England. I have never been able to account for this, even allowing for the cruelty and disregard successive British governments inflict upon the international poor. The same exploitation was now being performed in Wales. With the failure of the corn and barley crop through successively bad harvests all over Britain, Westminster was stripping Wales of food.

The effect of this was a country simmering into defiance of English rule: the onset of Welsh Chartism, the success of the Benefit Clubs, the springboards of the coming unions, were the direct response to English autocracy and cruelty: when the history of our time is told the hero will be the hungry man, and Wales, his starving mistress, the heroine.

The moon told me that it was midnight when I reached the slopes of Pen Milon, and there was an eerie, hook-nosed threat in the air of the mountains: soon, I thought, with a change of this wind it would be standing on the tails of twenty cats, for I knew this area.

Now, with Chancer breasting through high heather, we came to a little place of water known as Glyn Tarell: here a man was standing.

'Roundtowers,' I called to him, and immediately a dozen others rose up out of the heather, encircling me. All were armed with pistols, and I wondered at the wisdom of it; it was only transportation for grain-raiding, but the rope for carrying arms in defiance of the King.

'You lot on foot?' I asked, and a giant of a man with no neck and long arms cried at me:

'Our ponies are watering in Tarell.' He pointed downhill.

'Get them and follow me,' I commanded. 'Do you know what this is all about?'

'Do you, mister? That's what's worrying us.'

I gave him a grin, and Chancer pranced about in the moonlight while I waited: ten minutes later, at the head of twelve, I led them at a gallop around the skirts of Allt Ddu and up the slopes to reach the redcoat road.

'You're late,' said a voice on the redcoat road, and I knew it instantly – that of Paddy Ostler, he who had been kicked out of Blaenafon for cruelty to his horse: on foot was he now, and he rose up from behind a crag like a bear feasting.

'Any sign of the convoy?' I asked through my mask, and he came up to Chancer, this one, and peered up into my face.

'Hywel Mortymer, eh? I'd know that voice anywhere . . .'

'More fool you,' said the Swansea leader; he was big and fair and sat his old farm horse like a rider. 'What's the use of a mask if you blab a fella's name? Get off, ye big oaf!'

'I see'd 'em not two hours back, mind,' said Ostler, unabashed.

'The convoy?' I asked, reining in closer. 'Where?'

He said: 'Sorry about callin' you Mortymer, maister, but I anna clear in the head like some.'

I retorted: 'For God's sake! Where did you see it?'

He rose from his hunkers and pointed down the valley. 'Opposite Pencelli as the crows do fly, zur.'

The Swansea leader cried, wheeling his mare about: 'That's on the redcoat road?'

'Nigh on the redcoat, mun, and tidy. Ambush here – ye can't miss 'em.'

'How many?' I asked.

'Ten.'

'Soldiers?'

'Mules.'

'With panniers?'

'Christ Jesus, no, zur – carts.'

'And soldiers?' I repeated, for I didn't trust this one.

'They don't come none.'

'Ye what?' The riders bunched, staring down at Ostler and he gazed about them in his madman's daze, trembling.

'You'll not be hurt,' I said. 'Just tell us what you saw.'

He rose to full height, crying shrilly, 'Ten ole donkey-mules, I tell you I see'd 'em – and ten carts wi' bags loaded high – enough barley-mow for a regiment, and the donks were under the whip, an' all, for pullin' slow.'

'All right, all right,' cried someone. 'But how many soldiers?'

'None.' Ostler spun to him. 'I jist bloody told ye – *none*.'

'That can't be right,' said the Swansea leader.

'It be right sure enough,' cried Ostler. 'Do ye think I'm addled? And they're makin' up here for the Storey Arms.'

This was the ancient drovers' inn on the Merthyr road.

'Dismount and listen to me,' I said. 'You all know where we're taking the barley?' I pushed Ostler down the road as a sentry.

'Down to the Duke Well caves?' asked one.

'Llangattock, I heard say.'

'Jesus, mun, we're bloody miles from Llangattock.' They pushed and argued in whispers.

I said, my hand up for silence: 'We'll snatch it here, this is as good as anywhere. Sling the drivers off, and each man here drives a cart – tether your ponies behind. Get moving, too. Brecon Barracks is on a ten-minute tap and the dragoons are on exercise over by Sennybridge. I'll drive the first cart, the rest follow.'

'Where to, for God's sake?'

'A barge will be waiting at Tal-y-Bont wharf.'

'A wagon-train by canal? I never thought o' that.'

'You don't think o' nothing, boyo.'

They laughed together, chuckling at the ingenuity. Someone said, 'At two miles an hour? Those bargees are taking a chance, ain't they?'

'They're Nantyglo men,' I said. 'Their families are starving.'

'They'm caught, it's a rope for every one.'

'That's the chance they take,' I whispered, and stood up. 'Is that the old man waving?'

'It's Paddy Ostler, lest it's a redcoat.' And there came from the darkness, for the moon was shy, the song of a calling nightjar.

'That's him,' said the man from Swansea, and he went full length with his ear against the road. 'And they're coming – carts – old Ostler was right for once – hooves and carts, not pannier animals.'

'Get under cover,' I said, and we trotted the horses into a nearby quarry.

They came as if tomorrow would do; half-soaked; the men full of ale and the mules weary, their hooves dragging, their noses skimming the stone-laid road; this, the back-door military route from Brecon Barracks to Merthyr, the town of riots. In single file the wheat-train came pulled by mules, but donkeys were hauling the barley in the rear. And there came to me as I waited for the attack a sickening presentiment of disaster. The stakes were high; a few weeks' feed for the people of Nantyglo and Brynmawr if we won; or transportation to the blood-soaked triangles of Van Diemen's Land if we lost. I looked around the eager faces of the riders about me.

They were Swansea men, they'd told me; puddlers and refiners from Tregelles-Price's works down at Neath Abbey – under whom they ate respectably, for the Quaker ironmaster inspired loyalty; and the copper-workers of Port Talbot weren't doing so badly, either. But unionism among all workers was growing, and these were here to feed brothers whom they scarcely knew, and under the leadership of a man they had never heard of – me. Responsibility for their safety beat upon me. Nor was I happy about an unescorted convoy; there was always a first time, but this had not happened before. There was always the possibility of a counter-ambush.

It had begun to rain, gently at first, now in vicious slashes from threatening clouds; the wind rose, as I'd expected, battering in the quarry outcrops, sighing in dark places.

'Horses' arses, we can do without this,' said someone.

'I'd rather be back home in bed wi' my missus.'

The leading carts of the grain convoy came closer.

'Keep it loose,' I whispered, and raised my hand. 'Don't bunch up. And two of you keep the drivers covered while we get the carts free, remember.'

I brought down my hand; spurring Chancer, I took him into the roadway; crouching low on their mounts, the others galloped past me, and the convoy came to a halt. I saw in the light of the pumpkin moon the ten carts mounded against the rim of the mountain – instantly to die into blackness as the moon dropped her skirts; this is what saved us.

For, even as we surrounded the carts, dozens of redcoats rose out of the heather with levelled muskets, and a cluster of dragoons came prancing in from nowhere. A voice shouted: 'Hold fire, hold fire, men – I want them alive!'

Now there's a rumpus, with horses shrieking and commands being yelled in a bedlam of grinding wheels and stamping hooves. In the middle of the mêlée, Chancer went high, nearly unseating me, and I heard Paddy Ostler cry: 'Watch it, Mortymer – behind you!' and I reined, circling madly, in time to see a dragoon's silhouette take aim against the moon-lined clouds. I ducked, and the explosion of his pistol fanned my face as the ball went winging past me.

'Out of it, out of it, everybody!' I called, and I cursed Ostler in my soul, but not for saving my life. The same dragoon, finding me again, came in with a waving sabre; I saw the flash of its blade at the moment I fired my pistol. The shock of the powder flung him back momentarily, but I knew

324

I'd missed him when he came in again, his big horse knocking Chancer to his knees and throwing me off.

Men were fighting in little groups; others were streaming away from the counter-ambush as I scrambled back on to Chancer, and a voice cried beside me: 'Quick, mun – the lads are away, the bastards are fighting each other,' and I recognized the voice of the man from Swansea.

'Are they all clear?'

'All I can count.' He reined in beside me in the blackness, his mare steering Chancer into the quarry again. Somewhere among the carts a man was shrieking rhythmically amid shouts of anger: horses, many riderless, were galloping away in whinnies; an educated voice shouted above the babel.

'Settle yourselves, now come on! Outriders, outriders! Don't let them get away!'

'Are you all right?' asked my companion.

'Just about,' I gasped.

'God alive, that dragoon nearly had you. Go now!' he spurred hard and his mare wheeled in the moment before the moon, which had saved us, came out again, flooding the mountain.

'Good luck,' I said, and took Chancer fast, glancing back at the white stone road and the congested carts; the over-turned barley bags and the jumbling havoc of the soldiers and dragoons. I saw, also, a lone rider trotting clear of the confusion as if in pursuit of me. Another backwards glance and I saw him rein in; momentarily he seemed to lurch in the saddle, before sitting motionless, his horse stopped. This was the last enemy I saw as I took Chancer fast down the hill of Torpantau.

It would be a mistake, I thought, to get home too early; the safest thing to do would be to take the long way back past the Long Row in Nanty.

Early dawn fingers were curling in a mackerel sky as I took Chancer quietly along the sheep tracks of the Coity.

It had been a night of total failure; an informer had

doubtless been at work: vaguely, I wondered if it was Paddy Ostler, but I doubted this because Harry, his brother, was still living with an aunt in Pwll-du, and informers and their families got short shrift these days. One thing was certain; the people in Nantyglo would be on short commons until we had better luck with another grain convoy, and I wondered about the bargees awaiting us at Tal-y-Bont on Usk.

Within sight of the Whistle Inn, I took to the road because of Bully Hole Bottom, an area of ancient mining now filled with mud; in older times it had been fenced off, but not now, and the moon told me of the danger when I saw the ritual standing stone called Drum Boulder. Between here and the Whistle you could lose a horse and cart, never mind a sheep. Now, with Chancer's hooves clip-clopping on the stone road, I was wondering what excuse I had for Ellie this time, when a command rang out behind the berm: 'Right you, Mortymer – get off that thing and come down here.'

A man rose up before me, and I recognized him immediately.

Kent Mortimer. He waved a pistol at me.

'Down here, where I can see you,' and he chuckled. 'Dear God, everything comes to him who waits!'

I cursed my carelessness: my ineptitude had cost me the grain convoy – I should have checked for a counter-ambush; this mistake was likely to cost me my life.

Chancer whinnied behind me, and I realized that he was calling to the big black stallion that came out of the shadows.

We faced each other, Kent Mortimer and I, and I said: 'Right, man – shoot and have done with it.'

'Oh dear no, old chap – that would be far too quick. No doubt you took Musker, but you'll find me a different proposition.'

Behind him I saw a light go on in the Whistle Inn; probably Will Blaenafon and old Peg going to bed, or getting up. I said: 'You blow that thing off here and you'll raise the neighbourhood.'

He nodded. 'I've thought of that,' and he levelled the pistol at my stomach. 'Turn round, and get moving.'

Screech owls were quarrelling on the Coity: strangely, ring doves were sobbing from the cotes of the inn; right music for a funeral, I thought. Over my shoulder I said: 'At least I didn't shoot Musker in the back.'

'Frankly, I'm not particular. Does a bastard deserve anything better?' He prodded me with the weapon. 'Keep going.'

Clearly, he was taking me out of earshot of the inn, but now I began to wonder if he knew the area: initially, I'd supposed we were heading for the Bully Hole Bottom bog, where many a body, it was rumoured, had been dumped to hide the evidence.

Kent Mortimer said as we walked: 'For some time I've believed you were behind this grain-raiding, now I've had the proof.'

'Then why not hand me over?'

'Because this is a personal execution. Up to now I've left it to others, but now I'm taking a hand. An eye for an eye. Remember Tom?'

'I didn't kill your brother.'

'Perhaps not, but your father did.'

We went on. A light was bobbing along the Brynmawr road, but going away, not towards us. A coldness was stealing over me that was something more than the chill of the dawn wind; it was as if an unseen hand was claiming me; a mesmeric grip of the vitals, and in my throat there was a stifling dryness. Now the sheep track diverted and I took its left fork, which would lead us closer to the bog. For the thought had come to me that if I had to die I might be able to take Kent Mortimer with me.

I called: 'What about the botches you've made – Guto, my top-filler and the Jones twins – Christ, man, how many more have to die in this stupid vendetta? To say nothing of my girl and her baby . . .'

He answered behind me: 'You want to know? Then I'll tell

327

you. According to my father – and he makes the rules – every bastard issue of your father's line – the males first. Until he has stamped out the shame.' His voice rose. 'We are made with the veins of princes. Is there a man alive whose blood isn't stirred by tales of Mortimer's Cross?' and he prodded me forward again. 'We've ruled the Welsh Marches for the past four hundred years! Your own mother's heritage dates back, like mine, to Edmund's sister; and from her sprang Richard and his son who graced the throne of England . . .!'

'Jesus,' I said, 'you're going back a bit . . .' It was meant to anger him, and it did. For I'd heard in his voice a hint of mania.

'And then your father dragged my aunt's name in the mud – Lady Jane Mortimer – she hanged herself like a common felon! The plaything of a line of bastards. By God, you lot have something to answer for!' He was shouting now, and I was weighing the chance of turning for a dive at his feet when I suddenly flailed about, calf-deep in mud and water. Thinking it was an attack, he fired the pistol and the ball winged high, missing me by yards. But now he was floundering, too: with arms waving for balance he fell forward, shrieking in alarm. I knew the position of the Drum Boulder, and seeing it, clutched the vetch grass and struggled towards it.

Kent Mortimer went the other way, deeper into the bog, while I pulled myself out on to dry land. Safe, I turned.

Now he was waist-deep, and never will I forget the horror of his face as he sank lower. And, of a sudden, he yelled: 'My father will see to it – you hear me? As your first wife went, so will this wife and her children. Black be your house, you bastard Mortymers. One by one, my father will take them!'

I could have saved him, but did not. Covered with the mud of the bog, I crouched there, watching as he slowly slipped out of my sight, his arms waving; his mud-filled mouth babbled incoherently. I knew no pity, only relief; my children were safe at last: the bog sucked.

His pistol was lying at my feet; I picked it up.

The entire business had taken less than two minutes. One moment I was almost dead and buried; next moment Kent Mortimer was ten feet down in mud.

Back in Stack Square I washed down under the yard pump.

Ellie had left my nightshirt on the fireguard, and I pulled it over my shivering body; with my clothes in my hands, I crept up the stairs.

A beam of moonlight lighting her face, Ellie was sleeping like a woman embalmed. Impelled by thoughts of Kent Mortimer, I went barefooted into the children's room.

Edwina, down in the kitchen, was fast asleep; her clothes, meticulously arranged on a chair, as always, contrasted with Morfydd's, which were scattered upon the floor. Beside her slept Iestyn; both were breathing with rhythmic gentleness: he with the clothes tucked up under his chin.

Morfydd's beauty took my breath. My first-born, but a child no longer: two women in the house now, I thought. Three, soon, with Edwina coming on . . .

And then I saw something else, heard another sound, and peered down at the bed. Something snuffled under the blanket, and the face of a sucking pig appeared; one white-lashed eye regarding me with hostility. Then, as quickly, the pig turned over in Iestyn's arms, put its snout against his face, and slept.

Dear God, I thought: if Morfydd wakes up and finds that in bed with her, all hell will come loose.

Thirty-eight

A new forgiving summer, bright and hot with pleasant winds, fanned the peaks of the Skirrids in the year of 1825. The Sugar Loaf, as white as a Church of England sugar-cake at Christmas, dozed on her shoulder and smiled at Abergavenny. Our old Blorenge Mountain, decorated to the waist in purple heather, lay on her back in that bumbledore May and winked at the Coity, her breasts rising and falling over the valley like a sleeping woman. And early every morning, with the spit-gob spiders still slaving in the blackberry hedges, the morning shifts would go streaming up the Keeper's Road for work at the new ironworks being built – Garndyrus.

The building of this new Works below Pwll-du was for me a sign of coming prosperity. With the ending of the war with France, hints of better times were beginning to show. We still grain-raided and broke into the Company Shops, for Truck was always a major cause of complaint, including the practice of paying our wages in locally minted coin. (If you wanted coin of the Realm they deducted you 5 per cent.) But improvements in social conditions were beginning to show, and the foreigners got wind of it.

Until now the method of coal extraction had been mainly from drift mines and levels (the first shaft was sunk in Sirhowy in 1805), but now, with more coal available than was necessary for ironworking, the surplus was being sold on the open market. And speculators, quick to sense new profit, came bounding in.

With them, as always, came the immigrant Irish. In Blaenafon that year some three thousand workers got a living from iron, and only a third were Welsh-speaking. The town was crammed to the doors with lodgers; orphan and unwanted children wandered in droves, and in Stack Square humans were proliferating: Mrs Twelve Beynon was now Mrs Fourteen, and next door to her Mrs Pantrych, the wife of a farrier, raised a brood of six. With her came her sister, Mrs Dic Shôn Ffyrnig, whose husband, Dic Shôn, was the chairman of the new Hand in Hand Benefit Club. The treasurer of the earlier Faithful Friends Club had absconded with our funds.

Every married lady I came across – and many single ones – appeared to be in the family way that year; and my little plump Elianor was no exception.

Learning this, I lifted her high, dancing around the kitchen with her while she shrieked blue murder; then I kissed the little swell of her apron.

'Oh, Hywel, put me down, the very thought of it! Someone might come in!' and she ran like a rabbit for the scullery where I caught her again, whispering into her ear.

'No, *diawch!* What a terrible suggestion!' She blushed and wriggled like a maid. 'Down by here? In the middle of the day?'

I got her again as she ran up the stairs.

'In the kitchen, under the table?' She pushed and shoved and her hair came down.

'Come on, girl, we'll dance a jig for the Devil!' I said.

On the stairs, with the house empty, I got her again; panting, she lay against me. I said, breathless, kissing her mouth, 'We can be caught for twins as easily as one. Come on, my precious!'

'A madman and whooping you are! And me Chapel? Loose me!'

'My beautiful, my Elianor . . .'

'And you a deacon!'

It's a bit of a fumble getting under long skirts halfway up the stairs. She gasped against me, 'Oh dear, the children might come in. Oh . . .'

'The children are miles away.'

'Oh . . . oh . . .' said Ellie. 'Hell and damnation! *Ah!*'

I tell you this. I've never made love to a woman on a flight of stairs, but if my Ellie wasn't in the family way before, she certainly was now. Very successful.

This sort of behaviour appeared to be catching.

Look out of the window soon after dawn. Here comes Iolo Milk with Enid donkey and her milk float. Very fancy is Iolo first thing in the morning, with his hair and whiskers curling up black and gold on the chops, and him doing a hop-step-and-a-jump as he puts the jugs down with a flourish. Now a back-flip with his boots: now off with his cap, and he sweeps up the gutter at the feet of Angharad Evan, God help her.

'Morning, me darlin'.'

Got her nuts about her has Angharad, and goes scuttling; having heard talk of Iolo and his mate, Dai Paternity.

Now Iolo cries, his cap waving up, 'Morning, Morfydd, my beautiful! How's your love-life?'

Morfydd, not knowing I'm watching, curls and combs at her bedroom window in her new pink nightie.

Another word about her; she was the pester of my life.

Fifteen now, was Morfydd: serving at table in the house of Sarah Hopkins, and in good company, thank God, for she was dark in the eyes now, a woman of fire. 'My womb must have been aglow when I brought forth that one,' said Ellie.

Spare time she worked down Pwll-du drift, the Hopkins, seeing to the children as Annie Oh-No used to do, and if a child caught it screaming they always sent for Morfydd, for she could trim a stump as good as any doctor. Silent by nature, hers was a brooding quiet, with cold, hostile stares at anyone in authority, including down with the Royal Family and off with their heads. I could name six young hobnails who were losing sleep over her.

'Oi, oi, what you on with tonight, Morfydd Mortymer?' Iolo again now, stretching his breeches for a better look.

'Not you, that's for sure,' she calls down.

'What about an hour up the Coity?'

No answer. I could see her from the back where I was washing at the tub: and no blame to Iolo, either, for she was showing enough bosom to kill a cleric.

Very persistent is Iolo, bless him. 'You won't regret it, mind.' Beaming, his face cherubic and shining with soap. 'Give me ten seconds – that's all I need.'

'I'll settle for five,' calls Morfydd, and her window opens and her chamber comes up.

'No cause for that, mind,' says Iolo, dripping.

'No offence intended.'

'None taken, Iolo,' says I. 'Now bugger off.'

I tell you this: a man spins trouble when he takes beauty to bed, but he's asking for hell when he breeds it in a daughter.

'You're a great one to talk, aren't you?' said Ellie, coming down from upstairs. 'It's you she gets it from, Hywel Mortymer.'

Mind you, things come warmer in this direction when the sun comes hot and raging over the mountains and the corn waves ripe in seas of green and gold. All Nature is in love when the dormouse mates and the birds are playing their leap-frog games in joy. It is much the same with humans: the girls putting lavender water behind the ears, the young men riding the bucking stars in bosomy, fevered nights.

I tell you this – I'd rather be forty with a stomach coming on me than live again that damn palaver of, *Oh, please*, and *Get off*, and *If you do that again I'll tell my mam*, and half the time they hope you will and pray you won't.

So, in middle age, I come soft when I see the young ones ferreting around on the mountain; and being a man I suppose it's natural that I pity the fellas at the top of the list. For, though all the girls have got it, they're very loath to part with it. Talk has it that Dai Paternity actually broke a leg thrashing around after one of Mo O'Hara's girls, and I can well believe it.

But the best place of all for loving at forty is riding in a tram along the Rassau quarry road, with the old horse wagging along as if tomorrow will do: ay, ay – up there by Duke's Table, where the rim of the world meets the sky – on the day of the annual outing.

With your arm round the woman you love.

Ellie!

That spring day, looking back, was one of the happiest of my life.

The directors of the Blaenafon Iron Company had put me in charge, under Ephraim Davies, of the building of a new rolling mill at Garndyrus. The manufacturing chain was changing: Blaenafon furnaces would now produce pig iron; this would be sent by tram-road to the new Garndyrus mill for rolling.

More, an exciting new system of transport was being planned. Already Irish labour was cutting a new tram-road round the breast of the Blorenge; there, in the declivity formed by Nature, a marvellous invention of counterbalancing trams was being devised: a full tram of iron sliding down 2,000 feet to Llanfoist Wharf, pulling an empty tram up to the top.

Wonderful, I tell you, is the ingenuity of Man! From Llanfoist horse-drawn barges would take the wrought iron to Newport Docks; there to be loaded for the ports of the world. Sheet iron for the factories of the Argentine; rails for the railways of Spain; steel columns for the great houses of Peru; but – and this was the proudest order of all – 'Grade A' iron for use in the building of a great new viaduct at Crumlin in due course.

My world was complete; my ambitions fulfilled. From a lowly trammer down Hopkins to a gentleman puddler in a tall, glazed hat: and from there to site engineer of the new works at Garndyrus. All my fears for the safety of my family had died with Kent Mortimer.

Sir John, old now, was scarcely a threat. Talk had it that,

isolated and lonely in his Llanfoist mansion, he had been broken by the loss of his sons. Age had taken the fire out of his belly.

Thirty-nine

In the olden times, by the Celtic reckoning, summer began on the first day of May, and this was known as *Calan Mai*; similarly, the first day of November, called *Calan Gaeaf*, was the day that winter beckoned.

Such ancient terms sprang from the farms: most villages possessed a 'green', and it was on the first day of summer that this was officially opened for dancing. But we, in the industrial towns, having nowhere to play the harp and dance, chose *Calan Mai* for special celebration, and the date of this was our annual outing.

It was a time of shivering children. Had they been English, they would have celebrated Hallowe'en, which is the Eve of St John's; for us, May Eve was the time when the souls of the dead roamed the streets of our town; especially to be seen down *Rhyd-y-nos*, the 'dark as curtains' street, and most young ones spent the night of May Eve under the blankets listening to echoing footsteps which comforting parents asserted were human.

Not human at all; I myself have seen the spirits of the dead walking hand in hand from the cemetery, making for *Rhyd-y-nos*.

This being so, with weirdies and Irish banshees and ghouls about, it was necessary to take certain precautions on May Eve, and one of these was to light a bonfire at the entrance to one's habitation to keep the evil spirits away.

Nine men or boys were employed to make the fire, and Tomos, always a visitor to the ailing in Stack Square, was appointed to be in charge. All the children jigged and jogged about him, begging.

'Can I be one, Pastor?' Iestyn now, pushing other lads away.

'And me?' cried Mo Jenkins, the son of Big Rhys.

The families were already assembled in the moonlight; the trams and horses had been scrubbed up for the annual outing in the morning.

In the shadow of the Stack, with the furnaces simmering, nine of us turned out our pockets and placed all metal objects in a heap, including money, on the earth. All nine of us then searched Cae White for wood of nine differing sorts. These were then placed for kindling at Tomos's feet, and a coin was tossed to select the 'firer'. Young Mo won this, and knelt, rubbing together two bits of oak, and he set the flame. Then Gran Fat Beti, being the oldest there, brought a bag of flour into which she had mixed small cakes of oatmeal: filing up to Gran, all present had to pick a bit of this out of the bag; the one who got a piece of brown-meal cake had to jump three times through the bonfire, which was necessary to guarantee a full larder and good harvest for that summer. The shouts and shrieks of the girls with their clothes up you could have heard over in Waunavon. Edwina refused to do it in tearful protestations, but Morfydd made up for this – hers were up to the waist.

Gran Fat Beti, who ended her life freezing to death in a brick hollow at the entrance to Shepherds' Square one Christmas, explained that in far-off days, if there was disease in sheep or cattle, a lamb or a calf might be thrown into the bonfire as a sacrifice to the evil ones, but by my time this had ceased. However, all present then collected a handful of the wood ash to put on the mantel to guard against the cholera and typhoid: for all the time I knew her, my Rhia used to sprinkle some of this charm in her shoes.

Thus our May Eve ritual would ensure that the next day's Outing would be enjoyed without accident, and keep bad spirits away.

One, however, managed to slip through the net.

Few got any sleep that night in town. Ironworker families who were once farmers arrived in choirs before dawn to sing in harmony their *carolau Mai* (May carols), and fling furnace grit at the windows to get us up.

Now there's a palaver all down the backs of Stack Row, with Twm-y-Beddau naked at the tub and his kids throwing buckets at him, and Mr Pantrych shaving cut-throat in Number Five, singing the bass line of 'Mornings in May'.

Aproned wives were up cleaning windows – only to see what the others are going to wear, said Ellie – dear me, I haven't got a rag to my back.

Morfydd was in pink, Edwina in white and a broad-rimmed summer hat, and Iestyn strangling his crotch with tight braces and calf-length trews of Flannel Street alpaca.

Come seven o'clock we were away to go, and tidy, with Mrs Fifteen Beynon leading her brood to the waiting trams and Mrs Pantrych following, and outside the Drum and Monkey the brass band was tuning up: Mr Roberts on the kettle drum, Iolo Milk and Dai Paternity on flutes and whistles and making rude signs to the girls; Billy Handy banging the big drum and Afel Hughes on the ophicleide, with fat Mr Gwallter curled up in the serpentine. I tell you this – no brass band on the Top sounded quite like ours – never did discover what they were playing.

Into the trams now; squeals of delight from the kids and shrieks from the girls, with matrons carrying baskets of corned-beef sandwiches: there was Welsh cakes and lava-bread from Swansea market; wheaten biscuits and a cask of salted butter; ale barrels for the men and small-beer for the children from Selwyn ap Pringle's place. Free as air, most of this, bestowed by lovely Miss Sarah.

Tram after tram came up, and into them piled the waiting people. Bonnet-streamers were flying, 'kerchiefs fluttering; the women done up beautifully in grandma ribbons, even if it meant going into debt at the Tommy Shops. Lads in clogs, girls in lace; ladies in high-buttoned boots. Babies were yelling and being handed around for compliments; sucklers

338

on the breast, others being changed. And one by one the journeys set off, the first tram carrying the band.

Nigh twenty trams were out that May Day, I reckon, escorted by hordes of stumbling Irish with their arms thrust out for food, as usual. But we soon lost the poor things when we reached Black Rank, where Susie Obligato used to live. The tram-road stretched out like a needle of light before us. The sun burned down. The wind shafted the corn of Shant-y-Brain's fields and played do-re-mi in the up-shafts.

Now on, on, past the Whistle Inn where Peg Cuddle came out like a ship in full sail – Jesus, there's a size for you these days is that Peg Cuddle – assisted over the tumps by Will Blaenafon. And I gave a thought to Kent Mortimer spreadeagled below in the bog.

Will and Peg hauled aboard now, and we were off again. With the Baptist Chapel and Persondŷ left behind, we saw before us the whole of the Coity mountain lying on her shoulder. Cat's-ear and dandies painted up her voluminous skirts: cowslip and primrose decorated the banks; forget-me-nots, bright blue, waved their promise of summer from fields of early meadow-sweet, and their fragrance perfumed the mountain air. Never will I forget that annual outing! The morning was filled with happy chattering people: the soprano cries of the women and girls, the hoarse shouts of men and the shrill voices of children like my Iestyn piping up between. They talked much; they pulled at me for answers, but I didn't answer. It was enough to sit in that tram with my girl's hand in mine and enjoy the calm loving of her warmth beside me. It was a forgiving peace after the rioting with skin and hair flying: it was a benediction after the hungers, the skimping and the saving.

Cushy Cuddlecome and her two minders were awaiting us on the Brynmawr Corner, plus Grandfather Saul in his new Bath chair, and I must say I thought he looked a little older. Room was made for them behind the band tram, and Cushy sat in state, holding court like a great white seal in her frills and Sunday savageries, and she brought a ten-gallon cask of Allsopps with her for the males, she said, and within ten minutes the band was on its knees. Now over the Top, the highest place of the Valleys, and down to the Tredegar signpost where the trams swung right for the Rassau tramroad. Sirhowy folks were lining the road, clapping and cheering as we rumbled past, and Dot Popkin and Jenny Loom, having rustled up a pair of limestone cutters as lodgers, were waiting outside the Quarryman's Arms to pour us foaming jugs of home-brew in greeting.

Leaving Trefil behind us, the great Outing convoy snaked down the Quarry Road, and opposite Duke's Well we all piled out.

Never will I forget the sight of those excited people running over the moor to the Maypole, which the lads had erected overnight.

With Morfydd leading, followed by Iolo Milk and Dai Paternity, the Outing streaked over the common, there being a prize for the youngster who reached Duke's Well first.

'We want to watch those two,' said Ellie.

I'd already made a mental note to do so. 'Ach, they're only kids, *fach* – enjoy yourself – forget her.'

'A kid, is she? I know the look in that eye.'

Edwina cried, her eyes like stars, 'Oh, she is so beautiful! That is why the boys are after her! May I go with Mr Snell, Mam?'

'Mr Snell?' I asked.

'Sir, may I have the privilege,' said a little crow of a man pushing through the people: five-foot-nil, this one; frockcoat and gaiters, a polished high hat and acne, most unhealthy: English, too, by the sound of it. Somewhere or other I'd seen this boyo before . . .

'Where did you spring from?' I asked.

'O, Dada!' said Edwina, clutching herself.

'My name, Mr Mortymer,' said the stranger, 'is Snell.'

'Oh aye?' I helped Ellie down from the tram.

'Mr Snell, the seller of coloured Bibles, Mam,' gasped

Edwina, her hand to her chest. 'Church of England, mind, and he do fancy a walk with me.'

'Do he, now?' and I eyed him.

The little man bowed again, saying: 'You will forgive the presumption, Mistress Mortymer . . .' and such was the beauty of his voice that it came from a rent in his soul . . . 'but the pure loveliness of your daughter surely needs sharing. May I not walk with her? I who am over twice her age?'

'Oh please!' begged Edwina, swooning big eyes at him.

Down he went again with his starched collar around his ears, and said, 'My intentions, I assure you, are entirely honourable.'

'I should bloody hope so,' said I. 'She's only just thirteen,' and he drew himself up, his chest out like a bantam cock, replying:

'I will have you know, sir, that I am a man of God!'

'Lay preacher down in St Peter's, mind,' said Edwina, flushed, and sweat flew to her forehead.

Down went Ellie in a dying swan, and rose, saying, 'Our apologies to you, Mr Snell. We would be complimented were you to escort our daughter around the Maypole,' and Edwina, her eyes like twin stars, went down too, her white dress outspread.

Then she was off, her arm on his, her dress swaying like a lover.

Will Blaenafon arrived with Peg Cuddle then, winking after them.

'Tidy fella, Hywel – turn his hand to anything, they do say.'

'That's what I'm afraid of.'

'Ach, leave them be – an old frump you are,' said Ellie.

With my eyes skinned for Morfydd, this one was getting away right under my nose.

Now, with the band on the *oompa*, *oompa*, until little Mo Jenkins put an end to them by sucking a lemon, the maidens and men began 'threading the needle' – each one holding a

341

ribbon and entwining the pole with colour. Pretty that old pole looked, its top sprouting gay paper and evergreen branches to keep away the fairies.

Will Blaenafon dressed up as Fool Man and Dai Swipo, who had come for a feed, played *Cadi*; these two tried to trip the lads and kiss the dancing girls. Big-shouldered youngsters were carrying in the ale casks and small-beer; white-aproned wives were cutting sandwiches: Nellie Washboard and Meg Laundry were rushing around with trays of slopping pewters; it was a sunlit, happy scene. Watching it, smoking my clay, I thought of the great battle fought in this same place, when the sky was dark with Welsh arrows and the moors covered with English dead.

How strange and sad was the evolution of Man, I thought, in the hands of a loving God.

At midday, with the sun slanting down golden rays, Mamie Goldie and Billa Jam Tart arrived with their husbands, the two old soaks, Dai End-on and Mr Jam, Billa's cousin.

'Mind,' Billa used to say, 'he did catch me on a bad day, and old Dai got Mamie likewise. No washing in, kids howling, and the larder bare, ye understand?'

I could well believe it, for I remembered my first sight of Billa and Mamie, dancing a fandango on the cobbles of Llandovery – an age ago, it seemed – and their hearts as light then as an apricot blush.

Not so now; the four of them lived next door but six to us in Stack Square – Mamie with Randy, her early son, and Billa Jam with triplets and more on the way. And Dai and Mr Jam close enough to the Drum and Monkey to foam their whiskers from the bed – wives in one hand and Allsopps in the other. Sorry in my heart I was, for pretty little Billa especially. She said now: 'No Iestyn here today, Mam Mortymer?' and bowed.

'Back home with Dai One pig, and spots,' answered Morfydd. 'Poor soul, he's got a face like the rising sun,' and Ellie gave her a look to kill, saying:

'A touch of fever water, we think, Mrs Jam. How are you doing these days?'

'Just away to Taibach down south, Mrs Mortymer,' said Mamie Goldie. 'Dai and Mr Jam being copper-beaters they be goin' back to the trade, see? – good money to be made in Port Talbot, mind.'

'Come on, come on, you lot!' and up came Dai End-on supporting Mr Jam, and the pair of them tangling their boots at that time in the morning.

'God speed you,' said Ellie, and we bowed to them.

The last I saw of Mamie and Billa Jam were their backward, longing looks over their shoulders as the two old drunks, Dai End-on and Mr Jam, hauled them off down south, to the tub and the bed.

A caravan of Welsh gypsies was coming in from the Brecon Beacons after selling its wares on the great Van Rocks. Five rumbling hay-carts with ponies tethered behind; the women in gay coloured dresses and petticoats, the men virile, aggressive and curled-handsome, lolling on the footboards and winking at our Welsh girls.

These were the horse-traders of the mountains, people who owned no allegiance to King or country. They'd buy a half-dead hack in Tenby, brush him with tan stain, paint up his teeth, and sell him in Llaneilo for twice the money. Living off the land with their cans, pegs and fortune-telling, they moved by their wits from door to door. They were child-stealers, too. You could lose a baby from a pram outside Abergavenny market and find it labelled 'for sale' down Swansea; with advertisements in the *Clarion* to inform childless couples. Their youths, as handsome as Apollos, left a trail of swooners and wives with heart trouble.

Now they came down off the Rassau road and set up their hay-carts not a hundred yards from our Maypole. But we had the stream water, and they had none, so come afternoon a dark-handsome youngster, broad and tall, appeared by Duke's Table with shining white teeth, black curls to his shoulders, and two buckets for filling. Deep-chested and muscled, he winked at Morfydd and bowed to me.

'D'ye mind the waters for free, sir?'

'Take it and welcome,' I said, and I heard Morfydd sigh like the well of life going dry, and she knelt to save fainting off.

With his white shirt open to his waist and his dark eyes roving around our women stood the gypsy while the buckets filled; a saucy old air too, with his hands on his hips, and there was a fine arrogance in him.

Morfydd rose lazily from the midst of the women and smoothed her pink dress down over her body; and they looked, she and the gypsy, and I saw the wanting in their eyes.

God help me.

More May carols it was then, and down to the Quarryman's Arms for a final fling at the hops: the horses and trams were formed up for the journey home.

'Where's that Morfydd?' asked Ellie, as Mr Snell delivered Edwina, and made off.

'Nowhere to be found!' cried Iolo Milk and Dai Paternity, hot and bothered. 'Searched high and low, we have.'

So I ran down the line of trams loaded with sleepy people and wailing babies and came to the deserted Maypole.

Further down the moorland a gypsy camp bonfire was blazing under the rising moon, and from the circle of their carts I heard clapping and gypsy fiddles.

Unseen, I approached with care, for you could get your throat slit in this company: and saw in the light of the bonfire a pink skirt whirling and a girl's bare legs as it flared to her waist, and the man who partnered her was lifting her high in shouted laughter; round and round they went as the gypsies clapped the time.

'Jesus,' I breathed, and sank to one knee.

Higher and higher went the fiddles in shrieks; faster and

faster went their music: in and out of the bonfire they went, the pair of them – the youngster who had come to the stream for water, and my Morfydd. And as the dance reached its crescendo, the gypsies rose up in a body, shouting applause. The bonfire flared, shooting sparks to the stars: coloured dresses and waving scarves were a medley in the billowing smoke.

When I looked again, Morfydd and the gypsy had vanished.

This was my country; I knew it like my hand: I knew, too, of a cave grotto near by and the hay-loft within its opening where sheep sheltered from the wind and the farmers kept their upland feed: I made towards it across the open country.

Let this be clear, I trusted my Morfydd.

From the time when she bubbled and cooed on my knee, all dimples and wrist bangles, she was my girl. Also, it's right and fair to think the best of people, most of all one's daughter.

Oh no, it was the gypsy chap who bothered me; I was worried about him fizzing in the face of such virtue; and if he became too physical, for instance, my baby might not be able to handle it.

Also, I was perturbed lest Ellie hadn't told her the facts of life, for such things can come as a shock to the uninformed. So, my worries naturally subsided when, standing in the moonlight at the entrance to the hay-loft, I heard Morfydd's husky laughter.

Up the ladder to the top of the hay I went, and peered happily over the rungs, and nearly fell off backwards. For my beloved was lying in the straw as bare as an egg and the gypsy lad was wearing less.

'Dada!'

With hay-seed in her hair she stared at me, and her eyes, like saucers, threatened to drop.

She got the usual off Ellie when I ran her back to the waiting trams.

'Bad girl!' Ellie wagged a finger to impress the neighbours. 'Where've you been till now?'

And Morfydd, with her fingers entwined before her and her face cast down before their accusing faces, looked like St Joan must have done in Orleans before the howling mob. I interjected, 'Oh, come off it, woman, she was only watching the dancing.'

'I bet,' said Ellie.

Night. The town sleeps. Somewhere in Stack Square a baby is crying; there is no other sound but Dai One rooting around in his sty out the back. Even the furnaces beyond the stack seem to be dreaming in their hissing, simmering drowse. Snores and mutterings steal out on the cold, moonlit air: Mrs Fifteen Beynon gets out of bed over in Number Six to put somebody on the pot: the springs go down in squeaks as somebody else turns over.

Over in the yard of the Drum and Monkey, Belinda is letting the cat in. All down Staffordshire Row the shadows dance, for here the vagrants sleep, clutching each other against the cold; and Gran Fat Beti, chin on her chest and wrapped in newspapers, snores on her cubby-hole seat on Shepherds' Square.

But, contained by an unusual presentiment of approaching disaster, I could not sleep.

With Ellie breathing deeply beside me, I lay upon my back and heard the wind rising over Keeper's as if it, too, was disturbed by some unusual happening.

Then in a sighing of that wind, I heard it.

The sounds of slithering, marching feet and the chinking of chains: now the unmistakable clattering of hooves on the stone road. I glanced at Ellie; her eyes were open.

'What's that?' She sat up, pushing aside the Cyfarthfa blanket.

'I don't know,' I said, and got out of bed and went to the window.

With an officer at its head, a troop of dragoons was

346

approaching; behind the dragoons, guarded by foot soldiers, came a gang of eight or nine chained prisoners. It was a group of convicted criminals under escort being taken down to the Chepstow packet for transportation.

To my surprise the horseman did not lead them now up the Keeper's road for Abergavenny, but swung left and entered North Street. The clanking rose to a chatter as they neared Stack Square. Hoarse commands rang out as the party entered it.

Lamps were glowing in windows and doors coming open now; men with dangling braces, women in night-caps and hair crackers came out, crimping their toes to the cold, and what the hell's happening and it's those bloody English again, and you could have roasted a Christmas turkey on the language.

'What's happening, for God's sake?'

'Who the hell do they think they are?'

'What's it all about, anyway?'

'You'll soon find out!' cried the troop commander, his voice shrill, and he drew his sabre and waved it. 'I want all the men lined up – men and boys – come on, or we'll sharpen you! Right, Sergeant, search the houses!' and a beefy soldier ran past me with his musket at the ready, and through our kitchen and up the stairs.

'What is it, Hywel?' said Ellie, now beside me.

'An identification parade.'

Iestyn tugged at my arm. 'What's happening, Dada?'

'Now come on, pull yourself together,' said Ellie, for Edwina was in her arms shivering and weeping to float ships.

'Can they do this to us?'

'They're bloody doin' it, ain't they?' shouted Billy Handy, coming up. 'And my Belinda warming a welshcake – it's enough to give the child two heads. Who are they after?'

'Grain-raiders,' replied Morfydd, and put the Cyfarthfa blanket about Ellie's shoulders.

'Then I hope they bloody find them,' announced Dic

Shôn Ffyrnig, standing near by. 'It do give the town a bad name, I say.'

'And you a big belly,' snapped Morfydd. 'I didn't see you go short last winter!'

'Dear me, hark at it!' said Mrs Pantrych.

And Morfydd retorted: 'Aye, hark. For that's the trouble, isn't it? Too much talk and too little action. If I was a man I'd be raiding every night – and not their bloody grain-carts!'

'Morfydd! For God's sake,' said Ellie, wearily.

The soldiers were among us now, herding us into lines for marching past the drooping prisoners. Hatred welled up in me as I saw their bruised and swollen faces. Someone bawled: 'Right, you bloody Irish – get in line – and you, Welshmen.'

They threatened us with their musket butts; the young officer was riding his big horse round the Square, his sabre waving, and cried: 'All right, Sergeant, drive them past!' Somebody pushed from the back, and we stumbled forward. Pantrych and Dic Shôn were there; Tom Beynon and a few old sinkers from the Drum and Monkey, including Billy Handy.

'And you!' shouted the sergeant, and caught Iestyn by the collar and bustled him in beside me. Momentarily our eyes met, mine and the sergeant's.

'Easy, Dada,' said Morfydd.

One by one we filed past the prisoners, and I saw in their swollen faces the tragedy of my generation. Soldiers with torches flared them high as each man went forward; wearily, the prisoners raised their heads.

The sergeant bawled: 'Him, do you know him? By Christ, we'll get the truth of this, if we're here all night,' and he struck a man in the face. 'Don't worry, sir, he's somewhere in Blaenafon. If he's a town man we'll winkle him out.'

'Then sharpen them up, the packet sails at noon.'

In simmering discontent stood the Welsh and Irish; it was a powder-keg, and the soldiers knew it as they pressed back the women with crossed muskets.

If anything started it would come from the women, for

women start and finish rebellions, as they had discovered in France. They stood in the cold and fumed, these women, their eyes smouldering in their high-boned Celtic faces, and I noticed the officer rein in his charger and stop opposite Morfydd. Momentarily, she glared up at him, and then spat at his mare's feet. I saw him weigh her; indecision was in his face, and as I turned to face the prisoners again, shuffling by, I stared straight into the eyes of Paddy Ostler.

I was surprised, but he was not. No madness now, his calm blue eyes moved in his puffy cheeks; one was nearly closed by fist beating. I stared, he stared back; there was in those eyes not a flicker of recognition. The sergeant blundered forward, gripping him from behind.

'You know any here – any man – now come on, Ostler!'

Even the wind stopped to listen, I think: the torches flared, the moonlight poured down. Then a shrill laugh rang out, and a voice cried: 'Get off with ye, you silly sods, we earn good money now – nobody's a grain-raider here.'

It was Belinda Handy, carrying all before her. 'Do you think we've nothing better to do? Come on, Billy, back to bed.'

Morfydd laughed, then another woman – I think it was old Mrs Cooney, sister to the Pantrychs: then more laughed. Soon the women were shouting laughter. Even the prisoners straightened in their chains, grinning. The young officer, infuriated, was charging about on his mare; the sergeant, his cheeks purple, was bellowing commands, shaking his fist in the faces of the women. And in the middle of them, she who had started it, was Morfydd, stamping around in her bare feet, holding her sides. The Square echoed. The laughter spread down to the Row – even to Shepherds' Square, we heard later. The people were rocking to ironic laughter, even as the dragoons, with the prisoners clanking behind them, went up North Street and took the road to Abergavenny.

'Did you know that little man, the one they called Ostler?' asked Ellie, as we went back to bed.

'Never seen him before in my life.'

'That's strange,' she added. 'Surely he's young Harry Ostler's father – he used to be in the stables, don't you remember?'

'You're mistaken, surely – I'd have known young Harry's da.'

'Sent out of town for cruelty to a horse. Remember now?'

I shook my head, and her hand went out to me in the dark.

'Hywel, don't lie to me. Lie to those pigs, of course, but not to me. And no more grain-raiding. Please, *cariad*, for the sake of the children . . . ?'

And me thinking she did not know.

Forty

Everything seemed to happen to us that summer when Ellie was carrying our second son.

Iestyn the boy seemed to become a man overnight, with that proud dignity of walk that comes to a lad handy with fists. The girls at the kissing-gates giggled and ran at the sight of him; the other lads at school gave him a wide berth. He and Mo Jenkins, the son of Big Rhys, were hitting things up for a major outing, for they passed each other down Rhyd-y-nos street like hackled dogs, I noticed.

Then Edwina gave us a time of it, catching herself, said she, as she got out of the big tin bath – on the handle, said she – and the kitchen was full of wails and lamentations which sent Morfydd clumping in from the back and Ellie down the stairs at speed: even Iestyn got in on the act and was promptly booted out. And there was Edwina standing in a towel, crying, 'O Mama, O Mama, will I die?'

I knew what it was all about when I heard her cry: 'But don't tell Dada, please? Oh, don't tell Dada!'

Morfydd was the first to make an appearance, skipping and dancing into the kitchen and clapping her hands at the ceiling in delight.

'Oh, it's marvellous, Dada! We've got another woman in the house!'

'What's she on about?' asked Iestyn, glum.

'One day I'll tell you,' and I lit my clay.

'All the exciting things happen to girls,' said he, moodily.

And the look Morfydd shot at us was very droll.

Later, when she was dressed – and Ellie made her look

especially lovely that day, I took Edwina into my arms and held her.

'You're beautiful,' I said into her ear. 'There isn't a woman to compare with you in the whole of Blaenafon.'

Later that day we walked on the Coity, Ellie and me, and our world was bathed in sun. Below us the criss-cross, crazy obscenity of Crawshay Bailey's Cwm Crachen, the Valley of the Scab, rolled up its sulphurous clouds. Yet, around this evil, Wales had decked herself up in all her summer glory; the air up here was pure and bright with sunlight. Bobtail rabbits scampered; game rose lazily on clattering wings.

'It will be a boy, I know!' cried she.

'Rhiannon we will call her if it is a girl, and Jeptha if he is a boy – what about that?' I suggested.

'No, not Jeptha,' Ellie replied. 'For did not Jeptha sacrifice his own daughter to keep his promise to God? And this is a new life, my love, not death.'

'Jethro, then?'

Ellie screwed up her eyes to the sun, and her lips were red and her cheeks flushed; in full bloom was she that morning up on the Coity, and beautiful, as women always are when carrying.

'Oh, Hywel!' cried she suddenly, and clung to me. 'Hold me, hold me, for he has moved!' and she laughed in tears, clutching me, and I kissed her while she laughed and cried, which is the way of women when joyful. 'Oh, oh!' she said, 'he is at it again – clogs on, this baby!'

'What do you expect? Didn't I call his name?'

'Then Jethro he will be. Another son – I know it, I know it! Next November, God willing, I will hand you a boy!' And she held me at arms' length and with sparkling eyes looked me over. 'My,' said she, 'my boy is rising! Two sons, two daughters, and the manager of the new Garndyrus rolling mill!' On tiptoe she kissed me. 'Crawshay Bailey's right-hand man and two pounds fifteen a week!'

'Mr Hill's,' I corrected her. 'It was he who promoted me.'

'And starting tomorrow!' She laughed at the sun and clapped her little hands together. 'A pony and trap calling for you at eight in the morning – *Diawch!* That'll give the neighbours something in the eye!' and she strutted about. 'And give that damned old Pantrych and Mrs Dic Shôn something to gas about!'

'Good neighbours, though – be generous, Ellie.'

'Oh, my love, my precious . . .' said she, and put up her arms to me.

Up at Garndyrus on the road to Abergavenny, things were happening quickly. This was a new venture by the Blaenafon Iron Company. Balance ponds were sunk, puddling furnaces would be in blast there; the modern rolling mill would replace the drop-hammer system for making finished iron: Garndyrus iron would be the purest in the Eastern Valley, comparable only with that of Merthyr's genius.

Swarming with builders now, and under my management, the mill shot up: a row of workers' cottages were built opposite the Works, and a new cottage for me right opposite the Garndyrus Inn, later called the Queen's when Victoria came to the throne.

I supervised the boring of the Pwll-du tunnel that connected Garndyrus to Blaenafon, and through it came the housewives on their way to Abergavenny market: I planned Garndyrus Square of twenty cottages; the Row of fifteen more and the Ten Houses for the incoming Blaenafon specialists: I helped to build (but not design) the Blorenge Incline, down which poured 300 tons of finished iron a week for the journey by barge to Newport.

Garndyrus flowered and was profitable: its puddling fires lit the Usk Valley from Goetre Poorhouse to Crickhowell.

But I did not know, when Mr Hill appointed me as Manager, that the controlling shareholder of the new Garndyrus Iron Company was Sir John Mortimer, my uncle.

353

Garndyrus also provided a gainful opportunity to help feed the less fortunate.

With the Abergavenny to Brecon canal now extended to serve Newport, it was being used by inland farmers to transport wheat and barley to the docks by barge; the tonnage being under compulsory requisition by the central government at a fixed price. More, it was officially ordered that such barge loads be weighbridge-checked at Llanfoist, the Garndyrus Company's wharf.

By judicious interpretation of the tonnage vouchers, certain amounts of grain could be conveniently lost in transit: I had discovered that no weighbridge check was made on agricultural export at Newport Docks.

With every iron town on the Top owning its own wharf on the canal, it was a simple matter to convey such 'surplus' to places where the need was greater than in England. Thus began a system of minor theft which incurred less danger than raiding grain convoys, and no violence.

It was late in September when I returned from checking the barges to find a landau and its driver awaiting me outside the manager's office in Garndyrus.

It was a night of brilliant stars, mainly obliterated by the frenetic rush and tear of the compound: with three furnaces under blast and puddlers and their mates balling up at the forge, the iron was flashing to the molten glare: whips were cracking, team-wagons rolling; half-naked Irish labourers were bending to the strain, shouting their rhythmic, heaving choruses. Journeys of trams were being shackled up for runs round the Blorenge.

Off-shift ironworkers were hitting it up in the Garndyrus Inn; bawdy singing and piano accompaniment contrasting the roaring of the forges under blast as the iron was balled.

The first man I recognized in that baying redness was Idris Foreman. A good Union man this, one I'd learnt to trust. Diminutive, broad, he stared up.

'Somebody waiting for you, Hywel,' he said.

I gave the landau a glance. 'Looks important.'

'That's what I thought, so I let him into the office.'

'Who is he?'

'Don't know him from a crow, sir.'

I crossed the cinder patch and opened the office door.

Sir John Mortimer, my uncle, was sitting in my chair.

Age had wearied this one; struck him in the face. I reflected that it was some twenty-five years since the day I'd seen him last – in the Grouse at Abergwesym. A lot had happened to both of us since then.

'Well, well, well,' said he, and put his boots on the table.

'What do you want?' I asked.

Later, I flattered myself that I was calm, but turmoil was rising within me. Until now I had relegated this one to the back of my mind as a threat which could become reality; having heard nothing of him since the death of Kent, his son, I had lulled myself into a false security.

His face was skeletal and as yellow as old parchment; he was hairless, for the curse of wealth balds them quicker than scissors, my father used to say. It seemed impossible that this frail gnome could be the brother of my mother. Even more unacceptable was his claim to an ancestry of royal blood.

Sir John said, in a croaking voice, 'I have been ill, otherwise you would have seen me up here long ago.'

'Is that all you've come to say?' I opened the office door: immediately the iron rushed in; smoke, glare and the clanging of drop-hammers.

My uncle rose. 'It would appear that you don't understand the situation, Nephew. This office – this ironworks, indeed, is mine; if anyone is going, it is you.' In passing he kicked the door shut, then stood before me, slapping his leg with a small, silvered cane. 'Had you troubled to enquire,' he added, 'you'd have discovered that, upon the death of Thomas Hill last year, I acquired a controlling interest in the Garndyrus Iron Company from his stupid, profligate son. Hill may have appointed you as manager here – only a week

355

or so ago I heard of this. I shall now have the pleasure of discharging you.'

We faced each other across the little room, and the faint sounds of the works contained us.

He said: 'You killed my son.'

'I did not.'

'As your father killed Tom, my youngest.'

'You brought that upon yourself.'

Wandering the room, he said, 'Down the centuries it's been my family's misfortune to have to tolerate you insolent bastards. My sister brought you forth in sorrow; ending her own life like a common felon, to escape your rake of a father –'

'Leave my mother out of this!'

'She could have had her pick of the aristocracy. Instead she shared a bed with a charlatan of countless paramours and London larkery. By God, Mortymer, you and your bastards have something to answer for, and I have only been waiting my time.'

'We have nothing in common except insults, so go!'

'Ah no, we have much in common – it is sonship. You spew your seed in dark places, Mortymer. And I'll not end my days without making you pay in blood for my sister and my sons, to say nothing of my trusted Musker . . .'

'Have you finished the melodrama?' Catching him by his coat, I propelled him to the open door, and he shrieked, slashing at me with his cane and shouting.

'Bring forth your daughters, then, one after the other. I'll let them flourish, for they will not perpetuate your disgusting name. But your son, Iestyn, is precious to me; and if your woman spawns another, he will be precious, also. I will not leave this world until first they, then you, are six feet under.' Suddenly, he brought the cane down across my face. Tearing it from him, I hauled him through the door, and he tripped and fell full length.

From the ground he cried, 'A curse on your name, you hear me? This is not the beginning Mortymer, but the end.

Cursed are the bitches you mate with and the whelps they breech; one by one you will lose them, then I'll drive you out of these mountains!'

Plainly he was mad; his eyes were dilated and he was laughing as a lunatic. Mud was upon his face, and as his coachman lifted him, he stooped, filled his fists with furnace grit and flung it at me.

Slamming the office door, I leaned against it; bowing my head, I screwed up my hands, fighting to save myself from committing murder. The last I saw of him that night was through the soot-stained window. He was standing up in the landau, his whip cracking down on the backs of his horses as they galloped madly up the tracks. I watched until they were white smudges against the molten glare of the furnaces.

A knock came on the door behind me; Idris Foreman, screwing his cap, stood there.

He said, apologetically, 'The new master told me to come, sir. I . . . I'm to take over as manager immediately.'

'Are you, now!'

'Sorry, sir.'

'Don't call me that, Idris; from now on that's what I'll be calling you.'

He raised his pouched eyes to mine. 'Any time, mind – no hurry, is there . . . ?'

I gathered up my things and went home.

Forty-one

There is a wind-silence that comes in the night and brings calamity.

I have heard it within the explosion when fire and water meet. In the moment when the fire-box belches molten iron: I have heard it in dreams of burning witches; in the incantations of martyrs searched by the butcher's knife . . . before the coming of the braziers.

Always these dreams betoken fire.

I lay stiff and tense beside Elianor and listened to her breathing in the dark . . . and heard again the boot that scuffled in the yard.

In bare feet I tiptoed down the stairs and into the kitchen. And heard, in the moment before I reached the back door, a man's hoarse shout; the clatter of the tin bath falling from its hook down near the throne. And I swung back the door in time to see Iestyn clambering up, and beyond him the form of a man racing against the sky.

'What the hell's happening?' I said, and pulled Iestyn to his feet.

'Somebody trying to get in, Dada.'

'Why didn't you call me?'

'*Diawch*, mun, I can handle it.'

In his nightshirt he stood, all four feet of him, aged eight.

'Then why didn't you collar him?'

He made a child's face, his eyes like stars. 'Jesus, he'd have coffined me – he was over six feet.'

Briefly, I held him against me and noticed that his fists were still clenched for the strike.

'Come back to bed, and next time have a go. It's not the

358

size of the man, remember, it's the size of the fight in the man.'

'All right, but don't tell Mam and the girls – you know what they are.' He added, going up the stairs, 'Next time I'll have the bugger, mind.'

I thought: nobody, *nobody* is going to take this son from me.

Morfydd returned from her Nanty scrubbing in time for breakfast. Ellie, carrying all before her now, was cooking bacon; Edwina, always a dozy-Dora first thing in the morning, was dreaming at the window: Iestyn, his dark eyes everywhere, was packing in bread and drip; Morfydd, facing me at the other end of the table, raised her face to mine and gave me a long, belligerent stare.

The best thing about daughters, I reckon, is the knowledge that one day you can off-load them on to some unsuspecting man.

'Big Rhys came back from prison last night,' said she.

'Big Rhys?'

'The man who was once your friend.'

Ellie said, turning the bacon. 'Still our friend, as far as I know.'

'Oh no, he's not,' said Morfydd, and Ellie said, sighing:

'Look, girl. It's too early in the day to quarrel. Eat your breakfast and get off up to bed.'

'Eighteen months!' Morfydd rose and stamped about the kitchen. 'Swansea Correction, and the last six weeks on Beaumaris treadmill. And we didn't even know!'

'I knew,' I said, drinking tea.

'Then what did you do about it?'

'What did you expect me to do – organize a break-out?'

And Ellie said, coming to the table with my plate: 'Look, Morfydd. He grain-raided, they caught him, and he got eighteen months. He was lucky. Ten years ago they'd have hanged him.'

And Morfydd replied, her voice shrill with anger: 'Ten

years ago they had better men than now. God's blood! What kind of people are we?' She sat by the grate, her hands screwing in her lap, her eyes brooding a male malevolence. 'If I was a man I'd kick these bloody ironmasters from here to Risca.'

'Watch your language!'

'Safe houses make cowards,' said Morfydd. 'Down at Usk Correction they never stop the whippings, the treadmill's wearing out, and they're starving the paupers in Goetre Poorhouse. What's happening to our country? And what are we doing about it?'

'More than you think,' I said, eating.

'Is that a fact, Dada? Then I see no sign of it.' She flung out an arm, pointing. 'Last month you were the manager up at Garndyrus. This month you're an assistant puddler under Idris Foreman. Every kick, every damn thump you take lying down.'

'Don't shout at your father,' said Ellie, and Iestyn, I noticed, sighed and turned up his eyes at the ceiling.

'I'm off,' said he, and kissed Mam, winked at me, and went off to school.

Edwina, her head low, was quietly weeping, and Morfydd said, getting up again, 'Oh, dry up, for God's sake!'

'Always quarrelling these days,' sobbed Edwina, and I went round and got out a handkerchief and mopped her up. 'Always quarrelling,' she repeated, broken. 'It isn't Christian.'

'Matthew Twelve, twenty-five,' said Ellie. 'The child's right. ". . . Every city or house divided against itself shall not stand." Amen.'

'Isn't that what I'm saying, Mam?' On her feet again now, this Morfydd, sparring for a fight. 'Unless we make a stand Wales will go under. And men like Big Rhys Jenkins are trying to do it.'

'Meaning that I'm not,' I said, buttering bread.

'Meaning that I'd think a damned sight more of my father if he made a fight of it!'

'How dare you!' said Ellie, threatening her with a fork.

'She dares all right, because it is true,' I replied.

'Not true, Hywel, and you know it!'

Momentarily, we all stared at each other. I said, 'Finish this now, girls, let's have an end to it.'

For I knew them: get these two fighting-cocks going, and blood and hair would fly. Ellie would never accept an injustice.

'Oh, Dada!' cried Morfydd, her eyes bright. 'It is not like you! When they tell you jump, you jump – you only ask "How high?" The place is in rags. People are starving in this town. Big Rhys comes back after doing time for grain-raiding, and there isn't a man here to greet him. My God, what's wrong with you!'

I got up. 'Big Rhys will end on a rope the way he's going. As for the way I handle things here, that's my business. My responsibility is to the people in this house, and if you don't like it, you know what you can do.'

Which sent Edwina into a flood and racing out of the kitchen.

'Now look what you've done,' said Ellie. 'God help me! I think I'll go, too, and to hell with the damned old cooking.'

She began to cry, too, which got Morfydd up, smoothing and dabbing her dry, and don't take on so, Mam, Dada didn't mean it, did you?

Getting sick of it, me; what with one and the other of them.

One moment worried about her coming into the family way, now about to start a bloody revolution.

Daughters! If anyone wants a couple I've got them to spare.

But, much worse than this was to come.

The house wasn't only divided against itself, it was about to fall.

It happened six weeks after Sir John kicked me off the job as manager at Garndyrus.

❧

Gone was the pony and trap; gone were the managerial benefits, the cosy office, the forelock-touching respect from workmen: I was an assistant puddler again, stripped to the waist in the September frosts; one moment shivering cold, next moment frying in the heat of the furnaces. Idris Foreman came up; a North Country man.

'You're sticking it well, Hywel.'

'Got no alternative, have I? Half-pay's better than nothing.'

'Is there something between you and Sir John Mortimer?'

'Only a coincidence of names.'

'That all?' His small blue eyes regarded me in the shattered folds of his furnace-wealed face: a good man this; a sort of Ephraim Davies of Blaenafon.

'All I'm prepared to tell you.'

'What does Ellie think of it – you coming down the lines, I mean.'

'She thinks a lot but doesn't say much, that's Ellie. Right now she's got her hands full with her stomach.'

'When's the baby due?'

I rested on the firing-iron and nodded to the pull-up lad, and he dropped the chains and the furnace door slammed down; black smoke billowed up where once was molten fire; the bellows roared.

'Any moment now, by the size of her. Can you use another lad?'

'Who?'

The hauliers swayed on the rope between us; the wagons groaned, biting on the cinder-rail; there came the hoarse, Irish chanting.

'Iestyn?'

'Your lad? You're bringing him down?'

'Got to. The money's dropped and he's eating like a horse. Dai One will have to go, too, if this continues – he's a reasonable old pig – he'd be the first to see the sense of it.'

'Are you off that bad?'

362

I said, throwing down my iron, 'Who isn't these days? Can you start him?'

'On ironstone chipping, aye.' He eyed me. 'How old is he?'

'Eight. He's dying to get into it, he's sick of school.'

Idris spat and smoothed the spittle with his foot, and it shone like snail-crawl in the early light of the September dawn.

I said: 'I need the loot, Idris – another mouth to feed – I didn't have the last job long enough to save on manager's money.'

'Christ Almighty,' said Idris, and looked at the sky. 'What a country!'

'The country's all right, mun, it's the people running it,' and it was the last thing I said before the explosion.

'Bloody hell, what's that?' cried Idris, swinging about.

'Down in town,' I said, and we stood watching as a plume of fire-shot smoke rose lazily on the rim of the mountain. Faintly on the wind came the sound of the accident bell, a weary tolling.

'Sounds like somebody's caught it in Waunavon,' said Idris.

But it wasn't in Waunavon. Stack Square had gone up.

Had it happened earlier it would have got the lot of us in bed, because it blew out the front of our house, demolished the kitchen, killed Dai One, and landed the table like firewood at the base of the Stack. Had it happened an hour later, I would have been back off night shift, Morfydd returned from Nanty, and all of us would have been at breakfast. As it was it hit Grandfer Shams-y-Coed off the throne at the bottom of the garden, and Mrs Ben Thomas in Number Two had an assisted delivery.

Ellie was lying on the cinders of the Square when I arrived there breathless; Big Rhys was kneeling beside her, and Dr

Steel, still in his night clothes, had his bag open; Edwina was crying hysterically in the arms of Belinda Handy, who had run over from the Drum and Monkey; Iestyn, dry-eyed, was staring at the ground in horror.

Blood was on my girl's face.

With closed eyes she lay, the Cyfarthfa blanket heaped high over the mound of her stomach: nor did she stir when I called to her. All around stood the neighbours of Stack Square with blank eyes, shocked. The surgeon said: 'She is concussed, Mortymer; do not mind the blood, she looks worse than she is.'

'What happened, for God's sake?' I cried, and Big Rhys answered.

'It's the Stack manhole; somebody must have left shot-firing in the soot door, and it ignited.'

'Ellie!' I was kissing her face.

'Is there anybody else hurt?' asked the surgeon, and stood up, shouting, 'Now don't stand gaping, she's going to be all right. Come on, all of you, back to your houses!'

They obeyed instantly: loved and respected in our town, this one.

Big Rhys said, 'Leave her, Hywel, you cannot kiss her awake.'

'Are the children all right?' I asked, and Iestyn said, now beside me:

'The bed turned over when the floor came down, Dada. Mr Rhys came in and helped me get her out.'

'Couldn't sleep, see,' said Rhys. 'I was at my window and saw the manhole cover rise – I tell ye, it was an explosion in the soot door.'

Men and women running now with dousing buckets of water, forming a chain, for the piled debris of the kitchen was beginning to burn in gaseous flares.

'Ellie,' I said, and put my arms round her and lifted her against me, knowing the emotion of love and loathing: it restricted coherent thought, it stifled my breath.

And at that moment Ellie opened her eyes.

'There now,' said the surgeon; opening her mouth, he poured in laudanum. 'We are back, are we?' He elbowed me and got to his feet. 'Now take her somewhere warm. Hot, sweet tea, understand?'

An accident gambo arrived; three each side, we had lifted Ellie upon it just as Morfydd came.

'*Mama!*' With flying hair she came, like a madwoman.

Now there's a commotion, with Morfydd flinging people out of it and trying to get at Ellie, and neighbours barring the way, and she shrieked and shrieked – they heard her all down Staffordshire Row.

'Oh, my little love!' she cried. '*Mama fach!*' And she tore at the people holding her, kicking the men, belting the women.

'Let her through,' I said, and the gambo stopped at the North Street entrance.

People are strange. I have seen this one trimming a stump with scissors; giving lip and dirty banter to a collier who had a leg under a tram. Now she was holding her mother's hands and howling like a child with all its tuneless sounds.

'For God's sake, pull yourself together,' said Ellie. 'The neighbours are all eyes, damn them.'

We took her down to Shepherds' Square, where Mr Roberts and his missus were changing a bed; convenient for Mr Steel, this, being opposite his surgery. Then in came the neighbours, as usual; hanging on the walls like ivy, and who could have done it, leaving shot-firing about, and it couldn't have happened to better people. A pair of accident sheets arrived from Mrs Shanco Mathews; bandages and horse liniment from Belinda Handy, and a pair of breast phials from the skinny Mrs Gwallter, for things like this can always come in on occasions. Mrs Will Tafarn, whose chap used to beat her down in Aaron Brute's Row, brought honey-water from his hives; Iolo Milk came with six ladlings of free milk with the compliments of Butcher Harris, since deceased, and Sarah Hopkins's cook sent a bottle of French wine and an iron tonic for anaemia. Nellie Washboard came visiting with carbolic, and so did Sian Lewis. All this together with Nana Dorney's goat tethered outside for cream. I tell you this – you can go abroad in the world and never find neighbours like the valley Welsh. They even spread straw a foot thick on the bottom of North Street to deaden the hooves, so Ellie could sleep.

'Have you seen this child's hands, Mortymer?' Dr Steel asked.

Iestyn now; the palms blistered and blackened, and Big Rhys said, 'She was under the bed and the mattress burning; when I arrived he had his hands in the fire.'

As he tended Iestyn's hands in his surgery, I asked, 'What about the baby, Doctor?'

'It's not the baby I'm worried about, Mortymer, nor, indeed, your wife. Women in child – and the child they carry – have an infinite ability to survive calamity. The females of the species are the tough ones, this is why they live longer; that men are the strongest of the human kind has long been a mistaken philosophy. She will survive, and so will her baby.' And he frowned up at me over the top of his pince-nez as he bandaged Iestyn's hands.

'What concerns me far more is the astonishing nature of the accident. Shot-firer's powder left in a soot manhole outside your door? One could be forgiven for thinking that somebody might want you out of Blaenafon.'

Forty-two

I had to take some action to save the family.

Clearly, to stay on in Blaenafon, in the hope that my uncle would relent his stupid vendetta against us, was hopeless.

To leave the town without my employer's permission – Sir John's – would mean the Blacklist. With winter coming on, one could tramp from works to works without success; many a family had ended frozen to death in lonely mountain caves, or worse, in the Poorhouse: some in this predicament, as with the foresters of the Forest of Dean, had been reduced to beg for entry into Houses of Correction, in order to stay alive.

Ellie and I had but little money saved: anticipating the rewards of my promotion to Manager, we had spent on new clothes and things for the new baby.

There was but one possibility.

By the coming of November, Ellie was back on her feet again, swiping the dust from one place to another as women do, and like a clipper in full sail: bright-eyed and merry, she washed and cooked and mended in Number Three Shepherds' Square, into which we had recently moved on the recommendation of Dr Steel; and Twm-y-Beddau and his brood came next door, they having been blasted out of Stack Square at the same time as us. Within a week or so the baby would be born. When that happened, Iestyn would begin work up at Garndyrus with me, for his wage would be sorely needed.

This, I knew, would leave him unprotected. It was bad

enough working up at Garndyrus in the knowledge that Ellie, carrying the child, was exposed to attack except for neighbours; it was even worse to wonder what might happen if Ellie produced a son, another male to continue the hated Mortymer line.

Would Sir John act then, I wondered.

So far he had been quiet. Working in the furnace area at Garndyrus, I had not even seen him on the job, although Idris Foreman said he'd visited twice.

With the new baby due at any day, I decided to act.

There comes to a man a marvellous sense of peace when he watches his children sleep. Now I left the lamp by the door and went slowly to the bed where Morfydd and Iestyn slept – Edwina, because we had not yet properly settled in upstairs (and it was a grand upstairs in the Square, let me tell you) still slept under the kitchen table for warmth.

Iestyn, his nose turned up, was upon his back, sending up manly snores.

Morfydd, her black hair in thick, dark waves over her homespun nightdress, was awake; her dark eyes slanted up at me as I bent above her.

'You awake?'

She jerked a thumb at Iestyn. 'Jesus and Mary, do ye expect a woman to sleep during that bloody palaver?'

'Push him on to his front. And don't swear.'

'I keep doing that, but he comes back over. Oh, Dada, when can I have a bed to myself?'

'Marry an ironmaster and you can have one tomorrow.' I kissed her face.

It is a great pity for a man, I think, when the soft cheek of a puppy-fat daughter is exchanged for the firm, smooth shadow of a woman's face.

The colourless and cracked lips of winter vanish in the red curves of the woman's mouth; now fashioned for others. The scragged-back hair now falls in lustrous waves of beauty. No-Teeth-In-Front has grown twin pearls of shining whiteness; the throat is of swan-like alabaster.

One scarcely dares to touch now, the property being no longer father's.

'When we can find a pagan in the mountains we'll marry you off,' I said. 'A gypsy, for instance.'

'A lot you'd care!'

Bending, I kissed her another peck. Iestyn turned over in sleep as if expecting one, but I never kissed him.

This the boy–man; the good in him is me, the evil in him later, also. For this I believe – that while a daughter is the product of a womb's intimate manufacture, intrinsic in design of the female by the female, a wife who bears a son is but the vehicle of that birth. How otherwise come the bulging biceps, the wide shoulders and the javelin of the hunt that trembles to be thrown? While Morfydd was of Elianor, this, my son, was flesh of my flesh: with him I would know all my later days; live again in him, even into senility when the muscles sag and the water burns: he alone could rekindle the lost but eternal fire, the brooding aggression of the male.

And when the threat arrives, as now, it comes like the roaring of the tusk-horned mammal of the cave; the stink of the festering jaws that scatter the ashes of the primitive fire. I looked down at my sleeping son, and Morfydd came up on an elbow in the bed.

'You all right, Dada?'

I nodded, and left them, and her arms went about my boy in the belly of the bed as I closed the door.

This, I thought, was the end of it all; now was the certainty.

Going down to the kitchen, still warm and pervaded by the smells of last night's supper, I knelt near the door within a yard of Edwina's arm – flung out like a tram accident from under the table where she was sleeping – and raised a loose floorboard.

Taking out Kent Mortimer's pistol, I charged and loaded it, ramming home the ball.

North Street was black with him and near freezing, with

only a solitary light in Staffordshire Row, as I went up the Keeper's Road to Pwll-du.

Llanfoist House, Sir John's home, was a mansion situated below the canal bank, not far from the loading wharf. It was here that the Mortimers, having left Tregaron area for the industrialized South, made their family seat.

Here on the extensive lawns, under rose bowers, they entertained the county gentility. Here they stabled the hated yeomanry for the suppression of the rioting Welsh.

It was here, too, that the failing Sir John raised more sons from a second wife and sent them to English boarding-schools; once, therefore, this house has been full of children's laughter and a retinue of servants, grooms and two gardeners, one of whom was Eli Rodent, lately retired from the Forgehammer.

But now, apart from a cook, a parlour maid, Eli Rodent and a groom, my uncle lived in splendid isolation. At an age of more than eighty, he had abandoned his office of Deputy Lord Lieutenant of the County of Monmouthshire, for age had wearied him, and this had long been so. Perhaps the festering rancour of his hatreds, I thought, had led him into premature senility. Certainly, when I had last seen him at Garndyrus, he was but the wraith of the man who had taken every penny off my father at the Grouse Inn, all those years ago.

I could have used Chancer for the journey down the coach road, round Gilwern Hill and down to the canal at Llanfoist, but I did not. To have done so would have raised suspicion by his absence from the stables. Anyway, he was nearly on his last legs, said the ostlers: age, the smoke-filled tunnels and coal dust had taken a toll of his lungs: soon, I knew, regretfully, I would have to put down this good and faithful servant.

On the long descent I left the coach road and took across the fields. The two big furnaces of the Vale were going on the

370

night shift like marrowbones and cleavers; the Llanelly forge was whining like something from the pit of hell. Keeping clear of these, I cut over behind the new Navigation Inn and took to the towpath, concealing myself in wayside bushes as the barges went past.

In this manner, walking and hiding, I reached the fencing round Llanfoist House, and the road to Abergavenny was a purple ribbon below me in the moonlight. Strangely, a bonfire beacon was burning on the peak of the Sugar Loaf, and I hoped, because it was doubtless a signal, that it would attract dragoons: it did. Even as I reached the boundary fence, a troop of six yeoman militia galloped out of the house stables and took the road to the mountain.

Fate, it appeared, was delivering Sir John Mortimer into my hands.

Vaulting the fence, I was now within the grounds of Llanfoist House. Two lights were burning on its white façade; the entrance, dominated by immense Doric columns, flashed back its brown and gold embellishments; the gravel drive approaching it was emblazoned by a capricious moon just as I came out of the shadows.

Torture would follow my capture, should I be discovered in these grounds. With the country in a ferment of unrest, the authorities went to any lengths to obtain the betrayal of accomplices; a child of twelve could be hanged for stealing bread, and minor thieves executed in batches. My death would follow Sir John's imminently, if my identity was established.

But it was not death that was worrying me, it was the torture by flogging; better suicide before capture, I thought, than face 'marriage to the three sisters' – that is, roped to the whipping triangle – with a brain full of wanted names.

Big Rhys had been heard to say (but not to me) that he had seen living flesh sticking to the walls of the whipping-chamber in Old Beaumaris prison: that while on the nearby treadmill, he had watched the skin flying from convicts' backs after no more than twenty lashes of the cat-o'-nine-tails – while Ralph Rashleigh later recorded that '. . . after the first dozen strokes it was like jagged wire tearing furrows into my flesh, and the second dozen seemed as if someone was filling those furrows with molten lead'.

How many names would I spit out if subjected to such pain? I wondered. Does a man ever know himself until confronted with that ultimate decision?

No, I did not fear the pain, I swear it; but I feared my own inability to stay dumb in the face of torture.

Therefore, I determined to kill this man with my hands; the pistol I would keep for myself if all else failed.

Swiftly crossing a dancing lawn, I gained the south-west corner of the mansion; here, I had recalled, ivy grew in profusion, leading to a small, jutting balcony. From there I could reach a window-sash of the first floor, which was in darkness; a light was burning in a larger window of the floor above. Gripping the ivy, I swung myself upwards.

I was reaching up for the railings of the little balcony when light shafted the gravel drive below me. Clinging there, I watched a servant come out. He crossed the drive and went to the dancing lawn: here was positioned a pretty red-painted hut in an Oriental pagoda style; unlocking its door, the servant went within. Seizing the opportunity, I dropped lightly to the ground, paused for a moment, then darted through the half-open front door.

It was, I thought, as if Fate had decreed that Sir John Mortimer would die that night.

The hall floor echoed back a cold mosaic; instantly finding a drape of heavy curtains, I stood within them, waiting for the servant to return: he did, and as he closed the front door a clock in the village began to strike the hour.

Midnight; I counted the chimes. Then, my senses more accustomed to my surroundings, I heard bawdy chorus-singing of the canal navvies coming from the Navigation Inn; faintly I heard this, but it was then obliterated by the footsteps of the returning servant; he was carrying a heavy vase of flowers; in the light of the hall I saw his profile in a split second of recognition.

Eli Rodent.

I could have reached out, encircled his scraggy throat with my hand and drawn him, kicking, into the darkness of my hiding place. But I missed the opportunity, then as he pushed aside the draught curtain to open the door behind me and opened his mouth for the cry, I struck; all Eli Rodent saw was a fist coming out of the shadows, and he took it full. With the vase of flowers jammed between us, he slipped slowly down the front of me, and I lowered him to the floor.

Voices were coming from a room below the hall; probably the kitchen, I reasoned, for the voices were female. The cook and the parlour maid?

The hall stairway faced me now, a winding balustrade of polished timber with banisters of green and gold leading to the first floor; probably Sir John's bedroom: now up a curving staircase of scarlet, I ran swiftly along a landing carpet. The women's voices faded below me; the silence tingled.

Glancing down to the hall, I noticed my first mistake.

A boot – Eli Rodent's – projected obscenely from under the curtains of the hall; anyone coming up from below stairs would instantly notice it, and I made to return and cover it; only to flatten my body against the wall of the landing as a woman came clumping up the servants' stairs from the kitchen.

'Eli!' She did not call him harshly; indeed, she seemed to fear disturbing the place; an indication, I thought, that Sir John might be sleeping. The parlour maid. Watching her over the landing rails, I saw her hesitate: if she went to the front door to call from there, the man's outflung boot would trip her. With a thumping heart, I waited. The girl turned in a swish of skirts and went back down the stairs to the kitchen.

Door after door faced me on the landing. One by one I opened them, peering within: bed after bed I saw in the faint moonlight of the casement windows; all were empty of sleepers.

There came to me then, with a little shock, the cold reality of what I was about to do.

This would be the first time I had killed a man in cold blood.

On the coach road near the Clydach Cambrian public, I had killed Justice Williams, but it was not murder; it was a legal execution carried out in the cause of justice, and I had suffered not the slightest recrimination. This had been one who was a blemish on the face of his country, a sadist who had taken delight in inflicting punishments; branding, flogging, transportation and gory disembowelling, the filthy death Britain reserved for those she called traitors. It was for this I had killed him, not for his rape of Rhia, not even for Bimbo's bastardy. That was but the spark that had instituted an act of justice.

But this new business was different.

The murder of Sir John, I thought, kneeling in the shadows of the next door I opened, would be an act of self-preservation: sweat sprang to my forehead, and I wiped it into my hair.

Even the carrying of the pistol, I thought, was akin to cowardice; its use was a method of distancing myself from the murder – for murder, not an execution, this would surely be. While it had been easy to choke out the life of a criminal like Justice Williams, this man, my uncle, was no criminal; he was merely the instigator of the jigsaw of vendetta; a death-feud which had originated before I was born. Blood for blood was a disgusting malevolence; nothing could excuse the vindictiveness with which he had pursued it. But was I not now contributing to the rancour by retaliation? And would not I demand an eye for an eye if I had seen the rope-burn on a sister's neck? And known her husband's profligacy?

Yet, Rhia had died, and I kept seeing her face with irresistible clarity; her blood cried out to me from the grave up at Horeb. And remembering my son, this urged me onwards . . . until I came to the last door of the landing.

There was a glint of light under this one: I opened it with care, first cocking the pistol.

The bedroom door swung open, exposing a vast, carpeted room with large casement windows. Dark oak furniture lined the walls; an unlit chandelier hung from an ornate ceiling: beside a great four-poster bed half-veiled with purple drapes, a single candle burned.

In the middle of the bed Sir John lay sleeping.

I entered noiselessly on the thick carpet and, with the pistol held low, approached to where I could see him clearly. Conscience raised a shudder in me once again; to kill a sleeping man was no better than shooting him in the back, but I fought away the perfidy. Remembering Iestyn, I thickened my grip on the pistol, but then hesitated.

I hesitated, for I had seen in the face before me a hint of a defilement: the brow on the white pillow was too parched, the cheeks too sallow for acceptance of one merely sleeping. And as I bent closer, and listened, I could not hear his breathing.

The candlelight flickered, suddenly flaring: I saw more clearly the sensuous line of the nostrils, the thin mouth, and noticed for the first time, beneath the wrinkled, slitted lids, the white eyeballs.

This man was dead.

Disbelief struck me. Then, for an unknown reason, I was possessed by anger. Sir John Mortimer, my uncle, was already dead, and in death had brought my intentions to a lame and impotent conclusion.

I lowered the pistol, and, as I did so, I saw a woman standing by a door.

This was a connecting door to another bedroom; I had not noticed it before. Strangely, the sight of her standing there, as noiseless as an apparition, did not surprise or disturb me: it was as if she was a commonplace happening; a relative who had dropped in to a sick room in passing.

But then I realized that I had not seen the door open, nor heard her entry at a time when my mind was tuned to mouse-sound. And I straightened, peering across the coverlet of the bed where my uncle lay.

She was beautiful, this woman; the bright sheen of her youthful face was enhanced by the long mauve gown she wore: about her shoulders she wore a lace coatee of glowing whiteness, and upon this fell her hair in tight, black ringlets. She was tall and held herself with the dignity of a princess, and had she moved, I thought, her step would be soundless; but she did not move.

Beyond the woman the curtains were ajar and the sky was spangled by a canopy of stars: the woman moved then, shutting out the stars, raised her hand to me, and smiled. I saw in that smile a face I knew and loved: her every gesture I had seen before. In the moment before she faded from my sight, and phantasm diminished by my own recollections, I saw round her throat a necklace of rubies, but it was not rubies; it was the rope-burn. And I saw, in the second before she was lost to me, that expression of excited joy with which she had always greeted my childhood.

A moment later, as quickly as she had come, she vanished.

I touched the locket that held her portrait and knew that my mother, in death, would never be lost to me.

The dead do return to those they love, of course; unseen, they come to look; at times to warn or to share one's joys and griefs. As I saw my mother in that room I had seen her many times before in Tregaron – in summer I best remember her – going in a circle of delight, clapping her little hands together as she held a buttercup up to the sun: within an hour she was in tears because the buttercup had died. Had she come now, I wondered, to save me from the sin of murder: had she even brought about her brother's death?

A woman screamed in the hall below, and I knew they had discovered Eli's unconscious body.

Going to the window, I flung open the casement, swung

my legs over the sill and lowered myself into the little railed balcony. Then I went down the ivy hand over hand, and dropped to the drive below.

Up on the canal bank I ran along the towpath; then took the fields along the side of the Blorenge and over the top to Blaenafon, and home.

Ellie didn't stir as I undressed swiftly and slipped into the warm bed beside her, instantly falling into an exhausted sleep.

Forty-three

'True, is it, that Iestyn starts work today?' asked Edwina at the breakfast table.

'Aye,' I replied. 'What of it?'

She screwed at her hands like a penitent. 'The English preacher do say he is going up years before his time.'

'Does he, now?'

Morfydd was cutting bread; I saw her glance at me.

'Aye,' continued Edwina. 'And I heard him tell the owners straight that it is terrible to see the little ones on the Top in winter, and that heaven has no place for the father who sends them there.'

'Excuse me,' said Iestyn, getting down. 'I will start going.'

'Wait,' I said to him, and lit my pipe. 'Let us be clear, Edwina. Is it the English preacher saying this, or my daughter?'

'Little matter,' said Morfydd with a sniff. 'Everybody in town is thinking it, including me.'

'Good,' I answered. 'Now let it be said without English preachers and owners.'

Morfydd lifted dark, angry eyes at me, saying, '*Diawl!* Too young he is, and you know it. We are not like the Hughes or Griffiths – a penny a week less and they starve. You send a baby to work in iron in a house that is already taking thirty shillings a week. It is not Christian.'

I re-lit my clay. 'Take my shift at the forge today. Dressed in trews you might run the house better, I doubt.'

'Easy to say, but no answer,' came the reply, and she got up and stamped to the fire.

'Oh, please, do not quarrel,' whispered Edwina, close to tears.

Said Morfydd, 'Shut the snivelling. It do gain nothing. I say a bitch on every man who sends a child under ten to work with fire. God help us, the owners will be snatching them from their cradles soon, and that's not the only injustice. Half the town is in debt to the Company Shop, and the other half starving. The place is in rags at the height of winter. Over in Nanty we work like horses, here we live like pigs, and when the owner says grunt we grunt . . .'

'It is written,' I replied. 'As poor we must labour.'

'Aye, labour, and sweat by the bucketful. Right, you! Does Tomos Traherne tell you what else is written? Suffer little children and such is the Kingdom – that is written, too, he says. But Sara Roberts chips the ore when she is not as high as God's knee. Little Cristin Williams is buried with cold, and Enid Griffiths gets the iron over her legs at nine.'

'As poor we are born to suffering,' I said.

'*Whisht!*' cried she. 'Suffering all right and early for the Kingdom, by order of the masters and the preachers who take their money, eh? Listen! The God of Traherne is a pagan Christ. Sick to death I am of the bowing and scraping, and tired enough to sleep for a month, and if Iestyn goes to Garndyrus he goes without my permission.'

'This has been a long time coming out.'

'But not soon enough,' breathed Morfydd, coming back to the table. 'If there's not a man with the belly to lead us, we can soon find another out of town. Mr Williams comes from London to speak to us and there isn't a soul at his meeting –'

'Wait,' I interjected. 'What do you know of Williams?'

'That he stands for fair wages and decent hours like the workers are fighting for in London.'

'You've been to his meetings?'

'Yes, and not ashamed of it.'

'Nobody says you should be, but you will keep his talk out of the house or find another place to live, for I will not have it used as a political platform, and don't blame me if the

379

Baileys run you out of Nanty, for they are dead against lawyers.'

'The Baileys have more friends than they think,' whispered Morfydd.

'Oh, Morfydd!' breathed Edwina, her hands clasped.

'Yes,' I replied, 'for I'm a worker, and a good worker knows his place, and perhaps you'll tell me what we'd do without the Hills and Baileys, who have put their every penny into these mountains and are entitled to something back, even at the cost of sweated labour.'

My temper was rising, and I dared not let this argument continue; had Elianor been here she'd have put an end to it minutes back. The injustice of Morfydd's hints of my apparent weakness was burning deep in me. I wanted to shout that I'd been fighting against injustice before she was born: that I was one with her in everything she stood for, but dared not, for Morfydd had a tongue. Perpetually on the brink of outraged anger, she'd be one worse than Big Rhys when it came to secrecy. Until now I had managed to keep the house free of my politics, and intact. I didn't intend to risk its safety by sharing old secrets with an adolescent daughter; it was enough that Ellie knew of me . . .

But Morfydd had got the bit between her teeth, and she shouted: 'And perhaps you'll tell me what they'd do without us. The masters of these towns are bleeding us to death, and if Williams had his way he'd kick the backside of every ironmaster from here to England.'

I got up to leave. 'Easy in front of the children, please.'

Morfydd's face was flushed. 'Labour indeed! Crawling through the galleries where the masters wouldn't rear their pigs, and them sitting in the middle of their Company Parks paying wages in kind, and their prices in the Tommy Shops going higher every month!'

'Finish now,' I said, wearily.

'God help me, I'm not started,' cried Morfydd, and she swung to Iestyn whose jaw had dropped. 'Away to Mam and say goodbye, Iestyn, and remember that it was your father who sent you to work years before your time for pigs of ironmasters who have money to burn.'

'Enough!' I hit the table with my fist in sudden fury that sent the crockery rolling and Iestyn scrambling up the stairs, with Edwina sitting there howling like a dog.

Five minutes later Iestyn returned to the kitchen, his face bright with expectancy. Morfydd, hers now pale with anger, was waiting with a scarf.

'Round here, you,' said she, tying him up and sending me daggers. 'Freeze if you must, but do it in style. Eating-bag, tea-bottle, vest on, hair combed, scarf. Right now, away,' and she pushed him through the door. 'No fighting with the men, and keep off the women.'

'I will pray for you,' said Edwina from a corner.

'Aye,' replied Morfydd. 'Very warm he'll be after prayers. Move your backside, boy. Dada is waiting and scared to death of being late.' She tried to kiss him, I noticed, but he pushed her away.

Now, striding away into the darkness, I heard his pattering boots behind me, and he joined me with an upward, fearful glance. I said: 'Only one way to go to work, Iestyn – early. Please remember it.'

'Yes, Dada,' said he.

'Which shows respect for the man who pays you – Mr Crawshay Bailey of Nantyglo, who has been kind enough to take you on his books and lend you to Garndyrus.'

'Very kind,' said he.

We trudged along past Staffordshire Row: the moon was shivering; the pale stars looked cold in the frosty sky. The first day at work, I thought, was to any youngster a shock to the system; and for all his blatant masculinity, this one was still a child, and tongues and habits were rough in Garndyrus. I said to him: 'You're going to work before your time because of a new baby coming, do you understand?'

'Aye. Mam has told me now just.'

'A bit of a surprise for you, eh?'

381

He said, 'I . . . I heard the people talking, but didn't believe them.'

I nodded. 'Some things you must know when beginning work, Iestyn. Tonight, when we get home, the new baby may be with Mam. You know how it will come?'

'Aye, Dada. Out of the stomach and with pain.' He said this with a face cast down, and I know how he felt.

'Well done. And do you know how the baby was put into Mam?'

I hauled him into the middle of the road, for Mrs Tossach was emptying slops out of her window: very handy was she with a bucket of maiden's water.

'It . . . it was put by the seed,' said Iestyn, knocking off the drops.

'Well informed you are – who told you this?'

'Mr Tomos Traherne and Mo Jenkins, the son of Big Rhys.'

'There's a mine of information – does Mo know who put the seed into Mam?'

'Aye,' said he. 'Iolo Milk.'

I whistled long at the moon. 'Did . . . did he explain when this happened?'

Iestyn replied, uncertainly, 'On . . . on the outing to Abergavenny, you were on day shift and Iolo Milk took Mam up the mountain, and . . .'

'Continue,' I said, 'do not spare me.'

'And . . . and the seed from the heather went under her skirt and into her, because it was spring.'

I pulled out my handkerchief, blew my nose like a trumpet, and wiped the tears from my eyes.

'Is it sad with you, Dada?' His small boy's face was upturned.

'Upon my soul,' I said, 'it's a pity to spoil your innocence,' and spoke more to him of women and men; of the secrets of wives and respect for sisters: and there grew between us an affinity we had not shared before, so that I eventually took his hand.

'Nobody to see, my son,' I said to him. 'Two men together go easier up a mountain.'

The town was beginning to wake.

The little square windows of Engine Row were rimed with frost and a baby was crying in the house of Evans the Death, the undertaker: next door to him Marged Davis, a new girl, was getting dressed without pulling the curtains, as Mamie and Billa Jam Tart used to do; beautiful, she looked, waving her arms out of her nightie: Iestyn was staring, jaw dropped, so I hauled him on. There was no light in the house next door where Annie Oh-No used to live, and I gave a thought to her and her three lads. Where, I wondered, was the soul of Annie now?

Where, indeed, were many of those I had known and loved – the people of my town?

Susie Obligato, for instance, where was she? Was she lying in the arms of Bad Boy Gold, the husband who brought her to the straight and narrow? Or was he still in the chain gang while she nursed her baby in some wild place, with Aborigines for neighbours?

Where were Mamie Goldie and Billa Jam Tart, now they'd been captured by Dai End-On and Mr Jam? Were they scrubbing their fingers to the bone for drunkards' ale, their lives no longer engulfed in their gay, infectious laughter; for life to Mamie and Billa was an eternal joke.

Poll Plenty – what had happened to her? Talk had it that she had begged her way up to Coventry; doing a mite better than poor Bill Noakes, who now worked at the Royal Oak for Selwyn ap Pringle for food without wages, for he was tighter than a duck's bum, was Selwyn.

On, on, now, past the Drum and Monkey. Billy Handy and his Belinda were no longer in residence there now, having taken over the tenancy of the new Garndyrus Inn: but Mervyn Jones Counter was scratching his books in the window of the Company Shop there, Shop Row having

383

closed down up in Stack Square: at his best in confusion was Mervyn, smiling his rhubarb smile and giving short weight in the commotion.

I remembered last time I was in the Drum, when I beat up that Effyn Tasker, and one thing was sure, I reflected, we knew where Tasker was. A farmer digging down in Llanwennarth unearthed a skeleton, though Siwan, his woman, couldn't identify it.

A lot of things had happened in our town from time to time, like fresh flowers on the grave of Annie Oh-No and her lads, and nobody knew who was putting them there . . .

Cushy Cuddlecome had a turn down in the Prince, at Clydach, according to reports, but was fanned back to life by Ham Bone and Swillickin' Jock, her minders; but Grandfer Saul in his Bath chair was looking better than ever, folks said – that break down the Vale of Neath doing him a power of good, apparently.

A few had walked through the portals of the Upper Palace these past months – old Ma O'Hara, for one; leaving Pa to fend with a motherless brood. Tomos Traherne, the Pwll-du pastor, got a touch of the bronchials, and was nursed back to health by Miss Modesty Doherty, the harmoniumist, but Mrs Dulcie Bigg went into a decline during her platonic friendship with Selwyn ap Pringle, and expired from a dearth of affection.

Every window I saw on that walk, every rooftop, brought to me memories of the past.

Old Dai Swipo was last seen cutting paper dolls in the entrance of the Market down in Cardiff (where they later hanged Dic Penderyn for a crime he didn't commit), but on a happier note, Peg Cuddle, the layer-out up at the Whistle Inn, turned out twins with the assistance of Will Blaenafon. Better still, little Gwen Lewis fell in love with Dai Paternity. But Dai was absent at the altar; thereafter, going from bad to worse, Gwen Lewis became Wicked Gwennie Lewis.

Peep through the window of Mr Conky-Bum's cottage;

Meg Laundry is changing her little one on the bed, and how Conky managed it nobody ever knew, though Iolo Milk had a finger in the pie according to Eli Rodent, who, taken with an ague, followed Sir John to Llanfoist churchyard in under a month.

Pru Knock-Twice turned over a new leaf and used to stand outside the Jolly Colliers and the Miner's Arms, singing her tonic sol-fa and lecturing on the evils of strong drink. Mrs Di Eynon and her Albert emigrated to Australia, it being right and fair to civilize other parts of the Empire.

On, on we went, my lad and me; shivering in the bitter mountain wind we went, yet warmed in each other's presence.

'Before we go down to the compound, I want you to have a look at something, Iestyn,' and I led him along the rutted road to the Horeb at Pwll-du.

Together, we entered the lych-gate of the graves.

Who should be kneeling there at that time of the morning, but Ianto Idler.

'Morning, Mr Mortymer,' said he.

'Good morning, Ianto.'

He stood with his boots on backwards and his clothes on back to front, and screwed at his collier's cap. 'Just . . . just 'aving a word wi' my Doris before shift, like . . .'

'Of course,' I said, and Iestyn piped up, soprano:

'Just heard how you and Mrs Agnes Lewis 'ave got married, Mr Idler. Good news and good luck, Mr Idler,' and I cursed his soul, for Idler was a nickname, and said swiftly:

'But you are happy, aren't you, Ianto? Mrs Lewis is a fine woman. She will make you a wonderful wife.'

'Aye, that's right, Mr Mortymer,' and he backed away to the gate. 'Just that . . . well, ye never forget the first old girl, do ye?'

I held the gate open for him, saying, 'That's right, Ianto, you never forget the first one.'

'My Doris, see?'

The wind was bitter; tears sprang to his eyes. 'I mean . . . marriage is all right, ain't it? That's why I done it again.'

I nodded, and he added, 'Like you and your Rhia, ain't it, really speakin'?'

'Yes,' I said, and Iestyn, looking around the gravestones, suddenly cried:

'*Well!* Dada – look at this one. Same name as us. I've never noticed this one before . . . "Rhian Mortymer".'

'That's why I brought you here.'

'Where did you get those flowers?' he asked then, as I knelt.

'I had them under my coat.'

Some of these I spared for Annie Oh-No's three sons who lay together; for Annie, who lay outside the graveyard wall in unconsecrated ground, I had brought a bunch of garden daisies.

'Who's she?' asked Iestyn, reading the little wooden cross I had put there.

'One day I'll tell you,' I replied.

I thought, as I took him round the Tumble tram-road: there lies in this one, in all children, the innocence that the world has lost. And it was this very innocence that the world exploited.

On that dawn walk we found ourselves, as usual, surrounded by scores of children: half-asleep, ragged and unkempt, they rose up as if from holes in the ground about us.

These were the ore-scrabblers, vagrant Irish mainly, aged from six to fifteen or so, who worked in all weathers on surface veins, digging the iron off the face of the mountain. In their tatters they came, their empty bellies branded on their wan faces, their drumstick limbs projecting obscenely out of their clothes.

Lurching along beside us on the tram-road, in front and behind us, they slowly merged into a small tatterdemalion army; the trammers and hauliers of the Pwll-du levels: six-year-olds huddled against elder sisters to escape the mountain wind – they who raised the brattice doors against the creeping Foul; the furnace door-boys in their charred sleeves; the rag-cleaners and hookers, the hurriers and corvers, the skippers, gins, and the marrows.

And here was I now forced into the same exploitation through poverty. Morfydd was right; revolutionary creed was right, blind obedience was wrong. For this cruelty, still prospering in a disgusting Slave Trade, now sought new slaves – the young at home – through men who were on their knees to the god of profit. This greed existed in the churches and chapels, whose clergy saw rich horizons by supporting the ostentation of the rich; it flourished in the vulgar excesses of kings, courtiers, the parasitic despots of larkery, and the gilded robes of false priests. '"Receive the Holy Ghost," says the Bishop, then drinks a stirrup-cup and leaps a five-barred gate', said the Black Book of Wade, recently published. 'How can such a creature instil in me the sanctity of the Holy Scriptures in which he would have me believe?'

As I walked among that thronging child-labour, seeing them with a new eye now my own son was one of them, there grew in my imagination a mirage of beauty that supplanted the sum of the misery. It was as if a new revival of the human spirit had, for me alone, swept over the land. It exchanged the winter wind for the warmth of summer. It banished the hunger; it brought comfort to the aged and returned youth to the young.

Already, I realized that the conscience of the nation was stirring. Not seven years later, though at the defeat of Lord Ashley's proposed Factory Bill, William Cobbett was to say to the House of Commons:

The wealth of England, gentlemen, it would appear by your rejection of this humane amendment, is not based upon our merchantile trade; nor are our great banking houses the source of our prosperity; nor, indeed, do the landed estates form the basis of our international success in the world of trade. Aye, when all this is compared with one sixth part of the labour of three hundred

387

thousand little factory children – just two hours off their working day – mark me – and away goes the wealth, away goes the capital, away go the resources, and the power and glory of England!

My God, Gentlemen, what sort of land is this?

'Where do I start, Dada?' asked Iestyn, and I stooped, pointing.

'Report to that man over there. His name is Idris Foreman.' And I stood watching as he made his way from Idris to a nearby cave. So small and alone he looked, going into it; glancing back at me with childhood's indecision.

Eight years old. Twopence a day, and we needed his money. Christ, I thought, what a country! Was I any better, I wondered, than the greed of the masters who now employed him?

Stripping to the waist, I picked up my firing irons and went over the cinder compound to the furnace area. In passing, I paused by Iestyn's cave, and looked within.

An icy wind coming in from distant Beacons swept up from the valley.

In the cave, lit only by a single oil lamp, sat the ore-knockers: six or seven children, of whom the eldest was Sara Roberts, known officially as the ganger.

In rags was she, her tattered skirt scarcely covering her knees, and her arms were bare to the shoulders; she lived down the Tumble Bridge Houses with her mother, her father, once a farm labourer, and her twin brothers, one of whom, aged four, was working down Hopkins with Owen Howells on a second tram.

Beside her was Ceinie Hughes, and she was only six, there because there was nobody at home to care for her; her mother had taken molten iron over her back, and was lying in straw. Now Ceinie was trying to lift her chipping hammer, for until she could do so she drew no pay.

Seeing my shadow in the entrance, the children began to work diligently. Chip, chip, chip went the hammers; sitting astride the veins, they were knocking off the rock from the virgin ore, making it ready for the furnaces. Red light from the nearby fire-boxes flashed and beamed, lighting the interior of the cave, and I saw Iestyn. He was shivering with the cold. Chip, chip, chip . . . Near by was Mo Jenkins, the son of Big Rhys; beyond him sat Brookie Smith, the ten-year-old son of an Abergavenny trader; Brookie, who starved to death one Christmas morning.

I thought, turning away, this could not go on.

A gang of women hauliers went by, stripped to the belt despite the cold, their breasts vanished in the muscles of ash-hauling, and I thought of Rhia and the fumes of Clydach. Chanting an Irish song, they went, these women, their bodies stiffened like bars to the rope. But for the absence of a whip, these could have been the slaves of Pharoah.

No, I thought; it could not go on. Soon I would have to make the decision – the protection of my family or a fight to the end for freedom – no honour lay in hiding behind skirts and the bibs and tuckers of sons and daughters.

I was hitching up my trews for the furnace-raking when Idris Foreman appeared like a wraith beside me; his round face, with its old weals and furnace scars, grinned up into mine.

'Your Iestyn, eh?' He jerked his head at the cave.

'Aye.'

'Likely you can take him home again. Now that the old man's snuffed it, you'll be getting my job back, and I'll be off.'

'I doubt it. Sir John had a lot of influence in the Company.'

Idris said, 'But it's bloody wrong, ain't it? – these little kids working in the cold.'

'It's criminal.'

'Still, the only way we'll change it is to get together with the Union.'

'A Union in Wales? Don't be daft.'

'They've got 'em up north wi' the weavers.'

389

'We've got 'em down here,' I replied, 'if you count the Scotch Cattle ruffians.'

It angered him. 'Ruffians, did you say? It's ruffians we need to fight the ruffians. Sod the lads, you say? It's the family first and last, you say? You'd have no family at all if you left it to these bloody owners. Take it from me, Mortymer, the only way to get your lad back in the warm is by collective action, for while you're kicking one thief out of your front door there's two more bastards breaking down the back. Think on it, and I'll call round tonight with a Union card.'

'Keep it.'

'You're not interested? There's a speaker called Bennet coming down from London . . .'

'You know what you can do with him.'

He laughed, which surprised me, and said, 'Well, it was worth the try . . . for an educated man, you're a silly sod, Mortymer. But I tell you what – read this, will ye? Just to please me?' He gave me a handbill, and I stuffed it into my belt. He added, 'Ever heard of a fella called Heinrich Heine?'

'No.'

'You will one day, mun. A German, aye, but he speaks for the common man, for Europe and a band of brothers. His enemies are ours, Mortymer, the pimps and ponces of the landed bloody aristocracy from here through the lowlands and as far east as the Tsar.' His voice grew louder, and I was astonished by his eloquence.

'You think we're the only victims? By God, I wish we were. A hundred million children are starving on the streets of Europe while these bastards live in a profusion of luxury.' His voice rose again. 'They patronize churches of thieves and murderers, they wage unnecessary wars for profit; they conquer useless colonies for the employment of half-wits in plumed hats in the army, navy and the courts of law. They pay unmerited pensions to grooms of the royal bedchambers, while Welsh children labour underground and our women give birth at the face.'

'So what are we up to now, then?' I shouted back at him. 'A bloody revolution?'

'If necessary,' cried Idris, and I saw a new fire in him.

'You take to organized violence and they'll bring in the military.'

'Then let them come! And use it to prove your nationality, for the Welsh have never turned round on a fight. And don't talk to me of violence, Mortymer . . .' he wagged a finger up into my face, '. . . for violence is the tool of government. From the start of the Slave Trade – nay, long before – theirs has been the law of the whip, the rack and the art of hanging, drawing and quartering . . . Aw, Christ, what's the use? I'm talking to a fella who suffers in his kitchen. Don't rock the boat, eh? I'm all right, please leave things as they are!' He gave me a long, lingering look of dislike and hostility.

The wind fluttered the paper in my hands, and I looked past it to the dawn above the Golden Valley, for the sun was cutting the throat of the clouds and painting them up in rainbow colours.

And I witnessed a phenomenon.

The hills and vales began to move, as from some deep eruption below; as if the arrows of the pit-props piercing the country's vitals were collapsing in billowing dust. The sloping lands of Pen-y-fal and the Skirrids began to heave and stir: the sky darkened; small tummocky eruptions burst out in smoking wounds and fire. The whole of the fair country began to scintillate, throwing up rays of iridescent heat, now dazzling into a splendid, volcanic destruction.

Standing there I heard the shrieks of children and the shouts of men: aproned women were begging to men with bright sabres; muskets were cracking, cannon thundering in flame and smoke. And I saw the whole valley become as the desolate and outraged Pwll-du had become – a blackened cinder-tip; a refuse heap that once was beauty, before the coming of the Magnificent Greed.

Idris tugged at my sleeve, but I shook him away, for I was witnessing in my time what my son, Iestyn, would later witness in his – the outrage of my heritage in the name of profit.

Now the land began to glow, as the coals of a forge glow before shattering into nothingness and brilliant light. I covered my face with my hands.

Idris said, shaking at my arm, 'What's wrong, for God's sake, what's wrong with you?'

Large in the eye was he, and his furnace burns were bright weals upon the living flesh, and in that face I saw the face of my new son, Jethro, after the torment of his manhood by enemies who were not yet born.

He, too, I thought, like a million other Welsh children would suffer the quickening rape of this proud and savage land in their time . . . as I had witnessed it in mine. And a vision came to me of a score of children I had known and loved. Bendy Oldroyd, I saw, and he was hand in hand with Bimbo; Stella Popkin drooped before me, and Beth Ponty; one by one they reared up their heads – Blackie Garn and Susie Thomas who fell asleep at the brattice; Togo Walley, aged five, whom Blackie had to thrash; Gwen Lewis and Sian, Dai and Dodo, and Annie Oh-No's boys, who died under laudanum. All these, and more, came up from North Street with the starving Irish: rattling their begging-tins, they surrounded me.

And it seemed, standing there, as if a new dawn was breaking over the earth: one that held in its arms comfort, not only for my crucified generation, but for Iestyn's. Aye, I thought, the family first and last; for me this would always be. Yet I knew in my racing heart that this would *not* always be: that I was responsible for a million other sons; those that sprang from the loins of men and women who came after me, long after me, my sons and their sons had gone to dust.

One day, I thought, now strangely trembling, things would be changed. Wales would be purged of the cancers that had spread across her body: she would conquer and wash away the stains of defeat and rid herself of the foreign power that leeched her lifeblood.

Furnace Two – the one next door to mine – went into blast then, sending up a great, valedictory flame. And within her bowels the iron bubbled and moaned as the bellows sang and the heat tore the impurities out of the mass. Soon, I thought, when her suffering is over, the molten iron will flow out as pure as spring water.

I opened the handbill Idris had given me, and read in the light of the fire-box.

> What! Think you that my flashes show me
> Only in lightning to excel?
> Believe me, friend, you do not know me,
> For I can thunder quite as well.
>
> In sorrow you shall learn your error;
> My voice shall grow, and in amaze
> Your eyes and ears shall know the terror,
> The thundering world, the stormy blaze.
>
> Oaks shall be rent; the earth will shatter.
> Yea, on that fiery day, their crowns . . .
> Even their palace walls shall totter,
> Their domes and spires come crashing down!

'Mortymer, look! Look who's coming!' It was Idris again, bellowing into my ear above the furnace thunder, and pointing: turning, I dropped the firing-iron.

Morfydd, it was, racing over the compound towards me.

With her hair flying in the wind and her dress held up like a tent, she came at speed, and I would have heard her voice above the feet of marching armies.

She cried: 'Dada! Dada! Jethro! He's been born. Jethro, *Jethro!*'

Epilogue

Evidence of the Hated
Blue Books of 1847

The Blue Books of 1847, compiled by English Commissioners to inquire into the state of education in Wales, went beyond their instructed brief and published opinions as to the state of morality then existing among 'the poorer classes'.

The Commissioners, with the utmost prejudice, indicted the Welsh people, particularly Welsh women, for a degraded morality; referring to them as evil, savage, slatternly and rude, 'with scarcely a ray of spiritual intelligence'.

It is hardly to be wondered at, therefore, that the Welsh nation so furiously resisted the libel that a question was raised in the House of Commons and an apology obtained from the Commissioners.

However, such is the temerity and malicious bias of the reports that when the iron- and coalmasters are briefly (and clearly reluctantly) taken to task within them for their role in the exploitation of their workers, the real facts of the social conditions of the times shine through with unparalleled significance.

The following extracts from one Commissioner's report of the social conditions existing in Wales in 1847 may therefore be assumed to be of irreducible truth.

Even the physical condition of the people seems almost as if contrived for the double degradation and employers' profit. Some of the works are surrounded by houses built by the Companies without the slightest attention to comfort, health, decency or any other consideration than that of realising the largest amount of rent from the smallest outlay. I went into several of this class of houses in the north part of my district and examined them from top to bottom.

Men, women and children of all sexes and ages are stowed away in the bedrooms without any curtains or partitions, it being no uncommon thing for nine or ten people not belonging to the family to sleep together in this manner in the room. In one instance I found three men sleeping in a sort of dungeon which was about nine feet by six feet in dimensions, without any light or air, except through a hole in the wall not a foot square, which opened into another room occupied by some women. The houses are, many of them, so constructed that each storey is let off to different tenants. The necessary outbuildings in most cases do not exist at all. An immense rent in comparison to the accommodation is paid to the Occupier or the Master for these miserable places. Heaps of rubbish lie about in the streets and before the doors of the houses. There is neither drainage or even lights in the streets, although coal is close at hand. Tram-roads intersect and run along the streets of these places, which contain above 30,000 inhabitants. Nevertheless, these places are little worse than others, and, in some respects, superior to Brynmawr, which I described in my last Report. In many cases the Iron Companies have merely a lease of the estate, and have no other interest than that of making the most they can out of it.

Author's note: The districts to which this Commissioner refers are mainly the industrial regions of Monmouthshire (Gwent) and Glamorgan. The masters indicted being the Crawshays of Merthyr, Crawshay Bailey of Nantyglo, Sir John and Lady Charlotte Guest of Dowlais, Fothergill and the Rev. Monkhouse of Sirhowy and Tredegar, Homfray and Morgan, and others. Even the Quaker, Joseph Tregelles Price of Neath Abbey Ironworks is not absolved.

Evidence of Children in the Mines – Nineteenth Century

Little has been written by modern historians on the condition and labour of children working in the mines and ironworks of nineteenth-century Britain; indeed, such history was virtually undiscovered until recently: the result of this dilution of historical fact is that claim and counterclaim as to the veracity of modern statements were invariably challenged. Establishment historians have lied by omission.

Testimony of Phillip Phillips, aged nine years (his face badly scarred as a result of an explosion in one of the Plymouth mines). Questioned by the Inspector of Mines, Mr R. W. Jones, he said: *I started work when I was seven. I get very tired sitting in the dark by the door* [ventilating door] *so I go to sleep. Nearly a year ago there was an accident and most of us were burned. It hurt very much because all the skin was burnt off my face, and I couldn't work for six months. I have seven brothers and sisters, but only five of us can find work; none of us have ever been to school.*

Testimony of Mary Davis, aged six, also of Merthyr. She said, when found asleep: *I went to sleep because my lamp had gone out for want of oil. I was frightened, for someone had stolen my bread and cheese, I think it was the rats.*

Susan Reece, also aged six and of Merthyr and a doorkeeper, said: *I've been below six or eight months and don't like it much. I come here at six and leave at six at night . . . I haven't been hurt yet.*

Such young doorkeepers often rolled on to the line in sleep, and were run over by oncoming coal wagons.

Testimony of John Fuge, aged eleven, of Pontypridd, working down Maesmawr Colliery: *I began work when I was seven, cutting slates in Cornwall; came to Wales two years ago. This is a very wet mine, our feet are never dry. Pumping is hard work, so we only work eight hours at a time. Sometimes I get so tired I don't care about eating. When I'm thirsty I drink the mine water, and I earn thirty pence a week; I work every day, so I can't go to Sunday school.*

Richard Richards of Top Hill Colliery, Gelligaer, aged seven, told the Inspector: *I was six when I first came below. I work for about ten hours a day with my father; sometimes he lets me cut coal in his stall.*

William Richards, of Monmouthshire, working underground at Buttery Hatch colliery, appears to have been a character; he said: *I don't know how old I am, but I've been below about three years. When I first came down I couldn't keep me eyes open, but now I sits by the door and smokes my pipe. I smokes about 2 ounces a week, and it costs me twopence. I don't know what tobacco is made of.*

Another lad, the son of a clergyman, working in the same colliery, said: *My name's Josiah Jenkins, and I'm seven. Been down eighteen months and get threepence a day, but I haven't been hurt yet*; and Jeremiah Jerimiah, aged ten, had been down Buttery Hatch for five years. His father was dead and he had a badly disfigured face, caused by an explosion when he was five, and his friend, William Skidmore, aged eight, had a badly crushed hand – caused by a roof fall.

Ben Thomas, aged eight, worked in Broadmoor Colliery at Begelly, Pembrokeshire, hauling skips of coal – a 'very pitiful little fellow' said the Inspector, and Ben said: *I've been down here a year helping my brother to haul skips [sledge carts] of coal. Sometimes I get oatmeal broth before work, which is very hard and I am running all day. None of the boys in this pit wears shoes* – and Edward Edwards, who was aged nine, and was a carter in a colliery near Briton Ferry, described how . . . *I've been working down here three months dragging carts loaded with coal from the coal face to the main road underground; there are no wheels to the carts* [skips again]. *It is not so well to drag them as the cart sometimes is dragged on to us, and we get crushed often. I have often hurt my hands and fingers and had to stay home.*

In Dowlais, where the ironmaster was Sir John Guest, and his wife was Lady Charlotte, there was a level known as Penyard. One of the doorkeepers there was Zelophilad Llewelyn, aged nine, who told the Inspector: *I eat bread and cheese down there. I don't often lose my food to the rats, but they do sometimes steal the bags of bread and cheese from other lads.*

Finally, Tom Jenkins and his tram partner in the hauling, John Hugh, told the official: *We have no dinner time underground; I eat when I can; sometimes I get into the tram while my butty is hauling, and eat in there; he does the same when I push. My father is dead and my mother has seven children; one of these is aged seven and drives a horse. The trammers beat him and the others with whips when they do not mind to get the coal out quickly.*

Commissioner's note:

The boys called Carters are employed in narrow seams of coal in parts of Monmouthshire. Their occupation is to drag the carts or skips of coal from the working place to the main road underground. In this mode of labour the leather girdle passes round the body and the chain is between the legs, attached to the cart, and the lads drag on all fours.

Children in the Ironworks – Nineteenth Century

Much of the evidence taken by the Inspectors from children working in iron is a repetition of the preceding statements, with the constant addition of the statement, *I have not been burned yet*, or, as Young Morgan, aged nine, a puller-up at Anthony Hill's Plymouth Ironworks, declared: *I have been working here for two years now and sometimes I get burned at the furnaces. Sometimes, too, I get the stripes* [beaten] *for playing about*. John Brown, aged ten, said: *I work in the coke yard filling coke for my uncle, helping him to push the barrows down the furnaces* . . . And wagons filled with red-hot slag from the furnaces were dragged by 'cinder girls'. Thousands of such young children could be seen in the villages around the ironworks. Crawshay of Merthyr employed more than four hundred, fifty of these being girls, while Hill of the Merthyr Plymouth Ironworks employed, apart from a thousand men, a hundred and fifty boys and girls.

But life for children working in iron is encapsulated by a statement made by William Lloyd, the furnaces manager of Blaenafon, Gwent, who said:

I have about 37 children working about the furnaces under my charge, the youngest being about seven years old. I have some boys between eight and twelve years old helping the 'fillers' at the furnace top [tipping in the fuel and ore, a most dangerous task]. There are fourteen girls from ten to sixteen years in the coke yard and six lads in the casting-house and refinery of from ten to fourteen years, some of whom get burned, but not too badly: there are a few girls at the mines, working below; they all work twelve hours a day and the furnaces and refineries work all night.

This is the history that has been side-stepped in our time by 90 per cent of our Establishment historians; it is to be wondered if the crimes committed against the children of the Industrial Revolution are not being repeated, in a different guise, against the bodies of the children today.

The Commissioners' Reports (The Blue Books) of 1847 and the Commission of Enquiry into the State of Children in Employment (1840s) can be seen at the Public Record Office, Chancery Lane, London, wc2.

The writer urges the necessity for another such Parliamentary Inquiry into the state of today's children.